INVISIBLE AS AIR

Also by Zoe Fishman

Balancing Acts

Saving Ruth

Driving Lessons

Inheriting Edith

Praise for *Invisible as Air*

"With psychological acuity, Fishman . . . takes us to the place where there is beauty in brokenness, where there is light in the dark, and where we can find intimacy in our honesty. . . . From the first stunning choice to the last, I could not put this novel down."

—Patti Callahan Henry, *New York Times* and *USA Today* bestselling author of *Becoming Mrs. Lewis*

"Though it speaks to one of the most difficult issues facing our nation with wisdom and deep grace, this is not an 'issue' book. This is a book about people, flawed but striving, broken but hopeful. Once I started, I couldn't put it down."

—Joshilyn Jackson, *New York Times* bestselling author of *Never Have I Ever*

"Zoe Fishman writes with tenderness and urgency, with an ear attuned to all the silences, secrets and strain that frequently capsize modern family life. *Invisible as Air* is a memorable and compelling read about slipping into darkness and trying to find the light."

—Kristen Iskandrian, author of *Motherest*

Inheriting Edith

"A tragicomic delight. . . . Fishman deftly explores the intricate territory of mother-daughter relationships as well as the haunting specter of an Alzheimer's diagnosis . . . a delicious literary chicken soup for the soul."

—Mary Kay Andrews, *New York Times* bestselling author of *Sunset Beach*

"*Inheriting Edith* is a beautifully written story about what it means to remember and what it means to forget. Fishman masterfully portrays both a single mother and an older woman with Alzheimer's, as they are both struggling to come to terms with their pasts, their futures and each other. I loved this compelling and achingly real novel about friendship, family and second chances."

—Jillian Cantor, *USA Today* bestselling author of *In Another Time*

"A beautifully crafted story about second chances and life's big surprises. Warm-spirited and emotionally rich, *Inheriting Edith* celebrates the fine line between friendship and family. These characters will tug at your heart."

—Jamie Brenner, *USA Today* bestselling author of *Drawing Home*

"Fishman (*Saving Ruth*) combines relatable circumstances and delightful dialogue in this character-driven tale about forgiveness and acceptance, making it a quick read that's hard to put down."

—*Publishers Weekly*

Driving Lessons

"A charming and warm story about new adventures and old friends and how this likable heroine learns to embrace them both."

—Shelley Noble, *New York Times* bestselling author of *A Beach Wish*

"At turns funny and poignant, *Driving Lessons* is a refreshingly honest and insightful story of a woman whose questions about the direction of her life follow her from the big city to small country roads."

—Meg Donohue, *USA Today* bestselling author of *You, Me, and the Sea*

"Insightful and emotionally astute . . . Fishman demonstrates a rare gift for illuminating the interior lives of women with honesty, generosity and a whole lot of heart."

—Jillian Medoff, bestselling author of *This Could Hurt*

INVISIBLE AS AIR

A NOVEL

ZOE FISHMAN

WILLIAM MORROW
An Imprint of Harper Collins*Publishers*

This is a work of fiction. Names, characters, places, and incidents are products of the author's imagination or are used fictitiously and are not to be construed as real. Any resemblance to actual events, locales, organizations, or persons, living or dead, is entirely coincidental.

P.S.™ is a trademark of HarperCollins Publishers.

HarperCollins books may be purchased for educational, business, or sales promotional use. For information, please email the Special Markets Department at SPsales@harpercollins.com.

FIRST EDITION

Designed by Diahann Sturge

Library of Congress Cataloging-in-Publication Data has been applied for.

ISBN 978-0-06-283823-0

19 20 21 22 23 LSC 10 9 8 7 6 5 4 3 2

For my father, who taught me to never give up.

Ethan Michael Fishman
July 13, 1944–February 20, 2019

CHAPTER ONE

SYLVIE

Sylvie opened her bleary eyes and stared at the ceiling. Beside her, her husband, Paul, snored intermittently, his broken ankle wrapped in its dirty, beige cast. It was still dark outside, but a lone bird had begun to tweet, signaling morning's imminent arrival.

She dreaded this day every year because of the memories that arrived alongside it, landing with an ominous thud right in the center of her chest. Three years out, and it didn't get any easier to see it approaching on Teddy's school calendar, which hung lopsided on the side of the stainless-steel fridge.

Gingerly, Sylvie sat up and swung her legs over the side of their king-size bed, pausing for a moment to look at the clock. Five thirteen. Great. There were approximately fifteen hours left to endure, give or take.

In the bathroom, she ran a washcloth under ice-cold water

and plunged her face inside its folds, relishing the shock of its impact. Holding her breath, she held it there for a few seconds, imagining that when she removed it, her face would be young again. Her left eyelid, with its startling new Silly Putty consistency, would regain its elasticity; the permanent brow furrow her cynicism had cost her would smooth. She removed the cloth, hopeful for just a moment. Instead, her forty-six-year-old self stared back at her.

No, that wasn't fair, she thought next, grabbing her moisturizer from the shelf. She unscrewed its cap and took a generous scoop, massaging it vigorously into her cheeks, down over her chin, and back up over her closed eyes and forehead before finishing with the sides, careful not to smudge it into her hairline. It wasn't all bad.

She still had her big brown eyes and even bigger eyebrows, full lips and relatively lustrous head of black hair. She had never colored or straightened it, had barely blown it dry, and so she liked to think it was thanking her by staying shiny, with only the occasional gray surprising her. It hung in a wave against the faint outline of her collarbone beneath her olive, slightly rosy skin. Sylvie tried to smile at herself, but it felt too difficult, like the corners of her mouth were stapled to her chin.

She sighed, pulling open the immense drawer of their marble-topped vanity to retrieve her eye cream. An orange bottle inside rolled toward her, *click-clack*ing its way to the inside edge. She picked it up, considering its contents. Paul's pain pills. Say that three times fast. *Paul's pain pills, Paul's pain pills, Pops paint pits.*

He had fallen from his bike, her triathlete husband, and broken his ankle just two weeks before, although it seemed like two years. Sylvie had discovered that it was one thing to mother your son but quite another to mother your mate. She did not enjoy it, not one bit.

Several times a day she had to remind herself that this invalid version of Paul, this person who moaned and groaned through even the slightest shift of the pillow beneath his foot and frowned at the grilled cheese sandwich she made him for lunch claiming too many carbs, was not the real Paul. He was in pain, it was true, largely because he refused to take the pills she now held in her hand.

"I don't like the way they make me feel," he had said to Sylvie, handing the bottle over to her. "And anyway, you've seen the news. Oxycodone. What do they call it? Hillbilly heroin?" He shook his head, handing her the bottle. "Just give me some ibuprofen."

"How do they make you feel?" Sylvie had asked.

"What? Those?" Paul nodded toward the bottle in her hand. "Groggy. Out of it." He wrinkled his nose. "Not good."

"Okay, three ibuprofen coming up," Sylvie had replied, turning on her heel and walking toward the bathroom to retrieve them.

What was wrong with feeling groggy and out of it if all you were doing was sitting on the couch and telling people to bring you things? Sylvie wondered. You had to be cognizant for that?

She looked at the bottle now in her hand, the house as silent as a tomb around her. Her heartbeat sped up as she thought about how not being cognizant on this day, especially this day, might be nice.

Paul would approach her with sad, cartoon-character eyes, looking at her with the kind of manufactured sympathy she had always hated, even before she'd lost the baby. He'd put his hand on her shoulder, squeeze it ever so slightly and ask, *How are you today, honey?*, adding insult to injury.

She hated it when Paul called her *honey*—it felt so false, so pat. He couldn't come up with a better nickname? One that possessed a shred of originality? She supposed things could be worse—he could have been the kind of husband who called her *babe*—but still. Just use her own damn name.

It had been a loss for Paul too, she knew that, but the pain belonged to her. He shouldn't be allowed to access it. She had carried the baby, after all. She had had to feel her breasts fill with milk, engorged to the point of bursting, only to deflate in defeat a week later, with no baby to feed. What had Paul had to do? Sell the crib? Come on. She knew it wasn't easy, but it wasn't the same.

Sylvie hated today. Being out of it seemed like the perfect remedy. She touched the bottle tentatively. She had refused them after the birth of her children, the first time because she was lucky enough to not be in that much actual pain and the second time because she was on enough anxiety medication to tranquilize a horse afterward.

Now, Sylvie held up this new orange bottle to the light carefully, like it was an ancient Egyptian artifact. She had seen the shows about addiction, with people shooting up inside their cars in abandoned parking lots, nodding off midsentence and smacking their faces against their steering wheels. She had seen the same news Paul had, with the segments about entire towns turning into zombie villages on this stuff.

Sylvie put the pills back inside the drawer and closed it. She dutifully applied her eye cream, patting it gently into her skin. She opened the drawer again, replaced her cream and picked the bottle back up, the plastic warm from her incessant fondling.

No, this was different, she told herself. She was not going to be nodding off in her car anytime soon; she was just cutting herself a break on a tough morning in the middle of a tough month at the end of a tough three years.

She unscrewed the cap, took out one of the tiny, white discs and placed it on her tongue. With a grimace, she swallowed it whole, turned off the light and began her day.

* * *

"PANCAKES?" ASKED TEDDY, approaching the table with a bewildered look on his face.

A face that had just recently begun its maturing transformation from circle to square. Teddy was his father in miniature: same blue-gray eyes, same sandy blond straight hair, same button nose. The least Jewish-looking Jewish boy in the world, she had thought to herself from the moment she'd held his tiny, naked body against her chest.

"Why not?" Sylvie answered, smiling slightly at her son as he shuffled toward the table.

The morning light filtered in through the wall of windows

overlooking their deck, and below that the yard, which had burst forth with its green, purple, pink and yellow bounty months ahead of schedule thanks to the seventy-something-degree temperatures in February. Now, in April, dead petals littered the yard like confetti.

It had been almost two hours since she had swallowed the pill. Inside, Sylvie was an undulating ripple of goodwill, despite the fact that she was steeled for Paul's unwelcome reverence and splattered with batter. It was a miracle, truly.

Teddy dropped his backpack on the floor with a loud thud and scrambled over and onto the bench lining one side of the enormous wood table that Paul had repurposed. Once upon a time, it had been a barn door in rural Georgia. Now they ate pancakes on it.

She sat down in a chair across from Teddy, watching him eat like he always ate, as though he hadn't been fed in months. His hair flopped in front of his eyes slightly, and in the back, his cowlick stuck up and out, the same way it always had. If she squinted, he was four years old again, in matching pajama top and bottoms, the last of his adorable toddler tummy pressing against the patterned blue-and-green cotton of his shirt; his boneless feet swinging happily, nowhere near the floor.

To Sylvie's horror, tears welled up in her eyes. She pretended to cough and covered her face with one of the blue-and-white-striped cloth napkins she had tossed onto the table, wiping them away as she stood again.

Teddy looked up, chewing.

"These are good," he offered, as he forked three more onto

his plate from the white platter in front of him. "Thanks, Mom."

Sylvie nodded and placed her open palm atop his very warm head as she made her way back to the kitchen. She had forgotten her coffee. Sipping from her mug, she leaned against the enormous white apron sink, surveying the messy marble countertops covered with the remnants of her labor—a pancake-mix-covered yellow bowl and spatula, the still-slick griddle, an open carton of eggs.

"Syl?" Paul called from the top of the stairs.

For the first time in a long time, Sylvie did not cringe at the sound of his voice. And for the first time since he had broken his ankle, helping her husband down the stairs did not include a fantasy about "accidentally" pushing him instead. It was the pill, making her kinder, softer, more fluid. Bubbles of goodwill coursed through her bloodstream. It was a relief, to not quite be herself.

Her usual self was tired. Her usual self was complacent about what their marriage had become; what *they* had become: roommates with the shared responsibility of a child and a mortgage, not to mention the emotional baggage of a death. Her usual self was resentful about the fact that she worked full time, was the chief of Teddy operations and now nursemaid to a husband who shouldn't have been on that goddamn twenty-five-mile bike ride on a Saturday in the first place. A husband who should have been hanging out with his son instead.

She hadn't always claimed this as her usual demeanor toward Paul. When she had met him, she had fallen almost instantaneously head over rumpled bedsheets in love with him. He'd been fixing the sink of her then friend Ramona when she'd walked into Ramona's kitchen, his denim-clad legs and gray sweatshirt comically splayed out on the floor; his head hidden in the dark recesses of the cabinet as he did whatever it was one did to fix a sink.

This is him, Ramona had whispered conspiratorially when Sylvie had arrived, wet and cold from the rain. The two of them were supposed to be going to brunch; this new boyfriend of Ramona's was not supposed to be part of the equation. Sylvie had almost faked a stomachache and left—third wheel had not been on her agenda—but then of course Paul had squirreled out from his precarious position, victorious with wrench in hand, boy-like charm radiating from every one of his invisible pores. Sylvie had gone weak in the knees, had actually had to brace herself against Ramona's IKEA kitchen table. She'd gone to brunch. A week later, Paul had broken up with Ramona. Three weeks later he had moved in with Sylvie and Ramona had never spoken to her again. The rest, as they say, was history.

Teddy turned around, looking at Sylvie now with the same wry smile of his father's. Was that a smile of commiseration? Of empathy? Sylvie wasn't sure, but she would pretend it was. She and her son hadn't discussed Paul's neediness since his accident, only because they didn't discuss much of anything these days. Sylvie did a lot of talking at her son, but to call it conversation would have been delusional. To think that she had an ally in Teddy, that she wasn't a horrible person and maybe Paul had indeed become a pain in the ass, that was something to hold on to.

"Coming," she called, smiling back at Teddy.

She placed her mug on the counter and strode along the wood floors to the staircase, which wound up to the second floor like a giant corkscrew. Theirs was a house without any rooms downstairs, open concept before it was a bona fide concept since Paul was a contractor.

Vision Contracting, his business card read, a name they had worked on together so many years before. Paul had balked at it at first, saying it was too corny, but Sylvie had held her ground. She'd been right too. With every job he had taken, Paul's confidence in his instincts had grown, and not without good reason. He was very good at what he did. So was she.

Built-in bookshelves lined some of the gray walls of their downstairs, filled to bursting with books, myriad tokens from their travels and the occasional treasure that looked as though it came from somewhere exotic instead of the HomeGoods down the street. Paul called it cheating; Sylvie called it shopping.

An L-shaped, tan corduroy sofa with cushions like toasted marshmallows faced away from her, toward a television that took up almost the entire wall on which it hung. Flung about haphazardly over the painstakingly sanded and oiled wood floor were Persian rugs. Paul was in charge of their home's design, but he let Sylvie handle its wardrobe, albeit begrudgingly. Had it been up to him, they would have been living in a post-apocalyptic bunker.

Sylvie climbed up the stairs in her gray-and-pink-striped socks, to her husband.

"Good morning, P," she said, looking at his cast, and then his red plaid pajama pants, then his navy-blue T-shirt and finally his face, as she stood before him.

His face. Salt-and-pepper stubble along his square jawline and around his lips, which were a little on the thin side, Sylvie had always thought, but not weird Muppet thin, just thin. Hers were rather plush, so maybe her judgment was off. No one else had ever mentioned Paul's lips, not even her mother, who mentioned everything.

His nose was the same button nose as Teddy's, small and perfect. And his eyes—a blue-gray hybrid that could have been scooped out of a summer sky right before a rain. And lashes as thick as canopies; the same sandy blond as his hair, which was thinning now, around his temples and at the back of his head, a bull's-eye of age. For the first time in a very long time, Sylvie felt a swell of affection toward him.

"P?" Paul asked, taken aback. "You haven't called me that in years."

"I haven't?" asked Sylvie, snaking her arm around his waist to help him down the stairs. His impossibly slim triathlete waist.

Paul gave her a sideways glance.

"What?" she asked. "I'm feeling nice today."

"I like nice," replied Paul. He squeezed her shoulder as they began their slow descent. "Thanks. I know I'm a terrible patient," he added quietly. "I'm sorry."

Paul had always been an overapologizer, in Sylvie's opinion, but with his injury had come a sense of entitlement rocketing into the stratosphere. Or maybe she was just a terrible nurse. Either way, it was good to hear.

"Thank you for saying that," she said.

"You know what today is, right?" Paul asked, catching her off guard as they took the last step down.

Sylvie grabbed his crutches, which were leaning on the banister. "Oh, come on, Paul," she answered, shoving them toward him. Ah, there it was, her anger. Still there. Still Sylvie.

"What?" he asked.

She shook her head and turned away from him, back toward the kitchen. *Did she know what today was?* Unreal.

After the first few months following Delilah's stillbirth, Sylvie could not pretend her sadness away. The three of them had holed up together in a fortress of grief and shock, Sylvie and Paul doing their best to explain away the terrible unfairness of life to a nine-year-old but failing miserably under Teddy's wise gaze. He was too smart, too present, too invested in who he thought would be his little sister, to buy it.

They were all in it together. Until they weren't. At the three-month mark almost exactly, Paul had exited stage left, taking Teddy with him. Getting on with their lives as though her pregnancy—their almost family of four—had never happened. At least that's how it had felt to Sylvie, although she knew Paul would argue otherwise.

A beat later, Sylvie had moved on too, because what else was she going to do? But moving on for her was a commitment, full stop. She did not talk about Delilah, not ever, which Paul considered unfair. Sylvie didn't care if it was fair.

Back in the kitchen, she steadied herself against the counter and took a deep breath, her back to her family. She wanted the bubbles back.

"Hey, T," greeted Paul behind her. "Pancakes!"

"Err," Teddy grunted back, his mouth full.

Sylvie turned around, calmed by another wave of magic. Ask and ye shall receive, she thought, as it undulated throughout her body, unclenching her muscles one by one.

"Wow, Sylvie, thanks." Paul looked at her, his eyes pleading with her not to be angry with him. She gave him a small smile, indicating that the moment had passed. "I shouldn't, but I'm going to eat a million of these." He laid his crutches on the floor and sat down.

"Dad, they're pancakes, not meth."

"Meth! What do you know about meth, young man? I'll show you meth; give me those flapjacks." He speared three on his fork and plunked them onto his plate.

"Relax, nobody is doing meth."

The thing was, Sylvie had come close to talking about Delilah, almost always on this day. But then Paul would inevitably say something ridiculous, as he had just now, and the door inside Sylvie, the one that led to Delilah, would slam and lock all over again.

But what if today was different? Paul didn't mean to be insensitive; she knew that deep down, even as her anger still simmered from before. He just didn't know what else to say. And she was so sensitive. Too sensitive. Which for Sylvie manifested itself as defensive, angry, immovable. Until today. With this pill.

She whispered Delilah's name, testing it on her tongue. Each syllable was a relief, like loosening a too-tight belt. She would do it. She would commemorate the significance of the day. She would say Delilah's name out loud, not just whisper it. But how? When?

Sylvie considered her options as she watched Paul and Teddy eat, pleased to see Paul consuming gluten so voraciously. Since he'd started up with his running, biking and swimming nine gazillion miles—to nowhere, as far as Sylvie was concerned—few morsels of food passed his lips that hadn't been analyzed by the nutritional lab that had become his brain. And since he had been knocked off his bike, forget it. Sylvie was surprised she hadn't found him naked in front of the mirror, pinching his nonexistent muffin top like a teenage girl in trouble.

When Paul decided to become a triathlete, it was like he had invented exercise. On the rare occasions she wandered down into the basement that had been Teddy's playroom but had morphed into Paul's personal locker room and gym, she felt as though she couldn't breathe, like the bikes and sneakers and gloves and free weights were suffocating her. There was no room for her to take anything up, because his hobby took up their whole lives, all three of theirs. She couldn't so much as don a sports bra without Paul waxing poetic on the benefits of interval training. And don't get her started on the money he spent in the name of his newfound hobby. Sylvie hated it. All of it.

Still thinking of Delilah, Sylvie searched the kitchen, settling on the cabinet above the refrigerator. Quickly, before she could change her mind, she walked over to the cavernous pantry off the side of the kitchen and pulled open its levered door. Grabbing the collapsible stepstool from inside it, she walked it over to the refrigerator and set it up to reach her target. She climbed its three steps—Teddy and Paul with their backs to her, feasting still—and opened it.

The JCC, she called it, because that's where the yarmulkes and menorahs, challah covers and the Seder plate, kiddush cups and candlesticks lived. Mementos of a life they sometimes lived, or the life Sylvie had wanted them to live, anyway, in the beginning. She was Jewish, had grown up in a moderately religious home in New Jersey—synagogue on holidays and the occasional Shabbat, a disastrous summer at sleep-away camp, a Bat Mitzvah—and so even though she had fallen in love with an agnostic man who had no intention of ever converting, she had been determined to raise their children as such.

But something had happened to Sylvie's fervor as the years had gone by, as life twisted and turned its way forward. And certainly her faith had been challenged by the death of Delilah. Even so, she dragged Teddy to Hebrew School every week, sometimes by the scruff of his neck since he was so uninterested.

She wanted Teddy to know he was Jewish, to feel it in his bones the way she did, but lately she had had to face the fact that he just didn't. Whether it was his age or the impending

Bar Mitzvah he made no secret about dreading, she wasn't sure. But she knew she would rather it be that than her fault for marrying a goy, as her father had said so many years before. She hadn't spoken to him for four months after he'd said that. Finally, he had called her to apologize, which was a very big deal. Max Schwartz didn't apologize.

She and her father had resumed their relationship, he had paid for the wedding, he was even friendly to Paul. But there was a chasm there, always had been, between the two families: New Jersey Jews and Southern Baptists did not blend well no matter how many drinks you had, and Sylvie would know. She had done the research.

Sylvie rustled around in the cabinet, her hand searching for the small white candle encased in its glass votive. She found it, finally, her fingers closing around its circumference as she pulled it toward her. A thin layer of grime and dust had collected on its surface, a result of its two-year residency. Her mother had given it to Sylvie, on the first anniversary of Delilah's death, but Sylvie had shoved it into the back of the cabinet, annoyed.

She blew on it now in an attempt to clear the accumulated dirt, but it had embedded itself in the wax. She closed the door, candle in hand, and climbed down the stepstool.

"Mom, what are you doing?" called Teddy from the table, having turned around to see her carefully placing the candle on the countertop.

"Lighting a candle for Delilah," she answered, pulling open a drawer to retrieve a matchbook from a trendy, overpriced restaurant she and Paul had gone to on their last date night, a date so far in the past she couldn't even remember which month it had taken place in.

"What?" asked Paul.

She would not be irritated by the eagerness in his voice, Sylvie told herself. She would not. "A Yahrzeit candle," she answered.

"Wait for me," said Teddy, jumping up.

"What's a Yahrzeit candle?" asked Paul. "Get me my crutches, will you, T?"

Teddy held them out to Paul as he picked up his leg with both hands to forcibly move it over the bench, his cast landing on the other side with a slight thud.

"It's a candle you light to honor the dead," answered Teddy. "Right, Mom?"

He was beside her now, with Paul nipping at his heels. He looked up at her, just slightly since he was nearly her height, waiting for her affirmation.

"That's right, Teddy."

She squeezed his thin arm. Paul leaned forward on his crutches, eyeing the candle curiously and reminding her of a T. rex in the process.

Sylvie struck the match.

"Wait, we need to say a prayer, Mom," said Teddy, blowing it out before she could make contact with the wick. "Where are the yarmulkes?"

"I'll get them." So he was Jewish, this Bar Mitzvah–dreading son of hers.

She reclimbed the stepstool and snagged two black discs from the cabinet.

"Here," she offered.

"Could you put it on my head for me?" asked Paul, gesturing toward his crutches.

"Sure."

He leaned forward, and she placed it atop the bald spot that had gone from marble- to golf-ball-size in the past year, despite his best efforts. She liked that bald spot a million times more than his six-pack; she wished he knew that.

"Okay, T, do you want to start?" asked Sylvie. He took a deep breath and began.

Sylvie closed her eyes and mouthed the words along with him, a kaleidoscope of painful memories resurfacing. There was her belly, as taut as a drum, and there was little Teddy, touching it tentatively. And there was the pale blue of her hospital gown, the tops of her knees, her whole body shaking in those ice-cold silver stirrups. And Paul's face, his eyes as still as glass as he met her gaze.

"Mom?" asked Teddy. She opened her eyes, summoned. "Mom, I'm done. Was that good?" he asked, looking at her hopefully.

"Beautiful, Teddy. Really beautiful. Thanks."

The three of them stared down into the flame, Sylvie feeling its faint heat against her cheeks.

CHAPTER TWO

TEDDY

Teddy emerged from his front door reluctantly, the morning soundtrack of his neighborhood—birds tweeting, garbage trucks sighing, the occasional pair of moms in those weird skirt/shorts things he could never figure out shrieking in commiseration as they power walked by—blaring.

Man, what he wouldn't give for a phone to play music on, a pair of headphones to escape into, he thought as he began his walk to school. But his mom refused to buy him one, claiming he was too young even though every other kid in seventh grade had one. No wonder he didn't have any friends; he may as well have time traveled from 1800.

Teddy considered the possibilities of that story arc. Why anyone would want to find themselves in seventh grade again was beyond him. But maybe that was the point? A lord or baron dressed like Christopher Columbus, just plopped behind him in Spanish, sent ahead in time to save the world from Donald Trump. Teddy pulled his green notepad and pencil out of the back pocket of his navy cargo shorts, making a note. He liked to jot down the ideas he had. You never knew.

He was going to be a screenwriter, maybe a director someday—he wasn't sure. But he had ideas all the time, and sometimes they were decent. He had seen a lot of movies; he knew decent. He slid his notepad back into his pocket and continued on, pausing for a moment to face off with a squirrel, its entire body vibrating as it devoured the acorn it held in its front paws.

"Hello," he said. The squirrel stared at him a moment longer, and then scampered away, its bounty stored for later consumption. Great, he was talking to squirrels now.

He rounded the block, stepping around bags upon brown bags of lawn clippings and leaves hugging the perimeter of the enormous brick house on the corner. His house was big, but this house, it was like something out of *Gone with the Wind*.

He hadn't cared for that movie. It was too much for him, all the sighing and the way the actors spoke, like their noses were held together by chip clips. High up on a green hill this house sat, its redbrick exterior flanked by two concrete lions at the bottom of a staircase leading to its expansive porch and incredibly tall, like tall enough to imply that a giant lived inside, white door.

There were a lot of big houses in his neighborhood, but this one was the biggest. And as far as Teddy could tell, just an old couple lived there. What did they need all those rooms for, anyway? It had to be lonely, all that extra space, filled with what he imagined to be dark, heavy furniture no one was allowed to touch. What if they were vampires? Interesting. He pulled out his notepad again, making a note.

At the intersection, he pushed the *Walk* button. There was one four-lane road between his house and his school, but other than that, it was a fairly uneventful journey. He could do it with his eyes closed, which he knew, because he had done it more than once.

As he waited for the light to change, he thought of the candle his mom had lit for Delilah. It was the equivalent of aliens beaming down from outer space and into his backyard. She never did stuff like that. What had gotten into her? he wondered. Whatever it was, he liked it.

Behind him, he heard them coming. Taylor and Kai—girls from his grade. The most popular girls, if you were keeping track, and of course everyone was. It was just part of being in middle school, Teddy had noticed, this popularity percentage point phenomenon. Even he, someone who came in at a steady .02 on his best day, was well aware of the hierarchy that had become law the moment sixth grade had begun.

It was strange, the stock characters the popular kids had turned into, as though they had taken a summer class he hadn't enrolled in after fifth-grade graduation. For God's sake, Taylor used to eat her boogers in the first grade—Teddy had seen her do it—and now she was flipping her blond hair around like someone in a shampoo commercial.

The girls didn't even say hello as they came to a stop beside him, these girls Teddy had been in class with since kindergarten. He imagined a zombie walking up, ripping their heads off with his bare, purple and rotting hands and gnawing on their neck meat. *Neck Meat II: Tween Revenge.* A small smile played across his lips as he looked out into the traffic.

Teddy saw it happening before the drivers did, he was sure. An enormous white Suburban, with stick-figure replicas of a dad with a tie on, a ponytailed mom in a sun visor and three children in descending height spinning a basketball, wielding a baseball bat and holding pom-poms, respectively, pasted across its back window, veered into the left lane suddenly, completely sideswiping an unassuming gray Toyota Corolla in the process. Teddy thought of his mother. She hated those stickers with a passion. *Oh for Christ's sake,* she muttered every time they saw one, which was often.

Metal scraped metal as brakes yelped and glass shattered; the sound of the Corolla's side mirror slamming into the ground. The baby-blue Prius behind the Corolla stopped just short of slamming into its rear, as the driver tried to steer herself to the far lane, in front of the Suburban. There was no road shoulder to speak of, and so all around them, the other cars dealt with the accident's aftermath, attempting to get around the inconvenient mess and on with their day.

"Holy shit," remarked Taylor with zero emotion, her vocal cords as limp as boiled spaghetti noodles.

"Seriously," said Kai, her voice at exactly the same ineffectual register.

The light had turned in the meantime, and the three of them walked across the street together, single file, their heads turned toward the scene.

Safe on the other side, they stopped and looked at one

another. Teddy thought this was probably the first time Taylor and Kai had looked at him in two years. It was certainly the first time he had been up close to either of them in that long, probably even longer. Kai was pretty, he thought. He had forgotten the freckles spread haphazardly across both of her cheeks, like constellations.

"You want to go over there? Tell the police what we saw?" Teddy asked.

"Are you kidding?" asked Taylor. "No way. I don't want to be late. It was just a sideswipe, anyway; it's not like anyone is dead. My mom does it, like, twice a month."

"But we saw what happened," said Teddy. "It's our obligation to help."

"What are you, like a Boy Scout or something?" asked Taylor, flicking her hair again.

A blond strand escaped, floating through a sunbeam that filtered through the trees before disappearing onto the sidewalk. Teddy made eye contact with Kai for a millisecond before she broke, examining her white Converse sneakers instead.

"Come on, Kai. Let's go," commanded Taylor. Kai turned dutifully, and they strolled off at a quick clip, leaving Teddy alone.

He watched them leave. People, most people, were really just assholes, he had noticed. That was a good way to start a movie, he thought next, a voiceover saying just that as the camera panned in on this exact scene. He whipped out his notepad to jot it down and then pivoted left, toward the accident.

Teddy followed the sidewalk approaching the two women, who were out of their cars. The SUV driver was just as he had imagined, shorter than him, even, wearing a visor as her sticker had promised, her highlighted hair pulled into a ponytail, and dressed in head-to-toe spandex, the kind his mother couldn't stand. He knew this because she commented on it every time they were out in public together. Sometimes she treated Teddy like he was a girlfriend who would somehow understand her anger, instead of like a son who had no opinion about spandex to speak of other than that sometimes it looked nice on butts. Hers was not one of those butts, Teddy noticed.

Ahead of the spandexed woman a few feet, the other woman stood next to her Corolla, smoking a cigarette. He approached carefully. There was a girl on the other side of her, as skinny as a paper doll, scowling into the sky.

"Hello," Teddy offered tentatively, feeling self-conscious but also smug, since he was doing the right thing.

"Hey," the woman replied in a thick Southern accent, grinding out her cigarette on the sidewalk with the toe of her purple plastic clog.

She was dressed in pink scrubs with hyperactive puppies emblazoned all over them. Teddy was nauseated looking at them, the pancakes from that morning gurgling in his stomach, so he focused on her face.

It was heart shaped, like a cat, with wrinkles around her blue eyes that extended like tree branches. Her curly brown hair sat atop her shoulders crisply, shellacked into position by copious amounts of gel. It was a lot to take in, and for a moment, Teddy began to regret his piety.

The paper-doll girl regarded Teddy with a curious squint. Her long legs were encased in light blue denim and her pink T-shirt read *And?* in rhinestones. On her feet were fuchsia flip-flops. She had the same curly brown hair as her mom, but instead of being frozen into submission, it was wild and free, escaping in tendrils from the enormous bun she had piled on the top of her head. Her blue eyes were fringed with what appeared to be purple mascara despite the fact that the rest of her face was completely bare.

Definitely not from his school, thought Teddy, falling immediately and desperately in love.

"I saw what happened," said Teddy.

"You saw that bitch sideswipe us like we were in the goddamn Indy 500?" asked the girl.

"Krystal, if you don't watch your damn language, I swear," the woman barked at her. She looked at Teddy. "You saw it?"

"Yes ma'am," replied Teddy. "Just thought I'd come over here in case you wanted me to tell the police or anything."

The girl, he knew her name was Krystal now, regarded him with a degree more of interest, Teddy thought, but he couldn't be sure. Sirens heralded a cop's arrival, sending traffic scurrying like ants around an apple slice.

"That's nice of you," the woman in scrubs declared, squinting at Teddy as though she didn't know what to make of him. "See, Krystal? This boy is a good Samaritan. He could teach you a thing or two, that's the truth." Krystal rolled her eyes. "I'm Patty," she said. "And this is my daughter, Krystal, but I guess you probably know that already. Say hi, Krystal."

"Hi," she mumbled. Teddy blushed despite his best efforts. He had no control over his physical response to anything lately. It was horrible.

The cop turned off the wail of his sirens, but they continued their blue and red swirl in the morning sun. He got out of the car, looking young for a cop, Teddy thought. Like his English teacher, Mr. Case, who was just out of college and wanted everyone to call him Jack. Teddy just couldn't for some reason; it felt too strange, like seeing his parents hold hands or something. Not that he'd ever seen that.

As the cop walked toward them, Patty ambushed him, launching into her rendition of events a few feet from Teddy and Krystal. Teddy contemplated the ways in which he could start a conversation with Krystal based on what he had seen on film, but the only thing he could think of was "Do you come here often?" which, given the fact that they were stranded on the side of the road, didn't seem appropriate.

"Son?" the cop asked, motioning to Teddy.

"Yessir?" Teddy replied, shifting his backpack a little as he walked the short distance to them.

Krystal followed; he could hear her flip-flops slapping the concrete sidewalk behind him. The SUV driver had wandered closer too, finally off her phone. She looked at Teddy nervously, her eyes like two middle fingers of disdain, despite the forced smile on her face.

"Mrs. . . . ?"

"Platt," Patty answered, her voice gravelly and shrill.

"Mrs. Platt here was just saying how you saw what happened?" the cop asked Teddy.

"I did," answered Teddy, feeling nervous.

Would the SUV lady go to jail, right here on the spot? He felt guilty suddenly, thinking of those stick-figure children. But no, he had to do the right thing.

"I was on my way to school, waiting at the light," he explained, "when I saw her Suburban pretty much just run Mrs. Platt right off the road. Crossed into her lane like she wasn't even there." He could feel Krystal looking at him and straightened his shoulders.

"Is that your memory of the event, Mrs. . . . ?" he asked the culprit. *Culprit* was one of Teddy's favorite words.

"Sinclair," she volunteered, glaring at Teddy. "I had my blinker on," she began, before stopping abruptly. "She was in my blind spot." She shrugged her thin shoulders, surrendering to her guilt. "Yes, it was my fault," she admitted. Patty Platt smirked.

"All right, well, thank you, Tommy," said the officer.

"Um, actually, sir, it's Teddy."

"What?" the cop asked.

"My name. It's not Tommy; it's Teddy." The cop's eyes narrowed.

"Right. Teddy. You've been a big help, Teddy. You should be getting to school now, shouldn't you?"

"Do you mind writing me a note? Just to say that I was here?" asked Teddy, wishing he had anywhere to go but school. Into a pit of snapping alligators would even be preferable.

"Sure, kid." He ripped a blank ticket from his pad and began scribbling on the back of it.

"Thanks a lot, Teddy," said Patty Platt. He liked the sound of her first and last names together. "You saved us a big headache." She jerked her head in the direction of Mrs. Sinclair, who was on her phone again, yapping away.

"Yeah, thanks," said Krystal, moving closer to Teddy. Up close, her face was even more feline than her mother's, like she might start licking her paws at any moment. "She prolly would've tried to say it was my mom's fault."

"No problem," replied Teddy.

"Here you go," said the cop, handing Teddy his note. "Thanks again."

"Just doing my job," Teddy replied gravely. "Okay, well, guess I'll be going. Good luck." He turned reluctantly and began to walk.

"Wait!" yelled Krystal. "You got a phone?" she asked.

"Yeah," Teddy lied. "But it's at home."

"You got a piece of paper?" Teddy nodded, his heart beating so quickly that it shook his skull. He pulled out his green notepad. "I got a pen." She waved a purple sparkly one at him and snatched the notepad from his hand.

"What's all this writing?" she asked, thumbing through it with turquoise-chipped nails, bitten almost down to her white half-moons, which peeked out of the paint.

"Just stuff I think about," mumbled Teddy.

Krystal looked up, directly into his eyes. There was a sliver of green across each of her irises.

"Cool," she affirmed. No one had ever called Teddy cool. Quickly, she scrawled her number on a blank page. "Call me," she commanded, handing the notebook back.

Teddy nodded and turned toward school. Touching his notepad, which he had shoved back into his pocket, he smiled.

CHAPTER THREE

PAUL

Paul sat on the couch, his stupid foot propped up on the stupid ottoman, feeling sorry for himself and watching some not-altogether-unpleasingly-plump woman with brown hair and thick bangs cut in a very straight line across her forehead whisk eggs in a white ceramic bowl.

The sound was muted. He just liked to watch people cook; he didn't like to hear them yammer on about it. A book about triathlon training lay open on his lap, although he hadn't yet read a word of it in a week. Sylvie had brought it home from the library, holding it aloft like some kind of prize. It was a nice gesture, if not inherently inauthentic.

Why Sylvie was so threatened by his exercise regime, he still couldn't figure out. It wasn't like he hadn't asked her to join him on countless occasions, when he had first started out.

Paul had been in okay shape before, had played soccer and

basketball in high school and messed around with both in college, although not on a team or anything. He had never been good enough for that. But he was an athletic guy, which was why he went into contracting, actually—the thought of being on his feet was way more appealing than that of sitting behind a desk. A lot of people assumed contractors weren't the sharpest tools in the shed, that that's why they chose to work with their hands, but they were wrong. Paul was smart. Not to brag or anything, but he was.

He sunk farther into the couch, fighting his lids as they began to flutter. He had been like a newborn since he had broken his ankle, sleeping every two hours because what else was there to do? He hated it.

"How you doing?" asked Sylvie, padding up to him.

His eyes flew open, grateful for the distraction. He smiled up at her, noticing again that her face was not the frozen mask of resentment he had become accustomed to. When had the mask become her actual face? he had wondered just the night before, lying in bed with his ankle aching, the faint drone of the television show she was watching downstairs soothing him to sleep.

It would be easy to say that it had started with Delilah, but that wasn't true, though of course no one is ever the same after tragedy, himself included. And a shocking, sudden and unexpected tragedy like the kind they had all endured at that? Forget it.

If Paul had to pinpoint when exactly their marriage had taken a turn, he'd say it was when Teddy was around three. For years, Sylvie had been riding Paul to get his business off the ground, to go all in for their future so that she could have a break from her relentlessly depressing but bill-paying and benefits-providing job. But then when he had, she had hated him for it. He was never around, she said. He was always working, she complained. She'd had to change her schedule to accommodate his later hours and Teddy's activities, which meant, unfortunately, that he didn't get to see Teddy, or her, for that matter, all that much. But that was what she had wanted! He couldn't win.

Their grief had bonded them again initially, but then inexplicably, because she refused to talk about it, that glue had melted into nothing. Her affection toward him had become forced, for Teddy's sake only, Paul could tell. Then his triathlete training and subsequent equipment obsession that had made more than a small dent in their savings had erased even those, setting her mouth in a firm line whenever he appeared, her eyes cold and distant. And then when he fell and she had to take care of him, well, that had been the final straw, he guessed. She hadn't even made eye contact with him in the emergency room, she was so annoyed.

But this morning, she had actually greeted him with a smile. She had touched him. She had called him "P." She'd lit a candle for Delilah. What in the world was going on? he wanted to know but knew better than to ask. Because if he asked, forget it. Sylvie would get defensive and the mask would cover her face again, shutting off all her light. God, he'd missed that light.

"Okay," he answered, patting the beige couch cushion beside him. "Have a seat; take a load off. You're working from home today, I take it?"

"I'm supposed to be," she answered, landing with a thud that jiggled his ankle and made him wince. Sylvie worked in marketing, doing what exactly Paul wasn't sure, despite the fact that she'd been doing it for almost the entire twenty years he'd known her.

"Sorry," said Sylvie. "I have reverse body dysmorphia."

"Reverse?" asked Paul.

"Yeah, I think I'm much smaller than I am."

"Is that a thing?"

"Everything is a thing these days." Sylvie patted his knee gently and settled back into the cushions with a sigh.

Not a poisonous sigh either, but a contented one, Paul thought. It was very strange, what was happening. Paul watched the television, the woman now pulling a bubbling pan out of the oven with a red mitt, reminding himself not to say a word about it.

"What's she making? A quiche?" asked Sylvie.

"I think so. I turned the sound off, so it could be anything, really."

"Why do you mute it, anyway?"

"You know I don't cook," answered Paul. "I just like watching other people do it."

"Wish I had that luxury," said Sylvie.

"That chicken thing you made last night was delicious," said Paul.

"That was salmon."

"Oh. Yeah. That's what I meant."

"You want to go outside?" Sylvie asked. "I could set up a chair for you in the yard. It's a beautiful day."

Paul looked to one of the floor-to-ceiling windows overlooking the deck. The sky was as blue as the sea, not a cloud in sight.

"Okay," he agreed. Sylvie stood up. The sight of her ample backside aroused him, without warning. He pulled her back down.

"What?" she asked, considering his unspoken message with a raised eyebrow.

She could use a tweezer, his younger sister, Gloria, had said, the first time he had brought Sylvie home. He had blown up at her, telling her to fuck off, much to the chagrin of his churchgoing mother. He loved Sylvie's eyebrows; they were as unapologetic as she was.

"Here?"

"Why not?" Paul asked, smiling. Hoping. Sylvie looked around the room, realizing that she had no excuse to say no, Paul surmised.

"But your ankle. Are you sure you're okay?"

"Last time I checked, ankles were not involved."

He pulled her closer, gently. To say please was pathetic, but that's what he was thinking.

"Okay," she whispered. "But how?"

"Why are you whispering?" Paul asked. Sylvie shook her head, her eyes downcast. "Follow my lead," he said.

Paul took her face in his hands and kissed her lips, which tasted like coffee and syrup. It had been so long since their mouths had met. She surprised him by probing his open mouth with her tongue, tentatively at first and then with a bit more force.

Awkwardly, he lifted his foot off the ottoman and pulled at the waistband of his pants, not making much progress. Sylvie stopped to help him, pulling them down and over his cast into a plaid puddle on the floor. She stood up, laughing a little as she removed her own.

Usually, Sylvie's tendency to laugh during sex made Paul self-conscious and angry—a feeling that always led to an argument, because Sylvie couldn't understand why he took himself so seriously and he couldn't understand how she didn't take him seriously—but not today. Today he was just grateful that it was happening at all, and so he would keep his mouth shut.

She straddled him, guiding him inside her and slowly easing herself up and down with more than a slight degree of difficulty. He closed his eyes, focusing on the exquisite pleasure of something other than his hand doing this work, God's work, really, and surrendered to her familiar rhythm.

Within moments, he was done, exhilarated and embarrassed all at once but too exhausted and surprised by the fact that it had happened at all to care. She collapsed against his chest, inside of which his heart was beating so quickly it felt as though it might jump right out and dance a jig of happiness, right across the floor and out the door.

"That was nice," Sylvie said breathily.

"I'm sorry I finished—"

"Shhhh," she commanded. "Don't speak."

He grunted and closed his eyes. She was beginning to get a little heavy on his lap, but he didn't want to move. He was still inside her, after all, like a snail in its shell. Although he didn't like to think of his dick as a snail. He would move. Slowly, though.

"Oh, sorry. I think I passed out there for a second," said Sylvie. She rolled off and back into a sitting position on the couch beside him, pantless.

Paul stared into the kitchen, at the Yahrzeit candle on the counter, its small flame flickering inside the glass votive.

"That was nice this morning," he volunteered, encouraged by the rare intimacy of the moment. "With the candle."

"Yeah," agreed Sylvie quietly.

"Unlike you, though," said Paul, even as he feared he'd trip a wire with his comment. Sylvie shrugged.

"You know me. Full of surprises," she replied. She didn't sound angry, but her terse reply suggested that the conversation was over, unless Paul felt like losing an arm. He did not.

"Teddy seemed good this morning," he said, switching gears.

"Yeah," said Sylvie, sitting up.

"He's a good kid," he continued. "Except when he's being a jerk."

Sylvie laughed. "Our preteen," she said, shuddering. "Oh God, this is just the beginning too, you know. Stupid me, I thought boys didn't go through this."

"Go through what?" asked Paul.

"The silence. I mean, I knew physically we were in for a

shock with him, but emotionally I figured he would always be accessible."

"Accessible like me, you mean."

"Yeah, I guess so," answered Sylvie.

"But why should he be like me now? He's always been much more like you. Emotionally, anyway."

"What are you saying?"

"Forget it, never mind," said Paul.

"No, go on," urged Sylvie. "I promise I won't get angry." Paul made a face. "I'm serious."

"Okay, well, at the risk of losing my other ankle, I just mean that Teddy's never been one to talk about his feelings. Remember in kindergarten, when he had that bathroom accident and some of the kids were total assholes about it?"

Sylvie squinted, trying to remember. "Oh yeah, he pooped behind the art easel."

"Right. But we would never have known if his teacher hadn't called us in for a meeting. The kid was cool as a cucumber."

"Paul, he was five."

"Yes, I know he was five, but still. He's been that way all his life. When he was a baby, he'd twist up his face, looking like he was going to cry, but then at the most you'd get a tiny squeak of discomfort."

"Our stoic warrior," said Sylvie.

"Like you," confirmed Paul.

He bent down to pull up his pants but realized that he needed Sylvie's help. This damn cast was the bane of his existence. Before he had to ask, her hands were there, lifting his ankle and then his pants up and over it.

"Thanks," he said, handling his other leg.

Paul had assumed, when Sylvie was pregnant, that Delilah's personality would be more like his. He'd never gotten the chance to know, but he wondered about it still. If Teddy looked like him but acted like his mother, Delilah would have been the opposite. Logically it made sense.

Sometimes he'd see little girls and their dads out and about, certain girls with Sylvie's coloring, and his heart would hover in his chest, like a rickety elevator before reaching its appointed floor. He wished that she'd lived with every fiber of his being. He mourned Delilah's death, the girl who never got a chance to be; but more than that he mourned the family of four that never was, the innocence of his family of three and, going way back in time, the optimism of his marriage of two.

Sylvie stood up. Paul watched her gather her dark hair into a ponytail with one hand while sliding the black elastic that otherwise encircled her wrist up and over it in one fluid motion.

"Do you need help getting up?" she asked, turning to him with her arm outstretched.

He nodded gratefully. He did.

CHAPTER FOUR

SYLVIE

Sylvie ran to the stairs and up, up, up: *clomp, clomp clomp* in her tan clogs.

"Sylvie?" Paul called from upstairs, sounding alarmed. Sylvie couldn't remember the last time she had moved at this speed in his vicinity.

"I'm not being chased!" she yelled back, making a beeline for their bathroom. "I just really have to pee!"

She closed the door behind her and ran for the middle drawer. The bottle. She twisted off its cap and shook out one of her magic pills into her palm. Into her mouth it went, and then, thirsty at the faucet like she had been stranded in the desert for days, Sylvie drank.

She stood up, swallowed and ran out of the bathroom.

Shit. She ran back in, checking to make sure she hadn't left the bottle out on the counter. She hadn't. Okay. Okay. Good.

But wait.

Why was she leaving the bottle in the drawer anyway? Paul didn't want anything to do with the pills, but if he happened to see the bottle, he could notice that a few were missing, and if he hadn't taken them, then who had? And then he would approach Sylvie, and— She took the bottle out of the drawer and jogged to her side of the walk-in closet, which was just off the bathroom.

She turned on the light and scanned the crowded but organized room. Short sleeves, long sleeves, pants, skirts and dresses faced her. Shelved on the side were her jeans and sweaters, although she hadn't worn jeans since before Delilah. No, that wasn't true, she remembered, thinking of the photo of herself in them that had been the impetus to stop wearing them altogether.

Yes, there, she decided, her eyes landing on a red circular handbag hanging from a hook. Sylvie unzipped its interior pocket and carefully nestled the bottle inside.

If Paul asked, she would just tell him that she had thrown out the pills.

Good. Very good. All bases covered, thought Sylvie, feeling more than a little nuts. But it was okay. Just one bottle of pills her whole life, come on. Harmless fun. Did she not deserve a break from her brain?

She walked out of the closet, back through the bathroom, to the hallway, right into Paul. How he managed to creep around stealthily on crutches she would never know.

"You okay?" he asked.

"I'm fine," she answered. "Just had to pee before the meeting."

"Meeting?" he called after her, as she made her way down the stairs.

"Yes, the stupid PTA. For the end-of-year party," she explained, turning around to peer up at him. Paul seemed brighter somehow, like someone had pulled the string to a light bulb inside his chest. He was radiant, Sylvie thought.

The pill. It was working. She was so glad.

"Oh. Before you go, would you mind helping me down the stairs?" he asked sheepishly. "I go up and down on my butt while you're at work, but since you're here, I—"

"Yes, sure," answered Sylvie patiently. Patience: another virtue of her new medicated self. Normal Sylvie would have sighed heavily, perhaps even barked about how she had had to rush out of work early just to get home to make sure dinner was on the table because God forbid Paul cook something for himself and Teddy and now she had to go to this ridiculous meeting she consistently hated attending, that they always started exactly on time, and if she was late she'd miss the wine—but. Not this Sylvie. This Sylvie took Paul's crutches from him without so much as an eye roll, ran them down to the first floor and then trotted back up to become the human crutch her husband needed.

"Thanks," said Paul, as she snaked her arm around his waist dutifully, supporting him as he held onto the banister and slowly made his way, cast leg first, down to the first floor.

"You okay?" she asked, hoping he would say yes. Pill or no pill, she really was late.

"Fine," he answered. "Teddy here can take care of me." He glanced over to the couch, where Teddy was splayed out, watching *Splash* for the nine hundredth time that week. "Right, Teddy?"

Sylvie walked over to him, shaking his shoulder slightly.

"In five minutes, take a shower, T. Then bed." He nodded, not taking his eyes off the screen.

"Okay, I have to go," Sylvie announced. "Bye."

She kissed the top of his head, gave Paul a peck on the cheek and then, finally, she was out the door and into the warm spring air. It was the perfect jean-jacket-at-night-and-short-sleeves-during-the-day, end-of-April-in-Atlanta night.

Sylvie took a deep breath through her nostrils, feeling each particle of lavender oxygen filter through her as she walked briskly down the slight slope of the driveway. She had been enclosed in her tomb of an office all day, and then straight into the air-conditioned imprisonment of her car, and then into the house, running around like a chicken with her head cut off, scrambling to make macaroni and cheese out of a box and throw some fish sticks in the oven.

The smell of damp earth and grass clippings clung to her, and she was happy. Happy for the first time all day, because she wouldn't take any pills at work. That was crossing the line. That was cause for alarm. Not that she was performing brain surgery or anything—she was branding dog food, for God's sake—but still. She took another blissful inhale in and made a left toward Erika's McMansion.

Ahead of her, a lean woman walked her greyhound, its legs as spindly as matchsticks. It was true what they said, that dogs looked like their owners, she thought. What would her dog be?

As she passed them, she browsed through the limited catalog in her mind. She had never been a dog person, despite the fact that she forced Teddy to volunteer at a pet shelter. A bulldog, most likely, she guessed. Face folded into an accordion of frown; sturdy bordering on plump.

She hadn't always been like this, she thought, picking up her pace and wishing she had changed into her sneakers. Before Delilah she had been more like a—more like a what? Was there a dog who had no concept of death and tragedy? A bichon what was it called? Frise? The ones with the happy eyes and the Princess Leia buns for ears. No, that wasn't true. Sylvie had always been a bitch, just a clueless one. Oh, to be clueless again. Bubbles of drug-induced contentment popped in her belly. This was a close second.

She realized that she had reached Erika's house. It loomed above her at the top of an imposing hill of manicured lawn. Erika and her husband had mowed down the charming Craftsman that had once stood there and replaced it with what Sylvie was sure they considered mid-century modern but what looked to her like a schizophrenic bunker. Gray concrete, a steel stairway up to its apple-red double doors and a slab of cherrywood around its expansive middle like a belt. Paul shivered every time they drove by it.

"Here we go," muttered Sylvie under her breath, as she began her ascent. What would this meeting be like as the new version of herself? She was almost giddy to find out.

Sylvie Snow had never been giddy in her life.

"Sylvie! Hi, come in, come in," Erika chirped, opening the door and motioning her inside.

"Sorry I'm late," offered Sylvie.

She walked into their West Elm showroom. Erika's commitment to the brand du jour, whether it be the clothes she wore, the car she drove or, in this case, the furniture in her home, was a hallmark of her personality.

"Please," replied Erika, swooping in to give her a perfumed hug. "How are you?"

Erika's brown eyes were wide. Too wide. *Eye-lift,* Sylvie thought to herself.

"Oh good, you know, just—" Sylvie paused, hoping something clever would come to her, but her mind was as blank as Erika's impossibly smooth forehead. "Happy about spring."

"Oh God, I'm not," replied Erika. "No-sleeve weather is upon us, and my upper arms are as flappy as two flags in a hurricane." Sylvie glanced at Erika's arms, which were ensconced in camel cashmere.

Who cares, Erika! Sylvie wanted to scream. *We're almost fucking fifty years old! Isn't it our right to go sleeveless no matter the state of our triceps? Have we not earned that right just for simply existing for this long?*

But Sylvie did not scream; she just gave her weird, fake laugh, more like a hiccup than an actual laugh. She hadn't always been fake. There had been a time when Sylvie would have said exactly what she felt without a second thought. That time had been three years ago. The her before this.

A lot of people spoke and wrote about how grief cracked

them open like lobsters, revealing their bare, obliterated essence. One blogger Sylvie had read wrote about the unexpected empowerment of her grief, how although answering someone's "How are you?" with the truth almost always sent them scurrying away in discomfort, it actually gave her, the griever, strength. Because her truth was proof that her dead husband had actually existed. And every time she leaned into that truth, she was giving his life the recognition it deserved.

Sylvie understood what this blogger was saying; she did. But for Sylvie, it was different. By folding her grief deep inside her like an origami scrap, it was hers and hers alone. Because people had let her down, in the wake of Delilah's death. They had not been to her what she needed them to be. Not for long enough, anyway. And as she kept folding and folding that scrap, inevitably the rest of her had folded in on itself too.

Until now. With these pills. They released bubbles into Sylvie's bloodstream, and they were releasing something else: Sylvie. The old Sylvie.

"Girls! Sylvie is here!" Erika announced, presenting her to the group like a gift.

Sylvie forced herself to smile at the six women draped over Erika's monochromatic furniture, all balancing on their laps tiny paper plates crowded with orange cheese rectangles and purple grapes and clear plastic glasses filled with pink wine in their manicured hands.

She gave a small wave and darted right toward the kitchen island to pour herself her own plastic cup of chilled pink sociability. These pills were one thing, but these pills with a side of alcohol—that was something else entirely. Sylvie had discovered this the day before, when she had cracked open a beer while making dinner and shot into an atmosphere of goodwill she had never before known.

She placed the bottle back in its monogrammed sterling-silver ice bucket. Because you had to monogram your ice bucket. There were so many sterling-silver ice buckets around, you wouldn't want to get yours confused with someone else's.

Ellen Rhodes patted the tan leather couch cushion beside her. Sylvie sat. There was a conversation under way. Something about summer camp.

Sylvie took a big sip of her wine.

Paul couldn't understand why Sylvie involved herself at all in the PTA, considering every time she went to a meeting she was miserable, but Sylvie wanted to stay connected to her son, connected to his life outside of hers.

But what life? she thought now, sinking farther into the couch as the medicine flowed through her veins in a river of pink wine, undoing all the knots in her neck like a zipper, pulling the tab down as blue and yellow cartoon songbirds flew out.

Teddy hated school and, as far as Sylvie could tell, had no friends. She hadn't seen his two old faithfuls, Martin and Raj, in months. She'd been avoiding confronting this fact for so long that thinking of it plainly now was a revelation.

Here she was, planning an end-of-year celebration for a class of little shits who made her son feel less than, at a meeting she herself dreaded attending. What was the point? And why did she stay so damn quiet about it? Why had she chosen to cut off the blood flow to a part of her personality that she actually enjoyed? Sure, it might have gotten her into trouble on occasion but so what? Trouble was fun. Trouble was interesting.

"Ellen," Sylvie whispered, feeling another wave of warmth undulate through her.

Sylvie had known Ellen since her son, Elliott, had been with Teddy in pre-K. Her husband was an insufferable prick, and Elliott had had a biting problem for far longer than was acceptable. Sylvie had just seen Elliott the other day when she'd picked Teddy up to take him to Hebrew School; his long, unwashed bangs had hidden most of his face as he strapped on his headphones and clomped past her car, his mouth a tight line.

Ellen's life wasn't perfect either, but she was pretending just like Sylvie was. And why? For what?

"Mmm?" Ellen replied, leaning her head toward Sylvie but not taking her eyes off Erika. Her blond hair tickled Sylvie's nose. It smelled like a salon, like air-conditioned hairspray.

"Why are we here?" she asked Ellen.

"What?" Ellen replied, still keeping her eyes on the room.

"We're going to have to bribe our boys to even go to this party. Why are we here?"

The conversation around them had turned a corner toward hair removal. Lacey Ross's hand was in the air as she showed her armpit to Erika.

"I've been bribing Elliott to behave like a human being since he was in utero," Ellen deadpanned. "I'm in it for the free rose."

"No, but seriously," said Sylvie. Now Candace Mayhall had

pulled up the leg of her pants to show everyone her lasered shin. "Jesus, what is happening here?"

"If labia's next, I'm out," said Ellen. Sylvie laughed. Ellen was funny.

"Teddy doesn't have any friends," she admitted to Ellen. Ellen put her hand on Sylvie's knee and squeezed, looking at her finally.

"Honey," she said. "Elliott may be a bona fide psychopath," she admitted back.

"Shit," said Sylvie.

She had never had an honest conversation with anyone at one of these meetings. Not ever, not once. It was all lasered hair removal and who had an in with who for the school auction and where did you get those jeans, they're so cute. But never this.

When Delilah had died, Teddy had been nine. It had happened in the spring, and so mercifully Sylvie had been able to take quite a long PTA hiatus, through the summer and into the fall of his fifth-grade year, before returning.

And when she had, not one of these women, not even Ellen, had acknowledged what had happened to her. Yes, they had all—well, not all, *Lindsey Ferris, I'm looking at you,* Sylvie thought now—sent well-meaning emails and brought over food in the immediate aftermath, leaving it at her front door in insulated bags, but then, five months later in person, it was like it had never happened.

Sylvie had been pregnant, as big as a house the last time they had shared a couch with her, and then she wasn't, but there was no baby to show for it, so you would think that one of these women could have at least mentioned it to her face after the fact, at the very least told her they were so sorry for her loss even though she hated when people said that.

"I'm going to leave," she said quietly to Ellen, as Erika rang her monogrammed brass bell. Everything in this house was fucking monogrammed.

"What? Everything okay?" asked Ellen. Sylvie stood up.

"Guys, I'm sorry, but I have to leave," she announced.

Erika rested her bell on her lap. "Is something wrong at home?" she asked.

Had Erika's eyebrows been able to move, they would have been legitimately furrowed in concern; Sylvie believed that. Erika wasn't a bad person; none of these women were bad people. Except for Lindsey Ferris.

"Well, not really. Paul broke his ankle and is a complete pain in the ass. But that's not relevant to why I'm leaving." Sylvie took her last gulp of rosé. "I'm leaving because Teddy has zero interest in attending this party that we're planning. I wouldn't even know it existed if I wasn't part of the PTA, and to be honest, I'm going to have to bribe him to go. And you know, he's twelve, so shouldn't my bribing days be over? Shouldn't I just accept him for the cautious, shy, possibly antisocial but hopefully just not-comfortable-enough-in-his-skin-yet person that he is? Wouldn't that make everything easier?"

The women looked up at Sylvie, all their mouths slightly agape. She knew that as soon as the door shut behind her, Erika would take a sip of her wine and say something like, *Well, that was interesting,* and Monika Masuda would roll her eyes and utter something like, *Crazy much?* But Sylvie didn't care.

"Well," said Erika. "I don't really know what to say?"

"You don't have to say anything," answered Sylvie. "I'm certainly not mad at anyone." Sylvie paused. "Actually, that's not true. Lindsey Ferris, I'm mad at you."

Lindsey brought her French-manicured hand to her chest, the enormous diamond of her engagement ring catching the light and beaming it back to them, so much so that Monika Masuda shaded her eyes, using her own, considerably less expensive, hand as a visor.

"Me?" she squeaked.

"How come you never even sent me so much as an email when my baby died?"

Monika Masuda's hand dropped to her mouth.

"What?" asked Lindsey.

"You heard me."

"Sylvie, I—I." Lindsey took a deep breath. "I didn't?"

"No, you did not. You definitely did not. And I was just wondering why? I mean, you saw me pregnant, and then you saw me not pregnant minus the baby. Everyone else here at least had the decency to acknowledge what had happened."

"I sent you dinner," Erika volunteered.

"Yes, Erika, you did. Thank you. So what gives, Lindsey?"

"Well. I could have sworn I did—"

"You did not."

"In that case, Sylvie, I apologize. It's just that—I dunno—we're not friends. I didn't want to overstep my bounds, maybe? Honestly, I don't remember. It was what, five years ago?" Lindsey laughed nervously.

"Three years ago," said Sylvie. She felt surprisingly calm, the medicine still churning its pleasant Jacuzzi bubbles inside her. "Our kids have been in school together, Lindsey, since they were what, three?"

"Yes," answered Lindsey.

"So we may not be getting pedicures together, we may not even like each other that much, but we share a common experience, right? We're both mothers."

Lindsey stared at her blankly.

"Right?" asked Sylvie.

"Right," Lindsey said quietly.

"So the human thing to do when someone you know, even if they're just an acquaintance, goes through hell, is to send a damn email. Say you're sorry. Say you wish you could make it better. Say, 'If there's anything I can do for you, just let me know,' even if you don't really mean it." Sylvie collected herself. She was getting angry, pill or no pill. "Ladies, back me up. Am I right?"

The remaining six looked around at one another, mumbling their accords.

"I'm sorry, Sylvie," said Lindsey, her lip trembling. There was a tiny cracker crumb stuck in her pink lip gloss.

"Thank you. Apology accepted. And just so you know, the next time something terrible happens to someone you know, I don't care if it's the guy who cuts your grass, tell them you're sorry. Okay?"

"Okay."

Sylvie cleared her throat.

"Okay. Well, I'll be going now." She plunked her plastic cup onto the wood coffee table, avoiding a coaster on purpose. "Erika, if you want me to make my spinach dip for the party, call me. I can drop it off."

"The one in the bread bowl?" called Erika after her.

"Yes!" Sylvie yelled back, and shut the door.

Outside on the stoop, she stood in silence. The moon had arrived, filtering its silver light through the budding leaves on the trees. In the distance, an owl hooted as she began her descent down the driveway.

A smile crept over Sylvie's lips, tickling her teeth. Without warning, a single laugh erupted from her throat. And then before she knew it, she was happily hysterical, guffawing so hard that tears began to stream down her cheeks.

How liberating! She was free. She was finally free. And Lindsey's pious face, her stupid, boring face as she attempted to explain her self-absorption. Priceless!

What about Erika, her mouth hanging open like a goddamn mailbox!

Oh God. Sylvie felt so good. Would she feel so good in the morning, after this high had worn off? Not likely. But! That's what the pills were for. She would just continue to take them until they were gone, continue to live this pain-free, honest life, and then, when they were all gone, she would figure out how to be this way without their help. These pills were her training wheels; that was all.

She rounded the corner toward home, hugging herself against the slight chill, smiling still.

CHAPTER FIVE

TEDDY

Teddy couldn't get over it. Krystal looked exactly like Daryl Hannah.

The thought had first occurred to him as he walked home from school the day of the accident. He had been trying to figure it out, just who she looked like; it was someone from that movie about a mermaid his mother had forced him to watch a long time ago—what was the name of that movie? Crap, why couldn't he remember it?—when, just as he switched tracks to consider whether his mother had remembered to get his Honey Nut Cheerios at the store, *bam!* It had hit him. *Splash*.

He had rushed home, practically running—which for Teddy was unheard of unless he was in PE and being forced to do it—forgone his afternoon snack and scrolled through their vast streaming cue until he had found it.

Yes, he was right on the money; Krystal was the spitting image of the actress, whose name apparently was Daryl Hannah. Except for her hair. Krystal's was curly, like ringlet curly. And darker.

Now, four days later, Teddy had watched the movie six times: once on Friday, twice on Saturday, twice on Sunday and again, tonight. Monday night. He had practically memorized the dialogue, which was pretty funny, he thought, all things considered. And by that, of course, he meant the ridiculous plot. A mermaid on land in New York City, okay. But Tom Hanks was just great. He was really great.

Teddy wished he was like Tom Hanks and thought that maybe it wasn't such an unrealistic goal. It wasn't like Tom Hanks was some jock stud or anything. And he wasn't the best looking either. What he was, was charming. Teddy could train himself to be charming. Maybe.

He sat at his laptop in his room, his hair still damp from the shower, scrolling through Google Images of Tom Hanks. Old ones, when he was young. Why was it that when people got old, their bodies started to melt? Like candles or something.

"Hey, T," his dad said, catching him off guard. Teddy's heart jumped into his esophagus as he quickly slammed his computer shut. Could his parents knock, just once in their whole freaking lives? Was that too much to ask?

"What!" Teddy yelped back.

"Geez, Ted, relax," his dad replied, balancing on his crutches in the same blue plaid flannel pajama pants he had worn every day since his accident.

His mom had cut the left leg off to make room for his cast,

but still. It had been a couple of weeks; he could sacrifice the leg of another pair of pants for the sake of variety, Teddy thought.

"I'm not the enemy." He gave Teddy a look that said, *It's cool if you like eighties Tom Hanks. Who doesn't like eighties Tom Hanks?*

"Dad, come on," he replied, resisting the urge to kick the leg of his desk. "I know that. It's just like, could you maybe knock or something?"

"Yeah, yeah, of course. Sorry. You okay? Want to talk about anything?" He searched Teddy's face plaintively. His dad was all right, Teddy remembered. He was accidentally annoying, unlike his mother, who seemed to revel in it.

"No, I'm cool. Just, I really like the way *Splash* was shot, so I was just reading about it."

"*Splash*?"

"The movie?"

"Oh yeah, the movie. You're really into it, huh? Every time I walk by the TV, it's on lately. I just thought you were into Daryl Hannah. Or Tom Hanks, whatever. Either one is cool. I remember—" His father was on the verge of one of his rambles.

"Dad."

"Yes?"

"I'm not gay."

"Oh, okay. But if you are, that's okay too, you know?"

"Dad."

"Okay, okay." He loped the short distance to Teddy on his crutches. "Give me a hug."

Teddy stood up and hugged him, comforted by his father's familiar smell of toothpaste and bananas. He ate a banana every day, his dad.

"Get to bed soon. Your mom will kill me if you're still up when she gets home."

"'K. Good night, Dad."

"Good night, T." He closed the door.

Teddy raked his fingers through his hair, which was now almost dry. He rolled his chair away from his desk, which was really a drafting table, although his parents had presented it to Teddy as a desk for his eighth birthday.

He had drawn a lot then, mostly pictures of Stormtroopers and Darth Vader, so it had made sense at the time. But now Teddy was a writer, and he had homework, so he needed a more substantial desk. He eyed with distaste the orange plastic Georgia Aquarium cup that had become his pencil holder. A real desk with drawers.

His whole room needed an upgrade, Teddy thought. Or maybe he just needed to restock it. He scanned the shelves that climbed up the wall behind his desk, his blue-gray eyes squinting as he considered their contents. Harry Potter was so three years ago. And his mom had loaded his shelves with classics, as she called them: *The Odyssey, The Iliad, The Hobbit*—blah, blah, blah. Teddy was never going to read them.

There were trinkets too, placed here and there: Star Wars bobbleheads; a LEGO 747 that he and his dad had built together when he was seven, plus some artwork of his from elementary school his mother had framed.

Teddy swiveled around to face the other wall, the wall be-

hind his bed. It was filled by an enormous world map, which in theory was cool, but for, like, a doctor's office or something.

His bed wasn't bad, twin size with a gray-and-white-striped comforter. Not babyish.

Teddy stood up, crossed over to his closet and opened the door, revealing a full-length mirror nailed to its back. He needed new clothes too, he thought, surveying his own red-and-black-plaid pajama bottoms that revealed his ankles and beat-up yellow T-shirt advertising the science camp he had stopped going to the summer he had turned ten.

His face wasn't bad. Technically handsome, he guessed. Nice eyes, a small nose for a Jew—which was something he had heard his own mother, the Jewish one, say, so it wasn't racist, just fact—a square jaw. Not one hair on it, although Teddy searched for one fervently almost every morning in the magnifying mirror in his parents' bathroom. He had sprouted hairs elsewhere, which both embarrassed and delighted him.

The hair on his head was nice too. Plenty of it, although he liked to keep it short. A nice color, he guessed. Recently he had discovered gel and liked to spike it a little in the front, just to give it some character.

He wasn't all bad, he guessed. He went back to his desk, treading lightly over the muted gray, orange and yellow Turkish rug that stretched across the patch of wood floor between it and his bed. He sat and rolled back to his laptop, his heart pounding like it always did when he decided to google her name.

Krystal Platt.

A photo of her popped up on his screen. From her school, a public middle school not too far away that Teddy had heard of but now knew much more about since he had googled that too. It turned out that Krystal Platt played soccer, which had been a surprise to Teddy. She didn't look like the soccer-playing girls at his school, with their straight, blond hair pulled back in tight ponytails and impressive calf muscles, trotting up and down the field like tiny Clydesdales.

Sometimes, when Teddy daydreamed about their first date, he imagined himself saying to her, maybe sitting on a park bench, overlooking a sweeping vista: *Krystal Platt, you're full of surprises.* And then he would take her chin in his hand and kiss her.

He wanted to call her desperately. But there was one problem: he had no phone. Oh, how he cursed his parents! Screen time this and screen time that, and sexual predators blah, blah, blah. His computer had more locks on it than Rikers, which was an analogy he had stolen from Martin, whose parents were even more paranoid than his own.

Teddy had considered calling Krystal from his mom's phone, but it was surgically attached to her hand. Plus, what if Krystal didn't answer and then he didn't leave a voicemail and then she called back to ask who had called her and his mom answered? A terrifying probability that he could not chance.

He'd been eyeing his father's phone—he was on it way less than his mother—but until that afternoon he had been unsure of his passcode.

"So how many miles of swimming do you log on your app the first week versus running and biking?" Teddy had asked his dad, leaning over his shoulder as he sat on the couch.

"What?" he had answered absently.

He was reading a magazine called *Runner's World*, ogling a pair of sneakers that Teddy willed him not to buy. Since his father had taken up triathlete training, he had amassed a virtual sporting goods store of supplies, which had overflowed the basement and invaded every inch of the garage, so much so that neither his mother nor his father could park in there any longer. It was a bone of contention with his parents; Teddy heard their arguments late at night, when he was supposed to be sleeping, his covers pulled up over his head to block out the insults she slung at him, his father's silence on the other end.

"When you train for a triathlon," Teddy had answered, as though his asking about triathlons was a normal occurrence.

The truth was that he had been trying to figure out his dad's code for days, grabbing his unmanned phone when he wasn't looking and typing in every birthday, every name he could think of that might grant him access to Krystal Platt. Nothing had worked.

"Oh!" his dad had replied, flinging the magazine to the far corner of the couch in excitement.

Bingo, Teddy had thought to himself as his father searched for his phone. He had tried to garner his son's interest in this app at least a dozen times when he had first started using it: *Look how cool this is! Can you believe this interface?* he would say, swiping this way and that to no avail. Teddy hadn't cared one whit about it. Until that afternoon.

Teddy felt a little guilty, watching his father practically levitate with glee, but really, who was he hurting?

Teddy studied his father's long, tapered fingers as he typed in his code. 3-2-7-9. From the pocket of his pants, Teddy covertly pulled out his notepad and scrawled the numbers onto a blank page, his heart pounding as though he were robbing a bank. His code was 3-2-7-9? What was 3-2-7-9? That his father could prize a series of numbers that had no relevance to Teddy seemed hurtful, somehow.

But that hurt had faded as Teddy had endured his dad's interminably extensive explanation of interval training. Punishment for the crime, Teddy guessed.

Tonight, Teddy had eyed his father's hands as he helped him up the stairs. He hadn't been holding his phone. And there were no pockets in his pajamas, which Teddy knew only because he had seen them from every angle over the past couple of weeks.

So this was it. It was now or never. His father's phone had to be downstairs. All Teddy had to do was get down there, find it and pop back into his room before his mother came home. And stealthily too, since technically he was supposed to be in bed.

Teddy crept to the closed door of his bedroom and pulled it open slowly. Behind the closed door of his parents' bedroom, he heard the faint drone of the television. Downstairs was deserted and dark, save for a single lamp left on for his mother. His mother. The only possible foil to his perfect plan. He had to move at the speed of light.

Quickly, but not too quickly—the last thing they needed was another broken ankle around here, and the stairs were slippery beneath his socks—Teddy descended the stairs. At the bottom, he made a beeline for the couch. Not seeing the phone immediately, he began to frantically dig between the cushions. *Shit, it isn't here. Shit, shit, shit.* He plunged his hand into each of the remaining cracks, desperate for his fingertips' contact with cool, curved metal. Nothing.

"Goddamnit," he hissed into the silence, relishing the way it felt to say the word.

Teddy hit the cushion next to him with his fist, making a soft plopping noise that was not the least bit satisfying. That's when he saw it. The phone. On the kitchen counter, plugged into its charger.

He sprang off the couch and ran across the room to retrieve it. Just as he unplugged the phone from its power source, at exactly that moment, he heard his mother's keys in the back door.

He slid his sweaty palms down the sides of his legs, searching for pockets he knew were not there. As the door swung open, Teddy slipped the phone between the waistband of his underwear and his flesh and leapt over to the refrigerator, pulling it open to pretend he was eyeing its contents, even though his mother hated it when he did that.

"Teddy!" his mother trilled, opening the door and turning on the light.

He had braced himself for her disapproval, but her greeting was surprisingly upbeat. Too upbeat.

He adjusted the phone beneath his waistband, pulling it up farther before closing the door and turning around to face her.

Her cheeks were flushed pink from the spring air, her hair escaping a bun—or was it a ponytail? Teddy never was quite sure which was which—in soft tendrils. Her eyes were bright. She looked different, Teddy thought to himself. Pretty, he realized. Young. Was it weird to think these things about your mother? He decided no, since they were just innocuous, fact-based thoughts. Normally she did not look this way; that was an incontestable fact. Normally she looked like she was thinking about something else, even if she was talking to you. And her hair was down, a mass of heavy curls that seemed to, now that Teddy saw her hair up, add five pounds to her neck. She seemed so much lighter, his mother, standing in the kitchen with him now.

"It's too bright in here," she announced, flipping the switch she had just turned on. Purple air filtered in through the window over the enormous white porcelain sink, which was empty save for his father's water glass.

"You don't want to go to that end-of-year party, right?" she asked him. "God, I'm so thirsty." She took a glass from the shelf and crossed past him to fill it from the refrigerator's filter.

"What end-of-year party?" His mother stood before him, chugging her water noisily. Something was up with her, although Teddy had no idea what.

"At school," she explained, setting her drained glass on the counter.

"Definitely not," Teddy answered, envisioning exactly how that party would go, since it was the way it had gone every year since as far back as he could remember.

He would sit or stand in some corner of some classmate's basement, backyard or, horror of horrors, pool deck—the pool parties, those were hands down the worst—with Raj and Martin, although Raj wasn't a given now, thanks to his improved social status, drinking warm lemonade and talking about nothing.

"Oh good, that's what I thought. I mean, that's what I know," said his mother. "You've told me as much since the dawn of time, but every year I force you to do it anyway. And for what? If you don't want to go, you shouldn't have to go. You're almost thirteen years old; it's time for me to listen to you once in a while."

Teddy nodded his head slowly, slightly afraid. What in the world was going on with her?

"I never hear you, Teddy. I realized that tonight, sitting at this ridiculous meeting, feeling probably like you feel at all these ridiculous parties. Like, what is the fucking point?"

"Mom, are you okay?"

"Teddy, I'm more than okay, honey."

She swept him into an embrace. Teddy prayed that his father's cell phone wouldn't escape from its precarious position and clatter to the ground between them.

"I'm great. I just want us to try to really hear each other

more, you know? Accept each other as we are. Your father too." She released him.

"So I don't have to go to the party?"

"No, you don't have to go. Unless you want to go?"

"I don't."

"Okay."

Teddy and his mother stared at each other for a moment. Did she want him to say something else? He didn't want to. He wanted to text Krystal, and time was running out. He didn't know when she went to sleep, and if he sent the text while she was sleeping and then had to send a follow-up text telling her not to text back, it would just be too embarrassing. Code-red embarrassing. But that's where he was headed. The digital clock on the stove changed from 9:03 to 9:04.

"Well, thanks, Mom. I'm going to go to bed now."

"Sounds good. Me too soon. Probably watch some idiots on TV first, just to wind down."

"Idiots?" asked Teddy, sliding the phone out from his waistband and into his hand as he headed toward the stairs, his back to her.

It was kind of thrilling, stealing the phone even though technically he wasn't stealing it since he would be returning it to the same spot in which he found it. But the term *borrowing* wasn't thrilling at all.

"Yes, you know, my reality show idiots. Good night," his mother called after him.

"Good night, Mom," he called back.

If Teddy had to guess, he would say his mom had maybe smoked weed? He didn't know anything about smoking weed personally, but he had seen it in a movie or two. He peered over the banister, checking if she was assembling herself an enormous sandwich. No. Just settling into the couch, the remote pointed toward the screen. Who knew? Who cared? He didn't have to go to the end-of-year party, and he had successfully smuggled the phone upstairs and into his room. Two very good turns of events.

Teddy closed his door behind him, his heart pounding. He couldn't do it. How could he do it? What if Krystal didn't respond? What if she had given him the wrong number on purpose?

Teddy sat on his bed. *Calm down. Take a breath. She was the one who insisted you take down her number, remember? You didn't ask her for it. Why would she be trying to trick you?*

It made no sense, had zero payoff for Krystal. She didn't even go to his school, they didn't know the same people, there was no one she could brag to about making a fool out of him. Maybe she just liked him. Stranger things had happened.

He typed in his father's passcode, still puzzled by its origin, and up popped a picture, the rear view of his father on a bike, as narrow as a piece of paper turned upright and sideways, pedaling around the curve of a moss-hewn mountain, the sky gray and heavy. Who had taken this picture? Teddy had always wondered but had never asked. Certainly not his mother; the odds of her getting on anything with two wheels were zero.

A text popped up, startling Teddy for a moment.

Hey gimpy, how you holding up? it read. From someone

named "T.B." No first name, no last name: just "T.B." Tuberculosis. The dots hung and vibrated; Tuberculosis was typing more.

Miss you on the trails, it read next. And then an emoji of a woman with a blond ponytail on a bicycle popped up. So his dad had a female friend he rode bikes with, so what? She was probably on his training team. Teddy had gleaned that much, although he tuned out most of his dad's tri-talk because it was so boring. But could you, like, be married and still have female friends? Was that allowed?

No, Teddy! Focus! It was now 9:16. It was a roll of the dice whether Krystal would be awake at all, but a risk he had to take. Forget Tuberculosis lady and her dumb emoji.

He pulled his green spiral notebook off his nightstand and flipped to the page on which he had written drafts of both his introductory and follow-up texts to her.

With great care, Teddy pressed each digit of Krystal's number into the "To" line. There it was. Her number. Still holding the phone, Teddy lay back on his bed and squeezed his eyes shut. His stomach churned with anxiety, and for a moment he thought he might vomit all over his not babyish gray-and-white-striped duvet cover.

No, Teddy. NO, he reminded himself. *You are doing this. The worst that could happen is that she doesn't answer you and then who cares, you'll never see her again anyway. Okay?* He took a deep breath. Okay.

Teddy peered at his notebook, saying the words out loud as he typed them.

Hello, Krystal? It's Teddy. From your mom's car accident the other day? I helped with the cops?

Teddy took a deep breath and pressed the blue arrow, sending his message through the universe to what he hoped was Krystal's phone.

He held the phone in his hand, staring at the screen for what felt like an eternity, but when he looked at his clock, finally, only three minutes had passed.

Shit. It wasn't her. Or it was her and she didn't care. Or it was her and she was asleep. Or, or, or.

Teddy got up to brush his teeth in the bathroom that adjoined his room, still holding the phone. He switched on the light and placed it screen up on the counter, considering it carefully as he slid the white bubbles up and down, backward and forward over his teeth. He filled his blue cup with water and swished it through his mouth, spitting out the minty freshness in defeat. He ran the water again, cleaning the sink, replaced his toothbrush and cup on the counter and still, nothing. *Shit.*

He scowled at himself in the mirror, shaking his head.

He turned out the light and returned to his room, turning out the light in there as well. He set his alarm for earlier than normal because now, he had to return the phone to its charger before either of his parents woke. He thought about the blond emoji. The text. He worried.

Pulling back the comforter, he climbed inside and decided to feel sorry for himself. Now he had to send another text, telling Krystal not to text back, that it wasn't even his phone, that he was a moron who didn't even have his own phone. It was all too embarrassing, really the worst possible outcome he had envisioned—

Ding.

Teddy's heart leapt, and so did he, sending the phone clattering to the floor. He scrambled for it, clamping his hand around it in a death grip as he brought it back up to eye level.

I know who you are. Took you long enough. What's up, Teddy?

Teddy closed his eyes, this time in sheer exhilaration and gratitude. Oh, the tides were turning. Yes, they were.

He snuggled farther under his comforter and wrote back.

CHAPTER SIX

PAUL

Paul sat on the couch, feeling good. Well, not good as in the good of a month ago, when both of his ankles worked, but decent. He had showered by himself, sitting down on a white plastic stool Sylvie had brought home, his cast covered in a black garbage bag and packing tape. Sylvie had still had to help him get dressed and down the stairs before she left for work, but: progress was progress.

The temperature hovered in the mid-seventies, and so Paul could wear shorts, another reason to feel good. The pajama pants he had been wearing since he fell, the ones Sylvie had cut a leg off of, were like a flag for his state of one-footed despondency.

But here he was in his army-green shorts, smelling like his wife's expensive shampoo, clean-shaven, toes and fingernails clipped—again, Sylvie. He couldn't believe it, but she actually seemed content lately, happy almost. The Sylvie he had met and fallen in love with so many years ago. The Sylvie who liked to have sex with him, to touch him unprompted. The Sylvie who smiled when he walked into the room instead of just getting out of his way.

Sex. They'd had it all the time before it became laden with its intended purpose: to produce a child. It had taken them over a year to get pregnant with Teddy: fertility sticks and forced sex, doctor visits with no real answers as to why it was so hard and then finally: success. And then, one afternoon after an interminable drought, and at the ripe age of forty-two, after nine years of unprotected sex with no babies to show for it, Sylvie had gotten pregnant. It was one of those stories you'd never believe unless it was, you know, true.

When they had started discussing a second child, Sylvie had been adamant about the fact that if it wasn't going to happen naturally, then she didn't want it to happen: period. She had no interest in injecting herself with hormones or having Paul jizz into a cup. None. And what Paul wanted, she said, well, it just didn't matter. Because he wasn't the one all of this hormone injecting and turkey basting would be happening to.

So they had just taken it off the table. Until Sylvie had come out of the bathroom one morning, dazed, with a plastic pregnancy stick in her hand. She had shoved it at Paul, wordless. PREGNANT, it had read.

Paul had been overjoyed, but Sylvie, not so much. She had come around a bit, especially when they'd found out it was a girl, but mostly she just complained about how old she was, how tired she was. And this had irritated Paul. It was a miracle what had happened, he kept saying. Couldn't she just appreciate the miracle?

Arguing. And lots of it.

And then, when the dust had cleared after Delilah had died, they had never found their footing as a couple again. So much so that Paul had begun to wonder if they'd ever had it in the first place. So much so that the only way to fill the gaping void of intimacy in his life—other than cheat, which he would never do, because it just seemed like too much work, even though to say he hadn't considered it or even engaged in a meaningless flirtation with a twenty-eight-year-old woman on his training team would be a lie (but a white lie because it wasn't like he was ever going to do anything about it)—was to first: take up the kind of exercise that took up his entire life, and second: buy everything remotely acquainted with it under the sun.

Even more arguing.

But now, something was different about Sylvie. She was nicer, and so he wanted to be nicer. Just this morning, he had cut up two of his credit cards.

"Paul!" David boomed from the front door, vibrating the walls with his thick Boston accent, as thick as the day he had left fifteen years prior.

"My man, how are ya?" he asked, clapping Paul on the shoulder before plopping down beside him.

David was like a human version of Scooby Doo—short legs, an almost comically long torso, with a tightly muscled chest and arms, and an enormous head.

"Hanging in, brother," Paul greeted back.

David was Paul's friend. They had met five years prior, when Paul had hired him to help with some contracting work. But then David had fallen through a roof and shattered his leg, not when he had been part of Paul's team, thankfully. He didn't do contracting work anymore, but he did make beautiful furniture. Sometimes, Paul sold his pieces to his clients, to fill the new spaces he renovated for them. Paul was glad he could do this for David, because David had been cut a shitty deal, long before he plummeted through that roof.

His son had died in a hit-and-run, the bastard motorist not even stopping. And he and his wife had divorced shortly thereafter, angry shells of their former selves. She was remarried now, to some pastor guy in Tallahassee.

David wore his loneliness like cologne.

"Well, ya look good," David offered now, sitting beside Paul. "A little scrawny, but good."

"Thanks, man. How are you?"

"I'm alive," David offered with a wry smile. "Can I have?" he asked, motioning toward the white bowl of almonds on the coffee table. Paul nodded as he crammed an enormous fistful into his mouth. "Protein," David mumbled. A tiny almond shard flew through the air and landed on Paul's exposed knee.

"When you think you'll be back walking?"

"Another month, I think." Paul gently flicked the shard onto the floor.

"What about the bike? You must miss riding, huh?"

"I do," agreed Paul. Sometimes he dreamed about it, the wind against his face, the pedals moving beneath his capable feet, his neck tensed. "You been swimming at all lately?"

"My leg's been giving me trouble again. Hurts like a bitch even in the pool. I dunno," David replied. "Change of seasons or somethin', I guess." He shrugged. "So ya wanna sell some shit?"

"I do. All this stuff I bought for training—I don't use three-quarters of it," confessed Paul. "And it's overtaking the house, wrecking my marriage. You know."

"Yeah, I know," said David. "So let's see what you've got. I got a friend of a friend that can unload it for you, no problem. Gonna take a cut of the profit, but really, it's chump change."

"Who is this guy, anyway?" asked Paul.

"Just a minor detail," answered David, getting up to hand him his crutches. "Nothing you need to concern yourself with." Paul stared at him. "What? Trust me."

"What about Craigslist or something?" asked Paul. He stood up and tucked the crutches under his arms.

David dealt in shade. There was no way he was supporting himself on furniture sales and random gigs alone, especially at the excruciatingly slow rate he turned out his pieces. But Paul didn't ask questions of his friend. Which by definition made him a terrible friend, Paul realized.

They descended into the basement, David helping Paul.

"Jesus, man, it's like freakin' Sports Authority in here," said David, looking around at all the bikes and clothes and gear; the StairMaster and the rowing machine; the literal mountain of riding gloves, all still with their tags dangling from them.

"I got a little carried away," said Paul.

"I'll say." David let out a whistle. "All right, let's start with the big stuff first. What I'll do is, I'll take some photos on my phone, talk to my guy and see what he's interested in."

"That sounds like a plan," said Paul. "Can I help you?"

"With that ankle, forget it," said David. "Just sit there and look pretty." He pushed the boxes surrounding the rowing machine out of the way with the toe of his sneaker.

"So how's Sylvie doing?" David asked.

"She's doing really well, man. It's weird."

"Weird?" David started snapping photos.

"Yeah, she's been . . . nice."

"That is weird," said David. He looked over at him. "What gives?"

"I don't know," said Paul. "And you know, the anniversary of Delilah's death was a few weeks ago—"

"I'm sorry to hear that. Ya know, I thought it might be," said David. "I should have reached out. I'm a putz."

"It's okay, really," said Paul. "But, like, she commemorated it. For the first time."

"Whoa," said David.

"Yeah, she pulled out this candle, it's a Jewish thing or something, it's called a Yahrzeit candle?"

"Say what now?"

"It's an anniversary candle you light to remember the dead," said Paul.

"Does it smell?" asked David.

"What?"

"I dunno, like perfumy or whatever."

"No. It doesn't smell like anything. It's just a way to honor people who've died. And so she lit it, and Teddy said a prayer, and we all stood around and remembered Delilah together and it was nice."

David started to clear space around a stationary bike.

"No, I'm keeping that one. The other one, by the far wall, you can sell that one," said Paul.

"Well, that's a big fucking deal, the candle," said David, walking toward it, his broad back to Paul, the red and white stripes of his polo shirt stretched to capacity. "She hasn't so much as mentioned Delilah's name in years, right?"

"No," said Paul.

"What gives?"

"I haven't asked."

"Probably smart," said David, snapping away. "Whenever I tried to talk to my wife about Jeremy, she would usually end up taking a swing at me. Said it was all my fault that he was crossing the street, she wished I had died instead." His back was still to Paul, but his posture, it was slumped now. He had stopped taking photos, the basement silent.

"You don't believe that, do you, David?"

"I dunno. The kid refused to let me pick him up from basketball practice. Like, straight-out refused. Said it was embarrassing, he was eleven. What was I supposed to do?"

"You did what he asked you to do," said Paul.

If David had been the kind of person who hugged, and Paul's crutches had not been lying on the floor, Paul would have. But he wasn't, and they were. So.

"I guess." David turned around. His eyes were wet. "All right, is this it?"

"Sadly, no," said Paul. "There's more in the garage."

"Shit, man, you kidding me? How much you spend on all this?"

"Too much. Sylvie wants to kill me."

"Filling the void, huh?" asked David knowingly.

"Yeah."

"So where's the rest of it?" asked David.

"The garage. Here, there's a door to the outside; we don't have to go back up the stairs," said Paul. "Hand me my crutches?"

They went through the door and into the blazing sun, squinting against its merciless glare.

"How's Teddy?" asked David, as Paul pushed the button that slid the doors up.

"Good Christ, more bikes!" yelled David. He gave Paul a look. "You cut up your credit cards, bro?"

"Just this morning." That was not entirely true—Paul still had one and a secret debit card to a secret checking account—but all in due time.

"Teddy's good," said Paul, as David took more photos. "I think he has a girlfriend."

"Get out," said David.

"Yeah, he's been using my phone to text her; he thinks I don't know."

"Sexy stuff?"

"Oh God no, come on," said Paul. "Totally benign, tween shit. But still, it's good for him." Paul leaned on his crutches, watching David. His ankle began to throb insistently.

"Get him a phone already," said David. "You can buy yourself fifty bikes, but you can't get your teenager a cell phone? Come on."

"Technically, he's not a teenager yet. But you're right. It's Sylvie; she's the one so opposed to it."

"Well, maybe she won't be anymore, what with her new attitude and all. And the money coming in from your liquidation sale." David turned around. "You don't look so good, Paul. You okay?"

"Yeah, fine, just— I should have taken my Motrin, but I'm trying to wean myself off. My ankle is killing me."

"Wean yourself off?" asked David. "You broke your ankle, not your nail. Come on, I'll help you inside."

The doors slid shut behind them as David helped Paul up the deck stairs and into the house.

"There's no reason for you to be in pain, man," said David, as he settled Paul onto the couch. He dug into one of his pockets and came out with a small white pill. "Don't tell me you didn't get any of these from your doctor?"

"Not interested, but thank you," he said to David's hand, avoiding his gaze.

"Seriously, your doctor didn't give you any? You're supposed to take Motrin for a broken freaking bone? No way. Here. Just in case of an emergency." David placed it on the coffee table.

"Okay, thanks." Paul rubbed his eyes, hoping to erase the judgment out of them in the process, before looking up at David.

David had a problem with these pills, but he had told Paul he'd stopped with them. Now, here one was in his pocket.

"You got it. And if you need more, you need to demand them from your doctor. Jesus, the way the world works now, it's like, want a gun? Here's a gun. But if you broke your freaking ankle and it hurts, too bad. Am I right?"

"Yeah," Paul mumbled. He was very tired suddenly.

"Okay, be good." David clapped Paul's shoulder again, his signature hello and goodbye, and walked toward the door.

"You too," Paul called after him. "And thanks for everything today."

"You got it. I'll be in touch, after I talk to my guy," he said, letting himself out.

Who was Paul to judge David? David had a pill thing, and he, he had a spending thing. Neither was better or worse than the other. Except, of course, David's thing could kill him.

Paul settled into the couch and exhaled deeply. He would say something to David the next time he saw him. He would be a better friend.

But first: a nap.

CHAPTER SEVEN

SYLVIE

The sand beneath her feet was hot. When Sylvie had taken off her socks and shoes, surprised by the warmth of the morning, her feet had shone like white marble in the sun.

She walked now, alone, toward what she wasn't sure. She supposed the water, but it was the broadest beach she'd ever seen—sand bled right into the horizon. The sun beat down on her head relentlessly, and Sylvie wished for a hat. And that she'd worn sunscreen. Her skin was beginning to pink. Some water would have been nice too. Why was she so unprepared? That wasn't like her.

Exhausted, and embarrassed by that very fact—she couldn't have been walking longer than ten minutes—she sat. Just plopped down right in the sand, which was actually, now that she was in it, more dirt than sand. She scooped some into her hand and then watched it fall through her fingers, a salt-and-peppery mix. A cloud mercifully covered the sun, giving Sylvie a brief respite from the heat.

The ground beneath her began to vibrate. Like a train was running underneath her. Sylvie looked up. All around her was a vast nothing, just the dirty sand and the slight swell of would-be dunes. The vibration intensified, scaring her. She tried to get up, but she could not get her bearings, could not push herself up to standing.

That's when she saw them. Horses. A herd of them: black, white, caramel, spotted, freckled, gray. There were so many of them, their hooves stomping and slicing through the sand as they stampeded toward her.

They were still far enough away for Sylvie to appreciate the beauty of their wildness—their matted manes; their feral eyes, the whites yellowed. Their synchronicity. A pack.

But as they came closer, right toward Sylvie, her heart began to speed up. A pounding in her chest that echoed in her ears, louder than the stomping of their hooves, although she couldn't be sure which was which.

She couldn't get up, Sylvie realized. No matter what she did, she could not will her arms to work. She looked down, surprised to see a beach ball where her stomach should have been, a beach ball underneath the black T-shirt she was wearing.

Sand sprayed onto her arms and into her face. She looked up. The horses were coming; they were right in front of her, the ripples of their leg muscles like fish through water. They had come.

* * *

SYLVIE OPENED HER eyes, gasping for air. Above her was the white ceiling of her bedroom, from which a suspended steel fan swirled lazily through the pale-yellow light of very early morning.

She lowered her arms beside her, resting them on top of the damp sheets. Slowly, she regulated her breathing, slowed down her racing heart. That nightmare, it was the same nightmare she always had, and yet every time was like the first time; her subconscious just as easily fooled.

"Jesus Christ," she whispered, fingering the cotton of her T-shirt. She was completely soaked.

Beside her, Paul slept as he always slept, completely oblivious. Paul could sleep through a tornado tearing through the house, one that upended the bed with him in it. He would wake up in a dirt ditch somewhere, Sylvie was sure of it, the mattress on top of him, none the wiser.

When they had first started dating, Sylvie had found this quality endearing, but now it just pissed her off. Like a lot of things, she supposed.

She exhaled deeply, finally regaining her equilibrium back on earth. She was grateful it was only a nightmare, that she was not on the verge of being trampled to death by horses, that she was in her bed, alive. That was something; she was not always so glad to be alive.

She sat up, untwisting herself from the sheets, sighing because she was going to have to wash them. Gingerly, she put her feet on the floor, glancing at her stomach dejectedly.

She was always pregnant in that dream. But again, always surprised by it. And always, always sad afterward, to find it not so.

Slowly, Sylvie padded toward the bathroom, to the shower.

She turned the hot water as high as it could go and stepped in. Sylvie angled her face upward, closed her eyes, relishing it as it washed over her. The heat did not bother her; it was the only way she felt truly clean, to emerge as red as a tomato.

She felt through the steam for her body wash and squirted it onto her loofah. Slowly, she rubbed circles across her body, the smell of lavender filling her nostrils. *That dream. Wash it away. Forget it.*

She had other things to worry about anyway. Teddy's Bar Mitzvah, for one, which was a big fat nothing. The date of his service loomed large; it was now less than three months away, but as far as the party: nothing. No venue, no theme, no invites, no nothing. Part of this she could blame on Teddy's lack of interest, but only a small part. The rest of this failure was her fault.

But maybe, just maybe, she should take a page from her behavior at the PTA meeting a few weeks earlier. If the kid didn't like parties, why in the world was she throwing him a party? Because that's just what people did? That's what her parents expected her to do, like generations of Jews before them? Maybe, just maybe: screw it. Maybe listen to Teddy and do what he wanted to do. Not forgo the service altogether, she would never do that, but the other crap. If he didn't want it, if it would only make him miserable, why bother?

Sylvie squeezed shampoo into her palm next and rubbed

it vigorously into her scalp. But even before the Bar Mitzvah, she had something else to contend with. Something more pressing, something that had flooded her veins with anxiety from the moment she had discovered it.

Water poured over her head, the smell of vanilla and citrus overpowering the lavender, although it still lingered. Sylvie had been cursed with a superpower sense of smell. She said cursed because she would rather not smell so intensely every odor within a three-mile radius. She would rather not smell Teddy's sneakers by the front door when she was upstairs in her room. She would rather not taste tuna fish in her mouth days after she rinsed clean the aluminum tin and placed it in the recycling bin. Cursed.

The day before, when Sylvie had come home from work, she had found Paul snoring on the couch, sitting upright with his head against its back, his mouth open wide enough for a wayward bird to fly into.

The old Sylvie, the not-high Sylvie—she had downed a pill in her work bathroom right before lunch; she was going out with her boss, better known as the Weenie, and a client who made her feel like an underpaid kindergarten teacher in her last year before retirement and really just wanted to not feel that way, so she had taken it even though she said she wouldn't at work, but guess what? It had made lunch tolerable, and lunch wasn't technically work, so who cared? That old Sylvie would have been exasperated by the sight of her husband passed out, knowing he had been passed out while she worked, while she ran to the grocery store to supplement dinner, while she fought the interminable traffic to get home and make said dinner. The new Sylvie, the Sylvie who was still high, was not.

After she had set the bags on the kitchen counter in a dejected heap of beige plastic, she had walked over to wake him up, and that's when she had seen it: a round white pill that looked remarkably familiar. She had grabbed it on impulse, abandoning her plan and letting him continue snoring.

By the overhead light of the kitchen, she had examined the pill. It was one of her pills. One of *his* pills, to be exact. But what did it mean?

She had jogged up the stairs, to her bedroom and into her closet. She had dug into her purse, her hiding spot, relieved to close her fingers around the familiar, smooth cylinder. She had retrieved it, opened it. There had been two pills left. That's how many she had left behind that morning, wasn't it? Or had there been three? She could not remember and had promptly broken out in a cold sweat.

She had put the bottle back in her purse and stood in the dim light of the closet for a moment, considering all possible scenarios.

Scenario one: Paul had gone looking for his pills and, not finding them, ransacked the entire house, including every purse and every pocket of Sylvie's. Sylvie looked around the closet. It was as pristine as when she left it. This scenario was impossible. Paul rarely remembered to put the toilet seat down; he wouldn't have gone to the trouble to refold and rehang every article of Sylvie's perfectly. To be 100 percent sure, Sylvie crossed to her shelves of jeans she never wore.

All folded perfectly, all in color-coded order. Scenario one was out.

Scenario two: Paul had gone looking for his pills and, not finding them, assumed Sylvie had thrown them out. He had refilled his order. But how had he picked them up? His buddy David? Possibly, although why not just ask her? Unless he knew what she was up to. Which brought her to scenario three.

Scenario three: scenario two minus the Sylvie-throwing-them-out part. Paul was onto her, had noticed her complete personality change and wasn't buying any sort of natural reason for it. He had put two and two together. He was going to confront her, and what was she going to say?

More important, how was she going to get more pills? She had been counting on Paul's refill, because why not? A refill was meant to be claimed, and then she would stop. That's what she had told herself, but now the refill had been claimed by Paul. And Paul was wise to her.

Shit.

Panic had seized Sylvie. What was she going to do? What was she going to say? An outside observer of even the most distant variety, much less her own husband, would be concerned about the fact that she had stolen, hidden and taken a prescribed narcotic regularly for weeks, usually accompanied by a glass of wine. But it was a phase. Just a phase that had been handed to her. Like a Nordstrom gift card.

There had been only one way out of her swirling brain. Another pill. Sylvie had taken it, ashamed of herself for wasting what could be her next to last but seeing no other way to make it through what was bound to be a very awkward evening. She couldn't go to her own intervention sober; it defeated the purpose.

But to Sylvie's great surprise, Paul didn't say a word. All through dinner, not a peep. And even after, when Teddy had gone to bed: nothing. Sylvie had crept stealthily around him, a dazed smile on her face thanks to the pill but an unshakable pit of dread in her stomach.

It was so unlike Paul to bide his time with anything, to play the role of coiled viper planning his strike, but what else could possibly be happening? He hadn't even asked her about the pill on the coffee table, which of course she had forgotten to put back.

She had even sat next to Paul on the couch, pretending to watch a home remodeling show with him that featured a married couple who clearly hated each other, until she finally went to sleep herself.

After much tossing and turning and then the nightmare, here she was. She had to say something to Paul. She couldn't take it anymore.

Sylvie turned off the water and stood in the steam for a moment, reciting the lines she had written and then rewritten in her head. *Keep it simple,* she reminded herself, as she flipped her head over and squeezed water from her hair into the towel.

No eye contact, she told herself as she moisturized her legs.

She sat on the toilet seat and rubbed the lotion into the cracks of her heels. She really wanted a pill. But she had only two left, including the contraband from the coffee table. She should save them; she really should. For emergencies. They very well could be her last. Ever. Right, she would save them.

She hung the wet towel on the hook, avoiding her naked image in the mirror, and walked, head down, thinking, into her closet. Oh no, her stomach from this angle. No, this would not do. Sylvie stopped in her tracks and stood up straight, forcing her shoulders back. Better, much better. Not great or even good, but better.

She surveyed her clothing. It was Friday, a day once deemed business casual. But now it seemed that every day was business casual in her workplace of twenty- and thirty-somethings clad in skinny jeans and statement socks. Statement socks, for Christ's sake. She felt a million years old there and dressed the part, albeit expensively. A red-and-white-striped button-down and elastic-waist pants it was.

Her purse, hanging mere feet from Sylvie, her secret-stash purse, mocked her as she pulled on her underwear and strapped on her bra. Sylvie had never been able to understand the ads portraying women stepping daintily into their undergarments, fastening the hooks suggestively as though putting them on immediately implied taking them off in the company of a heated suitor. She always felt like she was putting on a suit of armor, heading into battle.

If you take a pill now, you'll only have one left, she chided herself as she buttoned her shirt. She pulled on her pants. But maybe this did qualify as an emergency. She could very well be about to walk the plank during this conversation with Paul. And the workday stretched long and endless before her, with no meetings on tap. Might as well be high, right?

She dug into the purse and took a pill. She couldn't believe there was only one left. Had she really taken thirty? Was that bad? No, it wasn't that bad. What was that, like one a day? Maybe two once in a blue moon? Now, three, that was different. Three was trouble.

She swallowed the pill dry.

On her way back into the bedroom, Sylvie stopped to massage moisturizer into her face and neck. The amount of lubrication it took past a certain age, just so your skin felt remotely pliable. It was criminal.

On the other side of the door, she heard Paul yawn. She knew he was scratching his balls, stretching—his wake-up routine was as familiar as her own.

It was time.

"Morning," she said, trying her best to sound casual, although it was hard to catch her breath.

On cue, the pill began to work its magic, slowing everything down, trapping time and space in Jell-O. Problems were suspended; she felt buoyant and young, and the light, inside or outside, it didn't matter, became almost comically ethereal.

"Good morning," said Paul, smiling with his eyes closed. "You smell good."

"Thanks, I showered."

Sylvie perched on the edge of the bed and then thought better of it and got completely on, adjusting her pillow in its white pillowcase against the low oak headboard and leaning against it, her legs crossed at the ankles on top of the gold blanket, her toes a turquoise that she had immediately regretted upon leaving the nail salon.

"Paul?"

"Yes?" He opened his eyes and turned his head, looking up at her. "You sound so serious. You okay?"

This was not a question someone on the verge of staging an intervention would ask, Sylvie thought. Paul was many things, but an actor was not one of them. Sylvie's nerves fluttered up to the ceiling like butterflies, leaving her only curious.

"I found a pill on the coffee table yesterday when I was cleaning up," she blurted out.

"Huh?"

"A white pill? It—" Sylvie stopped herself. Was she really on the verge of outing herself, of admitting to the fact that she knew exactly what the pill was? Idiot.

"Oh yeah, David gave me that. My ankle was hurting, and I told him Motrin was fine, that I didn't need one of those Oxywhatevers, but he refused to listen to me. I didn't feel like arguing anymore. You can throw it away."

"Oh. Okay. Sure." Sylvie closed her eyes, the last of the butterflies fluttering up, up, up. She was safe.

"That's what you did with my pills, right?" asked Paul.

"Your pills what?"

"The ones I was prescribed?" Paul rolled over slightly and pushed himself up, wincing a little.

Sylvie reached behind him and adjusted his pillow, helped him get comfortable.

"Oh yes. I threw them out. Are you sure you don't need them? Is the pain worse now?"

Sylvie was asking only because she knew Paul would continue to refuse them, continue to deny himself the pleasure of Jell-O suspension; and although there was a tiny part of her that felt bad for him because of it, mostly she was just glad that they were hers, all hers.

"I'm sure. Honestly, if I just stay on top of the Motrin, it's fine." He covered her hand with his.

"What's David doing with those pills?" asked Sylvie.

"Remember when he fell through that roof a couple years back? On the job?"

"Oh yeah," said Sylvie. "That was terrible. And he's all alone, right?"

"Yeah. After his son was killed, he and his wife split up."

"His son was killed?" asked Sylvie, covering her mouth with her hand.

"I told you that, Sylvie, come on."

"I don't think you did."

"I did."

"Okay, okay, it doesn't matter."

Paul glared at her.

"Okay, you did. Jesus. Sorry. I must have forgotten."

"So anyway, he ended up with a steel rod in his leg and I'm sure a lot of pain," Paul continued. "Voilà: a lifelong drug prescription and a free pass to addiction."

Paul pulled off the blanket and turned to get up, swinging his good leg onto the floor and then his cast with his hands. Sylvie crawled over to his side of the bed and hopped off to hand him his crutches, which were propped against the bedside table.

"That's a little extreme, don't you think?" She hated that she felt defensive on David's behalf, but she did.

"What?" asked Paul.

"To call him an addict."

"The guy's been taking these pills for years, so no," said Paul, hobbling into the bathroom.

Sylvie sat back down on the bed and stared out the window. She heard Teddy's alarm going off down the hall. A river of bubbles flowed through her veins as she watched a perched bluebird tweet from a tree branch. People were so quick to throw around the term *addict*.

Teddy's alarm continued to beep. She imagined his little hand searching for it on his bedside table, his eyes still shut, his smooth forehead scrunched into an accordion of frustration.

Except his hand wasn't so little anymore, her Teddy's. Just the other day she had noticed that he no longer had dimples where his knuckles should be. How she hadn't noticed before, she wasn't sure, watching him take a sip from his glass of water at dinner, his grown-up hand wrapped around its diameter.

She hadn't wanted Paul to confront her, to know about the pills at all. And he hadn't, he didn't. She was free and clear. She should be relieved. So what was this other feeling doing here?

"Syl, can you help me into the shower?" Paul called to her from the bathroom.

"Sure," she called back, getting up. She felt deflated. Disappointed. She watched her feet plod, one in front of the other, toward him.

What was wrong with her? Everything had turned out just

as she wanted it to. She was going to be able to continue this glorious charade for just a little while longer, with her husband, who had known her for twenty years, who she thought knew her better than she even knew herself, none the wiser.

She was as invisible as air.

* * *

SYLVIE PRESSED THE last digit of Paul's prescription number into the keypad of her work phone, holding her breath. Would it go through? It should; it read **1 REFILL** in bold on the label of the bottle. But what if it didn't and the doctor had to be alerted and then the doctor called Paul and then—

Hallelujah. It went through. Sylvie did a little dance in her cubicle and keyed in her pickup time. Nine A.M. the next morning. Easy peasy.

With this new bottle, she would conquer the Bar Mitzvah. Be done with it, finally. And then they could all move on into Teddy's manhood, together.

Sylvie got up to refill her coffee mug in the kitchen. Every day at work was like Groundhog Day. Come in, read some emails, send some emails, break for coffee, go to a meeting, go to lunch, surf the Web, fight traffic to get to the grocery store and then: home.

Repeat.

It was just so goddamn boring, Sylvie thought, as she snaked her way through the maze of cubicles, her cold coffee swirling in her mug. All of it.

"Open concept, open minds" was what her new boss, her

new child-boss, had announced last year, right before the holiday break. When Sylvie had returned, her beloved office with a door had been demolished, replaced with a cubicle the size of a shower stall, sandwiched between two of the loudest people on earth, although thankfully, one was currently on maternity leave.

Sylvie sighed. Her boss was thirty-two. Thirty-two! Fourteen years younger than her.

"Sylvie?"

She froze. Oh, how she hated small talk. Her pill had lost its initial intensity; she was not so sure she could socialize successfully without it.

Sylvie braced for she didn't know whom, since she didn't recognize the voice, and turned around in the hallway.

"Greg!" she answered, relieved. She liked Greg. She could handle Greg.

"How are you?" he asked, lifting his own mug in salute.

"I'm okay," answered Sylvie.

"Good for you," said Greg. "I'm certifiable. The twins have been sent from Satan himself to destroy me." He stroked the faint stubble covering his chiseled jaw and shook his head. "I don't even remember what it feels like to exfoliate."

"Greg, I haven't exfoliated since 1998."

"Sylvie!" Greg laughed. "How's Paul?"

Greg was in sales and the only person anywhere near her age in the entire office. He and his partner, Josh, had four-year-old twins: Agnes and Hank. He was the only person to acknowledge Delilah's death when Sylvie had returned to work, and she was infinitely and forever grateful for that small act of kindness. The only one in an office of near fifty people. It blew her mind still.

"He broke his ankle," Sylvie answered. "But he's a pro on his crutches. And I think the cast comes off in a month or so."

"That's terrible," Greg said, standing aside to let Sylvie into the kitchen first. "How?"

"Fell off his bike." Sylvie approached the coffeemaker and popped a pod into its mouth.

"Oy," said Greg. "And how are you?"

"Hanging in. Barely."

"I'm sure," said Greg. "If I even have a cold I'm the biggest pain in the ass on the planet. Josh has come close to poisoning me, I'm sure. How's Teddy?"

"I'm in the middle of avoiding planning his Bar Mitzvah."

"Teddy is old enough to get Bar Mitzvahed?" Greg whistled. "That's crazy. He was just a little guy, running around chasing Pokémon here, like, yesterday."

"Time flies," Sylvie murmured.

Her coffee was ready. She slid it out of the machine and cupped it with her hands, relishing its warmth and promise.

"Listen, I've been meaning to email you anyway. Josh and I are having a party of our own. It's our ten-year anniversary next week."

"Ten years!" exclaimed Sylvie. "A milestone."

"Exactly. So we're shipping the twins to Grandma's and having a night. You and Paul have to come. You must."

"When is it?" asked Sylvie, surprising herself by not being entirely opposed to the idea of attending. A party could be fun on her current cocktail of choice.

"Next Friday night. Eight P.M. until whenever. We're getting it catered, having a bartender, a deejay, the whole kit and caboodle. Y'all have to come."

"Okay," said Sylvie, nodding. "Okay, yes. Thanks, we will."

"Terrific," said Greg, giving her a big smile. He really was impossibly handsome. "Okay, let me return to the conference call I'm supposed to be on." He squeezed her shoulder and headed back to his desk.

She felt excited about a party for the first time in three years—maybe four, since who was excited about a party when they were pregnant? No one, that was who.

Sylvie used to love parties when she was younger. The primping, the dressing up, the scheming. Who would be there, what would she say, would she go home with anybody or would she sneak out early without so much as a goodbye? It was usually the latter; Sylvie hated party goodbyes. They took forever and were usually steeped in bullshit. *Let's get together!* Or *I'll call you!* No, you would not get together, and you definitely weren't going to call, so what was the point? But that had been fun too, the slipping out the door and into the night, the cab gliding through neighborhoods as she slumped in the back seat, peering at treetops and streetlamps and dreaming of her pajamas.

She had had a lot of girlfriends once. A lot of time to acquire and nurture those friendships that would inform a lot of who she would become as an adult. After all, she hadn't met Paul until she was twenty-six, which now seemed like infancy but at the time felt on the precipice of Medicare in terms of marriageability.

She wished she could go back in time and shake that former version of herself, tell her that she had all the time in the world. Not to rush. Not that she had felt rushed into her relationship with Paul, not at all. The moment she had met him, the moment he had popped his head out from under that sink, she had known. It was him.

But even still. Marriage was not easy. It changed things. Not the least of all her support system. Sylvie had left her girlfriends in the dust, and when she had finally resurfaced from the pool of passion and newness her relationship with Paul provided, they were all long gone. That was one of her biggest regrets.

Sylvie meandered through the hallway back to her desk, thinking of her past as the bubbles resurfaced inside her, vibrating pleasantly. She lost her footing for a moment and reached out to grab the wall for support, tumbling the coffee out of her mug and all over herself in the process. *Shit,* she thought, as the hot liquid bloomed brown against the red and white stripes of her shirt.

"Everything okay?" a voice behind her asked. The Weenie. Her child-boss. Of course.

"Oh yes, sure, I'm just a bit of a klutz today, I guess," she offered. "I'll get some paper towels from the kitchen, sorry about that."

"Here, use my napkin," he said, removing it from underneath the bowl he held in his hand. "Not that it will do much, but just a start."

"Oatmeal?" Sylvie asked, peering into what she assumed was his breakfast.

"Steel-cut oats," he corrected her, as though the term *oatmeal* was an insult.

"Right," she said, accepting the napkin and stooping down to blot the floor. Before she knew it, she had lost her balance entirely and was splayed out like a ragdoll.

"Jesus, Sylvie, you sure you're okay?" The Weenie stooped down to help her up.

"I think I forgot to eat anything this morning," she confessed, embarrassed and slightly alarmed by her blunder. The pill on an empty stomach had not been a good idea. Well, it had in terms of her demeanor, but as far as balance, not so much. *Note to self,* she thought.

"Here, you go back to your desk; I'll take care of the mess," he said, glancing toward his cooling oatmeal, which was beginning to look more like mortar than anything suitable for consumption.

"Are you sure? I can handle it," said Sylvie.

"No, no, go on back. Eat a protein bar or something. We have that FaceTime meeting with the dog-food people in ten minutes; you sure you're going to be all right?"

"Absolutely," she said, although she wasn't sure at all. "A protein bar, roger that. And thank you."

Sylvie walked slowly away, concentrating on her balance. Behind her, she could feel his Weenie eyes boring holes into her back.

CHAPTER EIGHT

TEDDY

Teddy stood at the sink, eyeing the sopping and soapy shih tzu–terrier mix with disdain. At least that's what Marcus, his boss at the shelter where he volunteered, had told him this dog was. She looked more like a large rat to him in this condition. Just bones and eyes, her mouth hanging open to reveal tiny yellow teeth.

He grabbed the hose and turned on the water, testing it first. He didn't like animals, but he wasn't a monster. He wouldn't burn it or anything.

Slowly, he washed the soap from her fur, guiding it off with his hands, which were encased in turquoise rubber gloves that went up and over his elbows. The kind of gloves you would dismember somebody's body with.

He had watched *American Psycho* on his computer the night before, the sound turned down to be barely audible, his blanket practically pulled over his head. His parents would kill him if they knew, but Krystal had told him it was one of her favorite movies, so what was he supposed to do?

It had occurred to him as he watched it that it certainly said a lot about Krystal if murder and dismemberment, along with unapologetic behavior from truly horrible characters, engaged her. After watching it, he wasn't sure they were going to make it.

It worried him now, still, as he toweled off the rat dog.

I like dark humor, she had texted him.

Teddy didn't think he was sophisticated enough to appreciate dark humor. He was more a Spielberg kind of guy. Or a *Splash* kind of guy. The dog blinked at him, now wrapped in a white towel. She was shivering beneath Teddy's hands.

"Okay, okay," he said as soothingly as he could. "Time for your blow dry."

He got to work, blasting her with a steady stream of warmth as she shook, sprinkling her wet-dog smell all over him. Teddy combed her fur with his free hand, and soon, she didn't look half bad. Much better than when he had first seen her, at least. Maybe now she would get adopted.

Teddy could see some little girl liking her. A little girl with blond hair. Straight. Maybe a pink bow in it. Six or so. He wondered what Delilah would have been like at six. She would not have had straight blond hair. She would have looked just like his mom; Teddy knew that somehow. A miniature version of his mother, complete with scowl.

Teddy picked up the dog and took her into Marcus's office for his approval.

"What do you think?" Teddy asked tentatively.

Marcus was never happy with his work. He was a former Broadway costume designer, or so he said, and favored viscose kimonos in swirls of fuchsia, tangerine and chartreuse over gray slogan T-shirts proclaiming things like "Rosé All Day" and "Indoorsy," cut-off jean shorts and slip-on sneakers in a variety of hues. He also expected Teddy to be some sort of dogmetologist and not, you know, a twelve-year-old boy volunteering for his Mitzvah Project against his will.

"I mean, I guess? Did you use the brush?"

"Yes, I used the brush," answered Teddy.

"The small one? With the boar's-head bristles?" Marcus countered.

"Yes," Teddy lied. He had used the big one.

"Here." Marcus made a big show of digging around in his desk drawer and getting up, like it was water torture or something. He approached Teddy and the dog with a tiny silver bow barrette. Sweeping some of her fur out of her face, he clipped it back against her skull.

"Hold her out," he commanded, taking a few steps back to consider his styling decision. "That works. What should we call her?"

Teddy was silent.

"Hello?"

"You're asking me?"

"No, I'm asking the dog."

Teddy swiveled her around in his arms so that he was looking directly at her.

"Barbara?"

"Barbara?" Marcus looked off into the distance, although the distance in this case was a wood-paneled wall six feet from his face. "You know what? I actually like that. Barbra it is, but without the second *a*. You can put her back in her cage; just make sure it's clean first." Marcus turned toward his desk but then pivoted back around. "I'll go out to the front, see what's what. Is Kirby here?"

"Yes," Teddy answered, as Marcus breezed past him and the newly christened Barbra. Kirby was another volunteer, but older. With a car. She wore the same lavender T-shirt every day. "Be the Person Your Dog Thinks You Are," it read across her quite ample chest.

Teddy was the only person there who kept his thoughts in his brain, where they belonged.

On Teddy's first day, when his mother had practically shoved him inside—she had asked him and asked him to come up with a Mitzvah Project of his own, but since he refused and time was running out, here they were, and he damn well better just suck it up and do the damn thing for a year—and sat in her car in the parking lot for the entire hour and a half to make sure he didn't escape, Kirby had been a little confused.

"A Mitzvah what?" she had asked him, as she showed him around.

"I'm getting Bar Mitzvahed," Teddy explained.

Kirby had looked at him blankly.

"I'm Jewish?"

"Oh right," she had said. "It's like a quinceañera, except you're, like, younger."

"And a boy. And Jewish. I read from the Torah," Teddy had said. Kirby had nodded absently.

"But yeah, other than that, just like a quinceañera."

The other dogs looked at him with resignation now as he walked by their cages with the new and improved Barbra.

"Okay, let's see if there's any poop hiding in here," Teddy mumbled, searching her cage with his still-gloved hands. No, clean as a whistle. He set her down and retrieved her bowls for food and water, closing the door behind him as he went to refill them.

This was a small shelter, only ten animals at a time. Most seemed to get adopted fairly quickly—Marcus was good at what he did—but the ones that didn't, well. Marcia the vet tech from up the road came to take them away in her white van. To kill them. Or what was the word, *euthanize*? That was a kinder word.

The few times Marcia had come while Teddy was there, Kirby had sobbed uncontrollably, so much so that Marcus had asked him to man the front desk while she collected herself. It was sad, of course it was sad, but if he had to choose between living in a tiny cage his whole life and going on to the great pet pound in the sky, he would undoubtedly choose the latter.

He put the replenished bowls back in Barbra's cage and petted her head awkwardly for a moment before closing the door again. That wasn't to say he didn't cross all his fingers and toes that someone would save these animals first. He was just being realistic. He looked at his watch. It was time to go.

"You headed out?" asked Kirby, as Teddy wrestled himself into his camouflage backpack next to her. He kept meaning to loosen the straps but never did.

"Yeah. Actually, wait. I should use the restroom first."

"Thanks for the play-by-play," said Kirby.

Teddy closed the door behind him, and the chemical scent of air freshener was like a punch to the face. He held his breath for a moment as he adjusted, and then wrestled himself out of his backpack and stared at himself in the mirror. He did not need to use the restroom, not in the technical sense. What he did need to do was make sure he looked okay.

He unzipped his bag and pulled out a fresh T-shirt, just a plain navy-blue one that his mom said he looked handsome in. He would never tell his mom that her opinion on such matters held any weight with him, of course, but it did, because what other opinion was there? He did not have any friends who were girls, and he certainly wasn't going to ask Kirby. Martin and Raj didn't even know about Krystal.

He took off the shirt he had on and grabbed his deodorant from his bag. As he swiped three times under each arm, he checked to see whether any new hairs had sprouted. No, just the same three on the left and five on the right. It wasn't much, but at least it was a bit of reassurance.

He retrieved his toothbrush and the travel-size toothpaste he kept in the front pocket and gave his mouth a mint makeover. That was the least he could do, really. Nothing like bad breath when you were sitting close to someone. Which he was about to do. Sit close to Krystal Platt.

Dating. Crazy. Teddy was going on a date.

He ran his hands through his hair and shrugged at himself in the mirror. This was him; this was it. It wasn't like Krystal hadn't seen him before. She knew who she was having a secret Saturday afternoon waffle with. Although in her case, it wasn't a secret. Patty Platt was dropping her off, Krystal had told him. This worried Teddy. Did Krystal have waffles with boys often? He put his backpack back on, turned off the light and closed the door behind him.

"Okay, now I'm really leaving," he informed Kirby.

"Au revoir," she said, not looking up from her book.

Outside, the air was warm. A wet-warm, the kind that had you sweating after three minutes. Teddy was glad he had reapplied his deodorant. It was a fifteen-minute walk to the Waffle House from the shelter and then forty minutes home; he had Google Mapped it on his computer the night before.

On the way to work, Teddy had told his mother that he would be staying later than usual, that Kirby would drive him home.

"Kirby? The young woman with the T-shirt? No, I'll come get you, it's fine."

"Mom, it's cool. She said it was no problem," Teddy had lied, looking out the window of the car to avoid her gaze. "Mom, seriously. Watch the road. It's fine."

"Okay," she had agreed, not sounding agreeable at all.

It wasn't that Teddy thought his parents wouldn't approve—as a matter of fact, he was fairly certain they would be overjoyed to know that he was going on a date—but Teddy wanted to keep it, wanted to keep everything about Krystal, his for now. There wasn't much he could call his own—his parents were the judge and jury of everything in his life—so he would have this, even if this didn't last past this waffle, for himself. Though he hoped it did.

He hoped that he was overthinking her dark humor. Probably. Teddy was funny; his humor was versatile. He would be more open-minded, he decided.

The yellow-and-black sign loomed ahead of him. Teddy checked his watch. He would be punctual, which might not be the coolest move, but Teddy was perfectly fine with the fact that he was not cool. Most of the time.

Through the glass door, he could see her. His heart fluttered in his chest. He was glad he was not see-through, although that was a good idea. A human who was entirely see-through in a world of regular humans: blood pumping, muscles contracting and releasing, emotions levitating organs. Quickly, Teddy moved away from the door and out of sight. He pulled his notebook out of his pocket, leaning his back against the redbrick wall to jot it down.

"You gonna keep me waiting all day or what?"

Teddy stopped abruptly, shoving the notebook back in his pocket. Krystal. Her brown hair was wild and free, curling up and around her head in a narrow halo before exploding into more defined ringlets down her back. She was wearing the same purple mascara. Besides that, her face was bare, the perfect heart he remembered. She had on a pink T-shirt and cut-off shorts, revealing her long, long legs. Daryl Hannah legs. On Krystal's feet were the same fuchsia flip-flops. Her toes were painted a glittery silver.

"Hi," Teddy offered, extending his hand.

"Are you fixin' to shake my hand?" asked Krystal, smiling broadly to reveal a gap between her front teeth that Teddy had not noticed before.

"I am," answered Teddy. "I didn't mean to do that; it just sort of happened." He was mortified. What was wrong with him? This was not a job interview.

"It's okay, don't get all red," said Krystal, taking his hand and pulling him inside. "It's cute. Now come on, I have a booth by the window." She walked in front of him, her hand a leash, still holding his. He was holding hands with Krystal; he couldn't believe it. She let his go, sliding into her side, over the cracked red vinyl of the booth.

"Have a seat," she instructed. "I already got you a water. Ice cold. Put a straw in it too."

"Thanks," said Teddy, struggling out of his backpack and shoving it toward the window. He slid in himself and took a big sip.

"Hi," he said, after he had swallowed. He took a deep breath. "I'm nervous."

"I'm Krystal," she replied. "Nice to meet you."

"Funny," he said.

"Well, I'm nervous too, duh! It's good to see you." She took her own sip. "You know, there's not one photo of you on the World Wide Web? It's crazy."

"Really? Not one?" This was not a surprise, he supposed. He didn't have any hobbies that involved other people, that involved obligatory photographs.

But. Krystal had googled him. She had looked for him.

Sitting across from her, it seemed even more impossible, but facts were facts. She liked him.

"I'm an international man of mystery," he said.

"Indeed."

"There's not much of you either, you know." A waitress came to their table.

"So he's here," she said to Krystal, smiling at both of them.

"He is. He loves the water. Thank you."

"Oh, my pleasure. Brewed it myself out back. Now what can I get y'all?"

"I just want a waffle," said Krystal. "Just a big ol' waffle."

"Me too," said Teddy, remembering that he had fantasized about saying *I'll have what she's having* too late. It would have been so perfect. Oh well.

"Two big ol' waffles comin' up." She turned and left. Teddy looked around. He and Krystal were the only people there, which he guessed made sense for 3:00 P.M. on a Saturday. It was too late for brunch, too early for dinner.

"So where were you?" asked Krystal. "Grooming dogs?"

"Yeah. For my Mitzvah Project."

"What's that?" asked Krystal.

"Well, if you're Jewish, you're supposed to get Bar M—" began Teddy, launching into the speech he gave every time someone asked.

"I know what a Bar Mitzvah is, genius," she said, rolling her eyes. "But what's this project business?"

"Oh, sorry," said Teddy. "That's cool, that you know. I feel like most people don't."

"Sure, I know. It's when you get your peepee snipped off and then there's a party with a deejay and stuff."

"What?" asked Teddy, choking on his water.

"What?" Krystal echoed, her voice faltering as her bravado cracked, just a little.

"That's a bris," said Teddy as gently as he could. "That happens when you're born. And they don't, you know, cut it off." He was red from the tips of his toes to the top of his forehead, he just knew it. "They just snip the foreskin." And now Krystal was red too.

"A Bar Mitzvah is when a Jewish boy reads from the Torah and becomes a man or whatever, according to Jewish law. Then there's a deejay," he explained.

"Oh my God, I'm an idiot," said Krystal, fading to pink. "I can't believe that's what I thought. I'm sorry."

"It's okay," said Teddy. "I'm not sure I've met someone, like, our age, who truly knows what it is."

"I mean, I did think it was unnaturally cruel to mess with teenage boys' peepees," Krystal whispered. "But I did know it was just a snip, not, you know, the whole thing."

Teddy nodded.

"Anyway, now that we've got that ironed out . . ." said Krystal, regaining her composure. The waitress arrived with their waffles, plunking them down on the table.

"Y'all need anything else?" she asked, refilling their waters.

"Nope, looks perfect," said Krystal.

"What about you?" she asked Teddy.

"All set, thank you."

"So you read from the Torah and you have a deejay," continued Krystal, pouring a generous pool of syrup into the center of her waffle. Teddy watched it spread, filling each crevice before overflowing onto the white plate.

"Basically. Plus I have to talk about my project." He set to work cutting his waffle.

"What are you doing?" asked Krystal, spearing a bite of hers onto her fork.

"I cut, and then I pour," Teddy explained.

"Interesting technique."

He nodded, continuing diligently as his stomach growled.

"So what's the Mitzvah Project all about?" she asked.

Teddy poured the remaining quarter of the syrup in the decanter onto the myriad golden squares decorating his plate and took a bite. "Mitzvah in Hebrew means 'good deed.' I have to do a good deed for a year and write about it. In a nutshell."

"But you said last night that you don't even like animals," said Krystal.

"I don't." Teddy shrugged and took another bite.

"Wouldn't you rather be doing something that you enjoyed?" Krystal talked with her mouth full, her hand with its purple fingernails almost but not quite covering it.

"But it's not about me," explained Teddy.

"But if you don't even like the dogs and cats or whatever, I mean, wouldn't they be better off with someone who actually enjoyed hanging out with them?"

"Krystal, it's not like I'm hurting them or anything, geez."

"I just think you should do something else."

"But I'm almost done," said Teddy. "I have, like, two months left."

"Two months is eight weeks. Why don't you do something with movies? You love movies."

"It's too late," said Teddy.

"You should host a movie night at the place my mom works," said Krystal, not giving up.

"Where does your mom work?"

"Twilight Manor."

Krystal had eaten all of her waffle at what Teddy considered an alarming pace and was now using her spoon to deliver the remaining syrup into her mouth.

"That old-people place?"

Teddy had driven past it hundreds if not thousands of times. It was big and cream-colored, with a fancy awning proclaiming "Twilight Manor" in bronze cursive over the entrance. A half-circle drive lay in front of it, like a frown.

"Yeah, she's a nurse there."

"What's with the name?" asked Teddy, taking another bite. "It's horrible."

"Yeah. But honestly, what are the options? Death's Doorway?" She giggled.

"Curtains Condos," said Teddy.

"No, but seriously," said Krystal, after they had both stopped laughing. "I'm there, like, all the time, waiting for my mom to get off work. I know a lot of the people there. Some of them are really cool."

"Cool?" asked Teddy. He didn't know a lot of old people.

His grandparents were technically old, but not Curtains Condos old.

"Yeah. I know at least five that would be totally down for a movie night. None of their kids visit them; it would totally be a mitzvah. And one you enjoyed. A double mitzvah."

"Mitzvot," mumbled Teddy, not entirely opposed to her idea. She had a good point.

"What?"

"Mitzvot. Plural of mitzvah," Teddy explained.

"Oh okay, whatever. Mitzvot." Krystal took the last sip of water through her straw, rattling the two remaining ice cubes in her glass.

"But how do I get out of working at the shelter? What do I tell my mom? And what do I do about my report?"

"I dunno," said Krystal. "I can't do everything for you. You're a smart dude; you'll figure it out. But here, I brought a card from Twilight, with the number and stuff. Call and ask for Jackie Jones; she's the boss. Tell her I sent you."

"Thanks," said Teddy, taking the card. "Have you seen *Splash*?"

"Who?"

"*Splash*, the movie? From the eighties?"

"No. Who watches movies from the eighties? See, this is why you would be perfect."

"It's about a mermaid who walks on land in New York City. Just for a little bit."

"I'm not into sci-fi," said Krystal.

"No, no, it's not sci-fi. It's a rom-com that somehow manages to suspend your disbelief. Like, I know and you know that mermaids don't exist, but the movie is so charming that you buy it."

"Okay, if you say so," said Krystal. "I'm not much of a rom-com girl. I'm more into blood and guts."

"And body bags," said Teddy. "I don't think I liked *American Psycho*," he admitted.

"So we agree to disagree. No big deal," said Krystal.

"Anyway, you look like the mermaid. Daryl Hannah," said Teddy.

Krystal smiled. "Oh yeah?"

"Yeah."

"I'll google her."

Teddy nodded.

"Listen, I have to go; there's my mom," said Krystal, pointing to the parking lot. Behind the glass of her windshield, Teddy saw Patty Platt furiously texting.

"After you," said Teddy. He was sad it was over. There was so much more to discuss.

He followed Krystal to the register, noticing unfortunately that she was indeed about an inch taller than him. He had thought as much from their initial encounter but couldn't be sure. He'd hoped he was wrong.

"Oh no, no, this is on me," said Teddy, jumping in front of her to hand the check to the cashier.

"Boy, this is 2019. I'm paying for my own waffle, thank you very much," said Krystal. "Give that back." She snatched it out of his hand and handed it over.

The cashier smirked as she rang her up.

CHAPTER NINE

PAUL

Paul stood in front of the mirror in his bedroom in only his boxer briefs, surveying himself. He was not happy, not happy at all.

His stomach, first of all. Where had the muscles gone? And from the side . . . was it? It was. A potbelly. He stood up as tall as he possibly could, lessening it considerably, but the moment he exhaled, there it was again. Shit.

And his arms. He needed to do some push-ups. They were as slack as udon noodles.

"Okay, Paul, relax," he told his reflection. "It's a body. It can be fixed. When your ankle is better, you will fix it." He felt slightly crazy.

Life was so short, and bad shit happened to everyone every damn day. A pretty bad something had happened to him, and here he was obsessing about a potbelly. His child had died before she even took her first breath outside the womb, but a potbelly was giving him a panic attack.

"It's bullshit," he told himself. "And you know it."

He had the sudden urge to log onto his computer and buy something. Anything.

"Paul?" Sylvie called from inside the closet.

"Yeah?" he yelled back, quickly moving away from the mirror as if she could see him, a jolt of pain like lightning running from his ankle up his entire left side.

"Fuck," he mumbled, grabbing his crutches, which were leaning against the wall.

In terms of furniture, their bedroom claimed only the mirror and a king-size bed, swaddled in white, which perched on a very low-to-the-ground wooden platform that had become the bane of Paul's existence, along with two matching chrome side tables and pale-green reading lamps.

Getting in and out of the bed with a broken ankle was torture on his worst day, comical on his best. But he couldn't complain about it because that had been exactly Sylvie's point against the expensive purchase in the first place, which Paul had ignored entirely.

Sylvie's bedside table held a few books, one collection of short stories that she owned and as far as Paul could tell had never even cracked open, a dog-eared novel from the library and her tortoiseshell glasses, which took up about two-thirds of Sylvie's face.

"They look like welding goggles," Paul had told her when she had first tried them on in the store, but Sylvie had just shaken her head in pity for Paul's apparent lack of eyeglass taste and bought them anyway.

Paul's bedside table held a copy of *Men's Fitness*, which mocked him now from afar, as he shielded his stomach with his free hand, and a Steve Jobs biography. He hadn't made it past page three and had been reading it for almost two years.

On the far wall were two large windows that were almost but not quite tickled by the branches of a dogwood tree in their front yard. The wall over their bed held an enormous abstract oil-on-canvas painting that his friend Ignatius had given them as a wedding gift. Fuchsia, navy, red, golden yellow and emerald splotches and splashes filled the frame.

Across from the bed, a giant flat-screen television floated on the wall. Once upon a time, Paul and Sylvie had been adamant about never allowing one into their bedroom, but that time had come and gone. Now, instead of having sex, they binge-watched *Breaking Bad*. Or, rather, Paul did. Sylvie slept.

Paul hobbled through the bathroom and into the closet to see what Sylvie wanted.

"What do you like better? This dress?" Sylvie held what looked like a navy pillowcase against her chest. "Or this dress?" She placed the hanger on the rack behind her and pulled another pillowcase, this one olive, off its hanger and held it up for his opinion.

"They're the same dress, no?" asked Paul.

Sylvie rolled her eyes. "No, they are not the same dress, Paul. The navy one has longer sleeves and a boat neck, and the olive one is shorter."

"Shorter, like, shows-your-legs shorter?" asked Paul.

"What other kind of shorter is there?"

"Legs all the way," answered Paul. "Skin, I like skin. Some sort of indication that there's a body underneath all that fabric is a surefire yes from me."

"Paul, really," said Sylvie, although she did laugh.

"Sylvie?" asked Paul.

"Yes," she answered, her voice muffled by the dress as she slid it over her head.

"I just want to say, and I don't want you to take this the wrong way or anything, but that you seem, I dunno, happier lately?"

Sylvie's head popped out of the dress, her eyes wide. "Happier?"

"Yeah. Are you, you know, happier?"

Paul braced himself. He wasn't quite sure how his wife would respond to his observation, but defensive was her usual go-to, or at least it had been since Delilah. No matter what he said, even if he intended it as a compliment, it got flipped on its back, its neck snapped in two between Sylvie's ferocious jaws.

"I think I may just be," she said. "But I don't want to jinx it, so can we not? At least until I'm ready?"

"Absolutely." Paul smiled as the tension in his body evaporated. She had not bitten his head off; it was a miracle. "I'm just happy for you. That you're happier."

"Thank you." Sylvie walked over to him and gave him a peck on the lips, but one that lingered longer than the usual two seconds. "Now get dressed; we're already fashionably late, but I don't want to be rude late."

They were going to Greg and Josh's anniversary party. Paul could not, and he meant this literally, remember the last party he and Sylvie had attended, much less without Teddy in tow.

"What should I wear?" Paul asked into the now-empty closet.

Sylvie had moved back into the bathroom, where she was peering into a mirror that magnified her flaws to one thousand times their actual size as advertised by the box it had come in. How was that helpful? Paul wanted to know, but then realized that he was the guy who had just been shirtless and near tears.

Paul's quarter of the closet was neatly organized by Sylvie, a sliver of blue oxford and the occasional stripe, a khaki in brown and olive and two suits: one gray and one navy. Two *J*'s came together to make a hanger for his seven ties and four belts. He never wore this stuff.

On the job he wore work clothes: stiff Carhartt pants and T-shirts, work boots with soles thick enough to bend rogue nails that sometimes littered work spaces, depending on the crew. These were neatly folded in three rows on three shelves, under which lived his five pairs of shoes. All his workout gear, which made up a quarter of his credit card debt—the machines made up the rest—was kept in a basement closet that Paul had made for himself after Sylvie had complained.

"It looks like Lance Armstrong threw up in here," she had told him one afternoon, when he had just started training. But that had just been the beginning of his foray into cyber stockpiling. Now he was up to his eyeballs in *things*. Things that were always meant to improve his life, but never did for longer than a week or two. And so: more things.

Paul sighed, surveying his options. He had thought he was excited to go out, but on second thought, it seemed like an awful lot of effort for a maximum of two hours, ninety-plus minutes of which he would spend on a couch somewhere, watching the world go by, because of his stupid ankle.

But no, he had to buck up. For he and Sylvie to be going on a date anywhere, much less to a party where they would willingly socialize with other people who had likely never known tragedy, whose lives were the equivalent of pink cotton candy, was too much of a unicorn to back away from. It was a big deal for them; of course he was going to get dressed in these clothes, uncomfortable or not, potbelly or not, and make it work.

Paul leaned forward on his crutches and swiped a blue button-down from the rack. The fabric was light and airy, and it had those tabs that would hold back his sleeves. He liked those, and Sylvie had an admirable talent for creating perfectly symmetrical folds.

He leaned his crutches against the shelves and buttoned himself into it, his foot perpendicular to the floor. He would have to put on his pants in the bedroom; he had to sit down for that.

"Oh shit," Paul hissed.

His stupid cast, with its moist, unforgiving grip on the entire lower half of his left leg an inescapable, itchy reminder of his limits. He couldn't even wear pants.

Sylvie would never let him cut a leg off his nice pants. *Let him?* Oh God. What was she, his mother or his wife? Paul winced and shook his head. Maybe he would just stay home, let Sylvie have fun without him.

"What's wrong?" asked Sylvie behind him, her timing impeccable.

"My cast. None of my pants are gonna work." He sighed. "You go ahead, I'll stay home with Teddy, watch a movie or something."

Sylvie put her hand around his shoulder. Her nails. They were red.

"You got your nails painted?" Paul asked incredulously. He had never seen her nails painted.

"Are they awful?"

"No, no. They're just different. Good different. What made you do it?"

"There's this place next to the grocery store, and I had a little extra time to kill. I thought to myself, Why haven't you ever gotten your nails painted before? And honestly, I couldn't answer the question. So, Slut Red it is."

"You're not a slut," said Paul.

"No, that's the name of the color. 'Slut Red.'"

"You're kidding."

"Nope. But back to your pants problem. Not to worry—just wear some nice shorts. Those navy ones are nice. With the flat front?"

"Shorts to a party?" asked Paul. "Sylvie. Come on. That's, like, a cardinal sin to you. Remember our first date?"

"I do. You wore cargo shorts. There almost wasn't a second date."

"But it was hot!"

"But it was a date. Listen, obviously it's nobody's first choice, but you broke your ankle, for Christ's sake."

"I dunno, Sylvie. I mean, these are two gay guys throwing a fabulous party and I show up in shorts? Come on."

"Paul. Honey. You need to get over yourself. You and I are not that interesting; we'll be lucky if anyone even notices us." Paul opened his mouth to protest her point, but Sylvie continued. "And that's okay. It's fine by me. I feel relatively pretty. I'm wearing makeup, I got my nails painted, and I'm not actively mourning the death of our daughter for once, so you know what? Fuck it. We're going to this party."

Sylvie was out of breath, panting slightly from her upchuck of emotion.

Paul dropped his crutches and turned toward her, pulling her into his chest as the crutches clattered to the wood floor. A bolt of pain traveled up his leg, and he felt as though he could topple the two of them at any moment, but he forced himself to stay upright.

Sylvie was not at all the same and yet completely recognizable as the woman he had married, and Paul wasn't sure how to react. To harp on it any further, he feared it would evaporate her breakthrough, dry it right up. But no, he had to. He had been waiting too long for the opportunity.

"Sylvie," he murmured, into the top of her head.

"Paul, I feel like we're gonna fall. Here, let me get you your crutches." She pulled out of his embrace and looked up at him. "You okay to stand for a second?" He nodded.

She handed them back to Paul, one at a time. They faced each other.

"What do you mean, you're not actively mourning her anymore?" Paul asked. "Here, let's go sit. On the bed." He started out of the closet.

"Oh, Paul, come on, let's not make this into a big thing," said Sylvie.

"I'm not making it into a thing," said Paul, swiveling around halfway. "Please." His eye caught something in the corner, on the ground. Something red. "Your purse is on the floor." He began to hobble toward it when Sylvie cut him off, practically shoving him out of the way to hang it back on its hook.

"Must have fallen when I was trying to figure out what to wear. I got it. Thanks." She looped its strap back over the hook and turned to face him again, her cheeks slightly flushed.

"So come on, let's talk, then." Sylvie marched out in front of him, taking the lead suddenly.

They sat on the edge of the bed. Paul wished he had those shorts on, but they could wait.

"So. Delilah?" he asked.

"Delilah," Sylvie repeated.

"How are you feeling?" he asked.

"About her?"

"Yes, about her. About what happened. About yourself?"

"Paul, you're taking that tone with me," said Sylvie. "Please don't take that concerned-therapist tone; you know it drives me crazy."

Paul sighed. "But I am concerned, Sylvie. What you said in the closet is a really big deal. But maybe *concerned* is the wrong word. I'm more interested than concerned."

"Lately, I don't know what it is, but I feel like I've moved into a new phase. Her death. It's not as heavy in my heart. It doesn't, you know, flow through my veins instead of blood anymore. I feel like I'm breathing again. Sort of," said Sylvie. She looked at him, her pupils impossibly opaque. Like black marbles.

"Sylvie, that's a really big deal," said Paul. He took her hand, still taken aback by their red tips.

"I know." She squeezed his hand. "I know you want more from me right now, but I just now landed here, in this spot. Can I just be in this spot for a while before unpacking all the rest? Please?"

Paul sighed. It wasn't fair that probing further, for the sake of their marriage, was not allowed. He had to wait, as he always had to, for her to make the first move. Never mind his feelings or his needs. He was so goddamn tired of it.

"I do love you, Paul." She searched his face, those marble eyes boring holes in his own.

"I love you too, Sylvie." He did, as hard as it was to love someone who made all the rules.

"Now let's get your shorts on," she said quietly, pulling away. "We have a party to go to."

* * *

"HEY, GUYS," GREETED Greg, pulling back his yellow door to welcome Paul and Sylvie inside. "So glad you could make it."

"You smell really good," Paul told him, as Greg moved to embrace Sylvie. "What is that?"

"Some cologne Josh brought me back from London." He rolled his eyes. "He said he went on a special outing to find it, but we all know he got it at the airport."

"Whatever, you smell amazing," said Sylvie.

"It's the thought that counts," added Paul. "Happy anniversary, by the way."

"Yes, happy anniversary." Sylvie thrust their gift at him. Paul had no idea what it was.

"Thank you. Come in, come in. Lots of folks here already. Let me intro—" More guests arrived behind them.

"No, no, we're okay mingling on our own," said Sylvie. "You have hosting to do."

Greg put his hands together in a praying position and nodded before being bombarded by the next couple.

"I need a drink," said Sylvie, as they continued inside.

"What were the prayer hands about?" asked Paul. "That was obnoxious."

"Maybe he's Buddhist now?" answered Sylvie. "Or maybe he's just drunk and didn't know what else to do with his hands. What's the big deal?"

"It was just obnoxious, that's all. Am I not allowed to have an opinion about what I find obnoxious? Even that's forbidden?" Paul snapped.

"Jesus, Paul." Sylvie turned to face him.

"Well, come on, Sylvie. Give me a break, already," said Paul. He was being a brat, he knew it, but so what? "There's the bar, on the deck. Come on," he said, hobbling in front of her to lead the way.

Partly covered so that Greg and Josh's kids could still play outside when it rained, that had been the goal of the deck, Paul remembered, as they stood in line for a drink. It had taken forever for Paul and his crew to build, but it was pretty magnificent, if Paul did say so himself. Sylvie had gotten him the job upon hearing Greg's need for a contractor, just swooped in at one of their office holiday parties and handed him Paul's card. It had been one of his first big jobs and had led to many more. Word of mouth is the best publicity, Sylvie had told him, and she was right. She was almost always right. Almost.

Tonight it housed a few round tables and two couches that they must have brought in, along with a full bar, complete with two bartenders. Delicate strands of twinkling globes were strung through and around the rafters, their gentle glow turning all the guests into their much younger selves.

"You sit. I'll take care of it," instructed Sylvie, pointing to an empty couch.

God, all he did was sit.

"No, I want to stand."

"But how are you going to hold your drink?"

"Shit, Sylvie, I'll lean on one of those tables out there or something, okay? I'll be fine."

He started through the room toward the sliding-glass doors that led to the deck. Three years of barely acknowledging him unless she was yelling or smirking at him, and now she was micromanaging his stand-to-sit ratio.

"Why are you so angry?" she asked, catching up to him.

"Because we're at a party, Sylvie. I'm a grown-up, remember? I know when I need to sit down."

"I was just looking out for you, that's all."

"I'll have a Jameson, neat," Paul said to the bartender. "I know," he said to Sylvie. "I'm sorry for overreacting, I just—I've got this. Okay?"

"Okay." Sylvie put her arm around his waist as Paul's drink appeared.

"Do you have tequila?" she asked, when the bartender shifted his focus to her.

"Tequila?" asked Paul.

"Oh yes, look at this. Fancy tequila. Perfect. Okay, I'll just have some of this over ice with some lime. Two limes. Thanks. What?" she asked Paul. "When in Rome."

They took their drinks to a table and stood, Paul perched on his crutches awkwardly, his ankle throbbing slightly.

"Hey, Ellen!" Sylvie called out loudly.

Ellen, a too-skinny blonde who was very tall but did not have any interest in being tall, as evidenced by the stoop of her shoulders, waved and then proceeded toward them.

"Sylvie," she said, going in for a hug, her very generously

poured pinot grigio threatening to slosh onto Paul's bare toes peeking out of his cast. The straw-colored liquid came just to the glass's edge and then, thankfully, retreated back to the pool from which it came.

"Hi, Paul," she said, putting down her wine on the table to shake his hand. Paul offered his right hand but was immediately embarrassed by the limpness of his grasp. Fucking crutches.

"Sylvie, I just want to thank you," said Ellen.

"For what?" asked Sylvie, taking a sip of her tequila.

Paul detected a very faint wince as she swallowed. Why the tequila tonight? Since when was she a tequila person?

"After that meeting, I went home and told Elliott that he didn't have to go to that stupid party if he didn't want to, and for the first time in possibly"—she paused and looked to the starlit sky overhead as though it had the answer—"seven years? He actually smiled. At me."

"Oh, that's nice, Ellen," said Sylvie. "Teddy seemed pretty thrilled too at the prospect. Although I can't help but feel a teensy bit guilty."

"Why?"

What in the world were they talking about? Paul wondered. His ankle hurt.

"The lack of school spirit, I suppose. Encouraging it and all." Sylvie rolled her eyes. "It's the good girl in me."

"No way," said Ellen. "Where's the school spirit if our boys are miserable? They've been miserable at these things long enough."

"I hope you're right," said Sylvie. "No, I know you are."

"Sorry, what are you guys talking about?" asked Paul finally.

"Sylvie didn't tell you?" asked Ellen. She took an enormous gulp of her wine, practically draining the glass.

"No." He looked at Sylvie, who shrugged her shoulders, although he could tell by her cat-that-ate-the-canary grin that she was pleased with herself, pleased by the attention.

"Oh, well, let me tell you then. Your wife stuck it to those PTA wenches a few weeks ago. She stood up for the little men, so to speak, meaning our little men."

Paul bristled. Teddy wasn't little.

"Oh yeah? How so? Sylvie, you didn't tell me this."

"I did. I told you that I told Teddy he didn't have to go to the end-of-year party if he didn't want to. I told you that, remember?"

"Well yeah, but you didn't mention anything about sticking it to anybody." Paul looked at her quizzically.

"I didn't really," murmured Sylvie, exchanging a conspiratorial look with Ellen.

"Get out of here!" Ellen squeezed Paul's shoulder, barely able to contain her excitement. "She stood right up in the middle of the meeting and basically told Erika and her cronies to fuck right off. In a classy way, of course."

Paul was shocked and a little turned on. Sylvie hadn't told anyone to fuck off to their face in years.

"I was just honest," Sylvie said. She had finished her drink.

He took a sip of his, suddenly feeling pressure to keep up.

"With myself and with them about Teddy. Like, why am I wasting time bribing him to be somebody who likes to go to school functions? What's the point? That's all."

"That's not all," said Ellen. "Stop being so modest. I love that you called Lindsey out. She really is just a terrible person."

Another woman called Ellen's name, and she waved her empty wineglass at her over Sylvie's head. She really was very tall, Paul thought. Probably as tall as him if he stood up straight, and he was six feet. Okay, five eleven.

"Anyway, I just wanted to thank you, Sylvie," she said. "You've inspired me. Could we get lunch or something soon?"

"Sure, just call me."

"Paul. Nice to see you. Feel better."

"You too," said Paul as she walked away. "How come you didn't tell me about this?" he asked.

"But I did," said Sylvie.

"Not the fun details. Not that you went all Norma Rae on them."

Sylvie laughed. "Paul, do you want to sit down now?" she asked.

He nodded.

"Look, the couch over there. It's empty. Let's go."

She took his crutches from him as he lowered himself onto the cushions, grateful.

"I need another drink," she announced. "Do you?" He held up his whiskey. It was still half full.

"Nope."

"A water or anything?"

"No, that's okay. Thanks."

"Okay." Sylvie turned to go.

"Wait. What did you say to Lindsey? What was Ellen talking about?"

"Oh, I just called her out for never acknowledging Delilah," she answered plainly. "I'll be back."

"Not acknowledging Delilah," he whispered into the night air, to no one, as she sauntered back to the bar.

Paul watched the party happen from the couch. The pretentious double air kisses, the fake laughs, the real laughs. Someone had turned on the music, and it floated out of invisible speakers, speakers Paul had painstakingly installed himself. He drained his drink, although he may as well have been drinking water. Sadly, he was not the slightest bit drunk.

Somehow, overnight it seemed, Sylvie's and his roles had reversed. She was the open one now, at least open on her terms; she was the one speaking her truth and enjoying life. He, on the other hand, was closing like a fist, buried in his pocket with no motivation to strike. Could it be as simple as the fact that without his exercise, he had no outlet? And without his freedom to click "Buy," no relief? Nothing to look forward to?

He pulled his phone out of his pocket and scrolled through his texts, landing on T.B., otherwise known as Tobi Bell. It was a rather absurd name, but she swore it was her real one, and to be honest it fit her, Paul thought. She was petite and spunky, with a voice that sounded a little bit like Peppermint Patty's: raspy and deep for someone her size.

He'd met her on his triathlon training team and immediately, without any rational explanation since he was (a) not cool, (b) significantly older than her and (c) married, she'd taken an interest in him. At first, Paul had been quick to assume that she was just that type of person—bubbly, overly friendly, a talker—and that he was easy prey: affable, eager to learn and a listener. But then, well, it became obvious that she had a crush on him, which was ludicrous but also flattering.

He did not indulge her flirting; he never took her up on her invitations for beers after a training run or stretched out with her despite her repeated attempts to ask him to join her on the ground, her legs sometimes over her head. Sure, it was a little over-the-top, her pursuit of him. But it was harmless.

Until the texts started coming. Sometimes Paul answered them, sometimes he didn't, but they always aroused him. Not because they were sexy texts, not at all. They were always banal, asking him about his day, a training exercise, whatever. But they came. And they were his secret. He had never told a soul.

He stared at her last text now and typed back, *Ankle healing. Crutches suck,* his whole body warm with both the knowledge that he shouldn't be texting back and the thought of her reading it.

"Paul, how are you, my friend?"

Paul looked up to find David looming above him, two bottled beers in hand. He closed his phone and shoved it back into his pocket.

"Mind if I have a seat?"

"Of course."

David sat and handed him a beer.

"What are you doing here?" Paul asked incredulously. David may as well have been a mirage. Maybe he was drunk after all.

"Cheers," said David, clinking his perspiring bottle with Paul's. He took a sip. "We kept in touch after the deck job," he explained.

"Cool," said Paul, taking a sip of his own. "It's good to see you."

"You too. I don't know a freakin' soul here."

"No date?" asked Paul.

"Not tonight."

"Well, the night is young."

"Not really," said David. "I'm tired. Where's Sylvie?"

"Somewhere around here," answered Paul.

"You okay?" asked David. "You sound a little down."

"I'm fine," said Paul. "Just tired too."

They sat together, nestled in the cushions of the couch, looking up and out at the rest of the world. Both lonely, together.

It was the best company Paul could possibly have.

CHAPTER TEN

SYLVIE

Thanks," said Sylvie to the bartender, feeling slightly dizzy but in a very pleasant way. Like the party was a hammock from which she swung slightly, suspended between two giant palm trees.

She giggled to herself, covered her mouth with her free hand. She really was stoned. She did not want to go back to Paul on the couch. He had been sulking since they had arrived. Frankly, he was killing her buzz. She felt guilty thinking that, since she was fully aware that she had been killing his for years. He was the nicer one, which was an incontestable fact, despite his flaws. She needed him to keep being that person.

She wandered through the party, nodding at people who smiled at her. Without planning it, she found herself at the base of the staircase, looking up to the second floor of the house.

Sylvie glanced around furtively. No one was watching her. As quietly and quickly as she could, she climbed the stairs, thrilled by the possibility of going somewhere she knew she shouldn't.

At the top, to the left, was a giant, open playroom straight out of a magazine. Every toy in its rightful straw basket, every basket tucked into deep wood shelves built into stark white walls. The floor was covered with a rug that burst with color: pink and chartreuse, orange and turquoise, emerald and lavender, baby blue and cream, all woven together to create a magical color palette that somehow managed to excite and soothe at the same time. A white tepee with swirls of navy splashed across its fabric stood in the corner, a tiny white wooden table with yellow chairs in the other. Two easels, for the budding van Goghs.

She moved on through the hallway. To her right, a door. She opened it and gasped, the force of missing what existed here—but had never for her—like a sucker punch to the nose. A little girl's room. Agnes's room.

She entered and stood rooted to the spot for a moment as she regained her composure, the room glowing slightly thanks to a nightlight in the shape of a fox's face plugged into the far wall, by the two windows. A twin bed lined the wall to Sylvie's left, a trundle bed, from the looks of it. White wood. Simple.

Sylvie approached it, stretching out her hand tentatively

to feel the softness of the lavender polka-dotted duvet cover. A stuffed ostrich lay against the pillow, its eyes comically wide, its soft feathers matted by the constant attention of four-year-old hands. Sylvie sat on the bed and hugged it to her chest.

Across from her was a low bookcase, with two rows of three cubbies. Books and bins of dolls and LEGOs, paper and crayons, blocks and impossibly tiny animals. In the corner, tulle and the recognizable sheen of polyester peeked over the edge of a tall woven basket. A cowboy hat lay on the floor beside it, the lone artifact out of place. Another beautiful rug, with fuchsia, navy, emerald green and gold threads woven through it, covered the floor. On the windows, pale-gray wooden blinds to keep out the light.

On the small white table next to the bed, a wooden lamp with an azure shade. On top of it, a glass globe plugged into the wall. Sylvie, still hugging the ostrich, switched it on, turning the room into a galaxy of hazy stars. Imagine, she thought to herself. Imagine if Delilah had lived.

What kind of girl would she be? This kind of girl, or a tomboy kind of girl? Would she have emulated her brother or forged her own path? She would have been three now. Would she have liked to have her nails painted? Sylvie wondered, looking down at her own red digits. Would she have been a snuggler or a wiggle-away kind of person? What would her voice have sounded like? What phrases would she have inevitably gotten wrong, making them her own each time she uttered them?

For the longest time, Teddy, instead of saying "for real,"

had emphatically uttered "for your real life, Mom" when defending a particular stance. It had given Sylvie so much joy, that turn of phrase. Sylvie had mourned when Teddy had outgrown it. She still did.

What would their life as a family of four be like? Sylvie kicked off her clogs, which landed with two muffled thumps on the rug. She placed her empty drink on the bedside table and lay back, her head against the pillow. Stars and planets were strewn across the ceiling like confetti.

Paul would be happier, with a daughter who adored him. He might never have taken up his training compulsion, and hence they wouldn't be thousands of dollars in debt and she might have been able to quit the job she hated.

And Teddy. Teddy would have been a great big brother because he was a sweet kid, but also because on the rare occasions Sylvie saw her son being able to exercise his authority—explaining a movie plot or a camera shot, for example, or more recently, picking out his own clothes (which killed Sylvie, but what could she do, he was twelve)—he puffed up with confidence, like a marshmallow in the microwave. And she? What would Sylvie be like?

The medicinal waves of serenity that had been rolling through her body all night were beginning to recede. Would that make it high tide or low tide? Sylvie wondered. No matter, she had another pill nestled in one of the giant pockets of her dress. She reached in and found it, a tiny disk in the bottom left-hand corner, waiting. Into her mouth, and with one commanding swallow, it dissolved into her body.

Sylvie would be an entirely different person, she figured,

if Delilah had lived. Being the victim of tragedy, it changed absolutely everything about you. Sure, you could smile again, eventually, laugh again and even forget for a while sometimes, that what once was was no longer. But even when you were happy, even when you experienced some sort of triumph, you were sad. Because wishing that things had turned out differently never went away. Even with these pills, that wishing never went away, as evidenced by the fact that here she was, in a four-year-old girl's bedroom, clutching a stuffed ostrich and sobbing.

Sylvie sat up. She patted at her eyes, knowing her mascara had likely run down her face. She stopped crying, as suddenly as she had started, as the blissful waves rolled again, smoothing over her unhappiness as they lapped and retreated, lapped and retreated.

Why couldn't she just get drunk at a party like everyone else, dance like an idiot to the hip-hop of her youth, which she heard thumping below, possibly spill her drink all over either herself or Paul, go home, have grunty sex and pass out? Why was she forever cursed with the weight of heartbreak, the bitterness of why her, why Paul, why Teddy, why Delilah? Try as she might, Sylvie could not push past it. But the pills. They helped. Until they didn't. And then she just took another.

Sylvie stood up. She smoothed the bed and placed the ostrich back in its spot. She switched off the globe, and the stars went out. She retrieved her empty glass. On her way out of the room, she pocketed a tiny kitten figurine, dressed in a pinafore and a red-checkered dress with a high, ruffled collar.

"Sylvie?" She stopped in her tracks, weaving ever so slightly on her feet, and grabbed the banister before turning her head to heed the greeting.

Greg. With his perfectly tousled hair and square jaw, he could have been a model in a J.Crew catalog.

"Greg, hey," she said. "Just using the bathroom up here. I hope you don't mind."

"Mi casa, su casa," he said, toasting her with his champagne glass. "Just being a terrible host, I'm afraid. I'm not much for parties."

"Really? But this is a great party." Sylvie turned around completely to face him, conscious of the tiny bulge of stolen property in her pocket.

"That's all Josh," he answered. "Happy husband, happy . . . I guess they don't have a trite cliché for that."

"I suppose not. How are you?"

"I'm okay, I guess. Nothing to complain about, but if pressed, I'm sure I could find something."

"Mazel tov on ten years," said Sylvie, lifting her own empty glass.

He approached her with a smile to clink his to hers. "Thanks, Sylvie. I can't believe it, actually. Went by like"—he snapped his long, tapered fingers—"that."

Sylvie looked at him. Really looked at him. His brown eyes were tired, underneath each a half-moon of gray.

"Greg?"

"Yes?"

"Has anything really terrible ever happened to you?"

Greg cocked his head slightly, considering the weight of her question.

"Yes." He paused. "My dad died when I was five. That was pretty terrible."

"That is terrible. I'm sorry that happened to you."

"I'm sorry it happened to him," said Greg. "He was only thirty-eight. Massive heart attack."

"How did you handle it?"

Greg poured some of his champagne into her glass. "I suppose the way all five-year-olds handle tragedy. Pretty resiliently. It wasn't until later, as a teenager, that I even knew to be angry. And that's a whole other thing, you know."

"How did your mother handle it?"

"She was a warrior," he said simply. "A stoic warrior. Raised me and my sister the best she knew how, went back to school for her master's in social work. Kept it moving. But not without her share of tears and rage, which I of course forgive her for. Then and now."

Sylvie took a sip of the lukewarm champagne. "Then?"

"Sure. Even at five, I could see how hard it was, to be a single parent."

"But don't you ever want to scream at the world? Like, 'Why did my dad have to die when your stupid dad is still here?'"

"All of the time. I still do. But that's what meditation and antidepressants are for. At least for me. And now, as a father myself, I feel like I have a chance to live the life he would have lived, if he had been given the chance."

"Greg, that's amazing."

"Is it? I don't know about that. It just is, for me. You know?"

Sylvie nodded. "You never needed to escape from that pain? All these years?" she asked.

"Sure. I smoked more weed than any pair of lungs has license to, did my share of psychedelics in high school and college. Looking for him, I guess, to appear and dispense some sage advice." He finished his glass. "Never happened.

"How are you doing?" he asked Sylvie. "How is your grief?"

"Mine?"

"It never goes away; I know that," said Greg.

"For the longest time, it was like carrying a boulder in my chest where my heart should be. It still is, some days. But lately, it feels more like a pebble. There's room to breathe. Sometimes."

Tears filled Sylvie's eyes as she admitted this, because who knew if it was even real? Without the synthetic lifeline she'd chosen, without this chemically induced euphoria, she was still struggling under that boulder's weight. She longed to tell Greg this, now, but she swallowed the urge. This secret was all she had.

"That's really good to hear," said Greg. "Have you found someone to talk to?"

"Yes, I found someone," Sylvie lied.

"Great. And Teddy and Paul? How are they?"

"Good. Great. Speaking of, I should probably find my husband."

"Good to see you, Sylvie."

"You too, Greg. And thanks for sharing that with me."

"You asked," he answered. "Not many people do."

"I wish more people would," said Sylvie. "I'll take a real question over bullshit chitchat any day."

"Me too." He smiled at her, a real smile, and Sylvie smiled back before making her descent back into the fray.

Slowly, she dodged in and out between the groups of revelers, now all more than a little drunk and dancing questionably to the nineties hip-hop that continued to bump over the speakers. There was Paul. Right where she had left him, his head back against the couch, his mouth open slightly. He was sleeping.

"Hi," she said quietly, sitting beside him. He sat up, dazed.

"Hi," he said, his saliva thickening his speech. "How long was I out? God, how embarrassing."

"You're fine," said Sylvie. She kissed him on the cheek and snuggled into the warmth of him.

They sat, the white linen couch a sailboat in a sea of revelry, watching.

CHAPTER ELEVEN

TEDDY

Teddy looked in his parents' full-length mirror in their closet for the sixth time. Was this shirt okay? It was his favorite T-shirt, but was it too babyish? He liked that it was gray, and soft, but it had *Jurassic Park* emblazoned across its chest, in orange lettering. It wasn't a baby movie, per se, but dinosaurs? Would Krystal think it was ridiculous?

"It's fine, you're fine!" Teddy hissed at the mirror, annoyed by his anxiety.

He turned away abruptly, almost tripping over something in the process. A red purse of his mother's. He didn't remember knocking it over, but if his mother saw one thing even the slightest bit out of place, she would know he had been in here. And then she would ask why. He picked it up to hang it back on the hook he assumed it fell from, only to hear a distinct rattle coming from inside it.

He unzipped it, curious. Inside, a pill bottle was nestled in the red leather. He picked it up, examined it.

Oxycodone, the label read.

He knew about this pill. In the fall, a woman with tattoos all up and down her forearms, which he knew because the sleeves of her blue shirt were rolled up, had come to speak to his class about drugs. Oxycodone had been her drug of choice, she said, and then she proceeded to weave her story of near-death and redemption. Teddy was not sure if becoming a talking head for middle schoolers around the country qualified as redemption, but to each his own, he guessed.

Afterward, all the popular kids around him had rolled their eyes. Drugs weren't the problem; it was the people who took them, he had overheard Judson Dearborn explain to his usual crowd of Klingons as he trailed behind them on their way back to class. Some people just couldn't handle them.

"Should I get a tattoo?" Taylor had whispered over him to Kai in Spanish class, as if he were invisible, missing the point of the woman's visit entirely.

Teddy had never really thought about drugs, but he had seen them in movies. He'd watched *Scarface* with his dad, one time when his mom had gone to Milwaukee for a work trip. But that was cocaine, which seemed like maybe the worst thing ever created. Why anyone would snort something up their nose to act crazy and sweat profusely was beyond Teddy.

Teddy thought the school may have been better off showing that movie than hosting Matilda, which was what the woman's name had been.

But here he was now in his parents' closet, holding a bottle of the very drug Matilda had warned them about and wondering why it was hidden in his mom's purse. He had always considered Judson Dearborn to be a narcissistic moron, but his words rang in Teddy's ears now. He felt nauseated, holding the bottle. He zipped it back into the purse, returned it to the hook and walked briskly out of the closet, turning around one last time to make sure it hadn't parachuted to the floor again.

Downstairs in the kitchen, Teddy looked at the digital clock on the stove. His parents had left for their party fifteen minutes prior, and Krystal was due to arrive in four. They had never said to Teddy, *Don't have anyone over when we're not here,* so technically he wasn't breaking any rules, but he still knew he was being bad. Which kind of felt good.

There was a firm *rap, rap, rap* at the door. She was here. It was happening.

Be cool, be cool, be cool, he repeated to himself as he strode purposefully to the door. *You're Indiana Jones. Hans Solo. Harrison Ford.* A young Harrison Ford, yes, that was it. He opened the door, trying desperately to assume his best well-what-do-we-have-here? smirk.

"Did you just barf or something?" Krystal asked, looking concerned.

"No."

"Oh good, I was about to hightail it out of here. Stomach bugs are the worst. I had one once that lasted five days. I looked like a skeleton in flip-flops." She paused. "In case you couldn't tell, it's my signature shoe."

Teddy took her in. A plain white tank top and pink shorts, her wild hair piled on top of her head like a woven basket. The left strap of her purple bra peeked out slightly, curving over her freckled shoulder. It took every ounce of restraint in Teddy not to reach out and touch it with his finger.

"Are you going to invite me in or what?" she asked. "I know your mama raised you better than this."

"Yes, of course, sorry, come in," replied Teddy, tripping over his words. Harrison Ford, he reminded himself. But it was no use. He was Teddy Snow, like it or lump it. He closed the door behind her.

"Woweeeee, this place is nice," said Krystal, as she moved through the downstairs. "It's so cool, how open it is. Did you say that your dad designed it?" she asked over her shoulder as she passed by the television, running her hand over the back of the couch. Her nails were not painted this time, Teddy noticed, and he felt a pang of appreciation for the beauty of their simplicity.

"Yeah," he mumbled, glancing again at a clock, this one on the far wall over the benched side of the dining table.

According to his estimate of what normal adults did at parties, he had given his parents two hours to socialize. But then again, his parents were not normal, so who knew?

"You're as nervous as a pig at a barbecue," Krystal announced, eyeing him.

"I know it," said Teddy. "Sorry, it's just if my parents come home unexpectedly, I'll be screwed."

"Don't worry, I can make a quick getaway. You can hide me in a closet and then when they go up to bed I'll just slip out, like I was never here in the first place. It'll be exciting." She smiled at him, her eyes twinkling like Christmas lights.

"But what about your mom? Isn't she coming to get you? Like, what if she's coming up the driveway at the same time my parents are or something?" Teddy felt faint. He hadn't thought any of this through. He slumped onto the bench.

"Good lord, Teddy, pull it together," said Krystal, opening the fridge and not seeming even the slightest bit fazed by the prospect. "I took an Uber here. My mom thinks I'm at my friend Nia's house, and technically I am, since that's where I'm headed after this. Relax."

She pulled an orange seltzer from the shelf and closed the door, opening it with a loud hiss.

"You're like a secret agent or something," he remarked with admiration.

"That's me." She held back the can and guzzled from its lip for a moment.

"Secret Agent Krystal Plaaaaattttt," she said, burping her last name loudly and then erupting into a fit of giggles. Teddy laughed too, freed from his anxiety by her wicked nonchalance.

He was a goner, he realized, not for the first time, wiping his eyes. Madly in love with Krystal Platt.

"Let's see the rest of this place," said Krystal. "If that's cool?"

"Sure," said Teddy, standing up. "I'll give you the grand tour. Wait, do you want anything to, you know, drink drink?"

He did not really want to ask Krystal this question since the taste of alcohol did not agree with Teddy—from what he'd experienced from offered sips from his parents' glasses on various but not many special occasions, he thought it was vile—but he felt like he had to. There was wine and beer in the fridge, a pantry shelf filled with bottles of clear and brown liquids. The memory of the pill bottle in his mother's purse came back to him suddenly, and he felt nauseated again.

"No, I'm cool," she answered, and relief washed over Teddy like an ocean wave.

"'K." He slid off the bench and walked to the fridge, next to Krystal. She smelled like raspberries. He took a seltzer of his own, guzzled half of it down and burped, "Aaaaafter youuuuuu." Krystal smiled at him, and his entire body burst into fireworks.

"Wait, just one second," he said, pulling out his trusty notepad. *Fireworks as special effect,* he scribbled quickly.

"You and that notepad," she said, shaking her head before leading the way.

"So this is the upstairs," said Teddy. "A guest bedroom that no one stays in because we never have guests."

They entered it. A queen-size wooden platform bed, a yellow quilt with pillowcases covered in gray. A small colorful rug lined with jagged blocks of purple, beige, emerald, navy and turquoise. A gray bedside table with a small brass lamp and eggshell-blue shade. A bureau. A window looking out onto the front lawn, shuttered with closed white slats to keep out the light.

"It's pretty," said Krystal. "How come no guests?"

"I dunno. My parents aren't much for entertaining, I guess."

"They don't have friends?"

"My dad has some," Teddy explained. "My mom, though, not so much. Or she used to, but not since—" Teddy stopped abruptly.

"Not since what?"

"This was supposed to be my baby sister's room," Teddy offered, surprising himself by acknowledging it out loud, to another person. To Krystal Platt, more specifically.

"Supposed to be?" she asked.

"She died," said Teddy quietly. "Well, she was born, but she was dead."

His explanation hung in the air, and the room transformed into what it had been three years ago: a nursery for a baby girl. A white crib, a yellow-and-white-striped rug, a gray chair that rocked back and forth with a silver leather ottoman.

"Teddy, that's so sad," said Krystal. She took his hand and held it, both of them still looking at the room but not at each other. "I'm so sorry for you and your family. That must have been awful."

"It was," agreed Teddy. "It still is. Her name was Delilah."

"That's a beautiful name," Krystal said softly.

"Thanks. It was my great-grandmother's name."

"Life can be very sad sometimes," said Krystal. She was still holding his hand. "My dad, he just took off when I was two. Left me and my mom and never looked back."

"That's terrible," said Teddy. "What kind of person does that?"

"A shitty one," said Krystal, finally turning to face him. Her blue eyes were wet underneath her purple eyelashes. "And a drug addict."

"I'm so sorry," said Teddy. "For you too."

Krystal shrugged. "Thanks, but it's okay. My mom says we're better off without him. But sometimes I think it would be nice to have a dad." She sighed. "Anyway, what can we do? Bad stuff happens every day, to every kind of person, you know? This is proof, this conversation we're having right now."

"I wish it hadn't happened to us," said Teddy.

"Me too." She unfolded her hand from his. "You're cute, but your hands are like lava mitts, you know that?"

I'm cute, thought Teddy. "Yeah, sorry."

"Nothing to be sorry about. My feet smell," she confessed. "Let's see your parents' room. I bet it's enormous."

"It's pretty big," Teddy agreed. "It's down at the end of the hall."

"Dang," said Krystal, taking it all in from the doorway. "This is like some Kate and Wills shit."

"Kate and Wills?"

"The Duke and Duchess of Cambridge? In England?"

Teddy had no idea what she was talking about.

"Do you do anything besides watch movies, boy? They're the future of England's aristocracy. And very chic. Also: rich."

Teddy blushed. Was he rich? He guessed he was. And he knew that Krystal was not.

"Wow, look at this bathroom," gushed Krystal, her flip-flops slapping against its marble floor. She opened a drawer.

"Oh my God, the makeup!" She scanned the bottles, picked up a compact and opened it to reveal a shiny mosaic of peach and bronze.

"Does your mother wear all of this?"

"No. At least I don't think so. Her face looks like her face." Not like the other moms he saw at his school or on television. Most of them looked like clowns, Teddy thought.

"You would know if she did," said Krystal. "Although I guess this stuff is so, like, nice"—she held up a different black compact and pointed at the word *Chanel* with her finger—"maybe the point is that you don't know. Like, you just think your mom looks rested and glowy and perfect naturally, but really it's this stuff."

"Nah, she doesn't wear it," Teddy announced, confident after Krystal's description. *Glowy* was definitely not a word he would use to describe his mother. "Tonight I think she was, though. For the party. She had lipstick on, that much I know."

The pills again. Teddy's mind kept circling back to them. Should he ask Krystal what she thought? She seemed to know everything.

"And look at this closet!" Krystal said, switching on the light. "Damn. This is like Neiman Marcus in here." She faced him, her arms folded across her chest.

"Teddy Snow, you are really rich," she announced accusingly. "How come you didn't tell me that?"

"I don't think about it," said Teddy. "I mean, no one has ever told me before, 'Teddy, you're rich,' like you just did. And anyway, it sounds like you're trying to make me feel bad about it." He shoved his hands deep into the pockets of his shorts.

"I'm not trying to make you feel bad about it," said Krystal. "Well, maybe I am a little. I'm just jealous. Let's be real, though."

"Don't be jealous. Having money doesn't make your problems go away. Or keep bad things from happening."

"True." She unfolded her arms. "But you can at least look better while they happen. And come home to your fancy bed to cry. My bedroom is the size of a shoe box. My whole house could probably fit up here, come to think of it."

"I think you look better than good," said Teddy quietly. "I think you're beautiful."

Krystal gave him a small smile. "You do?"

"Yeah." Teddy looked at his sneakers, embarrassed.

"Thank you," said Krystal.

He could hear her approaching, those damn flip-flops, but he didn't dare look up. The smell of raspberries was all around him, enveloping him like a fog.

"Look at me," she said.

Teddy looked up, and Krystal Platt kissed him softly on the lips. He had been certain she would taste like cotton candy for some reason, but her lips just tasted like skin. Soft, wet skin.

"Let's see your room," she said, brushing past him, back through his parents' bedroom and into the hallway.

If he died right now, right this very second, he would have lived, Teddy thought, and then immediately chided himself for being the corniest person on the planet. But he got it now.

He really got those cheesy romance movies, with people crying in the rain and making googly eyes at each other. This is what requited love felt like. Total and complete satisfaction mixed with terror that it would be taken away from you at any second. For now, Teddy would focus on the first part of that feeling.

"Looks like you found it," said Teddy.

He stood behind Krystal at the door to his bedroom, trying to see it through her eyes and hoping, hoping, hoping it looked interesting. A room was such a clear indication of a person's character, Teddy thought. A porthole into their soul, really. It felt deeply personal, for her to see it. To be inside it. The whole night did, and it had only been—he looked at his alarm clock next to his bed—thirty minutes. He had an hour and a half left, an hour to be safe.

"I love it," said Krystal, and Teddy's heart did a flip. She sat on his bed, facing him.

"Did you call Twilight Manor yet?"

"No." Krystal made a face at him. "But I will. Tomorrow."

"You have to do it. I mean, come on, Teddy. Movies are your passion. You have to share that with people who could use a little passion in their lives. That's the mitzvah."

Teddy smiled.

"Yeah, I looked it up. I know what a mitzvah is. And washing dogs' butts isn't it. At least for you. You have to do it, or the whole thing, this whole project, is just a joke. And then your Bar Mitzvah is a joke. If it has nothing to do with you, how is it yours?"

Teddy perched on the bed next to her, his hands practically

faucets. Sitting on his own bed next to Krystal. He slid them under his thighs.

"You sure are fired up about this," he told her.

"I am! I mean, the project is a nice idea, but not if it's bull-crap. Promise me you'll call tomorrow."

"I promise," said Teddy. He would. She was right.

God, he wanted to tell her about the pills he had found in his mother's purse. But he had already laid so much on her. And what if her response was the one he didn't want to hear? That his mom was in trouble? There really was no other response; he realized that. But hearing it out loud from Krystal Platt, who was this beautiful sage, wasn't something he was ready for. Because if she said what he knew she was going to say, then Teddy would have to do something about it. And he didn't want to. Not right now. Right now he wanted to kiss Krystal Platt.

And so he did.

CHAPTER TWELVE

PAUL

Paul stared at the ceiling fan going around and around, early-morning light peeking through the blinds. The air conditioner hummed softly.

His head throbbed slightly; he should have said no to his second whiskey, but when your friend hands it to you, saying no to a drink is just unnecessary martyrdom. He sighed and shifted slightly, noticing his wife's dark curls, the olive skin of her naked shoulder against the white sheets, the slow rise and fall of her back as she slept. He reached out to touch her hair but pulled back, remembering that he was angry.

She had disappeared for what had felt like hours during the party, returning to wake him up with nary an explanation. She'd been nice upon her return, sure, but to be frank: too nice. Something was going on with her. And damnit, he was going to find out what. Tobi had texted him back, as he knew she would, but he had deleted the string. And her number. It was ridiculous, what he was doing. And sad. And Sylvie's fault.

There was a rustling of the sheets beside him as Sylvie stirred. Paul kept his eyes on the ceiling fan. The bed shifted slightly beneath him as she turned over onto her back.

"Hi," she croaked.

"Sylvie, I have to know what's going on with you," he demanded, hoping he sounded commanding and not desperate.

"Good morning to you too," she replied, rubbing her hand over her mouth. "Jesus, my breath. My head. I drank too much."

"Sylvie, goddamnit, I'm serious!" Paul sat up, looking at her with disdain.

"Okay, okay." She sat up too and pulled the blankets around her chest.

"Where did you go last night, during the party?" he demanded. "You left me for hours, just sitting there like a buffoon."

"I thought you said David was there. And it wasn't hours."

"That's not the point!"

"I was upstairs," she said.

"Upstairs? What were you doing upstairs?"

"At first I was snooping," she confessed. "But then I found Agnes's room."

"Oh."

"I just meant to peek in, but once I saw all of her little-girl things, I couldn't help myself. I closed the door and climbed into her bed."

"You did what?"

"I know, I know. Creepy." Sylvie pushed her pillow against the headboard and leaned against it, pulling the covers even farther up, to her neck. "I thought about Delilah and what kind of girl she would have been, if she had lived."

"Oh," said Paul quietly, not expecting any of what she was telling him. "Well?"

"I don't know, I guess. But it was interesting to think about. I don't think she would have been a girly girl. More of a tomboy, I think."

"You think?" asked Paul, his anger fading ever so slightly. He considered a three-year-old Delilah. "I can see that. Because of Teddy, maybe."

"And you. I think she would have been a lot like you."

"You do?"

"Yes. You know, Teddy looks like you but has my personality, for better or worse, so it just makes sense that she would be the opposite."

Paul nodded. "Yeah, I've always thought that too, actually," he said.

"You've considered her, you know, as an evolving person too?"

"Of course. All the time. I see little girls everywhere, ones with your coloring, and have to catch my breath, thinking about what could have been. What was supposed to be but wasn't."

"Yeah," said Sylvie. "So that's where I was."

"Were you sad?" asked Paul.

"Sure," said Sylvie. "I cried a little, I think. But then I realized that I was very much in danger of passing out drunk in a four-year-old's bed and got my ass up." She sighed. "But it was nice, to give myself permission to think those thoughts."

"You've never done that before?"

"Maybe sometimes I've started to, but I always cut myself off. Or I *did*, anyway," said Sylvie.

"But why?"

"Because they're useless thoughts, Paul. What good do they do?"

"Thoughts don't always have to have a purpose," said Paul. "Sometimes thoughts are just a subconscious release."

"I'm starting to realize that, I guess."

"I'm glad," said Paul.

"I wish that I had seen Delilah," said Sylvie, practically whispering. "I'm angry at myself that I didn't."

Paul opened his mouth to say something, but she continued, staring ahead at the opposite wall.

"It just seemed too unnecessarily painful at the time. I had endured so much heartbreak in those few hours, the possibility of taking on any more, it just seemed wrong."

Paul had seen her. Delilah had had a thick head of dark hair, like Sylvie. She had long, dark eyelashes. She was plump. But she was also blue. His heart broke in two all over again, remembering.

He searched under the covers for Sylvie's hand and entwined his fingers through hers. He wasn't so angry anymore.

"I know I'm different lately. Obviously. I mean, we're sitting in bed talking about Delilah's death, for God's sake. You can't get much more different than that," said Sylvie.

"Yes," said Paul. "And it's wonderful, it really is. I just want to know how—"

"I'm on Prozac," Sylvie declared. She turned to look at him. "I started it about two months ago."

"What? But you've never even gone to see a psychiatrist. Or have you?"

"No, I got the prescription from my regular doctor. I don't know what it was exactly, but I was just so tired of being depressed. Which is an oxymoron, I guess, since being tired is a big part of being depressed. She was having me fill out those questionnaires they always make you fill out, like how often do you want to kill yourself or whatever, and for the first time ever, I answered them honestly."

"You want to kill yourself?" asked Paul, alarmed.

"No, no—bad example. Just those questionnaires, they're so obvious. At any rate, she asked me about my answers, we got to talking and she wrote me the prescription. At first I wasn't going to fill it, but then I did."

"Wow," said Paul. "I can't believe it."

"What? That I would be on an antidepressant?"

"That, but all of it. That you would admit to being depressed, that you would talk to your doctor, that you would have the prescription filled. All of it without so much as a word to me."

"You're mad at me?" asked Sylvie.

"Not mad," said Paul. "Hurt."

"Please don't be hurt," said Sylvie. "You know me; I need to work through things on my own first. This was one of those things."

"Fair enough, I guess, but I'm still allowed to be hurt. I'm your husband, for God's sake. We've both been in this together for three years, you know? A heads-up, just to feel included in your life, would have been nice."

"Sorry not to make this about you," said Sylvie.

"That's not what I'm saying at all," said Paul.

"Well, no, it is, actually. And you're acting like you've never had secrets of your own. Hello? The sports store downstairs? The thousands of dollars clicked away into the ether? And what's the problem, anyway? I may have filled the prescription secretly, but I'm telling you about it now."

"By the way, I'm selling most of that stuff," said Paul guiltily. "David is helping me. Would you have ever told me about the Prozac if I hadn't asked you right now?"

"Yes."

"Sylvie?"

"Yes, Paul. I was planning on telling you last night, but I got too drunk."

"So wait, what are the odds? You go on Prozac mere moments before I fall off my bike and break my ankle? That's crazy, the timing," said Paul. It did seem a little too hard to believe, that the universe had timed it all exactly right.

"It is," Sylvie agreed. "But maybe the Snows are finally being cut a break? Not literally, although you did break your ankle."

"Very funny," said Paul.

"Who knows how it worked out the way it did? I certainly don't. But I feel better, I really do."

"I'm glad," said Paul.

But did he feel any better? She'd given him an answer, a great, healthy answer, and yet he still felt uncomfortable.

She reached over to hug him, the blanket falling so that her bare chest pressed to his, and the pleasure her familiar warmth provided was almost too much to bear. He kissed her neck, and she kissed back, and then slowly, wonderfully, deeply, they were making love.

His discomfort was his own shit, he decided, pushing into her. He would work on it.

He would.

CHAPTER THIRTEEN

SYLVIE

Sylvie turned on the shower as hot as it would go and stood in the bathroom naked, waiting for the air to thicken. In her closed fist was a pill. She opened it and placed it on her tongue, smarting slightly at its acidic zing.

She kept her head down, avoiding the mirror, and got inside. The water was too hot. She played with the faucets, hot and cold, until it was still hot but not third-degree-burn hot. She stood under the water and closed her eyes.

Prozac. The lie had rolled so easily out of her mouth, like she had been planning it. She had not even given it one second of thought prior to that moment, that she would pick a decoy pill.

She was equally impressed and frightened by herself. She had lied, right to Paul's face, but not just a quick lie; she had thought of an elaborate one that had developed a backstory on the spot. Sylvie supposed it had been so easy because of course it was the way things should have gone, what she should have done if she was a healthy and mindful person rather than, well, who she was.

She had thought about scrawling "every single fucking day" across the top of the depression questionnaire her doctor handed her at her physical every year, sure, but decided instead to just circle the sometimeses and nevers and go on her way. And it was crazy too, because why was Sylvie so adamantly opposed to an antidepressant but gobbled these Oxys without a second thought?

There was nothing illicit about Prozac. There were also no bubbles, there was no escape, Sylvie thought, massaging shampoo into her hair. But was that entirely true? Antidepressants had to provide some kind of escape, or there would be no "anti" to speak of. Maybe she would ask her doctor for some when these pills were gone, she reasoned. Her lie had sounded so rational, so good. So healthy.

And Paul had bought it. Although why wouldn't he have bought it? It made total sense. And she was, for the first time, sharing her version of Delilah with him. That was what he had said he wanted for so long, and there Sylvie was, doing it. Cause and effect.

But the irony was not lost on Sylvie that her self-actualization, her decision to speak her truth, finally, was sponsored by none other than a big fat illegal secret. So there was that. But it was not going to last forever.

Sylvie realized too that her internal dialogue was beginning to feel a bit like *Groundhog Day*. So that was why, she decided, as she towel dried her hair, she was going to figure out this Bar Mitzvah business today, once and for all. She would press pause on the self-reflection, even if it was denial disguised as self-reflection— *Shit, there you go again! Just stop it. Stop it.*

She went to her closet and pulled a striped T-shirt over her head. It was like a memo went home from the hospital with all mothers: *For the rest of your life, horizontal stripes and linen will speak to you in a way you never before imagined. Fighting the impulse to clothe yourself in these fabrics is futile.* She pulled on a pair of sweatpants and stomped out, on a mission. First coffee, then computer. Bingo bango.

In the kitchen was Teddy. He was hunched over the table, shoveling cereal into his mouth.

"Aren't you going to be late for school?" asked Sylvie, pouring herself a cup of coffee.

"It's Saturday," Teddy answered, shaking his head. Sylvie thought that being disliked 98 percent of the time by a person you took care of 100 percent of the time was not a good way to feel.

"Oh right," she said. She walked over to the table, empowered by the heady mix of drug and coffee, and sat down on the bench across from him. He looked up warily.

Was that the beginning of a mustache across his upper lip? How did it happen? One day they were as plump and soft as Labrador puppies and the next, skinny reeds with Adam's apples and noses trying to figure out the rest of their face. But he was still beautiful, her Teddy. He could be as mean as a snake to her and she would always be madly in love with him.

"I'm going to Twilight Manor," he told her.

"Early retirement?" asked Sylvie.

"Very funny. No." Teddy sat up straight, pushed his bowl away. Sylvie had the sense that he was about to tell her something very important.

"I'm changing my Mitzvah Project," he declared.

"But don't you only have, like, two months to go?" asked Sylvie, knowing full well that this was the case.

"Yes, but two months is still sixty days I'd rather not be cleaning dogs' butts."

"Teddy, really. That's a little crass, don't you think? And dismissive. You've done a lot of good work there."

"Fine, but I haven't enjoyed one second of it. I couldn't care less about animals. All due respect. You're the one who made me take the job."

"Only because you refused to take any initiative on your own, and you had to be signed up for something," she said as calmly as she could. She would not yell. *Bubbles, don't fail me now.*

"I'm going to host a movie night at Twilight Manor, once a week," he said.

Sylvie blinked. It was actually a wonderful idea. One she wished Teddy had come up with eleven months earlier, but a wonderful idea nonetheless.

"I love it," she said. "It's perfect." Teddy's eyes lit up, pleased by her praise. There it was, Sylvie thought. Proof that she still mattered to him.

"Now, you know I have to ask you some questions—"

"Mom!"

"Because I am your mother and you are my twelve-year-old son," she continued. "Logistical questions only, I promise. Number one, have you told the Rabbi?"

"No."

"Okay, well, you have to let him know."

"Mom, I—"

"Teddy, you have to let him know. You have to explain your change of heart in a more tasteful way than describing your disinterest in cleaning dog butts and assure him that you have a plan in place."

"Okay," Teddy grumbled.

"Number two. Twilight Manor. Have they ever heard of you, or are you just planning to show up with a projector and popcorn?"

"Mom, come on, I'm not an idiot!" Teddy yelped. "Of course I've spoken to someone. The director. That's who I'm going to meet with today, to go over everything with."

"Teddy, I'm impressed," said Sylvie. "Where did this idea come from, anyway?"

"My friend. Her mom works there. She knows I love movies, so. It was her idea."

Sylvie's brain was like a cash register, its drawer opening with a ca-ching at the deposit of the words *friend* and *her*. The most crucial thing to do at this moment was to stay calm; she knew that. She placed her mug gently on the table, collecting herself.

"It's a great idea. May I ask, do you mind, who this friend is?"

"Her name is Krystal," said Teddy shyly.

Sylvie's eyes smarted. It felt like yesterday that Teddy had had his one and only girlfriend. During his preschool holiday break, three-year-old Teddy, in all his dimpled-knuckle and chubby-cheeked glory, just newly potty trained in superhero underoos, had mooned around the house gloomily for days.

"What's wrong?" Sylvie had asked and asked, to no avail, until finally, he had confessed.

"It's Leah. I love her," he had said plainly, his eyes as big as saucers.

The romance had been short-lived—Leah had moved to Wisconsin that summer, and Teddy hadn't even seemed to notice—but still. It had been nine years, and not a mention of a female since. Until now.

"Jesus, Mom, are you crying?" Teddy exclaimed. She was a little. Just a little.

"Krystal," Sylvie said, regaining her composure. "She goes to your school?"

She had never heard of anyone named Krystal, so it would have to be a new student, but this late in the year? Maybe she was a grade above him? An older woman! She considered the name Krystal and tried desperately not to judge it.

"I met her walking to school one day. I saw her mom get side-swiped by one of those enormous Suburbans. One of those with the family stick figure bumper sticker across the back window," he added.

"Oh God," Sylvie moaned. "You know how I feel about those stickers."

"I helped her mom out with the cops, and that's how we met."

"You never told me about this! An accident on the way to school! Was anybody hurt?" asked Sylvie.

Most of Teddy's life outside of these four walls was a secret to her, she realized. So they all had secrets.

"No, everyone was fine," said Teddy.

"How have you stayed in touch?" asked Sylvie.

"Computer," answered Teddy quickly.

"Oh right."

"And I've seen her a couple times."

"Dates?" shrieked Sylvie. "Sorry, I didn't mean to yell."

"I guess," said Teddy.

"But how? No, you know what? Never mind. You're a good boy, your grades are good, you're a good kid. You're twelve years old; of course this is happening." She spoke into the air, trying to talk herself off the ledge of hysteria. *This may be a two-pill kind of day,* she thought. *It may just be.* This was a lot to process.

"If she makes you happy, I'm happy," said Sylvie. "I really mean that. Just, you know—are you having sex?"

"Mom!"

"Okay, okay. But I won't apologize for that question because if you are, or if you're considering it, you have to come to me or your dad. Don't give me that look. You have to be responsible. It's your duty."

"Can we stop talking about this now?" asked Teddy.

"Sure. But I want to meet her. Can we have her over for dinner?"

"You don't like to cook," said Teddy.

"Sure I do." He narrowed his eyes at her. "What?"

"Fine."

"Do you need a ride to Twilight Manor? What time is your appointment?"

"Eleven," he answered. "I was going to ride my bike, but okay. Thanks. But you can't come in."

"Teddy!"

"Mom, I mean it. This is mine."

"Fine."

Sylvie understood *mine* and *yours* very well. She herself had never been good at sharing. It was going to be very difficult to apply this distinction to her son, but apparently the time had come.

"About your Bar Mitzvah," she said. Teddy rolled his eyes. "You have no interest in a party at all, do you?"

"Zero."

"Not even a small thing, with the family? And Martin? Raj? This Krystal person?"

"No. Well, I mean, maybe. Could it be here? Just like bagels or something?"

"Sure," said Sylvie.

She hated hosting, and now suddenly, she was hosting both a dinner for someone named Krystal, who had likely given her son a hand job, and a Bar Mitzvah brunch. Definitely a two-pill day. How on earth was she going to get more when this prescription ran out?

"I'm going back upstairs for a little bit, okay?" Teddy said, getting up from the table and taking his empty bowl with him. The spoon clattered against its insides as he walked to the sink.

"Maybe you could start writing out your thoughts for the Rabbi?" she said.

"Mom."

"Just a suggestion." She drained her coffee cup. "We should leave around ten thirty, yes?" Teddy threw his arm up in what she assumed was agreement as he walked toward the stairs. Sylvie got up to toast an English muffin.

"Hey, T," she heard Paul say.

"Hey, Dad. Need some help?" asked Teddy.

"Sure. Thanks."

Sylvie watched as Teddy helped his father descend the slight spiral of the staircase, marveling as she always did at just how much they looked alike. For the first couple of years of Teddy's life, she had bristled at the comment that everyone seemed to feel obligated to make: *He looks exactly like Paul,* they would say. *Spitting image.*

Sylvie would say, *No, he has my bone structure, look,* or *But we have the same eye shape,* or something equally ridiculous and mundane. Because it was hard to hear that the human you grew inside of you shared absolutely none of your physical characteristics. But eventually, Sylvie had given up trying to convince herself. So Teddy didn't look like her. So what? There were worse things, and didn't she know it.

"Hey," said Paul, crutching into the kitchen to pour his own cup before adding a healthy glug of almond milk to it. Almond milk. Sylvie hated almond milk.

"Here, let me carry that to the table for you, so you don't

give yourself a third-degree burn or something," said Sylvie. She got up and took it from him as he hobbled along behind her.

"That was nice, this morning," he said, smiling sheepishly at her as he sat down. Oh men, thought Sylvie. It really was that easy to put them in a good mood.

"What was Teddy talking about?" he asked.

"Nothing much."

She would let Teddy tell him. Right now, she would relish the fact that he had chosen her to confide in first. She walked back to check on her muffin; their toaster had a tendency to torch innocent carbohydrates. Sure enough, it was already turning a dangerous shade of dark brown.

CHAPTER FOURTEEN

TEDDY

He had told his dad too, about everything. He was glad his parents knew. About Twilight Manor, about Krystal, the whole thing.

For one, it was a long bike ride, and although that had been his original plan in terms of transportation, he had not been excited about it. Not only could Teddy not remember the last time he had ridden his bike, but he knew that extracting it from the garage, which was crammed to bursting with all his father's crap, would have taken a Herculean effort.

So getting a ride was a much better option, although he hadn't anticipated that both his mom and dad would be escorting him. He couldn't remember the last time he had been in the car with both of them at the same time. His father's bald spot was getting bigger, he noticed. Before it had been more of an Alabama shape, but now it was more like Texas. A shiny Texas.

And as far as Krystal went, it felt good to tell someone. If it had to be his parents, so be it. The night before had gone off without a hitch. Krystal had left before they came home, so there was no need for an illicit escape, but Teddy's anxiety had almost robbed him of enjoying their date. And it had been a date. They had kissed on his bed for seven minutes. Seven minutes. With tongue. Teddy smiled out the window at the green trees whizzing by. Tongues touching. An unpleasant idea in theory but in reality: wow.

Next he supposed he would have to come clean about his use of his dad's phone. But that meant asking him about this T.B. person, didn't it? Teddy had no interest in doing that.

He glanced at his mother, her dark hair piled on top of her head, clipped into its customary figure-six shape with her tortoiseshell clip, a horizontal slash of amber and brown swirls clamped across her black curls. Teddy had not forgotten about the pills. But maybe they weren't the catastrophe he was making them out to be in his mind. Maybe she had just stashed them there accidentally, en route to tossing them. No, that was ridiculous. But maybe they were, like, not the bad kind of Oxys. Maybe they just took the edge off, which is what Raj said his mom did, with her Xanax. And maybe they were just for emergencies. She seemed fine. Not like herself, but fine. Better than fine, even. Happy. Open.

Teddy decided that he would just keep his mouth shut about everything as far as his parents' secrets were concerned. It was the easier option. His mom turned the car into the circular drive of Twilight Manor, and Teddy pushed the thought to the back of his mind, out of the way.

"Should I just park over here?" asked his mom, driving into the back lot.

"Says Visitor Parking," answered his dad. "I guess so." He turned to face Teddy. "You're not an employee, right?"

"Dad, how could I be an employee if I'm not getting paid?" asked Teddy.

"Well, not an employee, but not a visitor," said his mom. "I guess we'll figure that out after you speak to, what's her name? Ms. James?"

"Ms. Jones, Mom," Teddy snapped, his affection toward her short-lived.

Why was it that every name of every person he ever told his mother about turned into something else? Jones became James, Raj had been Bob for a solid month before she had met him, and on and on. What would she do to Krystal's name? He could only imagine.

"Fine. And we're coming in with you," she added, parking.

"Mom! You agreed not to!"

"I know, I know, but we have to meet her, for God's sake. Make sure this isn't a crack house we're sending you to."

"Yeah, Mom, it's a crack house," snarled Teddy, undoing his seat belt and opening the door.

"T, watch your tone," said his dad.

They followed behind him, toward the vanilla-frosted birthday cake that was Twilight Manor. *I should have taken the bike,* thought Teddy, his annoyance with both of them an unscratchable itch deep within him.

"Please, just say hello and then let me do my thing?" he pleaded, turning around to face them. "Let me talk to her about Movie Night by myself?"

"Okay, no problem," said his dad. "This is your thing. Right, Sylvie?"

"We can't even suggest a few—"

"No!" Teddy yelled, now close to tears.

"I'm just kidding, honey," said his mom, pulling him toward her for a hug. "I'm just kidding. Sorry."

Teddy squirmed away; he did not want to be touched. When he looked back at her, her eyes were sad.

"Let's go in," he said. Her sadness was not his problem.

The glass doors slid open, punching him with a blast of air conditioning. He walked in tentatively, his parents behind him.

Twilight Manor was a series of concentric circles placed on top of one another, its circular floors dotted with apartment doors and rimmed with white wood balconies overlooking the lobby, where they stood now. It was filled with myriad bouquets of flowers in pale pink, white, lavender, fuchsia and green; a few stiff-looking couches in baby blue and off-white with gleaming cherrywood arms and legs and a baby grand piano in the corner. An elevator ran up the center of the circles, and at the very top, a huge, circular skylight, which bathed everything in a hazy, golden glow.

"Not a bad place to die," whispered his mother, all three of them silenced by its unexpected grandeur.

Where were all the residents, though? Teddy wondered. It was as silent as, well, a tomb, for lack of a better word.

"You must be Theodore," a deep voice rang out, making Teddy jump.

He turned to face the greeting, although no one called him Theodore, not ever.

"I am," he answered. She approached him at a brisk clip, striding across the room in fuchsia stiletto heels.

"Jackie Jones," she said, smiling broadly. "And you must be the proud parents of our young Spielberg," she added, extending her hand to shake his parents'.

Jackie put her hands on her patterned hips. She was encased in turquoise, red and chartreuse triangles that danced dizzyingly across the formfitting black backdrop of her dress. Her dark hair was cropped close to her head, hugging it save for a sweeping wave across her forehead. Her caramel-colored skin glowed, like it was lit from the inside. She was barefaced, with no jewelry, except for a neon-orange Fitbit encircling her wrist.

"So, Theodore, tell me more about your plans. Do you all want to join me in my office?"

"Oh no, we'll stay out here," said his father. "Maybe I'll try out the piano." Teddy gave him a small, grateful smile.

"'Chopsticks' is his specialty," his mother added. His parents suddenly seemed very small and very white to Teddy in the presence of Jackie Jones.

"Be my guest, but don't be surprised if Elmer appears out of nowhere to rap your knuckles with a ruler. He's our resident piano man, spent fifty years teaching and performing. Although Saturdays are slow around here; he's probably napping with his hearing aids out, so you're safe," said Jackie.

"Come on, Theodore," she said, quickly pivoting on the spikes of her heels.

Teddy followed her, reaching around to make sure his notepad was still in his back pocket. Making contact with its spiraled edge comforted him. He squeezed it slightly, its metal cold through the cotton of his chinos. His mother had insisted he wear these pants, and he had put up a fight, but now he was glad.

"So," she said, from behind her massive cherrywood desk. Two guest chairs sat in front of it, their seats covered in a shiny rose-colored fabric. Teddy perched on one of them, facing her.

"Are those your sons?" he asked, admiring the photo of four little boys in plaid shirts and bow ties, each one slightly taller than the next—all of them with Jackie's broad smile. Jackie threw back her head and laughed.

"Bless your heart, Theodore. Those are my grandsons." Teddy was shocked. Jackie looked younger than his mother, her face as unlined as the moon.

"I'm sixty-two," she told him. "Amazing what proper diet, exercise and nutrition can do," she said. "It'll turn back the clock."

Teddy thought of his own mother. He wasn't even sure he'd ever seen her drink a glass of water. On cue, Jackie took a long swig of water from an insulated silver bottle as big as Teddy's forearm.

"But let's get down to business, shall we? Movie Night at Twilight Manor, I love it. I just love it, and I know our community will too. Tell me what you're thinking." She placed her water bottle back on her desk with a thud. "Give me your vision, Theodore."

He was getting tired of being called Theodore, but he would worry about that later.

"Sure. So, I love movies. They've been my passion since I understood what they were," he explained. "And I have this Mitzvah Project. For my Bar Mitzvah?" He paused, assuming he would have to explain, since he always did.

"I know all about that. My son married a Jewish woman. You see that seven-year-old right there?" She pointed to the photo on her desk. "He's fifteen now. His mama made us go all the way to Israel for his, which you know I had something to say about initially, but in the end: the trip of a lifetime. Not that I'd tell her that." She pursed her lips. "Anyway, go on, Theodore."

"Oh, cool. I've never been," he said, referring to Israel. "But so, I've been doing the wrong thing for my project, something I don't even care about—"

"I know, Patty Platt told me." She wrinkled her nose in distaste. "I'm not a pet person either. All that dog hair all over my clothes? No thank you."

Teddy's cheeks warmed. Patty Platt, mom of Krystal Platt.

"Right. But I have a month of my project left, and I'd love to come here once a week for Movie Night. Maybe Saturday nights?" Jackie nodded, looking at the enormous calendar that covered the expanse of her desk.

"That could work, although we'd have to move Tai Chi. You're supplying the movies?"

"Yes ma'am. I have a lot of DVDs."

"Okay, I like a man who brings his own supplies. Perfect." She looked up from her calendar. "Theodore, we have a deal. Can we start next Saturday?"

"Sure," he answered.

"Great. Let me show you to the movie theater." Teddy's eyes widened. "Well, we can call it a theater for your purposes, but really it's just a big television with a bunch of chairs." She stood up and made her way out of the office. "Come on."

He followed her to the elevator, passing his parents, who looked up expectantly on the way. Teddy gave them a subtle thumbs-up, and they both beamed at him. Okay, he liked them again.

Jackie pressed the up button, and the elevator opened immediately. They got on, and she pressed three with a chartreuse fingernail.

"How come you like movies so much?" she asked, as they made their short ascent.

"They're like real life, but better," he answered. "Like everything you wish you could say and do in real time, but you don't have the agility or cleverness for it? Plus, there's always a happy ending."

The door opened.

"That's a very astute answer for a twelve-year-old," said Jackie.

"I guess," said Teddy.

He followed her down the hall, past a few apartment doors, their numbers on gleaming brass plaques, and into the TV room. A giant television screen filled the wall to his right, and in front of it, two brown leather couches were in a semicircle. Four navy-blue velvet chairs, their plump cushions slightly worn, sat behind them, also facing the entertainment. A few round cherrywood tables with two chairs each lined the remaining walls. An enormous Turkish rug covered the expanse of floor, a kaleidoscope of both muted and vibrant blue threads.

"This is the nicest retirement home I've ever seen," said Teddy. "It's also the only retirement home I've ever seen, but still." Light streamed in through the three windows lining the wall.

"Well, thank you, Theodore. And it is the nicest retirement home you'll ever see, by the way. I want our residents to feel good. Everyone calls them the golden years, but they hardly ever look golden."

Teddy thought of his Pop, his dad's dad, who sat in his leather recliner all day watching C-SPAN. "That's true," he said.

"Not so here," said Jackie proudly. "And you get what you pay for too; it's a pretty penny to live at Twilight Manor. So." She paused. "This movie night of yours has to be a class act, okay? I'm all for this Mitzvah Project, but no way would you be here without Krystal's blessing. I love me some Krystal."

Teddy blushed. "Oh yes, don't worry. It's going to be very classy," he replied. "And I'm grateful for the opportunity. Thank you, Ms. Jones."

"You can call me Jackie, honey," she said.

"Hello!" a man's voice bellowed from the doorway.

"Morty," said Jackie fondly. "Good day to you."

"To you as well."

Morty looked Teddy up and down through black-rimmed glasses, his blue eyes magnified comically by the density of his lenses. Above the tops of the frames perched two furry, wiry gray eyebrows that could have easily passed as caterpillars. His head was shiny and bald down the middle, paved on either side by the same wiry gray hair. He wore a navy-blue Brooklyn Dodgers T-shirt, which stretched tautly over his generous midsection, and khaki shorts held up by a wide, black leather belt. On his feet, navy-and-white-striped rubber slides over black trouser socks.

"And you are?" he asked Teddy.

"Teddy Snow," he answered.

"Morty Stein," he replied, pumping Teddy's hand vigorously, a slight smile across his lips. "Good handshake, Teddy. Very good."

Teddy puffed up, feeling proud.

"Are you the movie fellow?" he asked, his voice as New York as the Chrysler Building.

"I am." Teddy looked at Jackie for confirmation, and she gave him an encouraging nod. "I'll be hosting Movie Night here. On Saturdays."

"What about Tai Chi?" asked Morty, sounding alarmed.

"Gonna move that to Wednesdays for the month," answered Jackie. "No biggie."

"Okay. Good." He turned back to Teddy, visibly relieved. "I love Tai Chi," he informed him. "But I also love movies, so this is a good thing. What do you have planned?"

"Each night will be a surprise," said Teddy, devising his plan on the spot.

"But how will I know whether I want to come if it's a surprise?" asked Morty. A valid question.

"Oh, well, I guess you have a point," said Teddy.

"He does," said Jackie. "Theodore, you email me your list of what you're showing on what days and I'll have it printed up on a flyer for all the residents."

"Cinema Saturdays," said Morty, smiling. "That's what you should call it."

"I like that, Mr. Stein," said Teddy.

"I was in advertising," he offered. "Just comes naturally. And you can call me Morty."

"Oh okay. Morty."

"I'll go ahead and put out an APB, kid. This is gonna be big. Who doesn't love the movies?" He looked at Jackie. "We can get more chairs, right?"

"Of course, Morty. Okay, Theodore, are we good?" asked Jackie. "I'm going to need that list from you by tonight, so I can get everyone excited for next Saturday."

They both stared at Teddy expectantly, as though he had his list at the ready, which he did not.

"Sure, no problem," he said.

"Great. See you next Saturday, kid," said Morty, clapping him on the shoulder and making his way to one of the couches. "Time for some *Judge Judy.*"

The room began to fill with other Twilight Manorees, shuffling in for what looked to be a regular date. Old men and women: some short, some tall, all of them wrinkled and in varying degrees of cotton comfort. The scent of Bengay, coffee and baby powder filled the air.

Teddy took the elevator down with Jackie, wondering just what he was getting into. He didn't even know if he liked old people. Would he be able to command an entire room of them? What if they hated the movies he picked? He cringed, imagining what mutiny at the gnarled hands of octogenarians would feel like.

"Don't worry, Theodore," said Jackie. "They're pussycats, really. And they're lonely." The door opened onto the lobby, his parents reading the paper. "Their kids, they don't visit them like they should."

As the elevator closed behind them, Jackie shook his hand.

"Don't forget to send me that list tonight," she reminded him.

"Will do. And thanks again."

Teddy approached his parents, who were standing now, waiting for him. The way they looked at him sometimes, like they were amazed by his mere existence, he felt that. It was a nice feeling, to feel that kind of wonder directed toward him, but it was also too much. Sometimes.

"How'd it go?" his father asked.

"Good," said Teddy. "Let's go."

He led the way, his parents right behind him.

CHAPTER FIFTEEN
PAUL

Paul looked down at his leg. His pale, practically green, spindly leg. It looked like it belonged on a dining room chair, not on a man. Just that morning, he had had his cast taken off in the sterile examination room, both he and Sylvie recoiling from the dank odor his previously trapped limb had released. A giant exhale of stink.

"Oh my God, it smells exactly like the inside of a belly button," Sylvie had said, from behind the hand she had placed over her mouth.

"I don't even notice it anymore," said the doctor, without so much as looking up.

Paul sighed now, sitting on the back deck, out of the sun. Carpenter bees hung in the air around him and the air was filled with the smell of honeysuckle. Summer.

Seized suddenly by the urge to move, to ride, to do anything other than just sit there, Paul decided to transfer his stationary bike from the garage into the driveway. On the phone, the physical therapist had told him to take it slow, to not do anything too taxing with his leg prior to meeting with her, but screw it.

Limping slightly, he descended the deck's steps onto the lawn when his phone vibrated in his back pocket. Probably work—he was supposed to be supervising a project right now. He stopped, pulled it out. Reading the incoming caller's name, he grimaced. His mother. Should he, or shouldn't he? He didn't want to. It continued to vibrate, sending waves of guilt through the palm of his hand.

"Hi, Mom," he answered sourly, not able to screen her.

"Paul, what in the world am I supposed to wear to Teddy's Bar Mitzvah?" she began, launching right into it, as per usual.

His mother did not waste time, despite the fact that all she had was time to waste. She had retired from teaching after thirty-one years of reprimanding kindergartners, and from what Paul could tell, she nagged his father, went to the grocery store to buy Lean Cuisines and watched HGTV. End stop.

"I don't know, Mom. A dress?" he answered. He trudged into the garage.

"But what kind of dress? I'm in Dress Barn now." In the background, Paul could hear the faint rhythm of soft rock.

"Someone named a store Dress Barn? That's horrible."

"I know, I don't understand it either. And the dresses are pretty, so it's even more of a misnomer. Anyway, do I need to cover my arms? I read online that I can't show my shoulders or my knees."

"Mom, I think that's only for Orthodox Jews. That's not us. You can wear whatever you want."

Paul made his way through the boxes and boxes of shit he had amassed. Click, click, buy. Click, click, buy. Every time he felt useless or unappreciated or dismissed, it was click, buy, click, buy. And since that was most of the time, he had created quite a mess, literally and figuratively. It had taken Sylvie months to catch on, thanks to his covert maneuvering and the fact that he handled the bills, but then one morning she had gone down to the basement to look for who knew what, and the jig had been up. Boy, had it been up. He made a mental note to check in with David, to see what had been deemed worthy for sale.

"'Us'?" said his mother, as Paul cradled the phone between his ear and shoulder to push a very heavy box out of the way. Free weights. An entire box of five- and ten-pound free weights. What had he been thinking?

There was a tone to his mother's voice that he knew all too well, that he was going to ignore. He had been raised Southern Baptist, and his mother still was, although she had stopped going to church years ago. And although Paul hadn't converted to marry Sylvie, it was a bone of contention between he and his mother that she was forbidden to give Teddy gifts on Christmas or to send a chocolate bunny on Easter. Sylvie was adamant about it, and Paul certainly didn't care; he was an atheist anyway. But his mother was a different story.

"Mom, wear whatever you want, seriously," said Paul. "Is that it?"

He spotted the bike, pushed into the far-left corner, covered in cobwebs. Maybe he'd used it twice? He couldn't remember.

"No, that's not it," she answered curtly. "What happened to the party? Sylvie sent me an email. Heaven forbid she pick up the phone to call me."

"Teddy doesn't want one, so we're not having one. Just the service at the synagogue and brunch here after."

"And dinner Friday night at your house, but Sylvie's parents are coming Wednesday."

"We are? They are?" Wednesday through Sunday was a long time and broke the cardinal three-day rule. One minute—hell, one second—over a three-day visit with her parents, or his for that matter, never ended well. Never.

"Yes, don't y'all talk?" He ignored her question. "So what do I wear to that?"

"To what?"

"Dinner Friday, Paul! Good lord, this is like a game of *Who's on First?*"

"Mom," said Paul. "It's dinner, not the Oscars."

"Well, excuse me for wanting to be respectful," she answered in a huff. "I just don't want to show up looking like a fool. What do I know about Shabbat?" She pronounced it with a hard *a—Shaybat*.

"Mom, really, don't worry. You always look nice."

This was not true, but Paul appreciated her respect, even if it was halfhearted. He was sure he would receive the same phone call soon, from his sister, Gloria.

"Well, thank you. And your father? What should he wear?"

"I don't know, Mom! A button-down and khakis, I guess?"

"And we're staying with you?" she asked.

"Are you?" Paul's heart sank. His mother was silent.

"Yes, you're staying with us," said Paul.

Sylvie was not going to like this. He grabbed the bike by its handlebars, pulling it toward him.

"And what about Max and Barbara?" his mother asked.

"A hotel, I guess?" *I hope,* thought Paul.

"Fancy," said his mother. "Well, if they're coming on Wednesday, we're going to come on Wednesday too. We don't want to miss anything."

"Okay, Mom, I really have to go." Paul wasn't listening anymore. His ankle throbbed, but he was going to hose this damn thing off and have a go at it, come hell or high water.

"Okay, okay. Bye, Paul."

"Bye, Mom."

He slid his phone back into his pocket and dragged the bike out into the sun, covering both of his hands in dust and grime in the process. A spider crawled over his knuckles and he yelped, flailing his hand in exasperation and sending it flying into the yard.

Paul stood in front of the bike once he had it positioned just right, sweat dripping from his brow and pooling at the small of his back underneath his T-shirt.

"Shit," he said, getting a good look at it. He was going to have to clean the damn thing unless he wanted a spider to crawl up his shorts. He sighed heavily and turned on his heel, limping back up the stairs and into the house to get the necessary supplies.

Back outside, a wave of exhaustion swept over him. He got to work anyway, squirting a translucent blob of dish soap into the red bucket and then filling it with water from the hose; plunging a blue rag into it and then following the dusty and dirty curves of the bike until it turned back to its original color. Plunge, wring, rinse, repeat. He was really sweating now; his shirt stuck to his torso like a second skin. But he couldn't take it off, even though he desperately wanted to. He wasn't in shape.

Max and Barbara Schwartz. They had never liked him. He had always been not smart enough, not driven enough, not Jewish at all, and they had resented him for winning their daughter over anyway.

He plunged the cloth back into the bucket and wrung out the water onto the white cement of the driveway before starting on the bike's black leather seat, thinking.

When Paul had finally met Barbara and Max, after nearly a year of dating Sylvie, he had wanted them to like him. Of course he had. And he really wasn't worried about it; everybody liked him. Paul Snow was a likable guy.

But from the start they had been so cold to him, shaking his hand but barely making eye contact, asking Sylvie all about herself over brunch at the crowded restaurant she had picked. Barely even acknowledging that he was there. Despite this, when Sylvie had gone to the bathroom, Paul had told Max and Barbara that he wanted to marry their daughter. That had been his plan all along—he had bought the ring, he was doing it whether they gave him their blessing or not, but he was just being polite.

"But we don't even know you," Barbara had said.

"I guess you're going to have to get to know me, then," Paul had replied, his nerves shot to hell, but he wasn't going to let them know that.

When Sylvie had returned, they had all put on their best smiles and continued with their eggs Benedict and French toasts. Paul had finished his Bloody Mary in a single gulp.

And when they had gotten married, at some country club in New Jersey with two hundred people Paul barely knew, Sylvie's father had cornered him by the bathroom.

"You have to work hard now," he had told him, "now that you're her husband."

As if Paul didn't work hard in the first place. As if Max had made any effort to know him or his work ethic at all.

The bike gleamed in the sun, its silver paint revealed. Paul took a step back to admire it and then plunged the rag back into the bucket to tackle the spokes of each wheel.

Her parents had warmed to him only when his company had started to do well, when he and Sylvie had moved out of their tiny apartment and into the house they had bought for next to nothing: the worst house in the best neighborhood that Paul had renovated top to bottom by himself. And he would be lying if he hadn't felt satisfaction from that approval. But then they'd gifted them with a big check, for new furniture, Sylvie's mother had said, and Paul had been angry all over again.

"We can afford our own furniture. Hell, I can build most of it," he'd proclaimed angrily to Sylvie after she had waved the check at him, which had arrived tucked into a Hallmark card in the mail.

"Of course we can," she had said, "but why should we if we can use this instead?"

Sylvie didn't seem to understand the kind of obligation a check like that came with, the unspoken debt inked into the dollar sign. But Paul did. And when Sylvie had gotten pregnant with Teddy, the time had come to pay up.

"You're going to raise the baby Jewish," Barbara had told him, during one of their interminable visits. They were in the waiting room at the doctor's office for Sylvie's first ultrasound. Sylvie was signing in at the front desk, leaving them alone together.

That had always been the plan. Paul had no problem with it, but to be told instead of asked had sent him into a rage so blinding that he couldn't even see the screen when Teddy's tiny alien profile had shown up.

Paul was finished with the bike. Its silver chrome gleamed, the spokes of its wheels only slightly tarnished by time. Paul was very tired, every muscle in his body protesting further activity, but he was determined. He poured the dirty water out of the red bucket onto the green grass and draped the rag over the banister of the stairs leading up to the deck.

He got onto the bike. It was still the right height; his feet slid into the buckles on the pedals perfectly. The sun was high in the blue sky; he could feel it burning the back of his neck.

He pulled his T-shirt over his head and tossed it onto

the concrete. Fuck it, it was hot. He began to pedal slowly, forcing himself not to look down at his pale midsection. He could feel it bulging over the elastic waist of his shorts.

Max and Barbara. Paul had thought that surely Teddy's birth would transform them, the way all parents seemed to be transformed by the gift of grandchildren. Alas, this had not been the case. They were interested in Teddy, but in a removed way. Not once did they offer to babysit so Sylvie and Paul could go out when they came to visit. Instead, Barbara would take Sylvie to lunch, or she and Max would go to the movies after Teddy had gone to bed, as though they were on some sort of vacation. Sylvie had confronted them about it, but it had had no impact. Not much seemed to impact them. They were an impenetrable wall of self-involvement.

His mother had her faults, but at least she was a bona fide grandmother, taking Teddy for overnights when he was little, stuffing him with processed crap he never got at home, buying him ICEEs at the movie theater. Not so much in recent years, as Teddy turned the corner into tweendom, but that wasn't her fault so much as just the natural progression of things, of life.

Paul pedaled a little faster. And then: Delilah. What a disaster Max and Barbara had been. Just awful.

Sylvie's labor had come a month early, but they had gone in worried only about the baby's prematurity. Despite Sylvie's age, there had been no signs of distress; it had been a healthy pregnancy. Delilah had looked perfect and beautiful in each ultrasound. It had never occurred to Paul that she might be born with some sort of previously undetected complication, much less not alive.

Paul took a deep breath and held it for a moment, fighting the surge of emotion in his chest.

When the doctor had not found a heartbeat, when he had told them that Delilah was dead, Paul had felt as though a freight train had pinned him to the tracks and was roaring over him, the chug of its wheels so loud in his ears he couldn't remember hearing anything else. He had never felt so useless in his life. There was nothing he could do to change it, to bring his daughter to life. Nothing.

He'd watched Sylvie push, had tried to hold her hand, but she had swatted him away. She was not useless; she had a job to do, and she was going to do it, just like she always did. Paul had been a little scared and a lot in awe of her then, at her ferocity in the face of such sorrow.

When Delilah had arrived, Paul had seen her. He had touched her dark head of hair with his hand. But Sylvie had refused to look at her, did not want to hold her, just closed her eyes and shook her head.

And when the question of burial had come up, Sylvie had insisted on cremation. She wanted the hospital to handle it, to handle everything. When Paul had tried to reason with her, she had been as adamant as he had ever seen her, and that was saying a lot. Sylvie was adamant often.

"Let them handle it," she had said in a monotone, looking right through him with tired eyes. "Everything. I just want to go home. Please, just take me home."

Paul stopped pedaling, his head down. The tears, he let

them come. They rolled down his cheeks. So that's what he had done. He had not held Delilah either; he had refused the footprints and the photos as Sylvie had told him to; he had let the hospital handle her cremation. Because that's what Sylvie had wanted. It's not what he had wanted at all, but it's what she had wanted, and Paul's opinion held no weight in the wake of such unrivaled despair.

When Barbara and Max had found out that they had left Delilah behind, all hell had broken loose. They'd flown down, presumably to comfort their daughter and maybe, just maybe, him and Teddy too, because they had also suffered a tragic, life-altering loss, but it hadn't turned out that way. Mostly they had come down to yell at Paul.

How could he, why hadn't he called them, the baby should have been buried in a Jewish cemetery, did he have no respect for human life, how could he let Sylvie go through with her decision not to hold her, how soon did he plan on getting Teddy into therapy and on and on and on. Not one hug, not one *I'm so sorry, what a horrible thing to happen to you too,* not even the slightest empathy for Paul's position as Delilah's father. He would always hate them for that.

He knew he should let go of the resentment in order to move forward, but he just couldn't. Max and Barbara were assholes, and they would always be assholes, and he was allowed to hate them. He could hate them and still be perfectly cordial to their smug faces, Barbara's pulled so tightly that her mouth was never fully closed. That was his right.

Remember me? Paul wanted to yell into the empty yard. *I have rights too!*

His head still down, he eyed his stomach, thinking it was the perfect metaphor for how he felt. Defeated. Amorphous. Irrelevant.

Slowly, he dismounted the bike. His ankle was killing him. Overhead, gray clouds began to gather, covering the sun. He hobbled into the house just as the first drops fell.

CHAPTER SIXTEEN

SYLVIE

Sylvie!"

"Amanda, hi, honey," Sylvie replied, standing in the shade of Amanda's front porch. "You look beautiful."

This was a lie, but one that was required by law to tell if you were a decent human being. Which Sylvie wasn't even sure she was, considering her ulterior motive.

"Come in, come in," said Amanda. On cue, the panicked wail of a newborn began.

"So how have you been?" Sylvie asked, following Amanda into her living room, which was a virtual sea of discarded rubber pacifiers in an array of translucent colors and patterned burping cloths strewn over every curved surface. A pale-green, donut-shaped pillow, one that Sylvie recognized as one of the hundreds of items she'd had to send back after Delilah died, took up half of the gray micro-suede couch.

Sylvie sat down next to it and stroked it absently for a moment.

"I wouldn't touch that," Amanda warned, picking the baby up and out of what looked like a tiny vibrating spaceship. "She barfed all over it at some point last night." Sylvie withdrew her hand.

"Oh Sylvie, I'm a mess," confessed Amanda. "This is hard. I mean, I love her and everything, but this is hard." She unzipped her gray hoodie, revealing the white armor of her nursing bra. "And then, you know: this. Breastfeeding." She grabbed the green pillow and settled the baby onto it before releasing one of her breasts. Hungrily, the baby suckled.

Sylvie took a deep breath, counted backward from ten in her head. She hadn't been around a baby since she had lost hers, not in any tangible way, and here she was: smack-dab in the belly of the beast. What the hell had she been thinking?

The answer was she'd been thinking about one thing and one thing only. Paul's doctor had refused to refill his prescription again, so here she was.

Every new mom left the hospital armed with a bottle of pain meds, Sylvie had reasoned as she called her unsuspecting coworker to arrange a visit during her maternity leave. And Amanda was big on the whole natural water birth, all organic, blah, blah, blah; she hadn't shut up about it the whole time she'd been pregnant, and Sylvie would know since she sat in the cubicle next to hers. If there was anyone who was going to bring those pills home and let them sit in her medicine cabinet untouched, it was Amanda.

So here Sylvie was, premade frozen food from a fancy

gourmet shop in hand, her best supportive smile pasted on her face.

Four-three-two-one, Sylvie finished. *Okay*.

"Apparently, I have one nipple that works and the other, it's inverted or something," Amanda continued.

Her hair was lank, escaping her ponytail in slack brown waves that stuck to her neck. Sylvie felt for her, she really did. She vaguely remembered her first disconcerting and exhausting months with Teddy; if you remembered them clearly, you would certainly never decide to have another.

"I have to, like, attach a plastic donut to it for her to eat."

"Breastfeeding is a horror," agreed Sylvie. "But it gets easier." She paused. "Or it doesn't. My only piece of advice is to be kind to yourself. If it brings you more pain than pleasure for too long, hang up your nipples and buy some formula. Honestly, it's criminal how guilty they make us feel."

"Did you breastfeed?" asked Amanda, wincing as her daughter sucked.

"Yes. But it was very, very hard for a very long time, and in retrospect I wish I had given myself a pass. At the year mark, like, to the exact second, I stopped. And that was hell too, the engorged breasts like hot bowling balls, the leaking, the secret expression into the work bathroom sink, just so I could breathe again."

And the hormones. Sylvie had gone through it twice. But she wasn't about to tell poor Amanda that. Amanda had started at work only two years ago; she had no idea that Delilah had even happened.

"Here, I brought you some food," she said instead, holding up her two brown paper sacks of premade casseroles and fruit and cookies. "Should I put it in the fridge?"

"That's so nice of you," said Amanda, her dark-rimmed eyes welling with tears. "I can barely shower, much less cook."

"I know." Sylvie squeezed Amanda's knee. "I'll just put it away for you." She stood up, careful not to trip over yet another baby spaceship at her feet. "Would it be okay if I used your restroom?" Her heart was racing.

"Oh sure, of course, take your time," said Amanda.

"Can I bring you anything?" asked Sylvie.

"A seltzer would be amazing," Amanda answered gratefully. "This kid is literally siphoning all the moisture from my body. I feel like a raisin."

"You got it." Sylvie maneuvered around the spaceship and began walking. "So how's work?" Amanda asked.

Sylvie stopped herself from audibly gasping at the mess in the kitchen. The whole place, it was like a bomb had gone off. A breast pump and all its accompanying wires and plugs and bottles and shields littered one counter, and along the two others: dirty glasses and plates and papers and more burp cloths. The pile of dishes in the sink rose up and out of it precariously. Didn't she have a husband who could clean up? Christ, Sylvie thought.

"Oh, it's fine," she called to Amanda. "Same old. Same dumb clients. Same idiotic boss."

"So the Weenie continues to reign supreme with his weenieness?"

"Oh, and then some," said Sylvie, shoving the food she had brought into the crowded fridge.

"He gave me an Office Depot gift card at the baby shower," Amanda said.

"What!" screamed Sylvie.

"Exactly. I was like, *Thanks, Weenie, I'm sure Nina is going to need some printer ink.* He totally regifted it."

"Asshole," said Sylvie.

"Tell me about it. And I'm only getting six weeks paid leave."

"That's bullshit!" said Sylvie. "How is that legal?"

"Welcome to America," said Amanda.

Unbelievable, thought Sylvie, as she closed the refrigerator door. But why was she surprised? When she'd lost Delilah, they'd expected her back in two weeks. Sylvie had had Paul tell them to fuck off, his delivery far politer than what hers would have been. Three months later, she was back. Physically, at least.

Sylvie made her way down the hall, feeling guilty. Amanda needed the pills, probably more than Sylvie did. But, she reasoned, if Amanda wasn't taking them, if she was refusing to allow herself some relief, then who was Sylvie to convince her otherwise, much less let them go to waste?

She passed the guest bathroom and looked over her shoulder, in the slim-to-impossible chance that Amanda had gotten up to follow her. The hallway was as still as a statue, the whole house, in fact, silent save for the occasional grunt from the baby. Sylvie was safe.

Stealthily, her palms sweating, she continued on to the master bedroom, too focused to address the mess there too. The door to the adjoining bathroom was ajar. Slowly, she pushed it open, facing its expanse as though snipers lurked behind the toilet or in the shower. Then quickly she yanked open the medicine cabinet, scanning its contents. Nothing. Not one lousy pill bottle to be found. What kind of couple didn't even have one prescription medication to speak of in 2019?

Fuck, fuck, fuck. Seconds felt like ten-minute stretches. At any moment, Amanda would come wandering back here with the baby, a zombie on steroids the moment she found Sylvie rifling through her things. She had to hurry. It just couldn't be that there were no pills here. It just couldn't be.

Sylvie pulled open each drawer in the vanity underneath the sinks. Makeup, antifungal cream, moisturizer, all the usual suspects. But no familiar orange plastic bottles.

She checked again, just to be sure.

Near tears, Sylvie ran out of the bathroom. Fuck, fuck, fuck. Fuck Amanda for not having anything, fuck herself for being such an addict—there, she said it, she said it, okay?—and fuck the universe for getting her to this point in the first place. Fuck babies who actually lived, fuck the whole thing.

Out of the corner of her eye, over the mountain of laundry on the king-size bed, Sylvie noticed a bedside table. Amanda's bedside table, because it was piled high with parenting books with pastel jackets and various nipple ointments. Sylvie's last hope.

Sylvie ran to it, nearly getting tangled up in a pair of black stretch pants on the way. She pulled open the drawer, and there, next to a massive purple plastic vibrator, was the orange plastic bottle she had nearly given up on. Her heart pounding in her ears, equal parts guilt and elation, she picked it up. Jackpot. Quickly, but not too quickly—because what if the top flew off and the pills ended up everywhere? How would she possibly explain herself then?—Sylvie unscrewed the childproof cap and scanned the inside. It looked full, but not all the way full. Like two-thirds full. Sylvie would take six. Six would not be missed. She emptied them into her hand, wishing she could take more. She put the bottle back into the drawer, pushed it shut and stood up.

At the doorway, Sylvie stopped. Ten. She would take ten. How could Amanda possibly catch her? Unless there was some sort of nanny cam in here—Sylvie looked up and around at the ceiling corners. Nothing. And besides, they didn't even have a nanny—okay, she was fine. She ran back, shook out four more, placed the bottle carefully back in the drawer and ran out, her contraband in her pants' pocket.

"So sorry, Amanda. I ate something that didn't agree with me, I'm afraid," said Sylvie, wincing for effect as she sat back down.

The baby had been moved to the other breast, the plastic funnel Amanda had described earlier bobbing up and down on her nipple as she sucked.

"Oh God, sorry," said Amanda. "That's the worst. The other day I was literally nursing on the toilet while I had massive diarrhea. She wouldn't stop crying, and Doug just brought her in and handed her to me. I was like, Hello? I'm pooping?" She shook her head, her eyes on the baby. "But it worked, so. Hey, did you bring that seltzer, by any chance?"

"Oh God, I'm an idiot." Sylvie stood up. "Would you like it in a glass? With ice?"

"No, then I'll just have to wash it. Thanks, though, for the offer. I'll just take the can."

"Coming right up," said Sylvie.

She trotted to the kitchen, almost giddy with the knowledge that she had pulled it off. Although, ten more meant only ten more days. There was more than a month left before Teddy's Bar Mitzvah.

Sylvie returned to the living room, the wind knocked out of her sails. Amanda was gingerly slipping the baby back into her spaceship.

"Hey, Amanda, do you want me to sit with the baby while you shower?" asked Sylvie. Saint Sylvie, that was her. Amanda's eyes widened at Sylvie's offer. "Or a nap? Just anything that you've been longing to do today that you couldn't do because of her? I just remember, with Teddy in the beginning, it was so hard with Paul at work, I just—"

"Yes!" Amanda replied, almost but not quite yelling. "Sorry, yes! Yes. I would love to take a shower. I can't remember the last one I took alone. I always have to drag her bassinet in with me; it's just a mess. Are you sure you don't mind?"

"Not at all," said Sylvie. "Go ahead. You can even shave your legs."

Amanda smiled, a broad one that revealed all her teeth, and Sylvie could see the former version of her colleague in that smile, the version she would never be again on the inside—you were never the same on the inside once you became a mother—but that she would return to on the outside, more or less, once the newborn dust had settled. Amazing how you could fool everyone with your appearance. So few people had any interest at all in anything but the surface of things.

"Thank you, thank you, thank you," said Amanda. "She should pass out in a couple minutes anyway . . ."

"Go ahead, I've got it," said Sylvie.

And then she was alone with an infant for the first time since Delilah had died. A female infant, no less. Sylvie reached into her pocket and pulled out one of the pills, washing it down with the seltzer Amanda had left behind in her excitement.

The baby looked at Sylvie, her tiny body encased in pink-striped footie pajamas. Her hair was sparse and blond, her eyes a murky gray. She had no eyelashes to speak of yet, but her cheeks were full and pink. She was just beginning to bloom. Babies were so ugly when they were born, Sylvie thought. Teddy had looked exactly like Paul's great-uncle Beau, but not the younger version. The ninety-four-year-old version. And then, weeks later, his beautiful face had taken shape, his tummy had begun to press against his own footie pajamas, his elbows had sprouted dimples.

"Hello," said Sylvie, as the pill began to blessedly take effect. "I'm Sylvie."

The baby made an O with her tiny pink lips.

"Yes, oh," said Sylvie.

She settled back into the couch cushions as the baby dozed off, the sour scent of breast milk everywhere. What haunted Sylvie the most, the thing that went beyond even the layer upon layer of grief about Delilah that followed her everywhere like a shadow, that she couldn't shake, was the fact that she might, and she didn't know this for sure, but she might have been able to prevent it.

In the week leading up to Sylvie's labor, Delilah's kicks had stopped. Not that she had been that much of a kicker before anyway, but they had definitely stopped. And Sylvie hadn't done anything about it.

She hadn't told Paul; she certainly hadn't made an emergency appointment with her doctor, because she'd been too stupid to expect the worst, to expect the universe to ensure her daughter's safety.

Her maternal instinct had not trumped her sense of entitlement. There was a glitch in her system, and maybe, just maybe, that glitch had killed her daughter. Maybe earlier intervention would have saved her. Sylvie would never know, and this unknown would haunt her and haunt her. Forever.

She had never told Paul, and she never would. The maybe was too damning, too painful.

The baby was asleep. Sylvie stood up, before she could talk herself out of it, and jogged back to Amanda's bedroom. She could hear the shower still. One, two, three leaps to the bedside table.

Open the drawer. Take the bottle.

Back on the couch, panting, she dug into her pocket and deposited her first pilfer into the bottle before plunging it into the very bottom of her purse. The baby still slept. Only the sound of Sylvie's heart pounding in her ears and the water running through the pipes, the faint vibration of the spaceship. Sylvie closed her eyes.

It was wrong to have taken the whole bottle; she knew that. If she was lucky, Amanda wouldn't even notice they were gone. A little less unlucky, Amanda would blame her husband and they would get in a terrible fight that ended in an apologetic blowjob. Unluckier still, Amanda would accuse Sylvie herself. If that turned out to be the case, Sylvie would handle it the same way she had handled Paul. Prozac, for God's sake. She had pulled that one right out of thin air, on the fly. She would handle it.

The water stopped. In a moment, Amanda would return, refreshed and grateful, and Sylvie would leave, a mythic Mother Teresa who had given a new, exhausted mother the freedom to shave her legs without interruption.

Everything would be just fine.

CHAPTER SEVENTEEN

TEDDY

Teddy got off the elevator and made his way to the TV room, pretending as though he knew exactly what he was doing. The hallway smelled of burnt popcorn, gardenias and everything bagels. A heady mix, to be sure.

As he walked past Apartment 404, the door creaked open, giving him the distinct sensation that someone had been watching for him through the peephole.

"Early bird catches the worm. I like your style, kid," said Morty, shuffling toward Teddy in the same plastic slides and black socks pulled up to the middle of his hairless, white shins.

"Well, I wanted to set up first, you know," said Teddy. "Have you seen Jackie, by any chance?" He slowed his pace to match Morty's.

"Jackie? She's long gone. Busy lady. She's almost always

out of here by five. But she left me in charge, so don't worry, you're in good hands," he said as they entered the room together.

Six people surrounded an enormous bowl of popcorn on a table by the window, pecking at it like birds. Liter bottles of soda stood beside it, along with a sleeve of clear plastic cups. So much for being early, thought Teddy.

"People, our very own Siskel is here, may he rest in peace," Morty announced.

Teddy's underarms began to sweat profusely despite the room's air-conditioned frostiness. He didn't want to fail at something he cared about so much. He had mentioned as much to his mother on the way over, and she had said, not unkindly, *But what could fail?*

"But what if they don't agree with my opinion?" he had asked.

"So they don't agree," said his mom. "Then you have a discussion and you get to defend your perspective. And you have a solid perspective. I assume you've picked movies you love, so it's great practice for you. Arguing your point when you're actually informed is a natural high. And anyway, Teddy, these old-timers aren't going to come for you." She turned into the driveway of Twilight Manor. "Well, I take that back. Some might. But it'll be good for you, I promise. Just make sure they're fed."

Teddy eyed the bowl of popcorn now. A few stray unpopped kernels littered the bottom. The group stood before him and Morty, shoveling popcorn from their respective cups into their mouths. They reminded Teddy of a coterie of prairie dogs in the wild.

"Hello, everyone. I'm Teddy. Thank you for coming tonight."

"Welcome," trilled a woman whose white hair hugged her scalp like a glove. "I'm Beverly," she added, in a Southern accent as thick as peanut butter. She walked forward and extended a slender hand, her nails a bright red. Her black sweatshirt read #timesup in a bold white font. "Beverly Marlowe," she added, her brown eyes inquisitive behind thick turquoise-framed glasses. She was the coolest old person Teddy had ever seen.

"Morty says you're quite the movie buff," proclaimed another woman, this one in head-to-toe seafoam silk: pajamas, robe and slippers.

"Well, I don't know about that," said Teddy, "but I do love movies. And tonight, I brought a classic: *Back to the Future.*"

"Oh yes, we all saw it on the flyer," said Morty. "The last time I saw that movie, I think I was twenty."

"Well, that would have been impossible," said Beverly. "Since you're eighty-four."

"Eighty-four and a half," Morty said, correcting her. "I'm proud of every one of my years. I was just making a joke. Which is more than I can say for you, Beverly. Seventy-eight, my ass."

"Check my birth certificate!" Beverly said shrilly.

"Okay, okay, everyone. Simmer down," a voice called from the doorway.

Krystal stood there, her hands on her skinny, denim-cut-off-clad hips, and Teddy was never so glad to see someone in his entire life. His entire, almost thirteen years of life.

"Hey, Krystal," said the seafoam lady, her fuchsia-painted lips breaking into a giant smile. "What a treat. Your mama working late?"

"She is," said Krystal, strolling up to Teddy's side and nimbly retrieving the DVD from his hand. "And Teddy's my friend, so here I am. Y'all take a seat, okay?"

Everyone shuffled to their spots, lowering themselves carefully into their self-appointed spots.

"Thanks, Krystal," said Teddy, his confidence buoyed by her presence. "Does anyone want to know why I picked this movie?" he asked the crowd.

"Because it's great?" answered a man in a camel newsboy cap, pressed white shirt and creased khakis that appeared as stiff as papier-mâché. His long legs were crossed, his elbows resting on the arms of one of the chairs, his elegant, tapered fingers pressed together to form the perfect triangle.

"Well, yes, that," said Teddy, "but also because I like how Marty is able to go back in time and know his parents before they knew themselves. The idea of preventing them from making the mistakes he knows they're going to make, I really connect to that."

"That's heavy for a little guy like you," said Morty. "I disagree. That's never a kid's responsibility. Besides, I think our mistakes are meant to be made. How else do we learn?"

"Maybe," said Teddy. "But sometimes mistakes lead to

heartbreak, and why should anyone have to have their heart broken?"

"Oh honey, life is one big heartbreak," said Beverly.

"Maybe," said Teddy. "But not in the movies. That's why I love them."

"All right, let's watch the movie already, before we're all ten feet under," said Morty.

Krystal lowered the lights and slipped the DVD into the player. In moments, the room glowed, lit only by the giant screen. Krystal moved to the very back of the room and motioned for Teddy to join her.

"I shouldn't sit up front, in case they have any questions?" he whispered.

"Teddy, this isn't a lecture. It's a movie. They need to watch it."

"Thanks for coming," he said, sitting next to her on the sky-blue love seat. Its cushions were covered in velvet.

"Wouldn't miss it," said Krystal.

They stared at the screen. Quickly, before he could change his mind, Teddy took her hand. It was warm and soft. As soft as the cushions on which they sat.

"How are you?" she asked.

"Shhhh!" yelled Morty from the front of the room.

"Should we go outside to the hallway?" she whispered. "Morty's a hard-ass."

"Is that allowed?" Teddy whispered back.

Krystal stood up and pulled him with her out the door and closed it behind her. They sat, side by side, on the floor, their backs against the cream-colored walls, the wood floor cold beneath their bare legs.

"They're eighty-something, not eight," said Krystal. "I'm fairly certain they can watch a movie by themselves. You're going to ask some questions after, right?"

Teddy nodded. He had them all prepared, in his notebook.

"So it's cool. Now, where were we?" She took his hand.

"I'm okay, I guess," answered Teddy. "You?"

"I went to the pool today with my friend Marina, ate two hot dogs for dinner."

"I love hot dogs," said Teddy. "A summer staple."

His mouth salivated, thinking about them. Dinner had been some strange chicken and mushroom casserole his mother had felt compelled to cook. It had been pretty awful, although he had taken his obligatory five bites.

"Do you ever go to the pool?" Krystal asked.

"Like, my neighborhood pool?"

"Yeah, your neighborhood pool."

"I can't remember the last time I went," Teddy answered. "Maybe when I was, like, six or something."

"I bet all of your rich friends have their own pools, huh?" asked Krystal.

"I have two friends. Well, really only one now. And yes, he has a pool. But I don't think anybody swims in it."

"You have more than one friend!" said Krystal.

"Who?"

"Me, dummy. But I'm your girlfriend, so I guess that's different."

"You're my girlfriend?" he asked, barely able to utter the question.

"Sure. Don't you want me to be your girlfriend?"

Krystal faced him, her eyes bright, teasing him. Her confidence, it was contagious. It was one of the things he liked most about her. Loved. He could use that verb now without doubting himself. What a feeling. What an incredible, life-affirming, jump-up-and-dance-down-the-hall kind of feeling. He smiled at her.

"Yep."

"Okay then, it's settled." She leaned back against the wall, satisfied. "So why are you just okay?"

The door to the movie room opened, and the seafoam lady tiptoed out. She looked down, noticing them there, a small smile playing across her shellacked lips. What was it about old women and their lipstick? Teddy wondered. His Bubbe Barbara slept with it on.

"This movie is not for me," she offered. "Maybe next time you could show a romantic comedy. I love those."

Teddy nodded. "Sure," he said.

"Treasure these moments," she continued. "You blink, and suddenly, you're eighty-seven." She sighed. "Good night," she said, and glided past them toward the elevator.

"Good night," Teddy and Krystal called after her.

"That's Verna," said Krystal. "She just lost her husband, Troy, last month. They lived here together."

"That's so sad," said Teddy.

"Yeah. They were very in love. But then again, he was ninety-two. Who wants to live past ninety-two?"

"I guess you'd have to ask someone who's ninety-three," said Teddy.

"Fair enough. I'm still waiting, by the way."

"For what?" asked Teddy. "Oh, why I'm just okay." He sighed. "It's like I don't want to talk about it, but I also do."

"So go with do. I won't judge you, I promise," said Krystal.

"Well, it's not really about me," said Teddy. "It's about my mom."

"Is she okay?"

"I don't know. I don't think so."

"What's going on?"

"I found some pills. Hidden in one of her purses inside her closet. But they weren't her pills. They were my dad's pills, or at least the ones he was prescribed after he broke his ankle."

"What kind of pills?"

"Oxycodone?"

Krystal winced. "Uh-oh," she said.

"What?" asked Teddy.

"Those are bad news. Like, really bad news."

"At first, I thought, Oh she's just keeping them for him just in case, you know?" said Teddy.

"In case of what?" asked Krystal.

"In case his pain flared up or whatever and he really needed them."

"But why hide them in her purse? Does your dad have addiction issues?"

"Not at all," said Teddy. He thought about the machines in the basement, the boxes in the garage. "Well. Maybe. But not to drugs."

"But your mom does?"

"Does what?" asked Teddy.

"Have addiction issues," said Krystal.

"My mom has issues, but I wouldn't necessarily accuse her of being an addict," said Teddy. "Anyway, the bottle, it was full, or full-ish a couple weeks ago. And then, yesterday I went back in to check it. There were, like, five left."

"Shit," said Krystal.

"I know it," said Teddy. He unclasped his hand gently from Krystal's and rubbed his temples.

"Okay. Listen. Those pills are bad. I know it firsthand."

"How?" asked Teddy.

"My dad. That's why he's not around. Well, part of it, anyway. He started out on those things when I was a baby, and then a year later was nodding off on heroin, and then a year after that in jail and now, who the hell knows.

"Keep your mouth hanging open like that, a pelican's likely to fly into it," said Krystal, looking hurt despite her sarcasm.

"Sorry, I didn't mean— I'm just surprised to hear this, that's all. I'm sorry for you and for your mom."

"Thanks, but don't be sorry. We're better off without him."

Teddy took her hand again. "So what do I do? About my mom?" he asked.

"Has she been acting weird? Can you tell when she's on them?"

"I wouldn't say weird." Teddy considered his mother's turn of behavior in the recent months. "To be honest, she seems happy. Which for her is weird."

"Well, of course she's happy; she's high," explained Krystal. "She was sad before?"

"I wouldn't say sad so much as mad."

"Why? She doesn't like your dad?"

"No. Well, maybe. It's not that simple."

"Because of your sister," said Krystal.

She looked at him with pity in her eyes, but that was not what Teddy wanted. That look of pity had followed him around for a solid year after it had happened, and he had grown to loathe it. Because what did it do? A look was just a look; it didn't comfort or soothe or make anyone feel any better. What made people feel better was acknowledgment, and no one, not one person, had acknowledged his pain directly. Sure, he'd gotten presents shoved into gift bags from well-meaning neighbors and friends of his parents that his father had handed him awkwardly day after day until they stopped coming altogether. Even at nine, Teddy had wanted more.

"Yeah. I don't think she's been happy since, really. And now, suddenly, she is. I thought she had turned a corner or something, but you think it's the pills?" he asked Krystal.

"I'm no expert," she answered, "but I'm sure they're helping. I researched them online, just because I was curious. Like, their effect on the brain and stuff. You know what dopamine is, right?" she asked.

"Pleasure the brain creates," said Teddy.

"Right. So opioids create this false rush of it, supposedly. They release the floodgates. Happy is just the tip of the iceberg. And then, because they make the person taking them feel so good, they take more and more."

"Do I have to tell my dad?" asked Teddy. "I don't want to."

"But why?"

"I don't know."

He did not want to do anything at all; he did not want to be involved in the wherefores and whys of his mom's disappearing drug stash, but he had gotten himself into this mess by snooping, and now he had to get himself out.

"I better go back in," he said.

He stood up and then offered his hands to Krystal to pull her up too. Suddenly, she was before him, her face mere centimeters from his own. He kissed her lips. She tasted like bubble gum this time. Her phone rang.

"Sorry, it's my mom. She's ready to leave. Good luck in there."

"Thanks," said Teddy, remembering that he was nervous.

"And I'm glad you told me. About your mom."

"And I'm sorry about your dad," said Teddy.

"I gotta go," said Krystal. "Text me later?"

"Okay."

His parents had gotten him his own phone. He still couldn't believe it, but there it was, in his back pocket, the one opposite his notebook. An early birthday present, they had said.

He opened the door to the movie room. On the screen, the DeLorean took off into the unknown.

And when Teddy turned on the light, every person in the room was sound asleep.

CHAPTER EIGHTEEN

SYLVIE

She stared at the cookbook splayed open on the counter, thinking about how much she did not want to make the meal that stared up at her. Chicken Parmesan. It seemed like a lot of work when technically she could just defrost some frozen chicken patties, dump store-bought tomato sauce on top of them and cover the whole thing with cheese.

But she wouldn't; she had promised to make this from scratch, had made a big fuss about having Krystal over, and so she would. Plus, there were only two pills left, and she knew this because she had just taken her second of the day despite the fact that she had expressly forbidden herself from doing just that in the name of supply conservation. What was she going to do? She had to get more.

She laid the chicken cutlets on the cutting board and whacked one so hard that it all but disappeared into the board. Great, and now everyone at dinner would get salmonella and die.

"Sylvie?"

Paul. She bristled at the sound of her name being followed by a question mark; it always felt accusatory when either her given name, *Sylvie*, or her chosen name, *Mom*, was followed by a question mark.

"In the kitchen!" she yelled back. "Hoping I don't kill everyone at dinner," she mumbled to herself, as she transferred the defeated cutlets to a Pyrex and the cutting board to the sink.

"Syl, I hope you don't mind, but I invited David to dinner," said Paul behind her.

Her back was to him as she scrubbed her hands with soap, and she was glad. Because she was gritting her teeth. Goddamnit, that was all she needed, another mouth to feed with chicken that she would likely ruin, ano— And then, the bubbles snaked up her spine and into her brain, shaking it gently. Shaking her jaw loose and her doubts away. What was one more person?

She turned around to find Paul and David both.

"Sure, that's fine," she said. "Hi, David."

David stood before her, a triangle on steroids attached to two pipe cleaners for legs. The circles underneath his brown eyes were as deep as moon craters.

"Hi, Sylvie," he answered. "Thanks for having me. I told Paul he shouldn't have just sprung it on ya."

"No, no, it's fine. I'm probably making too much food anyway. Please stay."

"Thanks, Sylvie," David said.

"We're going to go to the basement and load some stuff onto his truck," said Paul. "We sold some of the bikes."

"That's great!" she said, and she meant it. It was a load off, knowing that Paul was in the process of reversing the havoc he had wreaked on their finances. "Thanks, David, for spearheading this."

As they turned to leave, she thought they could have been as young as Teddy in their gawky eagerness, but then Paul stopped.

"David, go on down, I'll be there in a second." David gave a salutatory wave without turning around and proceeded down the stairs.

"Sorry not to call beforehand," said Paul. "We were just on a site together and he got to talking." Paul lowered his voice, which was already low. So much so that Sylvie had to practically put her ear to his mouth.

"I think he's messing with those pills again. It's not good."

"Shit," said Sylvie.

"Yeah," said Paul. "I mean, I know selling this stuff is good news for us, but I think it might be good for him too. A distraction."

"Right," said Sylvie.

She rattled the mixing bowl on the island in front of her, hoping it was a subtle signal that she was busy, that she had a meal to cook, that it was time for Paul to scram.

"Okay. Call me if you need any help. I'm excited to meet this girlfriend." Paul turned to make his way to the basement stairs.

"Who?" she called after him.

"What?" he asked.

"Who are you excited to meet?"

"Krystal?"

"Oh right, yes, of course. Sorry, I have chicken Parm brain."

He left, and Sylvie glanced at the clock, her heart racing, but not because she had an hour and a half to finish what would normally take her four, give or take. She was fast at almost everything else, but when it came to cooking, Sylvie moved at a glacial pace.

David. Pills. Bingo. But how to get them was the question. She couldn't pop over there for a casual visit. Or could she?

As she beat the egg yolks, Sylvie considered her options.

* * *

"MRS. SNOW, IT'S SO nice to meet you," said Krystal. She handed Sylvie a wilting bouquet of red tulips. "Thank you for having me."

"Please, call me Sylvie. And we're thrilled to have you. Paul and I are just so curious about you. Thank you for coming."

Sylvie smiled, too broadly, she was sure, her cheeks hurting already. She was applying the age-old technique of killing with kindness, but the victim in this instance was her nasty old self. She was disappointed that Krystal wore purple mascara and cutoffs with flip-flops to meet her boyfriend's parents; that she spoke with a Southern accent; that her nails were painted glittery green; that her bra straps peeked out of her turquoise tank top.

Sylvie's initial impression was that this Krystal with a K was not good enough for Teddy and that she should just keep it moving right into teenage pregnancy with someone other than her son. She looked to Paul, trying to read his face for the same reaction. He looked thrilled.

"And I'm Paul," he said, extending his hand. "So nice to meet you."

Teddy, her Teddy—their Teddy—stood awkwardly to the side, but there was something different about his expression, Sylvie thought as she looked at him. Pride. Pride that this was his girlfriend, pride that he was introducing her to his family, pride in himself for having one in the first place. And wasn't that enough? Sylvie thought. It ought to be. She would make it be. *Shut up, you mean old bitch*, she told herself.

"This is David," she said to Krystal. "He's a family friend."

"Couldn't pass up a free meal," David offered. "Nice to meet you too."

They stood there for a moment, the five of them, in silence.

"Well, come on, the food is ready. Let's eat, shall we? I'll just put these in water first," said Sylvie.

She walked back to the kitchen, which sparkled from her manic cleanup, her wiping and rewiping of the counters with disinfectant as the chicken baked in the oven. It had come out looking edible too, which was more than Sylvie had hoped for. Her pill was wearing off; she could not take another, and so she would drink. A lot.

Sylvie pulled the stepstool out from the pantry to retrieve a vase, stopping to take an enormous sip of her rosé.

She grabbed the first one she saw, a glass rectangle, and filled it with water. On impact, the tulips drooped over its sides, exhausted. She drained the rest of her wineglass and poured another before facing them again.

"Sylvie, I was just telling Mr. Snow—sorry, I mean Paul—how gorgeous your home is," said Krystal. "It's straight out of a magazine."

"Oh, thank you," said Sylvie. "That's all Paul."

"You decorated it," said Teddy.

"That is true. That's very kind of you to say, Krystal."

"Can I help at all?" Krystal asked. "Do you need me to help serve?"

"Oh no, I think I'll just let everyone serve themselves. Less formal that way. You guys go ahead."

Sylvie sat at the table with her freshly poured glass of wine as the rest of them attacked the food. How to get to David on her own, or more to the point, how to get to his pills without causing alarm or even detection was on Sylvie's mind. It would not be an easy feat.

"It looks delicious, Mom," said Teddy, sitting down across from her. They were the only two at the table. "Thank you."

"You're welcome." And then, because she could tell that he wanted her to say something, anything, about Krystal: "She's very nice, Teddy."

"Yeah, you think so?" he asked, smiling.

"Yes." She did seem nice, that wasn't a lie, Sylvie reasoned. But nice was one thing; well suited was another.

Paul sat down. Sylvie thought about her own parents and the way they had treated Paul when she had first introduced them. Terribly. He wasn't smart or educated or funny enough. He wasn't Jewish. Her mother had even gone so far as to tell Sylvie that he wasn't attractive enough either. Sylvie had never forgiven them.

And now, look at Sylvie, doing the exact same thing. It was reprehensible, really. She took another gulp of her wine.

She looked at Krystal's plate as she sat down, piled high like she was a college football player. Sylvie pinched her own thigh under the table. *Stop it,* she told herself, wincing slightly from the pain. *Right now.*

"So how's your summer going?" Paul asked Krystal, after they were all seated and eating, including Sylvie.

"Pretty well," said Krystal, covering her mouth with her hand. She finished chewing. "I'm helping my mom out with some clerical stuff at work, but not a ton because, you know, I'm thirteen. I'll be working during the summers soon enough, might as well enjoy the pool while I can." She caught Sylvie's eye. "But I'm not being a total bum. I'm in a book club."

"Really?" asked David. "That's cool. What sorts of books?"

"All sorts. It's through the library, so we read whatever the librarian recommends. This month it's *The Catcher in the Rye,* which I've read before, but whatever."

"Great book," said David, before spearing half a chicken breast into his mouth.

How in the world was she going to get over to his house? Sylvie wondered.

"Are you excited about Teddy's Bar Mitzvah, Mrs.— I mean, Sylvie?" asked Krystal.

"I am. Our little boy becoming a man."

"Mom!" Teddy grunted.

"Sorry, I can't help myself. But yes, I am. A rite of passage. That reminds me, before you leave, I need your address, Krystal. I hope you'll come," said Sylvie.

"Thank you," said Krystal, blushing slightly beneath her freckles. She was pretty, Sylvie thought. If she could just scrub that mascara off her.

"Yeah, thanks, Mom."

"Sure, of course." Sylvie took a bite of the chicken.

"How many people you having here?" asked David.

"For the brunch? Let me think," said Sylvie. She did a quick tally in her head. "Maybe fifteen?"

Teddy looked up, his eyebrows furrowed.

"Oh, Teddy, relax. No more than fifteen," she repeated to David.

"Well, you're gonna need some extra tables. I have some at my place. I made 'em for a client a while back, but she decided she didn't want 'em. They're wicked nice too, if I do say so myself. Collapsible wood. Nice. You could use them instead of those ugly card tables I always see around. I got a couple of chairs too. They're all in my storage unit in the basement."

"David, that would be perfect!" said Sylvie, overjoyed by the offer—she hadn't even thought about the seating yet—and also about the access into his apartment. Into his medicine cabinet! It was almost too good to be true.

"I can pick them up, David, thanks a lot," said Paul.

"No!" yelled Sylvie, startling everyone. "Oh God, sorry. I didn't mean to yell. It's just that I need to see them first, to make sure they're right. You understand, don't you, David?"

"No sweat off my ball—my back. I can bring them by after you see them," said David. "If you like them, that is."

"I'm sure I'll like them," said Sylvie. "You do beautiful work."

"Cool," said David, smiling from the compliment.

"Does tomorrow work, David? In the morning?" she asked.

"Tomorrow I got a job, but Sunday works. Let's say around eleven?"

"Great," said Sylvie. She could make it. She could make it through the next day on one pill and then on Sunday, she could make it until eleven. She wasn't really an addict, for God's sake. She could do it.

"Sunday it is," she confirmed, depositing a bite of chicken into her giant smile.

CHAPTER NINETEEN

PAUL

"Thanks for having me, man," said David as Paul escorted him to his enormous truck.

"Our pleasure. Glad you could make it." The night air was warm and humid; an incoming storm hung in the air.

"Hey, you want to get a drink?" asked David. Even in the dark, Paul could see the loneliness in his eyes. Paul did not want to get a drink; he wanted to watch a *Shark Tank* rerun and go to bed.

"At a bar?"

"Yeah, at a bar. There's one a mile or two away, not far." There was a heavy pause as Paul considered all the ways David had been a good friend to him and all the ways he had been a mediocre friend at best in return.

"Sure," said Paul. "Let's get a drink. I'll just tell Sylvie. Be right back."

Paul hobbled back up the stairs, onto the deck and into the kitchen, where Sylvie was doing the dishes at the sink. It had been a long time since Paul had done the dishes, even before he broke his ankle, he realized, and immediately felt bad.

"Hey, Syl," he said.

She turned her head, still scrubbing, the hot water steaming as it poured from the faucet. "What's up?"

"You mind if I go get a drink with David?"

"Like a drink drink?" she asked. "At a bar?"

"Yeah. It's just, he seems really down, and he asked me to go, so—"

"Sure, go," she said, and swiveled her head back to her task.

"Are you mad?" he asked.

"No, I'm not mad," said Sylvie. "Why would I be mad? Go have a drink." She looked back at him. Her eyes did not look mad.

"Okay. I'll be back soon," he added.

"'K," she said. "Have fun."

As Paul walked back, he considered the fact that he had no male friends to speak of, other than David. He never had, really. Sure, he'd had the requisite buddies on the sports teams he'd played on in high school, basketball and soccer, but for the most part, throughout his life, he'd kept his head down and worked hard. From a young age he knew that his parents didn't have the money to send him to college and that he did indeed want to go, so that meant a scholarship, and a scholarship meant hard work. Paul Snow was a rational guy. Probably too rational, which explained the lack of friends. A party pooper, one might say. And *whatever* was what Paul would say to that.

He'd had quite a few girlfriends, though, once he'd gotten himself to college on the full scholarship he had worked so hard to receive. For whatever reason, women seemed to like him. He was all right looking, and he could fix things, but really, Paul figured his own apparent lack of interest was the real draw. Was it sexist to say that women liked a challenge? Probably.

"You good?" asked David.

"Yep, let's go."

Paul hoisted himself up into the passenger seat. His ankle throbbed. He wondered if it would throb for the rest of his life, a constant dull reminder of his mistake. Grief was like that, he thought. Just when you thought you were out of the woods, the ache of missing or what could have been started to pulse with its incessant emotional demand.

David made the short drive to a sports bar, the kind of place that Paul hated: televisions broadcasting myriad games everywhere, the stench of beer and chicken wings permeating the canned air. He took a deep breath and told himself not to be an asshole. It was one drink.

"So how are ya?" asked David, once they were settled into a booth, two frothy glasses of beer placed in front of them.

"Eh, you know. Fine," said Paul. He took a sip.

"Things with you and Sylvie good?"

"I wouldn't say *good*, necessarily," answered Paul. "But better lately."

"Better is better than worse," said David, taking a lengthy gulp from his glass.

"Better is better than worse," repeated Paul. "That's true. I'll drink to that."

He raised his glass and took another sip. All around them, other men—some alone and some in groups, some with women but most without—sipped the same lukewarm beers, their eyes glassy from the glare of the dueling televisions.

"You come here a lot?" he asked David.

"Enough," he answered. "It's something to do."

"What's up with the ladies?" asked Paul, regretting the question the moment it came out of his mouth. "Jesus, sorry," he said. "I've lost any modicum of coolness I ever possessed. Eighteen years of marriage will do that to you, I guess."

David whistled. "You've been married eighteen years? That's a lifetime."

"Tell me about it," said Paul.

"Wow. Cheers to that." David raised his glass again, but it had little more than a sip left in it. He gulped it down and motioned to the beleaguered waitress. "Want another?"

"I shouldn't," said Paul. "And what about you? I don't want you to drive home drunk."

The waitress appeared with two more glasses of beer, her perception of David's order eerily accurate despite the fact that he hadn't uttered one word.

"What are you, my mom?" asked David. "I'm fine. Beer is like water to me. And since you asked about the ladies, as you called them, I'm in a bit of a drought. Such is life."

"Tell me about it," said Paul.

"What do you have to complain about? You have a wife for sex."

"Uh, think again," said Paul. He was feeling the effects of the beer but started in on his second one anyway.

"Oh yeah?" asked David.

"I can count on one hand the times we've had sex in the past two years."

"Get the fuck outta here," said David, aghast. "That's torture. What's the problem?"

"The problem?" Paul took another gulp.

"Is it— Can you not get it up or something?" whispered David.

"God no. It's Sylvie. She has no interest. It's like I'm forcing her."

David raised his eyebrows.

"Not, like, *forcing her* forcing her. But she just has no sex drive. Not since Delilah, anyway. Or hell, maybe before that even, I honestly can't remember at this point."

David raised his hand to signal the waitress again, but Paul waved him off. "No more for me. I'm like a goddamn preteen, going on and on."

"Nah, man, it's good to get this stuff off your chest. Or else you go nuts. Listen, after Jeremy died, Brooke and I never had sex again. And we didn't divorce until three years after the fact, so. You do the math."

"Damn," said Paul. "How'd you endure it?"

"Not very well. We got divorced." The waitress magically appeared to set another glass in front of David. "Also, you know, she was having an affair."

"A minor detail," said Paul.

"Sylvie's not—"

"Oh, no way. No way in hell."

"You did say she was happier lately, though," said David. "Maybe it's the—" He made an obscene bed-creaking noise to illustrate his point.

"What are you, fourteen?" asked Paul. "That's offensive. And trust me, she's not having an affair. She's just not. She's on Prozac."

"What'd you say? Ball sack?"

Paul punched him in the arm. Hard. "Hey, man, take it easy. I mean it."

"Sorry. I'm sorry," said David. "I'm an asshole. Forgive me. Seriously." He put his glass down on the wood table, which was covered with what looked like centuries of beer rings, and stared at Paul until he met his eyes.

"We're good," said Paul.

"So, Prozac, huh? That's great if it's making her happier. I mean, that shit is poison, but whatever works."

"What do you mean, it's poison?" asked Paul.

"I mean, all of these antidepressants and antianxiety and this and that. Have there ever been any real studies on how they affect the brain? How do we know they're not, like, filled with cancer or some shit?"

Paul stared at him in disbelief. "Let me get this straight," said Paul. "Here's a guy who chews pain meds like they're gum and suddenly you're Dr. Oz? Come on, man."

"That's not fair," said David, his eyes narrowing. "Watch your mouth."

"You watch your mouth," said Paul. "Is what I just said not the truth?"

"I don't chew them like they're gum," muttered David.

Paul was grateful for the shift in conversation.

If there was a physical fight to be had, David would kick his ass, no question. And then where would he be? Bum ankle and broken ribs?

"And listen, we all know that shit I take is poison," David continued. "I'm just making the point that this other stuff that's supposedly good for us, where's the research on that? They're all doing the same thing, which is screwing with the chemicals in our brains."

"I'm sure there's lots of research, actually," said Paul, although he wasn't sure at all. "Anyway, man. How are you? With the pills?"

"Eh. I take too many," said David. "But I function. So what's the problem?"

Paul looked at his friend: his gray pallor, his tired eyes, the veins bulging out of his bony forearms. There were a lot of problems.

"Some chick over there is staring at you," declared David.

"What are you talking about? Do I have something on my face?" asked Paul.

"Just, you know, your face. No, she's really checking you out." David kept his eyes on the woman in question, but Paul refused to turn around. He was sweaty, very sweaty. "And now, yep, now she's walking over here."

"Get the fuck outta here," said Paul, just as he felt the table move slightly.

"Paul?" He knew that voice. He couldn't believe that he was hearing it, but he knew it.

"Tobi?" It was her, all right. Five foot three of sinuous muscle in a black tank top and very short white cutoffs, white sneakers on her feet. She was energy and fitness and fun and light. And trouble. A lot of trouble. Paul felt nauseated.

"What are you doing here, gimpy?" she asked, her voice raspy and flirtatious.

"Just out with my friend David here." He motioned to David, who gave a small wave.

"Hey, David, mind if I sit?" She sat.

"So how are you, Paul? No more crutches! That's great!" She was the human embodiment of an exclamation point, Paul realized.

"Yeah. Slowly but surely."

"Will you be back on your bike soon?"

"I hope so."

She was not wearing a bra. He wanted to run from the table and never look back. But he also wanted to stay. Sylvie had given him her undivided attention once. In the beginning. But now it was like a distant memory, like the dinosaur cake his mother had baked him for his fifth birthday. He had loved that cake.

"It's good to see you, Tobi," said Paul. "But I should really go. Sylvie will be worried about me."

"What?" asked David, looking at him incredulously. "You're leaving?"

"Yeah, I should go." Paul rooted in his back pocket for his wallet, pulled it out and threw two twenties on the table.

"Wait, wait," said David, chugging the rest of his beer as Tobi looked on, her brow furrowed in confusion.

"Do I smell?" she asked, sniffing her armpits.

"Not at all. You smell fine," said Paul.

"Like roses," added David. "But if my man says he has to go, he has to go. I'll drive you home, Paul."

"Well, nice seeing you," said Tobi as Paul got up, David right behind him.

"You too," called Paul over his shoulder as he rushed out.

In the parking lot, he traveled as fast as he could, narrowly avoiding falling flat on his face. Quickly, he scrambled into the cab of the truck.

"For Christ's sake, man!" said David, getting in and slamming his door. "What in the hell? Who was that?"

"Just a girl from my triathlete group." Paul struggled to get his breath.

"You're running from her like she's a demon from hell or something," said David, starting the engine.

"She is."

"She's into you, man." They pulled out of the parking lot and onto the road.

"I know," said Paul. "I can't be around her. It's not right."

"Whatever you say," said David. "It's all good, Paul. I've got your back."

They drove through the night, back to Paul's house, back to Sylvie and Teddy. When he got home, Paul would buy something. Anything.

The void was real, and it needed to be filled. Immediately.

CHAPTER TWENTY

TEDDY

When Harry Met Sally, huh?" Jackie sat behind her desk, extracting almonds from a tiny Tupperware container with a baby blue lid.

"Yes ma'am," answered Teddy.

"Why the change from"—she rustled through some papers on her desk to find the flyer she'd printed up with his initial schedule—"*Jurassic Park?*"

"Verna told me she wanted a romantic comedy," he explained.

"Ah, Miss Verna." Jackie smiled before placing her last almond on her tongue, as if it were a vitamin. She chewed it efficiently while dusting the salt off her fingers. "Well, shoot, I'm with her. I'll take that over dinosaurs any day. You know what, I might just show up tonight. Don't feel like going to spin class anyway."

"Have you seen it?" asked Teddy.

"Of course I've seen it," she answered. "A million years ago. But that's the kind of movie you think, You know what? I want to see that again."

"Oh good," said Teddy. "And again, I'm sorry about the late notice."

"You mean, the last-second notice," said Jackie, arching her eyebrow. "What's up with that? I hope we don't have a riot in the hallway, a bunch of octogenarians expecting to see T. rexes all up in arms over Billy Crystal."

"Tiny arms," said Teddy.

"Do what now?"

"You know, tiny T. rex arms?" He folded his own arm in an attempt to demonstrate his point. Jackie did not smile.

"Sorry, bad joke. And I know it's no excuse, but this week has been pretty hectic. I had to rewrite my Mitzvah Project paper—well, get it off the ground at least. It's in three weeks." Even as he said it, Teddy couldn't believe it.

"What's in three weeks?" asked Jackie.

"My Bar Mitzvah."

"Mazel tov. And I mean that sincerely, but listen up, Theodore. Rewriting an essay does not a hectic week make. Don't forget your responsibilities, now. Make a list. Check it twice. You feel me?"

"Yes ma'am," answered Teddy.

She was right, of course. And the truth was that although he was working a little bit on his paper, he was mostly spending a lot of time with Krystal. The day before they'd sat on his deck for two hours, playing Jenga and checkers, eating cold Popsicles in the muggy heat, not thinking about his mom or his paper or the fact that his father rode his exercise bike fifteen feet from them, his eyes maniacally focused on some imaginary finish line. "He okay?" Krystal had asked more than once.

"What time is it?" Jackie asked.

"Six," answered Teddy, looking at his watch.

"Oh, so we got a whole hour before the movie comes on? You goin' home and comin' back?"

"No ma'am, I figured I'd just stick around here, maybe work on my paper in the lobby or something, if that's okay with you."

"Wait, you know what?" said Jackie. "Here."

She flipped open her laptop and typed quickly. Seconds later, the printer hummed, emitting a single piece of paper. She handed it to Teddy.

Movie Night Change

"When Harry Met Sally"

No Dinosaurs This Evening

"Go take this to Morty. He'll get the word out. Lord knows how he does it, since no one here knows how to use a damn computer, but he does. Probably has some kind of Morse code system designed specifically for hearing aids."

"Okay, sure. Thanks." Teddy stood up. "What apartment?"

"Four-oh-nine."

"Got it. See you later?"

"Yessir. Close the door behind you, okay?"

Teddy made his way to the elevator. Dinner was winding

down in the cafeteria. Teddy could hear the clinking of utensils on plates and the faint murmur of voices, the scraping of chairs and walkers on the wood floor.

He got out on the fourth floor and made his way around the circular hallway to his destination. From inside 404 a woman shouted into what Teddy hoped was a phone; from 407 the familiar opening bars of *Law & Order*.

His mother loved that show. He stopped outside Morty's door, remembering the softness of her pink cotton pajama-clad legs underneath his head as he draped himself over her on the couch, wondering if nine was too old to snuggle with your mom but doing it anyway because she seemed so sad.

"You gonna stand out there all day?" barked Morty, opening the door with an unlit cigar hanging from his lips. Surprised, Teddy dropped the paper.

"How did you know I was here?" he asked, bending to pick it up.

"Kid, I know everything. Come on in." Teddy did as he was told, excited to see where Morty lived. "And I already know about movie night; I got the word out."

"Of course you do," said Teddy. "Thanks."

"Don't mention it. Myself, I'm not such a fan of rom-coms, but that one's pretty good. I like the writing; it's quick."

"Yeah, me too."

Teddy was surprised by the size of Morty's apartment. He'd known it was going to be small—he could tell by the number of them per floor—but not this small. The entryway was just a beige carpeted square of space outside the white kitchenette, which housed a tiny stove, refrigerator, microwave and sink, along with a few cabinets top and bottom, all in white. The kitchenette looked out onto a living room: more beige carpet, a lumpy green couch, a honey-colored wood coffee table, a black leather recliner, a flat-screen on a narrow table against the wall. Beyond that was what Teddy assumed were the bed- and bathroom. The entire space could have fit into his kitchen, Teddy thought.

"This is living, huh?" asked Morty. "Welcome to my humble abode, and by humble I mean, can you believe the rent I pay for this?" Morty sat in his recliner, the unlit cigar still in his mouth. "But what am I talking about? What does a ten-year-old know about rent?"

"I'm almost thirteen," retorted Teddy.

"I know that, just pulling your leg. Have a seat, make yourself at home," said Morty. Teddy sat.

On the white wall were hung two photos in gold frames.

"May I?" asked Teddy.

"Be my guest."

Teddy got up and walked over to get a better look. "Is that you?" he asked Morty, staring in wonder at the young, handsome man who smiled back at him in black and white.

Morty was in a tuxedo, and next to him: a woman in a wedding dress. She was smiling too. And pretty. Black hair frozen into those old-timey waves, a white lace gown that rose high on her slender neck, sparkling eyes.

"The one and only," replied Morty.

"And your wife?"

"Bernice. Love of my life."

"She's pretty," said Teddy.

"Pretty? Please. Try beautiful. A perfect ten. A knockout. No idea why she went for me, but she did."

"You don't look so bad yourself here either, Morty," said Teddy.

"Well, thanks, kid. I cleaned up nice."

In another photo, this one in color, Morty and Bernice stood in front of an enormous brick apartment building, holding a baby boy.

"You have a son?" asked Teddy, leaning in closer to get a better look.

Morty was thin and dapper, his dark hair plentiful and wavy, dressed in a short-sleeve white button-down and navy pants pulled up to practically his neck. A brown belt with a gold buckle circled his waist. He gazed at the boy lovingly, a broad smile on his face. Bernice, in a pink sleeveless dress, her hair looser and curlier than in her wedding photo, smiled at the camera. And the baby, chubby wrists and all, dressed in a red-and-white-striped T-shirt and diapers, was caught mid-giggle. Teddy grinned at them, their happiness contagious.

"I did," replied Morty quietly.

"You did?" Teddy turned from the wall. Morty had taken the cigar out, was rolling it between his fingers.

"It's complicated, kid," Morty said.

"Try me," said Teddy.

"His name is Michael. And when Michael was just a kid, not much older than you, his mother died," Morty explained. "What kind of God gives an angel like my Bernice cancer?" Morty shook his head, his voice grave. "It was devastating. And Michael, well, he didn't like the way I raised him after the fact. Says I was too distant, too this, too that. Not available enough. How available can a single father trying to put food on the table be? I tried my best." Morty put the cigar down on the table. "Anyway. He has a lot of anger toward me. Stopped talking to me after he graduated college, a college I put him through, mind you." Morty took off his glasses, rubbed his eyes. "Now he lives in New Jersey somewhere, with a grandkid I've never met. Anyway. I should stop. You're too young for this kind of talk."

"But I'm not," said Teddy. He crossed back over to the couch and sat down. "I had a sister. She died too."

"Oh for goodness sake, Teddy. That's just terrible." Morty leaned forward and put his hand on Teddy's knee. "I'm so sorry." For the first time, Teddy noticed that Morty was missing half of his index finger.

"Well, she never really lived, actually," Teddy continued, still staring at the nub where Morty's fingertip should have been. "She died inside my mom, I guess. But we didn't know until she was born."

"Heartbreaking," said Morty. "Just heartbreaking." He sat back on the couch.

"Her name was Delilah."

"That's a beautiful name."

Teddy nodded. "I don't think I believe in God either," said Teddy, as Morty handed him a Kleenex.

"Who said I don't believe in God?"

"You did, just now, when you were talking about Michael," said Teddy.

"I never said I didn't believe in God. I just asked what kind of God does that? That I can't tell you, but that doesn't mean I don't believe in Him. Or Her. Beverly would have my head if she heard me call God Him."

"Well, I don't believe in Him or Her or whatever you want to call it. And that's why my Bar Mitzvah just seems so ridiculous. Like, what's the point? Read from some roll of paper in a language I don't even understand to somehow prove that I'm a man? And who's a man at thirteen, anyway? I barely have pubic hair."

Teddy blushed, not quite believing the words that were tumbling out of his mouth in this spare apartment that smelled like leather and garlic. He had thought all these things, but he had never said them out loud before.

"Well, that's more than I needed to know," said Morty. He cleared his throat. "Listen, a Bar Mitzvah can be a lot of horseshit, sure. I've been to parties where parents forked out thousands of dollars just so they could look important. But I was Bar Mitzvahed, and my father and his father and his father, you see?"

"My dad isn't Jewish," said Teddy. "Just my mom."

"Okay, same difference."

"Well, not really," said Teddy. "Women have only been Bat Mitzvahed since 1922. I looked it up."

Morty shrugged. "The point is, it's a tradition. It's about saying, you know what, I've studied until my eyes crossed, I've dragged my ass to Hebrew School more times than I can count, and for what? To honor my forefathers and foremothers by reading the same Torah they did. *L'dor vador.* You know what that means?"

"No," said Teddy.

"Continuity," Morty replied. "Generation to generation."

"But what does that have to do with God?" asked Teddy.

"What am I, a rabbi?" asked Morty.

Teddy sighed.

"Listen, do I think God really gives a shit whether you get Bar Mitzvahed or not?" said Morty. "No. But I think the ritual brings you closer to God, just because for this year, this important year when you're on the precipice of puberty, it forces you to make your Judaism a priority. When you'd rather be doing anything but studying the Torah or sitting here listening to an old-timer like me jabber your ear off, here you are. Talking about God. See?"

"Maybe I'm thinking about God, but that doesn't mean I'm any closer to believing," said Teddy. "How come you believe?"

"I can't tell you, kid. It's just a feeling I have," said Morty. "Or maybe it just gives me hope, to believe. After Bernice died, I had a tough time with God. I thought, *How can this be?* And I still do, I always will. But there's been enough beauty and joy in my life before and since to keep the idea of Him—or Her—alive."

Teddy looked at Morty, in his black tube socks and plastic slides, and just didn't know. He wasn't sure what he wanted as proof of God's existence—maybe a burning bush?—but he wasn't buying it.

"And what's this whole becoming a man, becoming a woman thing about?" he asked Morty. "I feel like my childhood ended for me when my sister died, three years ago. When I was nine."

"Fair enough, Teddy, but let me ask you this," said Morty. "When you were nine, when you were forced to stare death and all its unfairness right in the face, did you have the wherewithal to ask these complicated questions or to think the thoughts you're thinking now?"

"No," Teddy admitted.

"So there you go. Manhood in a nutshell. Along with a couple of other unmentionables, obviously. It's time, your forefathers knew it was time, and so you put on a jacket and tie, you read from the same script they read from, you have a nosh and that's it. Next chapter."

Morty pushed a button underneath the arm of his chair, and it slowly began to lift off its foundation, transitioning him into a perpendicular position to the ground.

"All right now. Chop-chop, it's time for the show." He shuffled toward Teddy and, without warning, wrapped him in a very warm and brief hug.

"I'm very sorry for what happened to your sister. I'm sorry for you and for her and for your parents, you hear me?"

Teddy nodded, feeling his chest tighten. "And I'm sorry about Bernice," he said in return. "And Michael."

Morty squeezed Teddy's arm. "Thank you, I appreciate that." He led the way out of his apartment, slowly, and Teddy fell into line behind him.

"I want an invitation to your service, kid," said Morty over his shoulder. "And Beverly too."

"Are you and Beverly . . . ?"

Morty turned around to face him, right outside the door to the movie room. He lowered his voice. "We are what we are, kid. Life gets lonely at this age, let me tell you. She's a blessing in my life. Beauty and joy, kid, you see? When I thought my shot at that was long over. Is that God?" Morty raised an eyebrow. "Why not?"

As Teddy set up the DVD player, he contemplated Morty's thoughts on manhood. He'd never considered the transition to be so figurative, to be more about the way you looked at the world rather than the way you looked in it. It made much more sense to Teddy, Morty's perspective.

What he really needed to do, Teddy decided, if this Bar Mitzvah was going to mean anything to him in the long term, was go back to the moment when Delilah was born but not born, when he learned what death was in the waiting room of that cold, sterile hospital, when he learned that she was gone, he would never meet her, she was never going to be. He needed to go back there and bridge that experience with the boy he had been then and the man he was becoming now.

It would take a little bit of planning, and he was not at all equipped for the journey, Teddy knew that, but it was also not impossible to both imagine and complete. He could do it.

"*When Harry Met Sally*!" cried a disgruntled Movie Night attendee at the door, who apparently hadn't gotten Morty's memo and was now eyeing the Scotch-taped flyer with great disdain. "I'm here for dinosaurs, damnit."

Teddy exchanged a glance with Jackie, who sat with a bowl of popcorn on her lap, her shoes off to reveal neon-orange-and-black-zebra-striped ankle socks.

"My apologies," said Teddy. "Let me explain."

And so he did.

CHAPTER TWENTY-ONE

SYLVIE

Sylvie turned off the ignition and sat in the parking space marked "Visitor" in white stenciled letters, staring at the vast apartment complex. So much red brick. It went on and on, the same building after the same building save for the numbers on the doors.

She pulled down her visor and slid over the mirror's plastic cover, examining her teeth for stray food. All clear. She slid the cover back, flipped the visor up, took a deep breath and opened the door.

The heat and humidity was suffocating, like a plastic bag over her head as she made her way to David's apartment. This was her first day without a pill in almost three months, she had checked the calendar to confirm, and couldn't quite believe it. That was a long time to be taking drugs.

Yeah, she said it. In her head, at least. Drugs.

Sylvie knew she was in trouble, but this was it. Her last hurrah. The Bar Mitzvah was less than a month away, and after that, she would get her ass into therapy. Okay?

Okay.

Number fifty-six. Brass numbers on a black door. She knocked.

He opened the door, stared at her, a bemused expression on his weathered face.

"Hey, David," she said.

"Sylvie," he returned. "Come on in."

"Thanks."

She followed him inside, noticing with relief that it did not look like a junkie's lair as she had feared. The living room walls were a soft, subtle gray, the floors bare wood, the couch a darker gray, expensive looking, in the shape of an L. An oak coffee table that looked as though it had just been sawed right out of a tree, sanded just so. Sylvie recognized it as David's work. He was talented, there was no question. Not a junkie. Or hell, maybe everyone was a junkie today; everyone was on some pill or another.

Sylvie didn't know anymore. Her head was really pounding.

"Could I have a seat?" she asked. "Sorry, I'm feeling a little out of it."

"Sure, of course," answered David. "Can I get you some water or something?"

"Water would be amazing," she answered, her mouth so dry it was like talking through mud. "Thank you."

She stared at the enormous television hung on the wall,

noticing that there were no pictures in the room, no art. She wondered if there were pictures of his son anywhere. Sylvie had lost a child she never had the chance to meet, but he had lost a child he had known, he had raised. That was worse, she thought, thinking about Teddy but then shoving the thought out of her mind with brute force. She would not think about Teddy or Paul.

Stay focused, Sylvie, she told herself.

"Here you go," said David, returning with her water.

"Thank you," she said. She tilted her head back and drained the glass in an instant.

"Everything okay?" asked David, looking concerned.

He was wearing camouflage cargo shorts and a tight navy-blue polo shirt, his feet bare. The uniform of someone much younger—he could almost fool you into thinking he was in his twenties if you didn't look at his face.

His eyes were sunken into his sockets a little, like he hadn't quite woken up. Wrinkles spread out from the corners of them like wings and across his forehead like the rake tracks in one of those Zen sand gardens. Sylvie had the same wrinkles, you were supposed to in your mid-forties, but there was something about the pallor of David's skin—gray with an undertone of yellow—that put him almost but not quite nearly on his deathbed. And the patchy, salt-and-pepper stubble lining his jaw didn't help either.

That wasn't nice, Sylvie thought to herself, the deathbed comment; she took it back. Besides, somehow David had managed to hold on to all his hair, every last strand. The fact that he wore it in a coarse gray ponytail was unfortunate, but Sylvie understood his attachment to it. She wished he would cut it, though.

"So you want to take a look at those tables and chairs?" he asked, reminding Sylvie of her excuse to be there. "I apologize, I wanted to get them out of my storage unit in the basement before you got here, but time got away from me."

"No, no, don't apologize," said Sylvie. "Happy to pop down to see them."

"Cool," said David. "Shall we?"

"We shall."

"You have a really nice place," she told David's broad back, following him down the stairs at a close clip. *You have a really nice place, can I buy some Oxys off you?* That's what she wanted to say, she needed to say. The sooner she got it out, the less weird it would be. But how?

"Oh yeah? Thanks," he said over his shoulder. "I want to buy some art for the walls, but I dunno the first thing about art buying. My wife, she had the taste in that department. Took it all with her when she left too."

They had reached the first floor. David turned around to face her, his sunken eyes glassy. He was stoned right now, Sylvie realized. He was probably always stoned. Why would he share his pills with her? This was a bad idea; she should just okay the tables and chairs and get the hell out of there, weather this withdrawal and go back to her real, chemically independent life.

"Paul and I, we can help you pick out some art," she offered. "He has a friend, an artist here. We have a piece of his in our bedroom."

But she didn't want to go back to her old life. Well, her most recent life, anyway. Her life since Delilah had died.

"Okay, cool, sure. That'd be nice, thanks." He smiled at Sylvie. "Just over here, these are the stairs down to the storage units."

She followed him again, across a sidewalk that burned bright white in the hot sun. In the distance, she could hear splashing, the shrieks of kids playing.

"Your complex has a pool?" she asked.

"Yeah," said David. "Way over there. When I moved in, I made sure I was as far away from it as possible." They approached a heavy gray door.

"Too loud?" asked Sylvie.

"Too many kids," he answered. "It's hard for me to be around kids or hear them playing and having a good time or whatnot." He paused to look at her, his hand on the silver crash bar.

"I understand," said Sylvie. "I can't be around little girls really, especially babies." *Unless I'm stealing their mother's drugs.*

"Yeah," said David. "You get it."

"I get it," said Sylvie.

He pushed on the bar and the door opened, emitting a welcome blast of air conditioning. Sylvie followed him in, down another flight of stairs.

"If you don't mind my asking, how old was your son when he died?" Sylvie asked.

"You mean, when he was killed? He was eleven."

Sylvie shook her head behind David, her eyes smarting. Eleven.

"I'm so sorry, David," she said. "What a shitty thing to have happen to him, to you, to your wife, to your marriage. I'm really just very sorry."

"Thanks," he replied.

They had reached the storage units now; they stretched in front of them, numbered black door after numbered black door lining the fluorescent-lit, steel-gray hallway. Sylvie had never been in a morgue, but she thought that this was what it might look like. Except in this case, dead belongings instead of people.

It was interesting, the things people held on to. The actual material goods. Paying rent for an apartment of belongings they would likely never need or touch again but couldn't bear to part with. Sylvie had emotional baggage galore, and lord knew she was paying her own type of rent to house it, but as far as stuff, she was very good at throwing things out. Maybe too good.

She had thrown out her wedding dress, which in retrospect seemed kind of harsh. But the dry cleaning and the paper-bust business, a virtual coffin for it to reside in as she grew older and fatter, it just seemed like a waste of money. And if the daughter she was going to have—because of course she was going to have a daughter, her naive self had figured without a second thought—was anything like Sylvie, she would have no interest in wearing it on her own wedding day.

"Sylvie?" asked David. She was so deep in thought that she hadn't even realized he'd been holding the door open for her.

"Oh sorry," she replied. "My head. I'm on Mars."

"No worries."

She walked into what was essentially a generous prison cell with shelves, David following. It was remarkably neat, everything in boxes and labeled. Sylvie wondered what was in them, even as she sensed that a lot of who his son had been was here, in this room, packed away. Sylvie had these same boxes too, of course. Metaphorically speaking. The real stuff, the tangible gifts and things for Delilah, she had had Paul return, sell and donate. In that order.

"The stuff is back here," said David, pushing past her slightly to the far wall. "I have six of these," he said, pulling a table from the stack leaning up against it. "Much nicer than those run-of-the-mill card tables, right? All wood."

"They're gorgeous," said Sylvie. "Is this oak?"

"Yeah, sanded it down and sealed it, but that's it. They each sit six." He paused. "But unfortunately, I only have twelve folding chairs." He shrugged. "I didn't get around to making the rest. They're right here."

"Those are gorgeous too. And that's okay," said Sylvie. "I can rustle up the rest."

Her head was really pounding now. Coming up to the close of their meeting and how in the world was she going to segue into a drug deal?

"Okay, cool," said David. "I'll bring 'em by in my truck this week."

"Thanks," said Sylvie, feeling desperate. How, how, how? "That sounds great, and I really appreciate it.

"I'm so sorry, would it be okay if I used your bathroom before I go?" she managed to squeak out.

"Sure, of course."

Out of the unit, up the stairs, back along the sidewalk, up the other set of stairs, into his apartment, down the short hall and into the bathroom. Sylvie yanked open the mirrored cabinet door, knowing she wasn't going to find anything. An addict didn't store his bounty out in the open; he hid it. Like she did, she realized, thinking of her red purse. Fuck.

Just a few more weeks. She closed the cabinet and sat on the toilet, thinking. She would just come out and ask him. Point-blank. Pill enthusiast to pill enthusiast, friend to friend. Like there was nothing to be embarrassed about. If he balked, if he refused, that's when she would, well, she couldn't even think it. She just had to do it. Or not. Maybe good sense would find her at last, she thought, hoped, even as she knew it would not.

Sylvie stood. She washed her hands at the sink but would not look in the mirror. *Here we go,* she thought. She opened the door and walked purposefully down the hall. David was standing at the counter in the kitchen, drinking a can of Coke.

"Oxys," Sylvie blurted out.

David swallowed his sip, coughing slightly at her outburst.

"Oxys. Do you have any I could buy?" she asked as confidently as she could, as though this was a perfectly normal question for her to be asking him.

"You serious?"

"Yes," she said, relieved to have finally asked. "Yes, I am serious."

"What the hell, Sylvie?" David furrowed his brow and put his can down on the counter, avoiding her gaze. "I'm not a drug dealer, for Christ's sake."

"No, I know you're not," said Sylvie, although she had no idea if he was or he wasn't, and she really didn't care.

Either he did this all the time or he would make a one-time exception for a friend; she didn't care. She just wanted the pills. So badly.

Just these few hours without them in her system, her world was too much. Edges were sharper, the sun was hotter, her unresolved emotions too present. Sylvie much preferred the alternative. She would do what she had to do.

"David told me that you had offered him one, is all. I just thought maybe you had access to more." She perched awkwardly on the barstool across from him.

"What happened to you? How'd you get into this?" he asked.

"Paul's pills. When he broke his ankle, the doctor prescribed them for him, but you know Paul, ever the martyr. Ever the health nut. He had no interest in them. And I wouldn't have imagined that I would either until I made the mistake of trying one, just to see what all the fuss was about."

"Shit," said David.

"Shit is right." She laughed awkwardly. "So now I know."

"You know this stuff is the devil, right?" asked David. "No good can come out of taking them for the wrong reasons."

"Oh, I dunno, I feel pretty good taking them," said Sylvie. "Better than I've felt in years, maybe ever."

"Sure, but it's so fleeting," said David. He drained the can into the sink and put it in his recycling bin, his back to her. "And pretty soon you need more to do the same job, and then you can't function without them." He turned around. "But what am I telling you for? Look where you are. In my apartment, sniffing around for pills. I'm preaching to the choir here."

"Well, I mean, it's not a lifetime thing for me," argued Sylvie. "As soon as this Bar Mitzvah is over, it's curtains for me with this stuff."

"Sylvie."

"I'm serious! I just need to get through the Bar Mitzvah, and I have no interest in doing it sober if I don't have to."

"What's the problem with the Bar Mitzvah? I thought it was a celebration. A party," said David.

"I suppose it is, if you actually feel like celebrating anything. If you have the capacity for happiness, I bet it's a great party."

"Right," said David.

"So do you?" asked Sylvie. "Have some pills?"

David sighed. "How many are we talking about?"

"Thirty?"

"Thirty! Jesus, Sylvie. I don't have thirty lying around." He raked his hands through his lank hair. "What do you think this is? CVS?"

"Okay, okay. Twenty?"

David put his elbows on the counter, his head in his hands.

He was beginning to bald after all, just a little, around his crown, Sylvie noticed. "I mean, shit, Sylvie. That's still a lot."

"I have the money. Just tell me what it costs."

Sylvie sensed he was on the precipice of caving. Her renewed sense of optimism sent a welcome surge of adrenaline throughout her tired body.

"I can't do it. Paul would kill me."

"Oh come on," said Sylvie. "Paul is not my keeper. Trust me, he'll never know. He hasn't the first clue about me; he hasn't for years, and it's fine. It's totally fine."

To her disbelief and embarrassment, a lump had formed in Sylvie's throat. It was not remotely fine.

"It's just wrong," said David. "You have a family, Sylvie."

"Oh for fuck's sake, David, give me a break," said Sylvie. She was getting angry now. She had not expected a lecture. "I'm not asking you for a bag of heroin! Just twenty pills. That's it. I'll never rat you out. I'll never bother you again about it, okay? I swear on my son's life. It's a onetime thing." She was pounding her fist on the counter, Sylvie realized. "Sorry." She unclenched her hand and laid her palm flat on the cool white surface.

"Sylvie, I can't do it," said David.

"I'll fuck you," she said.

"What?" David looked scared. Sylvie was scared of herself, to be honest, but she pressed forward anyway. She had nothing to lose.

"I will fuck you for twenty pills," she said calmly. "And I will never breathe a word of it to Paul. It's a win-win, David." Sylvie channeled every seductress she had ever seen on-screen. "Fucking me sounds good, doesn't it?" David's mouth was parted slightly. She had a chance still.

"Sylvie, I—"

"Shhh." She stood up and walked around the counter until she was standing right in front of him. Close enough to smell his breath, which was slightly sour.

Don't break, she told herself. *If you break, if you overthink this for just a second, you're screwed. Keep going.*

"What do you say?" she asked him, putting her hand against his crotch. He was hard. "Hmmm?" David moaned slightly. "Do we have a deal?"

He nodded.

"Oh good," she said. "Goody."

She unzipped his shorts, pulled down his underwear and lifted herself up onto the counter. She pulled up her dress. She was not wearing any underwear; this had been her backup plan from the moment he had mentioned the tables at her house.

As he entered her, shame overtook Sylvie. She squeezed her eyes shut against the image of Teddy's smile, the sound of Paul's laugh, the silence of the delivery room after Delilah had been born, the dancing cactus in her cubicle at work. This was where she was. Screwing her husband's best friend for pills.

He thrust once, twice, three times and then collapsed into her, almost pushing her off the counter and onto the floor. She put an arm behind her to brace herself. At least she hadn't had to kiss him. At least it had taken less time than brushing her teeth.

David stood, but he kept his head down. He pulled up his underwear and his pants. Sylvie stayed absolutely still. For a moment, she had a crazy thought that he would refuse her the pills, still. Then she would have to kill him.

He walked out of the kitchen and down the hall to his bedroom. *Jesus, I'm really nuts,* Sylvie thought. *Kill him?*

She hopped off the counter and stood up. As she straightened her dress, his semen ran out of her, stickily coating the tops of her thighs. She had some wet wipes in the car, she remembered.

"Here they are," said David. He looked at her, his eyes sad. "Twenty."

"Thank you," said Sylvie.

"Don't ever come back here," he told her.

"I won't," promised Sylvie. She took the orange bottle from him, her heart pounding with gratitude. It was fine; it was all going to be fine.

"Oh, what about the tables and chairs?" she asked, her hand on the doorknob, her back to him and what she had just done. "Are we still good with those?"

"I'll drop 'em by," said David quietly.

"Excellent," said Sylvie.

She opened the door and let herself out.

CHAPTER TWENTY-TWO

TEDDY

Today he was thirteen. Today he was a man.

Teddy gazed at his scrawny bare chest in the bathroom mirror, his peach-fuzzed face, which had debuted an angry red birthday pimple on his forehead overnight. He certainly didn't look like a man.

He grabbed his toothbrush and squirted the requisite glob of minty blue onto its bristles. His parents hadn't even mentioned today, he thought as he brushed. He wondered if it would get lost in the Bar Mitzvah madness, his actual day of birth. He hoped not. That was a week away. And he wasn't so sure his parents would feel much like celebrating him at that point. Teddy had some plans.

There was a knock at the door.

"Yeah?" asked Teddy, through a mouth full of toothpaste.

"Birthday pancakes downstairs in three minutes!" his dad yelled triumphantly. "Hurry up!"

Teddy smiled before spitting into the sink. They hadn't forgotten.

"Be right there!" he yelled back.

For as long as he could remember, his mom had made him pancake numerals on his birthday. And even before he could remember, there were pictures of him warily examining a golden number one, a single birthday candle plunged into its fluffy depths. It was tradition.

Teddy made a pit stop in his room for a T-shirt and shorts change before hustling down the stairs, following the scent of pancakes, eggs and turkey bacon like that cartoon skunk. What was his name again? Pepe something?

"Well, well, well," said his mother from behind the stove, spatula in hand. "If it isn't our birthday man."

She smiled, a real smile from ear to ear, one that lit up her face and made her pretty, and Teddy wondered if she was on those pills. If she was stoned.

He smiled back tentatively and decided not to think about that, even though he had checked the red purse last night and discovered a new bottle, the prescription made out to David Conway. He knew David Conway. That was his dad's friend. It had bothered him all night, and it bothered him still. But what was he going to do? He didn't know.

"Morning," he mumbled.

He hadn't told Krystal about this recent turn of events, but Krystal kept harping on the fact that he should tell his dad. Teddy still didn't think that was the way to go. He looked at him now as he brought him a glass of orange juice, limping ever so slightly, freshly showered after what he assumed was a vigorous workout against doctor's orders, and knew his father was screwed up too, in his own way. It seemed to Teddy that that was the true hallmark of adulthood: being secretly screwed up while appearing completely normal and productive. Great. What a future to look forward to.

"Thanks," said Teddy, taking a big gulp.

"Happy birthday to you," sang his parents, as his mother carried a platter displaying his one and three pancakes, a single lit candle in the three. She placed it in front of Teddy as they finished the song.

"Make a wish," she demanded. Teddy did not, out of spite, but blew it out anyway.

She kissed him on the forehead, tilted his face up to hers. With his eyes, he tried to tell her, *I know about the pills. Cut it out, Mom,* but she was oblivious to his telepathic attempt.

"Beautiful boy," she said. "Excuse me, man. This face, I could eat it up I love it so much!" She kissed him again. Teddy felt loved, he did, even as he felt anger. It was so complicated, this man thing.

"How does it feel to be thirteen?" asked his dad, putting plates filled with eggs and bacon in front of him.

Teddy grabbed the syrup and doused his new age with its sugary sweetness, until the numbers were submerged in a pool of amber. He thought of Krystal, of their first date. He thought about the texts on his father's phone.

"Different than twelve," he answered, spearing a triangle

with his fork. His dad helped himself to some bacon and eggs.

"No pancakes?" asked Teddy, still chewing.

"Gotta lay off the carbs," he answered, patting the heather-gray material of the T-shirt draping his midsection.

"Yes, your father doesn't want to lose his modeling jobs in Milan this fall," said his mother with a smirk. "All the designers are depending on him." She plopped down on the bench beside Teddy with two pancakes of her own.

"Come on, Sylvie, give me a break," said his dad, not looking at her. "My pants don't fit, okay? And I want to wear them for the Bar Mitzvah. Is that something I should be made fun about? Jesus."

Teddy stopped eating, his stomach suddenly full. His parents didn't so much argue when they argued; his mom just lobbed firecrackers while his dad retaliated with water balloons.

"Sorry," said his mother, surprising Teddy. "I'm sorry, Paul. Of course it's not. I just think you look great, is all. I didn't realize your pants don't fit."

His dad looked up from his plate. His mother did not do apologies. She was definitely stoned, Teddy thought. So these pills, they made his mother a nicer person. Why were they bad again?

"Yeah, they're just a little tight. Enough to make me uncomfortable."

Teddy went back to eating, his appetite restored. He knew why the pills were bad; he'd done lots of research online. Over time, if you kept taking them and taking them, your brain forgot how to be happy on its own. And then you became an addict. And then your liver exploded and you died.

"Whatever happened with David's tables and chairs?" his dad asked. "Are we using them here for the brunch?"

His mother began to cough.

"Hands up," Teddy and his dad said at exactly the same time. It was the family's verbal Heimlich and always seemed to work. His mom complied, reaching for the ceiling.

"Yes," she answered, when her coughs had stopped. "He's bringing them by sometime this week."

"So they're nice?" asked his dad.

"Who's nice?"

"The tables and chairs?"

"Oh yes. Very nice."

"Great," said his dad.

Teddy kept shoveling food into his mouth despite the fact that he was no longer hungry. David Conway. With the tables and chairs. And the pill bottle that had now taken up residence in his mother's red purse.

"Hey, speaking of tables and chairs, your senior friends are coming," his mom said to Teddy.

"Senior friends?"

"Yes, the ones you asked me to invite? From Twilight Manor: Manny, Bonnie, Janet. They're coming to the synagogue and the brunch."

"Who?"

"Your friends?"

"Mom! It's Morty, Beverly and Jackie. What is it with you and names?"

Teddy was pleased to know they were coming, even if the idea of standing on the bimah in front of them chanting Hebrew and then schmoozing them over lox and bagels made him itch all over.

"I don't screw up every name. Like Krystal, for example. She's coming. And her mother. I'm excited to meet her. What's her name again, just so I get it right?"

"Patty," mumbled Teddy.

Patty and his mother were night and day. He did not envision that going well. And his Bubbe was definitely going to have something to say about Patty Platt's hair. Teddy realized, swiping the remaining syrup off his plate with his last square of pancake, that he had never seen Patty Platt in anything but scrubs.

Tonight he was going to their house, however, his first time. Patty and Krystal were making him a birthday dinner. Maybe tonight he would see her without scrubs. He blushed involuntarily. Out of context, that was a very strange thought. In regular clothes, of course is what he meant.

But he did not want to do any of this. He did not want to read from the Torah; he did not want to make a speech to that cavernous room of pew after pew, all the expectant faces he knew and didn't know lined up in rows, all staring at him or, worse, their watches. He did not want to come home and watch his parents stumble through the social graces of hosting, which was something he had seen them do maybe three times in his life. He did not want to speak up about David Conway's pills in his mother's purse. He did not want to ask his father about that string of texts from

T.B., which bothered him still. He did not want to do any of it.

"So you'll be getting a lot of presents at your Bar Mitzvah," said his mom. "And of course there was the phone. But I just wanted to get you a little something extra." She got up from the table and walked to the pantry.

"We," said his dad.

"What?" she asked, returning with a box wrapped in blue and white stars.

"*We* wanted to get you something," he repeated. "You said *I*."

His mother paused. Teddy wanted the earth to open up and swallow him whole.

"Did I? I'm sorry," she said, regaining her composure. "We. Of course." She handed Teddy the present.

"Thanks," he replied, the pancakes settling in his stomach like lead.

He ripped off the paper to reveal a long white box, and then he ripped off its top to reveal a sea of white tissue paper and then dug through the paper to find two very unsatisfying somethings: a light-blue button-down shirt and a navy tie.

"What's this?" he asked.

"For your Bar Mitzvah," his dad explained.

"You have to look nice," his mother added. "You know that. I thought these were nice. Not flashy or stiff, you know? Just nice."

"A tie?" asked Teddy. "Really?"

"Really," said his mother. "It's a big day."

"I'm wearing a tie too," said his dad. "It's kind of fun sometimes, getting all dressed up."

Teddy sighed and set the box on the bench next to him. He did not understand why tying a virtual noose around his neck qualified as dressing up.

"Thanks," he mumbled.

"You're welcome," his parents said in unison, causing both of them to laugh. A laugh! His birthday had been saved by the Gap.

"I'll teach you how to tie it," his dad offered. "Later."

"Okay." Teddy realized this was the perfect segue into something he needed to ask him.

"Hey, Dad, do we still have that tent?"

His mother dropped her fork, and it clanged against the side of her plate and then fell back against her lavender shirt, smearing syrup and scrambled egg particles in its wake as it came to a stop in her lap.

"Shit," she mumbled.

"Uh, yeah, we should. In the garage. Unless, Sylvie, you—"

"I haven't thrown it out," she said, examining the stain, not making eye contact with either of them. "I don't even go in that garage anymore; no one can move, it's so filled with your crap."

"I told you, I'm in the process of selling it," said Paul. "David sent me a text; he's already sold the rowing machine and two of my bikes."

"That's great," said his mother, chugging her water.

This David sure was around a lot, Teddy thought. Maybe his dad knew about the pills all along. Which was even more screwed up. Teddy wanted to go back to being eight, now more than ever. He knew too much. It was enough already.

"I was thinking I want to camp out one night, in the backyard," said Teddy. He was not a good liar, so he kept his eyes on his plate as he stood up to clear the table. He knew from movies that this was a good tactic, to keep moving as a means of distraction.

"Oh, okay."

Teddy knew his father was exchanging a look with his mother behind his back as he carried dishes to the sink, but that was a good thing because that meant they were buying it. Teddy was as outdoorsy as an ice cube. It was a hard sell.

"Can you show me how to set it up?" he asked, coming back to the table to retrieve the empty glasses.

"Sure, no problem. It's not hard. At least I don't think it is. We never actually used it." His dad handed Teddy the now-empty plate where the turkey bacon had been.

"Can we do it now?" asked Teddy.

"Uh, sure. Sylvie, is that okay with you?"

"Sure," she answered. "It's fine. I'll get the rest." She smiled weakly.

"Thanks, Mom," said Teddy, giving her a reluctant hug, just because she looked like she needed it, not because he wanted to.

"You're welcome, honey. Happy birthday. I can't believe you're thirteen. A teenager." She hugged him tightly. "I love you," she said.

"I love you too, Mom." He did love her. He was mad at her, for taking those stupid pills, but he still loved her.

He followed his dad out to the garage. His father pushed a button and the door slid up, the sound of metal scraping metal ominous.

"Sorry for the mess," said his father. "But I'm fixing it. I'm selling most of this stuff."

"Why'd you buy it in the first place?"

"Because I could, I guess."

"Oh."

Teddy thought that anybody with a credit card could technically buy anything they wanted, right? But to buy things just to buy them, and then to never use them, well, that was weird. That was a problem. And even though he had heard his mother yelling at his dad about the money, Teddy thought that was just the tip of the iceberg.

"Anyway, the good news is that I think I know where the tent is," said his dad, pointing to the back left corner.

He and Teddy squeezed their way over to it, facing the cobalt-blue nylon backpack in which it was stored.

"Man, it's been a long time," said his dad. He put his hand on Teddy's shoulder as he sighed. "All right. See, the great thing about this tent is that it's all crammed in here, poles and all. Modern efficiency at its best."

They continued to stare.

"Well, go on," his dad said finally. "If you want to use it, you have to get it out of the garage first."

Teddy grabbed it forcefully, expecting it to be heavy. But it was not, and he lost his footing, almost falling.

"How much did this thing cost?" he asked, straightening himself. "It's as light as air."

"Too much. I thought we would use it more than we did. Or we have. So it's good that you're interested in it. Means it was an investment rather than me being impetuous. For once."

They walked out of the dark and cool garage and into the glaring sun, both wincing in exactly the same way at exactly the same moment of reentry.

"God, it's hot," said his dad. "Let's go over by the side of the house, where it's shaded, or else we'll both be baked potatoes by the time we finish.

"Here, drink some water," said his dad, producing a bottle from somewhere as he lay the bag down in the grass. Teddy hadn't even seen him bring it outside with them, but of course he had. His dad was never without water.

Teddy took a long swig, relishing its chill as his father knelt on the ground and began to empty the backpack. He pulled his notebook from his pocket, flipping quickly to the empty page on which he planned to notate the ins and outs of tent construction. TENT, he scrawled across the top. And then: WATER!!!! He couldn't forget it.

Teddy looked down at the ground, at the pieces of the tent, and decided right then and there that he would not be using it after all. No way. Spread out before him was what may as well have been the components of a brain surgeon's operating room tray.

"Oh God, Dad, never mind," said Teddy.

"No, no, it looks worse than it is, I promise."

His dad sat back on his haunches and searched for the

bottle of water. Grabbing it, he drank. It was just one night under the stars, Teddy thought. A sleeping bag was fine.

"Did we— Was Mom in trouble while we were camping?" Teddy asked quietly.

His father looked up at him.

"I can't remember," Teddy explained. "Like, did you have to take this whole thing apart while she was in labor with Delilah?"

"Oh God, no," said his dad. "Here, sit." He patted the grass next to him.

Teddy hadn't expected to say anything about Delilah, but her name had begged to be spoken, he felt. And so he had.

"We were about to set up, but then your mom didn't feel well. We got the last ferry back."

"I remember now," said Teddy.

An image of his mom's face, twisted slightly in worry and discomfort from behind the glass as he and his father stood outside on the stern of the ferry, the water spraying them as the boat sliced through the waves back to land, came to him. He could sense, even as his mom smiled at him when she realized he was watching her instead of the water, that something was wrong.

"Dad?"

"Yeah?"

"Did the trip make her sick?"

His father turned to face him. He looked right into Teddy's eyes.

"The doctor said no," he answered, dodging the questions.

"But what do you think?" Teddy asked.

"I don't know, T, to be honest. I don't think one day walking in the heat can cause a miscarriage, but on the other hand, if we had been able to get to a doctor sooner, maybe we could have saved her?"

"What does Mom think?" asked Teddy.

"She doesn't know either."

"Why'd we even go on that trip?"

"I wanted to do something nice, just the three of us," said his dad. "That's all. Before the baby came. I just wanted us to have a memory of us as three that would make us all smile." His dad's breath caught, and Teddy looked over at him. He was crying. It had been a long time since Teddy had seen him cry.

"I get it, Dad," said Teddy. He patted his father's sweaty forearm. "Don't blame yourself."

"I don't, and I do," he said. He wiped his eyes and put his arm around Teddy's shoulder. "Thanks, buddy."

Teddy thought of Morty, about the way his wife had died. Death came in all sorts of shapes and sizes. It didn't care who you were or what your circumstances were; it had no interest in fair or unfair. And its repercussions, they stretched into infinity.

"You know, I realize we've never really talked about Delilah like this," his dad said. "I'm sorry about that. In the therapy I did with Mom, right after, the psychologist advised us to not put any thoughts in your head, to let you bring up questions on your own, but maybe that was bad advice."

"It wasn't bad advice," said Teddy. "I mean, you talked about it with me when it happened. I remember that."

He did remember sitting in the hospital waiting room with his father, whose eyes were red, whose voice was shaky.

"Your sister died," he had told Teddy, and the words had rung in his ears. "I'm so sorry."

And he had pulled Teddy close; he could still remember how his father had smelled of sweat and sadness. You wouldn't think that sadness had a smell, but it did. Dank, like the garage, actually, now that Teddy thought about it.

"Maybe we could have talked about it more, you know, since, but I understand."

"Would you like to see somebody now, to talk about things?" his dad asked.

"Maybe. I'll let you know."

They stared at the disassembled tent in the shaded grass. A white butterfly fluttered by, landing on one of the poles.

"Forget about the tent, Dad," said Teddy. "It's more work than I was banking on."

"Are you sure? Really, it just takes some practice. Or I can just set it up for you here, if you want to have Krystal over."

"What?"

"Have Krystal over? In the tent?" His dad cleared his throat. "I assume that's what this is about?"

"Dad! No!" Teddy dug his heel into the ground, dislodging a patch of dark soil underneath. The butterfly flew off.

"There's nothing to be embarrassed about, T. You're growing up. It's normal. Listen, I want to give you this." His father dug in the pocket of his shorts and came out with a square box.

"What the hell is that?" asked Teddy, despite knowing exactly what it was.

"Condoms," his father explained. "Do you know about condoms?"

"Dad, Jesus!"

"Well, do you?"

"Of course I know about condoms."

"Do you know how to use one?"

"Yes." Teddy had a notion—it wasn't rocket science—but he didn't know for sure. But he wasn't going to ask his father to show him, for God's sake.

"Okay. So here. If you're going to have sex, you have to use them. And it's not only pregnancy you should be worried about; it's your own health too. Do you know about STDs?"

"Dad! Enough."

Teddy took the box and shoved it into his own pocket, even though he felt ridiculous. It's not that he hadn't thought about sex with Krystal, he had, but he didn't need his parents involved. Although he did wonder how exactly it worked. Like, he knew, but he also didn't know.

Teddy stood up. "Dad?"

"Yes?" His father looked up at him from his seated position on the grass.

"Who's T.B.?"

"T.B.?" His father's face turned just the slightest bit pink, and Teddy's stomach dropped.

"She's no one. Well, not no one. She's a human being. From my triathlete training group. Why do you ask?"

"Why is she texting you?" Teddy demanded. He was scared of the answer.

"How do you know she texts me?"

"That's not the point, Dad."

His father sighed. "She texts me because she likes me, I guess. But nothing has ever happened, and nothing ever will happen, if that's what you're worried about. I'm not interested."

"Does Mom know about her?"

"No. But only because it's nothing, T. Truly. You have to believe me. I—I suppose if you want to know the truth, and I have no idea why I'm telling my twelve-year-old son—"

"Thirteen, as of today," Teddy reminded him.

"Right, sorry. Thirteen-year-old son, excuse me. The truth is that for a moment, I liked the attention. It's silly, really, but it's the truth."

Teddy eyed him warily, not really believing him.

"I've deleted her from my phone, you know," his dad said. "Want to see?"

"Okay." His father pulled his phone from his pocket, scrolled through his contacts, and sure enough, T.B. had disappeared, just as every disease should.

"Okay," Teddy said again. "Good."

God, how he wanted to tell his father about his mom at that moment, to unload the rest of their baggage, but he could not. Not now. This was enough, to know that his father was his father and not some gross, cheating father like

Martin's, who now lived in a chrome-encrusted condo in Buckhead and had hair implants.

"Do we still have a sleeping bag?" he asked, remembering why they were out in the yard in the first place.

"We have three," said his father. "In the garage, right next to where the tent was."

Teddy looked at his father, still sitting on the grass.

"Do you need help putting it back?" he asked. "The tent, I mean?"

"No, I've got it. It's your birthday."

"Thanks," said Teddy. "Sorry I got so mad, about the condoms. I wasn't prepared for, you know, the big talk."

"It's all right. And I'm sorry you've been worried about those texts. I'm glad you came to me. Please, always. Come to me. Okay?"

Mom has David's oxycodone prescription in a red purse hanging from a hook in the closet, Teddy wanted to say. *Do you know about that?*

Instead he just nodded and made his way through the grass, back to the house.

* * *

"YOU SURE KRYSTAL'S mom is okay with driving you home?" asked his mom, as she idled in their driveway.

Teddy had never been to Krystal's house before. He wasn't sure what he had been expecting, maybe something a little less green. And by green, he meant the actual color of the house. It was painted a faded chartreuse color that reminded Teddy of Slimer from *Ghostbusters*.

"Yes," he answered.

He and his mother both gazed at it. It was small, with a screened-in porch. The paint on its concrete base, a slightly darker green, was flaking off in spots. There were flowers planted alongside it, little bursts of purple and yellow and pink.

Suddenly, two enormous silver foil balloons, a one and a three, floated out of the porch door and bobbed in the early-evening sky. Krystal followed, holding them by their ribbons, smiling broadly. Her bare arms and legs were like Popsicle sticks.

Teddy smiled back and opened his door.

"That's sweet," said his mom. "Please give Krystal and Patty my best." She put her hand on Teddy's arm. "Have a nice time."

"Thanks, Mom." He had asked her to stay in the car.

"Hey, birthday boy! Hey, Sylvie!" yelled Krystal from the steps. His mother waved, backed out of the driveway, and Teddy felt a profound sense of relief. Being around her lately was exhausting, knowing what he knew.

He approached Krystal, feeling shy. She was so pretty. Always so pretty. He blushed, remembering the conversation he had had with his father.

"How are you?" she asked, handing him his balloons.

"Good. I'm a man now, you know," he replied.

"I know, I can tell. You look different," she said.

"I do?"

"No. But you do look handsome."

"Thanks."

They stared at each other for a moment, ready to talk and talk and talk but unsure of where to start in this new environment, with Patty Platt just behind the front door.

"Well, come in, I guess," said Krystal. "My house could, like, fit in your living room, but whatever."

"Krystal," Teddy replied. "Don't be dumb."

"Mom, Teddy's here!" she yelled into the house, holding the door open for him.

Teddy followed her into a small living room. A flat-screen television sat on a chrome stand to his left, and across from it, an L-shaped and lumpy brown leather couch. The wall in front of him was adorned with an array of framed photos, all of Krystal and Patty, and right in the middle: a very large, very gleaming brown wood cross.

"My mom is into Jesus," Krystal explained. "But she's cool with you being Jewish, so don't worry."

Teddy wondered how this fact about Patty Platt had somehow escaped mention in the hundreds of conversations he and Krystal had had. They'd certainly talked about his Jewishness enough.

"Hey, Teddy," said Patty, coming out of the hallway that led to the rest of the house. "Welcome to our humble abode."

She wore a pair of jean shorts and a gray T-shirt with Snoopy and Woodstock emblazoned across its front.

"Thank you for having me, Mrs. Platt."

"Teddy, please. Patty. Didn't we have this conversation before?"

"I'm sorry," said Teddy. "It smells amazing in here," he added. It did. Like fried food and frosting.

"Thank you. I made my famous fried chicken for you. Have to pull out all the stops for the boyfriend, you know."

"Mom!" shrieked Krystal. *The boyfriend,* thought Teddy.

"Now you guys hang out or whatever, let me finish with this mess."

"Come on, Teddy, come see my room," said Krystal. "You can leave your balloons at the table; I'll just tie them to your chair. Here." She took them from him and wound them around the armrest at the head of the table.

He followed her down the hall, the kitchen to his left with Patty Platt inside and first a small, pink-tiled bathroom and then Krystal's room on the right. Five feet from his face was another door, one that led to Patty's room, he assumed.

Teddy thought of his own house, the vastness of it, all the space they never even used, and felt ashamed.

Inside Krystal's room was a twin bed covered in various shades of purple, pushed against the far wall under a window shuttered with fuchsia blinds. Along the wall was such a vast collection of stuffed animals, there was barely any room to sit on the bed, let alone sleep in it, and all with giant eyes. Eyes as big as plates, all staring at him.

"I'm really into Beanie Boos," said Krystal.

"Into what?"

"Beanie Boos. These guys." She gestured toward the bed.

"I can see that," said Teddy, surprised.

Krystal came off as so tough, and yet here she was with

an army of stuffed animals to protect her in a room that reminded him of melted crayons. There was a turquoise desk and chair against the other wall, and a light-pink faux-fur rug across the scuffed wood floor. It was a lot of room for such a small space. But then again, Teddy thought, Krystal was a lot of personality for such a small person.

"Sit with me," she said, making room on the bed for them both.

"So how's your day been?" she asked, her eyelashes shellacked in their signature purple. Teddy was suddenly annoyed, filled with an urge to scrub her face and redecorate her room.

"Okay," he mumbled.

"Your parents treat you to lunch at some fancy restaurant or something? Give you a car?"

"Give me a car, what are you even talking about?" asked Teddy.

"I see you judging my Beanie Boos. Don't be a snob, Richie Rich."

"Richie Rich?"

"You're being a jerk. You should see your face, all scrunched up like something smells in here," said Krystal.

"It's not," Teddy countered, although he guessed it probably was. "Okay, but that's a lot of Beanie Boos looking at us. I mean, a lot. And their eyes are so, you know, big." They both turned their heads slightly to take in the crowd.

"I can turn them all around, to face the wall," Krystal offered, her voice softening.

"That would take hours," said Teddy. She reached out to

shove him playfully in what would have been his biceps, if he had one. Teddy tightened it reflexively anyway.

"Sorry if I'm coming off as rude," he said, grabbing her hand as it fell away. "It's been a weird day, but that's not your fault. And I'm really glad to be here. I can't believe your mom made fried chicken. And that you got me those cool balloons. Thank you."

Krystal moved closer to him.

"Sorry I called you Richie Rich. I didn't mean it. What was weird about today? Your mom?"

"No, not her so much." He took an animal from the pile, an iridescent violet-and-emerald dragon with folded wings, and squeezed its stomach gently.

"You know why I'm so into movies?" he asked her.

"The same reason I'm into these guys," she replied. "They make you feel safe."

Teddy was startled by the accuracy of Krystal's answer.

"You're an emotional savant," he said. "Like Rain Man or something."

"Who's Rain Man?"

"It doesn't matter." He squeezed her hand. "But, yeah. Movies make me feel safe."

"Safe from what?"

"Sadness, I guess. After Delilah died, I watched them all the time. My parents, they were both so sad." Teddy spoke quickly. He just wanted to get it out.

"And what about you? Were you sad?" asked Krystal.

"Well, I was nine. I was sad that I wasn't going to have a sister. I was worried about my parents, who cried all the time. But I was also alone. A lot. So movies became my babysitter."

"Didn't your parents talk to you about what had happened?" asked Krystal.

"A little. But mostly I just watched movies, and that was enough. Or it was at the time, anyway. Lately, though, with my mom and the pills and my Bar Mitzvah coming up, I don't know. I'm thinking about her death, my family, all of it. A lot more. And today, my dad and I talked about it. About Delilah."

"How was that?" asked Krystal.

"It was kind of nice," said Teddy. "Until my dad went off on a tangent. But that's another story. But it got me thinking about my mom. I mean, sure, this happened to all of us emotionally, but physically, it happened to her."

"Something like that is sure to screw you up," said Krystal.

"Exactly," said Teddy. "Did you know that fetal DNA becomes part of the mother? It's crazy."

"What's so crazy about it? Women, like, grow human beings," said Krystal.

"Right. I guess I never understood the scope of the feat before."

"Men," said Krystal.

"Anyway. I have a lot more sympathy for my mom now than I did."

"Uh-oh."

"What?"

"You're not going to let her keep taking those pills, are you? Those pills are not fixing her," said Krystal.

"I think I'm going to back off," said Teddy. "It's getting too complicated for me."

"What's complicated about it? She's taking drugs that aren't hers. What's happening to her stash? You checking?" Teddy grabbed a stuffed flamingo from the pile and squeezed its neck.

"Hey, take it easy!" Krystal snatched it back. "The pills are gone, aren't they? She took 'em all?"

"They're not gone," said Teddy. "There's a new bottle."

"A new bottle?" Krystal shook her head. "How do you know it's new?"

"It's someone else's prescription. Not my dad's. His friend's."

Teddy stared down into the olive-green fabric of his lap. He did not want to be spending his birthday discussing this with his girlfriend in a pile of alien animals; it was so hot in this room, and the smell of oil from the chicken frying in the kitchen made his stomach turn.

"Teddy," said Krystal quietly. "This is bad."

"I know."

"You have to—"

"I know! I know what I have to do, I know what it looks like and probably is. I know, okay!" yelled Teddy.

He did not like Krystal looking at him like that, her eyes wide with sympathy, her mouth in a tight line. He wished he had never told her. Why had he told her?

"Guys! Dinner's ready!" Patty Platt hollered.

Krystal got up from the bed. Teddy touched the flamingo again, his hand lingering on its giant head for a moment, and then he got up too.

CHAPTER TWENTY-THREE

SYLVIE

If Todd Weiner were an animal, he would be an anteater, Sylvie thought for not the first time.

He had a very long and narrow nose, small eyes, and ears so far back on his head that they were practically touching. He also had generous straight black bangs that were pushed to the side by what Sylvie could tell was some sort of hair product, but nevertheless an escaped clump always hung limply across his forehead.

He walked briskly, his shoulders rounded, his too-long-for-his-short-torso arms swinging slightly, as though they were propelling him through the hallways.

How advertising and branding were different, Sylvie still didn't know, but the latter apparently was more of a bait for millennial business, and that's what the Weenie, better known as Todd to those who didn't work for him, was. A millennial branding genius.

As Sylvie made her way through the sun-drenched office to her cubicle, she broke into a very serious flop sweat. So much so that she was forced to stop mid-stride and remove her white linen blazer. Winston, their IT guy, looked around the rectangle of his computer screen and smiled at her.

"Hot as hell in here, right?" he said.

"It's like the surface of the sun," Sylvie replied.

She folded her jacket neatly and draped it over her arm. Sylvie had just taken her pill in the parking lot; she had waited until the last possible second since she had to conserve her supply. She hadn't planned on it, but then the Weenie had sent her an email last night, requesting a meeting with her first thing. Really, she'd had no choice. She certainly couldn't endure it sober.

She glanced at her watch and picked up her pace. The Weenie did not take kindly to tardiness.

"Amanda?" Even as the waves of relaxation began to course through Sylvie's system, although they had become less pronounced as of late and were more like ripples, Sylvie panicked. Now her chest was sweating too; she could feel the narrow rivulets streaming into the cups of her bra. "You're back already?"

Sylvie had not seen Amanda since she'd emerged from her shower, sitting on her couch in a stoned daze as her baby slept, pretending to be a kind and responsible coworker instead of what she really was: a pill-popping thief.

"I only had six weeks, remember?" Amanda replied, not really looking up from her computer screen.

"That's ridiculous," said Sylvie.

"Tell me about it." She still wasn't making eye contact with Sylvie, which made her very, very nervous.

"How's the baby?" asked Sylvie, hoping to lighten the conversation. She had forgotten her name.

"Good." Amanda continued to type.

"Do you have a photo?" asked Sylvie, desperately hoping that she sounded like she cared.

She had two minutes before her meeting with the Weenie. Todd. She had to remember to call him Todd to his face.

"Uh, yeah," said Amanda. Finally, she met Sylvie's gaze. But she did not smile. She pulled out her phone, and a picture of the baby popped up.

"Oh, she's beautiful," Sylvie dutifully cooed, even though the baby was all forehead. "It's good to have you back, Amanda. You look great, by the way."

She did, it was true, Sylvie noticed with jealousy. All the weight had melted off her since Sylvie had seen her last; she looked exactly like her old, pre-baby self, except with eye bags. Sylvie was still carrying her weight, three years later, from the birth of a baby who didn't exist. A lump rose in her throat as big as a bowling ball. Sylvie choked it down.

"Thanks." Amanda returned to her typing.

She knew, Sylvie realized. Amanda knew what she had done. Shit.

Sylvie draped her jacket over her desk chair and hustled to the Wee—no, Todd's—office.

Todd's assistant, Marlena, sat just outside Todd's office. She was online shopping.

"Hi, Marlena," said Sylvie.

"Oh, hey, Sylvie. You scared me."

"Big sale?" Sylvie pointed at the screen.

"I don't know what you're talking about," Marlena replied, shutting the window down.

"Okay," said Sylvie.

"I'll let him know you're here."

"Cool."

Sylvie's shirt was now sticking to her, and she was reminded of the nights after Delilah, when she woke up soaked from head to toe, as though she had showered when she had not; her body expelling all the maternal hormones gone to waste.

"He's ready for you," said Marlena, returning.

"Marlena," said Sylvie through what felt like plastic wrap coated in Elmer's Glue. "Could I possibly get a glass of water?"

"I wish. Budget cutbacks. They took our water cooler away."

"What? When?"

"Last night."

"Jesus. Okay then, guess I'll make it work." She braced herself, noting with relief a familiar ripple of chemically induced relaxation, and walked in.

"Sylvie, hi," said Todd, getting up from behind his massive desk.

"Hi, Todd," she replied, summoning all the false cheer she could muster. They hugged awkwardly, only their collarbones touching, each of them patting the other exactly three times on the back.

"So, how are you?" he asked, returning to his chair.

"Good, good," said Sylvie, settling down into the swamp of her lower half as she sat down across from him.

"That's great," said Todd.

He leaned forward and put his elbows on his desk, forming a triangle with the thumbs and forefingers of both hands. He rested his chin on his thumbs, and Sylvie knew, much to her horror, what was coming next. Even before he uttered the words, she knew.

"So, Sylvie, we've had a real come-to-Jesus moment with our budget. As you and everyone else knows, the world is basically on the brink of apocalypse, and the economy, at least for us, is unfortunately no different."

"You're not—"

"I'm so sorry, Sylvie, but I'm afraid I am. You're at the top of the food chain, salary-speaking, and we just can't afford you anymore. Not if we want to meet our bottom line."

He unfolded his finger triangle and placed his hands on the desk, facing her with what Sylvie was sure he considered his empathic smile, one he had probably practiced in front of his bathroom mirror that morning.

"Are you seriously trying to tell me that eradicating my salary is going to keep this company afloat? Let's get real here, Todd. Let's fucking get real."

"Okay, Sylvie, I can understand that you're upset, but there's no need for foul language."

"Then be real, you ass. I'm not buying this salary bullshit for one second."

Sylvie was terrified at the prospect of not having a job, with

Paul's debt and their lifestyle, plus who knew how long it would take her old ass to get hired anywhere else. But she was also filled with—and this was likely the drugs talking—a kind of unexpected elation. It was the same elation she had felt at that stupid PTA meeting. Freedom to say exactly what she was thinking, hurt feelings be damned. And this was even better because the Weenie had no feelings! She had nothing to lose.

"You're firing me because you can and because I'm too much of a threat for you to keep around," she declared.

"A threat?"

"Yes, I'm smarter than you. I'm smarter, and I'm quicker on my feet, and every great idea you come up with and claim as your own has come out of my mouth first. That's the truth."

"No," said Todd. "I'm firing you because you hate being here, because you are disrespectful and rude to me and because, quite frankly, your work sucks and has sucked for a long time. That, on top of your exorbitant salary, is why I'm firing you."

"You little shit," said Sylvie.

Thankfully, her anger had magically released her salivary glands and her mouth had resumed its normal function. She hated him—he was indeed a bona fide shit—but he was also, for once, right.

"Also—and this will remain just between us because I'm kind enough to do you and your reputation a solid—Amanda told me about you swiping her pills. She doesn't feel safe working with you, and frankly, neither do I," he said.

"Get out of here," she muttered. "That's ridiculous. I did no such thing."

"Sylvie."

"Todd."

"Look, I don't want to get into it. I trust her word. Plus, you've been suspiciously, shall we say, wobbly around the office."

"What are you talking about?" asked Sylvie.

"The falls?"

"Once!" Sylvie shrieked. "I fell once! And I went over there to see her baby. Do you know how hard that was for me? Do you even remember what happened to me? That I lost my own baby three years ago?"

"I'm sorry for your loss," he said.

It took every fiber of Sylvie's self-control not to hurdle his desk and choke him to death.

"I went over there to be kind. I didn't touch her fucking pills."

"Sylvie. I think this discussion is over. It is what it is. You are no longer needed here."

"You better be giving me some severance. I've worked here for eight years."

"I can give you two weeks."

"Two weeks? Are you insane?"

"Thank you for your time here, Sylvie. We have very much appreciated your efforts and contribution to the team. Terry from Human Resources will be in touch. And we've taken the liberty of clearing out your desk. Marlena has your things outside for you."

"Marlena knew this was happening? Do you know that bitch online shops all day long? Do you?"

Todd stood up as if to escort her out.

"Don't you even think about muscling me out the door, Weenie. Everyone calls you that, you know. The Weenie. There is not one person here who thinks you're qualified for anything but ordering Danish and bagels for morning meetings. Not one."

She stood up and turned briskly toward the door, almost tripping over her feet in the process.

Outside, Marlena held a box of her things in her arms, which Sylvie promptly snatched.

"That was shitty," Sylvie told her. "You couldn't even give me so much as a warning? Where's the sisterhood?"

Marlena shrugged.

"And let me tell you something else," said Sylvie. "All of your clothes are two sizes too small."

Sylvie clomped down the hallway, her high long gone. She passed Amanda, who was cowering in her cubicle.

"I didn't steal your fucking pills, you idiot," Sylvie lied.

"Give me a break."

"I had the runs."

"What you have is a problem."

"And what's this about not feeling safe? I mean, honestly, Amanda."

"What? You stole from me. I don't feel safe."

"You know what?" said Sylvie.

"What?"

"Your kid is ugly."

And with that, Sylvie walked out the door.

CHAPTER TWENTY-FOUR

PAUL

Paul sat on his exercise bike in the driveway, the sun practically setting him on fire. David's truck came up the driveway, and for a moment, Paul considered being run over and how that wouldn't be the worst thing. But with his luck, he would probably survive and be a paraplegic, which would just be terrible.

Paul stared at the hot asphalt beneath him. As a bead of sweat rolled down his nose and landed with a splat, he swore he heard it sizzle. He was having all sorts of thoughts lately, morbid thoughts, and he didn't like it. He knew he was depressed, but a middle-aged married couple with matching Prozac prescriptions was too much of a cliché for him to bear. Exercise should do the trick, he had reasoned. Except it wasn't.

"David!" yelled Paul. David waved from behind the glass of his windshield before turning off the engine.

"Hey, man," said Paul, getting off the bike. "This is a nice surprise. What's up? Everything okay?"

"Oh yeah, I'm just dropping off the tables and chairs." David looked just to the left of Paul's gaze, not directly into it. "I didn't think you'd be around, was just gonna take the equipment I sold for you to free up some space and leave 'em in the garage."

"The stationary bikes and the rowing machine?" asked Paul.

"Yep," answered David. "You've got around six hundred and fifty bucks coming to you."

"That's all? I easily spent fifteen hundred on those, all told." Paul was annoyed.

"Yeah, but once the guy takes his cut and I take my cut, that's what's up."

"Your cut?"

"I can't do this totally for free, man, come on," said David. He still wasn't looking at Paul.

"Fine," said Paul. Who was he to complain? It wasn't like he had taken any initiative in the matter other than suggesting it to David. "You sure you're okay?"

"I'm fine, man," said David, finally looking him in the eye. But he didn't sound fine; he sounded angry.

"Okay, okay. Sorry." Paul walked over to the garage and pressed the button that opened its doors. "Thanks a lot for letting us borrow these. On the one hand, I'm relieved that we don't have to go through the bullshit of some giant, expensive Bar Mitzvah party, but on the other, well, now I have to have everybody at the house. In my space. Not my specialty."

"Yeah, I'm sure," said David. He motioned toward the truck bed. "You want to help me get them out and the machines in? As long as you're here?"

"Of course." Paul followed David around to the back of the trunk.

"What's with the bike in the driveway?" asked David. "It's a hundred degrees out." David hoisted himself up into his truck bed, his skinny calves like broom handles poking out of his rather enormous and blindingly white Nikes.

"I'm an idiot," confessed Paul, taking a table from him. "I thought it would up the ante on my workout, but I'm exhausted. I just can't get my groove back lately."

"Oh yeah?" David hopped down with two tables of his own, and they walked together to the garage. "I'm sorry to hear that."

"Haven't seen you in a minute," said Paul.

"I'm just busy," said David, resting his tables against the outside of the garage.

"What, the Riley house is practically finished," said Paul.

"Yeah, that's been all me, by the way," said David. "The other guys on the team are a bunch of lazy asses."

"Really? Why didn't you tell me?" asked Paul, following him back to the truck for their next round.

"Not that big a deal. I'm telling you now." They passed the next sweltering twenty minutes in silence, emptying the truck bed.

"Is that it?" Paul asked, when the bed was empty.

"That's it," said David. "Now, let's get the machines I need and load 'em up." He wiped his brow with his forearm. Paul didn't know if he could do it. His muscles were quivering, they'd been out of use for so long.

"Could we take a little break?" he asked David, embarrassed.

"Nah, we have to keep it moving. It's only three things." Paul looked at him beseechingly. "We stop now, we're never getting started again. Trust me. Come on, man, I'll do most of the lifting."

Paul nodded, fighting the urge to collapse onto the lawn.

First, they had to stack the boxes up and out of the way. There were so many of them. A food scale, a people scale, riding gloves, protein powders, a blender as big as Teddy's head, Speedos on sale, goggles, spandex everything, four different pairs of the same sneaker; it went on and on, Paul's browsing history come to life. Click, click, buy and then he tracked the package maniacally: two more days, today! And then the thing would arrive on his doorstep, he would drag it into the basement away from Sylvie's prying eyes like a lion with its kill, rip open the box and be satisfied for exactly ten minutes.

"Rowing machine first," said David, when a path had been cleared. Paul nodded. "Count of three. One, two, three," and they were carrying it, Paul's back on fire, his ankle throbbing, sweat dripping from every pore. The same with a different stationary bike, and finally, mercifully, the last thing of all the things, for the moment at least, a backup trail bike for the trail bike Paul already had.

David closed the bed of the truck and they both leaned against it, panting. Paul more so than David, but he was relieved to notice that yes, David was panting too.

"You want a beer?" Paul asked.

"I can't," said David. "Gotta take off."

"Where to? Come on, one beer."

"I really can't."

"Listen, I don't want to seem out of line here, but are you . . ."

"Am I what?" asked David.

"You're not, with the pills again—"

"For fuck's sake, Paul. No. And you've got a lot of nerve talking to me about pills. Mr. Shopaholic."

"Okay. I guess I deserve that," said Paul. "I didn't mean to offend you. I just think you're acting a little strangely with me today, that's all."

"Sylvie came sniffin' around for pills," David blurted out.

"What?" Paul didn't want to know what David meant, and yet he knew exactly what he meant, and despite the heat, he suddenly felt cold.

"My oxys."

"What the hell are you talking about?"

"The other day when she came for the stuff, she asked me for some pills. I didn't want to tell you, but how can I not tell you, you know?"

"I need to sit down," said Paul. "Will you come inside with me and sit down?"

"Okay," answered David.

Paul walked slowly; he was seeing spots, whether from the onset of heatstroke or shock that wasn't exactly shock—it was more like *of course that's what Sylvie has been up to, you idiot*—he wasn't sure.

"I'm a little bit confused," said Paul, taking two beers from the refrigerator and handing one to David.

"I shouldn't, man," said David.

"Drink the fucking beer," said Paul.

"Okay."

"She told me she was on Prozac," said Paul, when they were both sitting at the table and he had taken a long swig from his green glass bottle.

"I highly doubt that," said David.

"So what the hell happened?" asked Paul, although he knew David had no answer.

"Whatever happened to the Oxys your doctor prescribed you, when you broke your ankle?"

"I didn't want anything to do with them. I told her to throw them out."

"And did you see her throw them out?" asked David.

"What am I, a fucking detective? No, I didn't see her throw them out. But she's never messed with pills before, or any drugs, for that matter. Why wouldn't I trust her to throw them out?"

Paul put his head in his hands and closed his eyes and thought. Ever since he had come home from the hospital, ever since he had given his wife the task of disposing of the pills he had no interest in taking, she had been different. There was the Yahrzeit candle, for one. The talking about Delilah for two, a giant egg of three-year silence just cracked open like it was no big deal. Sylvie's psychobabble about honesty. Her acceptance of Teddy's Bar Mitzvah terms. And the spaciness that had replaced her resentment like a thief in the night. A thief Paul had appreciated. Her resentment of him was an exhausting emotion to go up against each morning, like climbing Machu Picchu in flip-flops.

God, he was so stupid. Prozac, for Christ's sake. He sat up.

"Did you give them to her? The pills?" he asked David.

"I did. And I'm sorry. But she was desperate. And she swore to me that she just had to get through the Bar Mitzvah and then she'd get some help. She swore." David shrugged. "I should know better, but I believed her. Except now I don't."

"You don't?"

"No. I think she needs help. I know these pills. When you get to the point where you need one to get through the day, the point where you're begging people you barely know for some, you're in trouble. This Bar Mitzvah business is a load of shit. There will always be Bar Mitzvahs if you're an addict, you hear what I'm saying?"

"I hear what you're saying," said Paul. "I just can't believe you gave them to her."

But he wasn't mad at David. None of this was his fault.

He looked at David, and David opened his mouth to say something else, but then promptly closed it again.

"What?"

"Nothing," said David. "I'm sorry I gave them to her. And I'm sorry I'm telling you like this. I know you have a lot on your plate."

"I don't have a thing on my plate," said Paul.

"You depressed?" asked David.

"Yeah, I think so. I think that's about right."

They both sat on the couch, the hum of the air conditioner the only sound in the otherwise empty house. Outside, the sky began to darken as a summer thunderstorm approached.

"I should get going," said David.

"Okay."

David stood up. "I love you, man. I want you to know that," he told Paul. There were tears in his eyes.

"David, it's okay, really," said Paul, standing up too. He put his hand on David's shoulder, a sign of solidarity. "I'm glad you told me. I'll handle it. It's not your fault." He paused. "But can you please get your ass back into rehab? You're worth more than these stupid pills, you really are. You have to learn that. Like, truly learn that."

"Okay."

"Okay like okay, or okay like whatever?" asked Paul.

"Little bit of both," said David. "But I hear you."

"I'll see you," said Paul, as David walked back toward the French doors leading to the deck.

As he opened them, the front door opened at exactly the same moment. It was uncanny, the timing. Bracing himself, Paul turned. But it was Teddy. Thank God, it was Teddy. He could not face his wife yet.

"Hey, Dad," Teddy said, making a beeline for the kitchen.

"Hey."

Thunder cracked outside, and then moments later a bolt of lightning lit up the sky. Rain began to fall. Softly for a moment and then, in sheets, beating down on the hot earth mercilessly as David backed his truck out of the driveway.

"Your bike is going to get ruined," said Teddy, standing at the sink and staring out the window. He crunched into the red apple he had just washed.

They both watched the bike being pummeled by the relentless rain, out there alone on the driveway.

CHAPTER TWENTY-FIVE

TEDDY

Teddy looked at the clock on his mother's car's dashboard. It was 3:33. Make a wish, he thought, and his wish was that this whole stupid Bar Mitzvah would just be swallowed by a sinkhole.

"Mom, where the fuck are you?" Teddy's mom barked into the air, the magic of Bluetooth connecting her to his grandparents, her parents. He glanced over at her. Her lips were pulled back, her teeth bared like a rabid wolf. They had been circling the airport for near thirty minutes, combing Zone Three because that's where his grandmother, his Bubbe, claimed they were.

"Oh, you know what? We're in Zone Six. Not Zone Three."

Sylvie looked over at Teddy and shook her head in disbelief. Then she pounded her fist against the wheel and hung up.

"I'm not going to be able to do this," she said, looking straight ahead. "They drive me absolutely fucking nuts."

"So don't do it," said Teddy. "I don't know why we're having this stupid Bar Mitzvah anyway. Everyone hates everyone else, and I couldn't care less."

Plus, you're on drugs, Dad's miserable and getting texts from girls named after diseases and I'm fighting with the only girlfriend I'll probably ever have. He really missed Krystal. It had been three days since they'd spoken, since the delicious but awkward dinner at her house, when she wouldn't even walk him out.

"You know what, get out," said his mother. She screeched over to the curb, cars she cut off in the process blaring in protest. "I've had enough of your attitude. This is Zone Six, where your idiot grandparents supposedly are. Find them and bring them to the curb. That is, if it's not too much for you. I wouldn't want to put you out."

She reached across Teddy and opened his door, her eyes as angry as he had ever seen them. He supposed she had not taken a pill today. He also supposed that he was kind of being an asshole. He got out.

He could hear his grandmother squawking from yards away, something about her bag. His mom couldn't stand his Bubbe's designer luggage.

"She treats each piece like a goddamn newborn," she had said on the drive over, gearing herself up to be annoyed.

"Bubbe?" he called out into the crowd.

It had been a few years since he had seen his grandparents;

they had visited when Delilah had died, and then he and his mother had flown to New Jersey to visit them a year or so later, but save for the occasional FaceTime and birthday or Chanukah card, it was radio silence. Teddy had not thought he cared, but seeing them now in person, from a distance even, he realized he was angry.

But then his Bubbe turned, her comically stretched face breaking into a smile that did not move a muscle of it, her dark hair shellacked into a bob, her nails a deep, dark red and her wrists adorned with gold and diamond bangles that shone in the afternoon sun, and Teddy's anger subsided. She was a character, his Bubbe, and she made the best matzoh ball soup and always, always told him he was the most gorgeous boy in the whole wide world. She was all right.

"The most gorgeous boy—no, the most gorgeous *man*—in the whole wide world!" she shrieked, causing the soon-to-be passengers rolling their bags through the revolving doors to stop in their tracks, the weary just-traveled to crack smiles.

Behind her, his grandfather stood, tall and thin, a wry smile of his own playing across his lips. His bald head shone in the same sun, his eyebrows as expansive as his mother's, although far less groomed. He was wearing his usual uniform of blue button-down and flat-front khakis, a gold Rolex on his remarkably hairy wrist and brown loafers on his feet.

Before he knew what his feet were doing, Teddy was running to them, as though he were five and not thirteen, longing to be enveloped in the heady scent of honey and vanilla that was his Bubbe.

"Let me look at you," she cooed. "Such a face," she exclaimed with delight. "Max, have you ever seen such a handsome face?"

His grandfather came closer and palmed Teddy's chin, lifting it up so he could peer into his eyes.

"Never," he agreed.

"Mom's on the warpath," said Teddy. "Let's move to the curb." He took the handle of his Bubbe's suitcase and began rolling it behind him.

"Careful!" she yelled. "That luggage costs more than you have any right to know!"

And then, there was his mother, out of the car in a flash of malcontent, no hellos to his grandparents, nothing but huffs and sighs as she loaded their things into the trunk and ushered them into their seats. Once back behind the wheel, after she had guided them out of the maze of cars, she finally spoke.

"Zone Six is not Zone Three, Mom. You almost got us killed," said Sylvie.

"I'm sorry," his Bubbe replied. "It's nice to see you too."

"Mom, that's not what I meant," his mother said with a sigh. "It's just, like, how hard is it to read a sign correctly?"

"Hey, Sylvie, give it a rest, okay?" said his Zadie. "We said we were sorry. Traveling is not so easy for us now; we're not as young as we used to be."

"Fine," said Sylvie. "I'm sorry. I'm being a bitch. I'm just stressed out about the Bar Mitzvah, I guess. Sorry."

"That's okay, Sylvie," said his Bubbe, reaching forward over the seat to squeeze his mother's shoulder with her bejeweled hand.

Her veins rose like skinny green snakes from her sun-spotted skin. It was funny what you could do to a face to hide your age, but your hands always told the truth, Teddy thought. He looked down at his own, which were folded in his lap, as taut and smooth as gloves.

"God, it's hot here," said his Zadie. "I've been *schvitzing* like a *schmendrick* since I got off the plane." Teddy pulled his notebook out of his back pocket to copy down his grandfather's Yiddish. It was the most wonderfully weird language he had ever heard, and he only heard it from them and, very occasionally, his mother.

"It's definitely hot," his mother agreed.

"I hope the synagogue is air-conditioned," said his Bubbe.

"Of course it's air-conditioned, Mom. Where do you think we are?" Sylvie snapped back.

"Oh, Teddy, I can't wait to see you on the bimah," his Bubbe said. "You'll wear a tie and jacket, yes?"

"I dunno," Teddy mumbled.

"Yes you do," said his mother. "A tie. No jacket."

"No jacket?" asked his Zadie. "For a Bar Mitzvah?"

"Dad, leave it alone."

Teddy stared out the window at the hot sun baking the asphalt of the road, the people crammed into their cars with their windows rolled up, blasted by a steady stream of frosty air inside. Everyone looked miserable, he thought, as he passed a man digging so far into his nostril it was a wonder he didn't run straight off the road.

"The yard looks nice," his Bubbe said, as they pulled up the driveway at last. "You ready for Saturday?" she asked.

"Ready as I'll ever be," answered Sylvie.

"Well, we'll stay with you tonight and tomorrow, but then we'll head out to our Air Beebee to give you some space," said his Bubbe proudly.

"Airbnb, Mom, not Air Beebee," said his mother.

"Potato, potahto."

"And thank you, for that," his mother added. "It's going to be an absolute shit show here once we start setting up for the brunch. I wish Paul's parents had the same sense of—"

"Hey, isn't that Granny and Pop's car?" asked Teddy as they pulled up.

"What!" his mother shrieked. "What in the sam fuck!"

"Sylvie, really, watch your language," said his Zadie as they idled next to their maroon sedan.

"But what are they doing here?" asked his mother, seething. "They're not supposed to be here until Friday! I'm going to kill Paul."

Everyone was silent in the car for a moment as they watched his mother process this information. This was not going to be good. Not at all.

"Let's just go inside and see what's what, shall we?" asked his Bubbe. "Even though we know what's what. Really, the nerve of them. We never get to see our grandson; you would think they could at least back off for two days," she mumbled under her breath. *But you never visit,* Teddy thought. *You could, but you don't.*

Out they all tumbled, his Zadie taking the bags from the trunk and handing his, a beat-up, proper suitcase instead of the pristine, patterned and oiled small vehicle his grandmother claimed, to Teddy.

"Hi," said Teddy's father, opening the door. Sylvie stormed past him and into the house.

Teddy wished Krystal would appear. He needed to see her, to hold her hand, to absorb her as defense against the passive-aggressive hysteria that was the hallmark of the few times in his life his parents' families had gotten together. And all for what? For this Bar Mitzvah he didn't even care about. He was angry again.

"Hello, Sylvie," said his Granny, standing behind the marble island over a bowl of something white and gelatinous. "I brought French onion dip and some chips!" she offered cheerily.

"Teddy, look at you, all grown up," she said. "I can't believe it."

She shuffled clumsily over to him, clad in turquoise Bermuda shorts and a fuchsia T-shirt with a bedazzled parrot woven into its fabric, its sleeves cuffed. Her short brown hair was frosted and hair-sprayed into place, both sets of nails French manicured.

Teddy loved his Granny too, this polar opposite of his Bubbe. She let him eat Cheetos and made banana pudding, the kind with Nilla Wafers rimming the circumference of the bowl like synchronized swimmers on the precipice of a plunge.

"Hi, Mary," said Sylvie. She put her purse down on the counter, his other grandparents standing awkwardly behind her, like penguins at the zoo. "I'm sorry, I didn't realize you were arriving today." Teddy saw her glare at his father.

"Oh, I'm sorry, I asked Paul if it was all right, and he assured us that it was," said his Granny. She stood, her arms by her sides.

"Paul? You never mentioned this to me," said Sylvie.

"I didn't?" His dad threw up his hands. "I'm sorry if it slipped my mind. Barbara. Max. Good to see you. Let me take your bags to your room for you."

"Careful with—" said his Bubbe.

"Your bag," finished his father. "I know, I know."

"Well, hello, Mary," said his Zadie. "You're looking well. And Paul Senior, is he here too?"

"Oh yes, just comatose in front of the television, as per usual," said Mary.

"Hey, Sylvie," said a slightly familiar voice from the living room. Moments later, his aunt Gloria had joined them. "Guess it's a real party now, huh, Teddy?" she asked.

"I guess so," Teddy replied.

He had not seen his aunt in years, even though she lived with his grandparents. She was thirty-nine, recently divorced for the second time and a perennially unemployed nail technician. When Teddy had overheard his father expressing displeasure at the fact that she had once again moved into her childhood room, his Granny had replied, *What's the big deal? It's not like she takes up any room.* And she was right. His aunt Gloria was as thin as a needle. Teddy had never seen her eat. What he had seen her do, however, was smoke. A lot. And that's where she was headed now, her pack in hand.

"I hope you don't mind, Sylvie, I'm using one of your mugs as an ashtray," she announced to Teddy's mother as she passed by her.

"My mugs?" Sylvie was irate.

"Nothing a good run through the dishwasher won't fix," Gloria replied. "By the way, you're looking thin, girl. Good for you."

His mother blushed. Her jaw relaxed. "Oh. Thank you."

"I was going to say the same thing," said his Bubbe.

"Let's have some of that dip, shall we?" declared his Zadie, moving toward the bowl.

"Really, Max, your cholesterol," Teddy heard his Bubbe murmur to him.

"When in Rome," he murmured back.

"I'm just going to run upstairs to freshen up," said his mother. "I need a minute." His father was avoiding her gaze. As she took the stairs, Teddy watched her closely. He knew exactly where she was headed. To the red purse in her closet. It was now or never. He followed her.

He found her in the closet, just as he had suspected, and his heart felt like it might burst from disappointment and fear. Disappointment that Krystal had been right and fear because now he had to do something about it. It shouldn't be this way, a thirteen-year-old having to parent his parent, but here he was, standing silently behind his mother in her closet as she dug for her fix. He watched her pull out the orange bottle in the dimness; she hadn't even bothered to turn on the light.

"Mom," he said quietly.

She unscrewed the cap, her back still to him. She hadn't heard his voice.

"Mom," he said again. This time louder.

She shoved the bottle into her right front pocket quickly, its white top in her left, before turning around.

"Jesus Christ, Teddy, you scared me!"

She looked weird, like a marionette puppet whose mouth was being manipulated by an unseen source. Teddy felt so many emotions at once—sadness, anger, fright, pity—that he thought he might disappear into thin air. Yet still he stood.

"Mom. I know about you and these pills," he said.

"Teddy, what are you talking about?" she had the gall to ask, with the bottle bulging out of her pocket.

"Cut it out, Mom," he said, and his voice broke. Goddamnit, he was crying. That had not been part of his plan.

"Teddy," she said, in the voice he knew as that of his real mom, not this weird, lying drug mom. The mom before Delilah, even. And of course, that made him cry harder.

She reached around behind him and closed the door to her closet before pulling him to her in the pitch-black darkness.

"Oh, T," she said. "Shit. Here, let me turn on the light." She did, and there they were again. "Let's sit," she said. She pulled the bottle and its top out of her pockets and stood them up on the floor beside her as they faced each other, cross-legged.

"Mom, why are you doing this?" asked Teddy.

"I don't know," she answered. "Because they make me feel good and I haven't felt good in a really long time?" She put her head in her hands. "Oh my God, what a nightmare. Here

I am, telling my son that drugs make you feel good. This is really the bottom. Like, this is it. Teddy." She looked at him. "I am so sorry. How did you—"

"I was in your closet for some reason, I don't even remember why," said Teddy. "The bag fell, and when I picked it up, I heard the pills rattle. I read the label. And then I kept checking, every week or so, to see if the pills were disappearing. And they were. And then there were more from David, Dad's friend." Teddy sighed. "What the hell, Mom?"

"What the hell, indeed. Listen, these pills are horrible, okay? I'm not going to lie to you about facts I'm sure you already know. I took one of your father's on a whim, and I haven't looked back. And it's a problem, okay?" She reached forward and grabbed his hand. "But it's a temporary one. I swear to God. As soon as the Bar Mitzvah is over, it's over. The whole thing is over. I swear."

"Why do you need drugs to get through a Bar Mitzvah?" Teddy asked. "You're the one who's been so adamant about this thing and now here you are, hiding from it? None of this makes any sense."

"I know it doesn't to you, T. See, the thing is, I'm terrible with emotions. Or I have been, since Delilah died. I never dealt with it, is the bottom line. And that was stupid. Because the whole time, she was haunting me. She still haunts me. And an event like this, which is supposed to be about family and joy and transfer, it just has me all shook up inside. Worse than before. But these pills, they make me less so. Less impatient, less of a bitch, more of my old self before grief knocked me sideways."

"So, Mom, you're telling me, your son, that drugs are the answer when life gets too complicated? You realize the insanity of this conversation, right? I mean, this is like, How Not to Parent 101," said Teddy.

"I'm being honest with you about why we're sitting here in this closet together. About why my thirteen-year-old son is staging an intervention with me. I am mortified, okay? But I can't lie to you," said his mom. "I'm fucked up. And this is an incredibly fucked-up way for me to deal with that. And I will pay the price when it's over. But now, with your Bar Mitzvah three days away, is not the time to stop."

"Mom, I want you to stop."

"I know you do. But I can't right now. The withdrawal alone with my parents, Mary and Paul Senior? And Gloria? Can you imagine, Teddy? I mean, someone could die by my hands. I can't have that." Despite himself, Teddy smiled.

"So listen. I'm going to take the rest of these to get me through this. And then it's over. I swear to God."

"You swear to God?" Teddy asked.

"I swear," she replied. "Your father doesn't know, does he?"

"No, not that I know of," said Teddy.

"Okay."

He watched his mother put a pill on her tongue and swallow it whole. She stood up and reached out her hands to help him up too.

"I love you," she said, hugging him. "I'm so sorry you have to deal with this. I'm ashamed of myself, but I don't know what else to do but to be honest with you at this point."

"You swore to God," he reminded her, looking her straight in the eyes.

"I did. Now come on, let's go get sick on onion dip."

"You go ahead," said Teddy. "I need a second."

"Okay," she said. She put the bottle back in her bag and hung it on the hook.

When he could no longer hear her footsteps, Teddy turned out the light.

CHAPTER TWENTY-SIX

SYLVIE

Today is Thursday, thought Sylvie. She was in the bathroom, just out of the shower, and could make out Paul's shape shifting beneath the covers of the bed. She was going to be upbeat. She had just taken a pill, which left her with only seven, and she had today and then tomorrow and then the next day to get through and then it would all be over.

The day before had been a bottom, although Sylvie realized with a fair amount of shame that every time she reached her supposed bottom she allowed herself even a few more thousand feet to fall. To be confronted by her thirteen-year-old son in this very closet about her drug problem—she couldn't get much lower than that. To have him beg her to stop taking them, lower still. But! She was going to stop; that had always been the plan, and now she had sworn the same to Teddy, so it was fact.

Still. It was shameful, and Sylvie was mortified that the conversation had had to take place at all. She hadn't learned that her parents weren't who they claimed to be until her early forties, that the code of ethics they expected her to follow had no real place in their own lives. Sure, it was on a smaller scale than, say, illegal drug use—Sylvie had realized that her mother had the follow-through of a gnat, despite the fact that she had been riding Sylvie to *finish what she started* since she was in diapers and that her father had had a short-lived affair with his secretary back when you could call them secretaries—but her former ignorance had been a sort of bliss.

Poor Teddy. He had experienced too much pain for his age, and it was all her fault. Because first her body had failed her, and then, her self-control.

She combed her hair and faced herself in the mirror. *Don't do this now,* she told herself. She would also not think about how she had screwed up her son right now; or about David, whom she had not seen since she had prostituted herself for his pills; and certainly not about her job, which she currently no longer had. She would not.

Not when she had a house full of people to host—she could kill Paul for inviting his parents and sister early—and entertain. She had never really liked Mary, but Delilah's death had turned her dislike into outright hatred. She had actually had the gall to say that *God needed Delilah for something else*. To Sylvie's face, as though that was a perfectly plausible explanation for her granddaughter's death. *Oh really, what did God need an unborn baby for?* Sylvie had screamed back before Paul had ushered his mother out of their bedroom.

So there was that.

Sylvie took a deep breath as the pill began to take effect, calming the tornado of rage and anxiety that swirled within her. She considered her hair dryer but then decided against it. It was too much work; her hair was curly, it had always been curly; deal with it, world. She applied her foundation, her concealer, her bronzer and her blush. She curled her eyelashes and dutifully painted them a deep, dark black. She swiped her lipstick over her lips.

There had been no further movement from Paul. She would let him sleep. She moved to the closet, selected a striped blouse that floated over her stomach, creating the illusion of flatness, and pulled on a pair of expensive designer chinos that she had driven to the mall and treated herself to after being fired. She was ready.

Turning off the bathroom light, she made her way quietly to Teddy's room. She wanted to give him a hug, to tell him she was proud of him, to try her best to assure him that she was still his mother, still capable, still there despite the fact that she had let him down.

"Teddy," she whispered, opening his door.

The room was darkened by his drawn blinds, but she could see that his bed was already made. It was unlike him to be up so early, but it made sense. He was awfully nervous about

Saturday; the night before he had barely spoken to anyone at dinner. Then again, that could have been her fault and had nothing to do with the impending Bar Mitzvah, Sylvie thought. *Stop it,* she told herself.

Down to the kitchen she trotted, and there were her parents, fully showered and dressed, her mother's makeup painstakingly applied. It wasn't even 8:00 A.M.

"How long have you been up?" she asked.

"Good morning to you too, dear," replied her father from behind his mug of coffee.

"Have you seen Teddy?" she asked.

"No, not a soul," said her mother. "Do you have a grapefruit, by any chance?"

"Grapefruit? What is this, a Disney cruise?" asked Sylvie.

"What?"

Sylvie looked around. Where was Teddy? A profound sense of dread filled the pit of her stomach, but she quickly told herself that she was being ridiculous. Maybe he had gone over to that Krystal person's house. She grimaced. *That Krystal person.* She sounded exactly like her mother, something she had vowed never to do. All things considered, it was the least offensive of the many vows she had broken lately, but still.

She looked out the kitchen window. Paul's stationary bike was still, inexplicably, there. When she had asked him why he had dragged it into the driveway instead of, you know, taking an actual bike ride on one of the five nonstationary bikes he owned, he had just shrugged at her, as if she was a nag. Something was up with him, she thought, but then, so much was up with her that she had left it at that. But today, it had to be dragged back into the garage because: Saturday.

Sylvie left her parents at the table and searched the rest of the house for her son. She lingered at the guest room doors of her in-laws, but there was nothing but the sound of snoring coming from Paul Sr. and the faint but specific smell of cigarettes from Gloria. She padded back to her bedroom.

"Paul," she said from the door. He did not stir, just an angular lump under the white duvet, curled into himself, his back to her.

"Paul," she said. Louder.

"Yeah?" He rolled over quickly and sat up, his cowlick pointing west. "What's the matter?"

"It's Teddy. He's not here."

"Jesus, Sylvie, what time is it?"

"It's 8:07 A.M.," she replied, looking at the red numbers of their alarm clock. Paul lay back down and groaned.

"I'm sure he's at Krystal's or something."

"This early? Seems a little unlikely."

"Well, maybe he snuck out, to sleep over."

"Teddy? Our Teddy? No way."

"Sylvie, he's growing up," said Paul. "There's a way." He sat back up, rubbed his eyes. "Do you have your phone? Have you called him?"

Sylvie shook her head.

"Isn't that why we got him that stupid phone? Call him."

"Okay. You're right." Sylvie walked over to her bedside table and unplugged her phone from its charger.

She felt her heart beating wildly in her chest as the phone rang and rang, whether from the idea that her son was having sex or that he had run away because she was an epic failure as a mother, she wasn't sure.

"He's not picking up," she told Paul.

"Okay, then call Krystal." Sylvie made a face. "Sylvie, stop being such a snob. Call her."

She walked into her closet and called Krystal.

"Hello?" Krystal answered.

"Krystal?"

"Yes, this is her."

This is she, thought Sylvie.

"Hi, Krystal, this is Teddy's mom. Sylvie?"

"Oh. Hi."

"Listen, is Teddy with you?"

"With me?"

"You can be honest; please, there's no judgment. It's just that he's not here, and I'm, we're, a little concerned," Sylvie said.

"He's not with me," she answered. "We haven't spoken in a couple days. We had a fight."

"You had a fight?"

"Yeah."

Sylvie wanted to know what the fight was about but also knew that it was none of her business. But if the subject of said fight might lead her to Teddy, well, that was a different story.

"I hate to be nosy, but is there anything about your fight that might give you an idea where he is this morning?"

Krystal slurped on the other end of the phone. "Sorry, just finishing my coffee," she said.

A thirteen-year-old drinking coffee, thought Sylvie. But she was an unemployed forty-six-year-old drug addict, so who was she to judge? Temporary drug addict. Temporary.

"Sure, go ahead," she said to Krystal.

"Well, I don't think it's cool to divulge all our argument's details, but I guess the relevant one is that he was speaking of, of, um—"

"Go ahead," said Sylvie.

"It's a bit awkward," said Krystal.

Sylvie sat down as her insides turned to warm syrup, her blessed drug doing what it did. It was going to be okay. Teddy was probably down the road—down the road! Yes, that was it! With his Twilight Manor movie buddies.

"Oh, I know where he is!" Sylvie cried. "He's got to be at Twilight Manor. He's got a special thing going with that one older man, what's his name? Manny?"

"Morty."

"Yes, Morty. Oh, thank God," Sylvie said, convinced with no evidence.

"My mom is working today. Do you want me to call her and see if Teddy's there?" Krystal asked.

"Oh, Krystal, would you mind? That would be such a huge help. I have so much going on here—"

"For the Bar Mitzvah?"

"Yes. You're coming, right? You and your mom? Please, I hope a little fight won't prevent us from seeing you." This was not entirely true. Sylvie was not looking forward to explaining Krystal to her parents.

"Of course. I love him."

Sylvie gulped. A female other than her was not allowed to say this about Teddy with so much conviction; the possibility of hearing it wasn't remotely on her radar, but there it was.

"Right. Okay. So yes, please, could you call your mom and then call me right back?"

"Will do."

"Thank you very much, Krystal."

Sylvie hung up. She was certain that Teddy was at Twilight Manor; he seemed to have a sort of Mr. Miyagi/Karate Kid thing going with Morty from the few details he had shared, but checking his room a little bit more thoroughly couldn't hurt.

"So what's the word?" asked Paul, coming out of the bathroom in a towel, his hair damp. There was a tone to his voice, a tone of contempt. Even in the simplest exchanges between them lately, that tone hung in the air like sulfur.

"Pretty sure he's at Twilight Manor hanging out with that old guy, his friend? Morty? Krystal is calling to confirm; her mom's working there this morning."

"I told you he was fine," said Paul dismissively.

Sylvie rolled her eyes and went back into Teddy's room. She opened the blinds. It was as neat as a pin, something she felt a slight sense of guilt about since she was fairly certain her tendency—no, full-blown obsessive compulsion with cleanliness—had been absorbed by her son's brain.

When his preschool teacher had told them during the requisite parent conference that Teddy insisted on stacking the blocks in an exactly congruent way within the constraints of their plastic container, Sylvie had winced. Since then, she had mostly convinced herself that keeping things clean and organized was not a bad trait to pass on, mostly because it hadn't seemed to stifle Teddy's creativity. That had been her chief worry. Because she wanted for him what she hadn't had, and Sylvie's creativity was limited to fabric swatches.

She meandered over to his desk and tapped the *R* on his laptop keyboard. The screen came alive, its picture familiar. Sylvie sat down, her heart beating at the sight of the still-familiar logo, although the last time she had taken a bus had to have been over twenty-five years ago. In college.

It was a Greyhound schedule. Bus times from Atlanta to St. Marys. And in another window, the ferry schedule from St. Marys to Cumberland Island.

Sylvie slumped in her chair. Teddy had gone back. The bravest one of the three of them by a long shot. He had gone back. A lump rose in Sylvie's throat as it so often did, but this time she did not choke it back. It erupted from her in a scream.

"Jesus, Sylvie! Are you all right?" Paul ran in, his eyes wide with concern.

"Paul, look." Sylvie pointed to the screen.

"What?" Paul read it, and then he put his hand to his mouth and reached for the edge of the bed.

"Shit," he said.

Sylvie's phone rang.

"Hello?"

"Sylvie, it's Krystal. My mom says he's not there. She's looked everywhere, and Morty hasn't seen him." Krystal sounded panicked.

"Okay, thank you, Krystal. I think we know where he is, but thank you."

"Where? Is he okay?"

"I don't know. I hope so. I'm going to go get him. Everything will be okay, Krystal," Sylvie assured her. "I'll have him call you as soon as we have him, okay?" Sylvie hung up before Krystal could ask her anything else.

"So I'm going to go," Sylvie announced. "He has to be there. I'm going to get him."

"You're not going alone," said Paul.

"No, I have to go alone. We can't just leave everyone here to fend for themselves."

"Sylvie, they're grown adults; they'll manage. You're not going there to retrieve Teddy by yourself. Forget it."

"What's with you lately?" hissed Sylvie. "You bark at me."

"That's for another time."

"What's for another time?"

"My barking reasons."

"Tell me now, for God's sake, before we're locked in a car together for five hours," said Sylvie.

"David told me."

Sylvie felt the blood drain from her face, down through her body and into the floor. "He told you what?" She kept her voice as neutral as her beige toenail paint.

"About the pills, Sylvie, what do you think? He told me

that you came to his house asking for his pills, like some kind of housewife junkie."

"Housewife junkie? Excuse me?"

The room was beginning to spin, ever so slightly. Sylvie put her hands on her thighs, sitting across from Paul on the bed, whose eyes were on fire with anger. But was that all that David had told him? That was the question.

"That's what he told you?" she asked again. "He told you that I asked him for his pills?"

"Isn't that what I just said?" said Paul. "What are you, a parrot? A parrot and a junkie?"

"God, Paul, you're being so fucking mean!" yelled Sylvie, feeling and sounding exactly like her former fourteen-year-old self. "I have a problem, obviously. Would a little compassion kill you?"

The nerve she had, asking for his compassion, she thought, when what she had done was much, much worse than beg for drugs. When their own son had staged an intervention with her not twenty-four hours earlier. But here she was.

"I'm sorry," said Paul, his shoulders slumping slightly. He looked at the floor for a moment. "I suppose on some level, I should have some compassion for you, you're right. And don't mistake my anger for lack of worry. There's plenty of worry here, believe me. But to go to a friend of mine, an addict, no less, behind my back and hit him up for pills—that's like, well, to be honest, I'm embarrassed. Angry and embarrassed and worried. You've been taking these things regularly since that first prescription I came home with? From the hospital?"

Sylvie nodded.

"Jesus, Sylvie, that was almost four months ago."

"It was?" She sighed, composed herself. "Yes, I'm addicted to them at the moment, okay?" she said. "It's true. I can't go a day without at least one for a variety of reasons that I'll share with you later, perhaps on this road trip we're about to embark on, but right now we have to focus on just that. The road trip. Because we have to make the ferry. Because if we don't make the ferry tonight, we won't get back in time for this goddamn Bar Mitzvah with any time to decompress, and Teddy won't be sealed in the Book of Life and we'll all burn in hell."

"Book of Life? What the hell are you talking about, Sylvie? And I thought Jews didn't believe in hell."

"We don't. Not in the afterlife, anyway. Current life, definitely yes. Anyway, we have to pack; we have to go. We have to brief everyone."

"Okay," said Paul. "All my stuff is in the basement. I'll go down there and throw it in a bag."

"What about your ankle?" asked Sylvie.

"What about it?"

"Can you, like, trek through the wilds of Cumberland Island with that thing?"

"I'll make it work," said Paul. "Don't forget: long sleeves and pants. The mosquitoes there are like land sharks."

"I remember," said Sylvie. He left her in the closet.

Paul was right about the sleeves and pants, but she just couldn't bear the thought of enduring the heat that way. She would buy bug spray at a gas station on the way. Oh God,

Teddy. What had he worn? Her heart sank, imagining him covered with welts. Mosquitoes had always loved them both.

"For fuck's sake, Teddy," she mumbled, pulling her backpack, which hadn't seen the light of day since the last time she'd visited Cumberland Island, from the dark recesses of her bottom shelf and threw a pair of shorts, a T-shirt, a sweatshirt, a change of underwear and some socks into it.

"Sylvie!" her mother called from below.

"What?" she yelled back.

She pulled off her carefully curated outfit, shimmied into a different pair of shorts and pulled a too-tight tank top over her head.

"What's going on? What's wrong?"

"One second!" Socks. Sneakers. Check. A hat. Check. Okay, she was ready.

Her memories of the last time she had packed this bag, as she zipped it closed now, they bubbled just below the surface of her consciousness, but she did not have the time to even acknowledge them, much less dwell in them. Her pills. She dug through the red purse and pulled out the bottle, shoving it deep into her backpack's front pocket.

"Sylvie!" her mother called again.

"Coming! Jesus!"

She ran down the stairs, backpack in tow, just as Paul was coming up from the basement, dressed like a deranged beekeeper. Everyone was in the kitchen now: her parents, Mary and Paul Sr.—the latter two still in their pajamas, their hair askew. Outside on the deck, Gloria smoked, watching them through the glass of the French doors as if she could read lips.

"Good morning," said Paul. "Sylvie, what's with the shorts? Do you want to get eaten alive or what?"

"What's going on?" asked his mother. "Paul, honey, why are you dressed like that? It's nine hundred degrees outside."

"Everyone," said Sylvie. "There's a situation."

"What kind of situation?" asked her father, perking up. He loved situations.

"It's Teddy."

"What's wrong with Teddy? Oh my God," said her mother, putting her manicured hand to her chest.

"He's taken a trip. Without asking us."

"He ran away?" Paul Sr. asked.

"He's gone to Cumberland Island," said Paul. "We have to go get him."

"Cumberland Island?" asked Mary. "With the horses? Isn't that where . . . ?"

"Where I lost Delilah? Yes," said Sylvie.

"Oh, for God's sake," said her father. "Why would he go back there?"

"Well, obviously he has some unresolved issues," said Paul coldly. "He was on that trip too, you know."

"Know? Of course we know," said her mother. "Why you would take a trip like that, camping, of all the things, at eight months pregnant, is beyond me—"

"Mom, shut up," said Sylvie.

They had had this conversation once before, right after it had happened, right after Sylvie, Paul and Teddy had arrived home, trapped in a fog of disbelief and fear. That her mother would turn their tragedy into an *I told you so* moment was not unexpected, but it was reprehensible nevertheless, and Paul had all but swung a machete at her head in response.

"Okay. So. We're driving down this morning to make the ferry, find him and bring him back in time for the Bar Mitzvah. At least that's the plan," said Sylvie.

"How are you going to be able to find him?" her father asked. "Does he have a tracking device implanted in his head or something? That's a big island, isn't it?"

Sylvie hadn't considered this, but of course he was right.

"We'll find him," said Paul.

There was a knock on the front door.

"Who's that?" Gloria asked, joining them.

"No idea," said Paul. He walked as quickly as he could, his ankle dragging ever so slightly, over to it. Outside stood Krystal, strapped into a backpack of her own. A purple backpack.

"I'm coming with you," she declared. Her wet eyelashes were bare. She looked like a thoroughbred colt standing there, all arms and legs.

"And who is this?" asked Sylvie's mother.

"You're not coming with us," Paul told Krystal. "It's pointless. We'll be back in twenty-four hours."

"Sweetheart, we barely know what we're doing; we can't be responsible for you too," explained Sylvie, ushering her in and closing the door even though they really had to go. "Does your mom know you're here?"

"I'm Teddy's girlfriend," Krystal said to everyone. "Krystal. Nice to meet you."

"Hello," everyone murmured back.

"I love him. I'm coming with you," she told Sylvie and Paul. "Besides, I know how to camp and also, when he was in the bathroom one day, I put a tracking device on his phone."

"A tracking device?" asked Paul, exchanging a look of concern with Sylvie.

"Sure, so I could always know where he is. Controversial, I know, but in a time like this: hello, I just saved us from wandering around like feral raccoons in the dark for ten hours. I know exactly where he is."

"Feral raccoons?" said Barbara.

Sylvie met her mother's gaze over Krystal's head: *Not Jewish, but I like her,* she mouthed. *Smart.* Barbara tapped her own head with her ring finger to illustrate her point.

"You know where he is? Where? Show me," Sylvie said to Krystal.

"Oh, no way," said Krystal. "I'm not falling for that trick. Let's get in the car and then I'll show you."

Sylvie looked at Paul, whose face underneath his hat looked strained. He shrugged slightly.

"Okay, fine," said Sylvie. "You can come. But you have to tell your mother."

"My mother drove me here," replied Krystal.

What kind of mother not only grants her daughter permission to join the road trip from hell to a wild horse island enshrouded in dark dysfunction and trauma but delivers her upon its doorstep willingly? thought Sylvie, as she hugged everyone halfheartedly and headed out the door. What kind of mother was a secret pill-popping prostitute? *Glass houses, Sylvie,* she reminded herself.

"I'll call you," she told them.

"Be careful," said her father. "I don't trust that island."

They had never spoken outright about Delilah's death; her father had only pushed her hair away from her forehead one afternoon as she lay in bed a week later, still unable to move, the blinds shutting out the sun. His hand had felt as dry as sandpaper. It was the closest he had come before or since to comfort.

"I will, Dad," Sylvie said.

"Paul, what are you doing?" she asked as he loaded the tent and two sleeping bags into the trunk of their car.

"Teddy didn't take the tent, so who the hell knows where or how he's planning to sleep?" said Paul, his voice thick with worry. "He did take a sleeping bag, though. We only have two, so—"

"I'll sleep with him," Krystal interjected, throwing her backpack into the car.

"Like hell you will," said Sylvie. "You'll sleep with me in mine." Krystal shrugged from inside the car, her curls draped across the back seat.

"Sylvie, take it easy," said Paul. And then, "Are we ready? We can stop for water on the way."

"Ready," said Sylvie, throwing her backpack in the trunk before he closed it.

"I'm worried," she said to him.

"Me too," he answered, but there was no softness there. Their concern was not enough unification to make him forget about the pills, Sylvie realized, as she looked him in the eye.

This was going to be the longest drive of her life.

CHAPTER TWENTY-SEVEN

TEDDY

Teddy stood on the deck of the ferry as it pulled in to dock, glad he had remembered a hat to protect him from the unrelenting sun. He popped the last of the weird packaged cinnamon roll he had purchased from a vending machine into his mouth and hoped he would not suffer for his culinary sin later, alone, on an island with no bathrooms to speak of. The roll had appeared to be older than Teddy was, but he had been starving in the St. Marys bus station, so what could he do? He slugged back the Styrofoam cup of coffee he had also purchased right before boarding. He had never drunk coffee before and had been revolted by his initial sip. Six packages of a powder that claimed to be coffee's mate later and it was mildly recognizable as a beverage people would willingly consume. How his parents were addicted to this stuff, he had no idea.

Addicted. His mom. Their conversation. It was all so surreal and unfathomable, that he would be the one asking her to cut it out and that she would be refusing—temporarily, as she had sworn, although Teddy wasn't sure he bought it—but it had happened all right. And now here he was, trading one intervention for another but hoping this one was more successful.

He was terrified of the day and night that stretched out in front of him, but he figured if he had made it this far—if he had snuck out of his house in the middle of the night, taken an Uber to the bus station, hopped on said bus to St. Marys and boarded the ferry all by himself—then he was going to be okay. And if he came out on the other end with some closure, feeling better about the man he was supposedly on the cusp of becoming in two days, then all the better. *L'Chaim*, as Morty would say.

He knew his parents were freaking out. They had called his cell phone fifteen times. Krystal had called six. But he had not picked up. He had to do this alone. It was the only way it would work. Five minutes prior, feeling guilty, he had sent them all a text telling them he was okay, he was on a mission, he would be back the next day, please don't worry or call the police. Then he had turned off his phone.

His fellow shipmates began to disembark, all in various degrees of preparedness. There were around two dozen or so of them on this 9:00 A.M. boat, the first of the morning, all of whom Teddy had eavesdropped on, his notebook at the ready.

One family—two moms and their two daughters—were covered in camel-colored hiking gear complete with zippers placed at their elbows and knees in case the sun's merciless heat won out over the danger of its dangerous rays. Three were red-haired and freckled, one of the mothers brunette and olive. The redheaded mom was Mommy and the brunette mom was Ma. The two girls were Charlie and, for some reason, Rabbit, which Teddy had double-checked. He hoped it was a nickname but then had realized that who was he to judge? He was named after a bear.

Another couple, Tammy and Ron—young, maybe in college or just out, Teddy had surmised—were tattooed practically from head to toe, and he knew this because they were wearing such little clothing, which was shocking to Teddy at first but then kind of liberating as he began to sweat even in the cool breeze, even at just 9:15 in the morning. Tammy had horses galloping up her left leg, which explained their trip. If she had a thing for horses, Cumberland Island was the place to go. They never left your memory once you'd seen them, those horses—wild eyes and matted manes, their sinuous muscles just beneath the glossy surface of their coats.

Tammy and Ron were not even remotely ready for the island, however. Both of them were as white as ghosts, and yet Tammy had refused sunscreen. And they were both in flip-flops. If Teddy hadn't had work to do, he would have followed them around just to see them fall apart firsthand, as a kind of plot exercise for a future screenplay.

Not that he was that prepared himself. Teddy had left the tent behind but attached a sleeping bag to his backpack, thinking he would sleep under the stars as part of this entry into manhood. As his feet, encased in high-top sneakers, made contact with dry land, however, and the first mosquito made direct contact with the exposed skin of his neck, he realized he had forgotten perhaps the most essential tool of all for this journey: bug spray.

He began to panic a little as he walked, the beauty of the island lost on his addled mind, which was taking stock of the supplies he had had the good sense to stash in his backpack in an effort to make himself feel better. Three bottles of water, almonds, apples, protein bars, sunscreen, a change of clothes, some underwear, a travel bottle of shampoo in case he got to shower. A bathing suit just in case. A small towel. A sleeping bag.

A mosquito landed squarely on his forearm and he swatted it away, but not before it had gotten its fill of him. A red welt puffed up in its wake.

But no bug spray. Idiot.

Teddy forced himself to look away from the bite and up, to take stock of the untouched nature surrounding him. It was magnificent here; the trees alone with their wide trunks and dense branches that reached up, up, up into the sky were enough to make you marvel. Up ahead were Tammy and Ron snapping a selfie of themselves, the illustrated canvases of their skin already beginning to pink, even in the shaded canopy the leaves provided.

Teddy grabbed a water bottle from his backpack and took a hearty swig. He put it back in, rezipped it and began again, the trees his umbrella. He reached back into his mind and remembered the last time he had been here, walking this same path of dirt and rocks.

His mom. Her body had been so warm to the touch when she was pregnant; just holding her hand was like putting on a mitten. *I'm an incubator,* she had replied as Teddy had told her this, helping her off the ferry.

He had climbed a tree, Teddy recalled, eyeing the majestic arch of one now, feeling its weathered bark against his palm. He had hauled himself up and over the low, thick branches as his dad struggled behind him, his mother shrieking in fear below.

Teddy dropped his backpack on the ground and climbed again. The bark felt rough and warm beneath his hands; he could feel its ridges even through the fabric of his pants as he clung to it. Sideways and up, sideways and up, and then he stopped. He sat, swinging his legs underneath him, watching the swoosh of his blue Converse going back and forth. People milled below, adults and kids laughing and talking, the distant notes of their conversations like bubbles rising to the surface of water. He thought about the horses. Hiding in plain sight. He climbed down after a few minutes, resisting the urge to stop and eat. It was not yet eleven o'clock, and he hadn't packed enough food for unnecessary snacks.

The tree-shaded path ended abruptly, depositing him without warning into an open green space mottled with patches of sand and dirt. In front of him were the charred remains of a mansion, its long-lost grandeur still apparent even in the hollowed-out brick shell of what remained. The Dungeness Ruins.

Teddy wandered its perimeter, imagining the life that once inhabited such a place. Fancy dinners and parties and maids in scullery caps; butlers and gardeners. A family of four, like dolls in very stiff clothes, looking out the windows. Maybe a little girl with blond ringlets down her back on a rocking horse, diligently watched over by her governess. Governess. Whatever had happened to that word? They probably still used it in England, Teddy reasoned.

He kept walking. He shifted his backpack and realized that underneath it, where it met his shirt, was soaked with sweat. He also realized that he had forgotten another thing. Deodorant. Great.

He wondered what Krystal was doing. Since their argument, he had been composing what he wanted to say in his green notebook, choosing words and then erasing them, picking others and then erasing those too. He didn't have much written down. What he wanted to say and what came out were two different things.

I'm scared, he wanted to say, *about my mom. I don't know what to do.* What he had written down was: *My mom is not your dad.* And then: *I did it.*

Krystal was probably with her friend he had never met at her neighborhood pool that he had never seen. He imagined her lying on a chaise lounge in the sun, her eyes closed. Did she wear a bikini? A surge of heat flowed through him, separate from the sun. He had never seen her stomach in the light of day, but he had touched it. Her skin was impossibly smooth.

He found a shaded area and sat down. He had to eat; his stomach was growling like a tiger in a cage. A protein bar and an apple. Some water. That should do the trick. Teddy removed his backpack and set it against the trunk of a tree, positioned his sleeping bag for a bit of lumbar support and leaned against it. That was better. He took off his hat and wiped the sweat off his face with his hands. He drank and drank from one of his bottles of water. He began to eat, too quickly at first, and then he reminded himself to slow down. The last thing he needed was stomach cramps.

His parents were definitely losing it right now; he knew they were. They would have no idea where he was, but he hoped they had taken his text to heart. He hoped that they trusted his word that he was okay, that he would be back. His mom had probably had to take an extra pill, just to deal. And his dad? Who knew. Teddy was mad at both of them, he realized, for the secrets he felt compelled to keep on both of their behalves. It was messed up.

Trudging through the white sand toward the beach felt like walking on the surface of the sun. It was just after noon; Teddy had checked the watch he had borrowed from his dad's vast collection of time-interval, stopwatch, BMI/step-counter plastic behemoths. It looked and felt more like a satellite dish than a means of time measurement on Teddy's skinny wrist, but he was glad he had it. Otherwise, he would have had to turn on his phone and read what he was sure were nine hundred texts from his parents, each one more agitated as they continued to go unanswered.

The sun beat down so forcefully on Teddy's head that he felt it might burst into flames. He kept his eyes on his feet, and as he watched his blue sneakers move through the sand, he remembered complaining, crying in dramatic despair when he was nine, enduring this same seemingly endless trek. His father had told him through gritted teeth to buck up; his mother had looked at him with a mix of pity and annoyance.

"Come on, T," she had said. "I'm as big as a house. If I can do it, certainly you can. Look at my ankles, Teddy; they're like balloon animals." And they were.

His parents had walked on when Teddy refused to budge, leaving him behind until he had no choice but to keep moving, lest he be stranded alone in the sand.

There were lots of times in his life that Teddy had been acutely aware of the fact that his father, and sometimes his mother too, wished he was a tougher kid. The kind of kid who didn't stand on the soccer field daydreaming as the ball rolled right past him, a gaggle of boys kicking at one another's shins in an attempt to redirect it. The kind of kid who wanted to ride his bike. He knew that when his dad narrowed his eyes and massaged his temples with his thumb and index finger that he was frustrated with what he saw as Teddy's laziness. But Teddy didn't think he was lazy. He just wasn't interested, and wasn't that okay?

It was so hot.

Onward Teddy trudged, and then, mercifully, the sun ducked behind a cloud and he was granted reprieve as his sneakers moved onto the wet sand of the shore. Tentatively he sat, sinking slightly into the ground.

The water was as gray as the horizon, and just as still. Dragonflies darted in and out of the air all around him. Teddy drew his knees to his chest and waited.

In the stillness, a tribe of horses walked in front of him,

their hooves making small splashes in the tide. They had appeared out of nowhere, it seemed. Like ghosts. But they were as real as the wet sand on which Teddy sat. They whinnied and snorted as their matted tails cut through the thick, humid air, swatting at the flies hovering around them.

There were four of them, walking in a line. The leader was the color of syrup, the second a chocolate brown, the third white dappled with gray and the last a deep, dark, midnight black. They were completely unconcerned with Teddy and couldn't have been more than fifteen feet away from the toes of his sneakers. He did not move.

How could you not believe in God when nature like this, in its purest form, existed? thought Teddy. How else to explain this beauty? How did these horses even end up here in the first place? Had their ancestors been born under the care of the millionaire who had owned the now-decrepit mansion? Had they lived in barns stuffed to the rafters with golden hay, been fed carrots by their owners, been meticulously groomed by the staff until they shone like marble? And when all that wealth and grandeur had disappeared, they continued on, still? The white-and-gray dappled one stopped suddenly and stared at Teddy with her rheumy black eyes, directly into his own.

What had Morty said? *L'dor vador*?

Yes.

Teddy could see the window of the hospital waiting room, feel the scratchy sofa beneath his curled-up legs, remember the fear that had kept him wide awake even though it had been so late. Later than he had ever been awake in his nine years of life. He had been alone for hours in that room, and he had been terrified, even though he had pretended he wasn't because his parents, in another room down the hall with a closed door, were too. And he had never seen that before either. He had never seen them scared by anything, and yet his mother had been trembling and crying when he hugged her goodbye, and his father's eyes, above the pale green of his surgical mask, had been as wide as saucers.

The horse snorted and broke its gaze. The tribe of four continued on down the shore.

As he watched them walk away, sobs rose up inside Teddy like small earthquakes. He erupted in tears, damp and sweaty and sandy, all alone just as he had been in that hospital waiting room. He cried for his mother. He cried for his father. He cried for Delilah, who never even got the chance to see the world. But mostly he cried for himself. He'd been robbed of a sister he'd never known, but he'd also been robbed of the parents he'd once known. They had never been the same.

And now his mother was a drug addict because she couldn't bear her own reality. A reality in which she hated his dad. A reality in which his dad secretly texted with women who used emojis and poured his money down a giant cyber hole, all the while running, cycling and swimming away from the void that threatened them all. And Teddy watched movies on a loop. Because anything was better than the void. Anything.

That night three years ago, Teddy had finally fallen asleep underneath a mauve blanket a nurse had draped over him in that waiting room. In the wee hours of the morning, his father had returned, sitting down next to him. The shift of the cushions had woken Teddy.

"Hi, buddy," his dad had said softly. Teddy remembered it as clearly as if it had been the day before. "Come here."

His father had pulled him close. Teddy had looked up, his eyes blurry, not quite sure where he was. His father looked different, not like his real self. His real father was not the color of putty; his real father's eyes were not bloodshot and ringed by blue circles. And yet Teddy could tell by his hands, his long, tapered fingers, that it was indeed him.

"Delilah didn't make it, buddy," he had said, choking back a sob.

"Didn't make it where?" Teddy had asked.

"She died, Teddy," he said. And then his sobs came, his tears melting into Teddy's hair.

"She died?" asked Teddy, not believing him. His father nodded his head.

"Did Mom die?"

"No, no. Mom is okay. Mom is fine. I'm so sorry, T. I'm so, so sorry."

"I'm not going to have a sister?" Teddy had asked, stunned.

"No."

And they had sat like that for a while, his father crying and Teddy's head swirling. He had never known someone who died. And even though he had never met Delilah, he had felt as though he knew her. She was his sister.

"Can I see her?"

"No, honey, I'm sorry. She's gone."

Teddy hadn't understood this. "But she was born? And then she died?"

"No, she died inside Mom."

And that had been the extent of the explanation. Teddy had accepted this, stored this confusing information in his brain, clinging to his father like a life preserver on that scratchy couch as the sun came up through the window, turning the world pink.

CHAPTER TWENTY-EIGHT

PAUL

What do you mean, there are no more ferries today?" Paul asked the very overweight, pimply-faced teenager behind the desk. Her head sat directly on top of her bare shoulders, separated only by an impressive swell of chin flesh.

"There are two ferries that leave every day, and three that return. The second and final one left almost two hours ago." She sighed heavily. "As I just explained to you."

"There's no need to get huffy," said Sylvie, who was standing next to him. "Our son is out there, so we're understandably concerned for his well-being. Excuse us if we want to be absolutely clear on the schedule."

"Did the third and final ferry come back already?" asked Krystal.

Paul was continually surprised to hear her voice, to see her beside them. She had barely spoken during the interminable car ride, just put on her headphones, plugged them into her phone and sulked out the window as he and Sylvie exchanged very minimal and terse commentary about their strategy once they, if they ever, got to the goddamn island.

"The last one returns here at 5:30 P.M. Like I told you."

"Did you see a young boy this morning? Skinny? Twelve years old? With a backpack and a sleeping bag?" asked Paul.

"He's thirteen," said Krystal. "He had a birthday?"

Paul glared at her. Sylvie grunted.

"I wasn't working the morning shift, so I didn't see him get on. If he did get on. And I don't, like, examine the people getting off. I have a life?"

"All due respect to your *life*, our son is in danger," said Sylvie. "Is there someone you can call and ask? The guy who worked the first shift?"

"Why do you assume it's a guy?"

"Oh, for fuck's sake!" Sylvie hissed. "Could you try to be a little less of an asshole? Would that be possible? It's our runaway kid who has no idea what he's doing out there, okay? Is a little empathy too much to ask for here?"

"So can you call him or her?" asked Krystal, interjecting with an apologetic tone. "Is that possible? Just to see?"

"Tony doesn't have a cell phone," the teenager answered. "And he's at his jujitsu class anyway."

"They have a jujitsu class here in the middle of Bumfuck?" mumbled Sylvie.

"I heard that," the attendant replied angrily.

"Okay, thank you very much for your time," said Krystal. She moved away from the desk and waved them over.

"We need to find someone to take us over," she whispered, leading them out of the office and into the blazing sun. "Obviously Teddy boarded the nine A.M. ferry; the last tracking I have for him shows him here at eight thirty A.M., right after he sent us that text. Either his phone died, or he turned it off himself."

"Take us over to the island?" asked Sylvie.

"No, take us over to Alcatraz," said Paul. "Of course the island. What do you think she's talking about?" He eyed his wife angrily. These pills made her dumb.

"Oh, look, a comedian has joined us!" Sylvie snarled. "Are you practicing your set?"

"Guys, pull it together!" yelled Krystal. "Fighting isn't going to help us now. We have to act as a team."

"Krystal," said Paul, dropping his enormous backpack with its tent and sleeping bags hanging from it like fishing lures onto the concrete, "you're not even supposed to be here. As a matter of fact, I'd like to know why you're here."

"Because I love your son. And furthermore, I'm the only one here who's clear-headed." Krystal raised her eyebrows.

"What's that supposed to mean?" barked Sylvie.

"It means she knows about the pills," said Paul, not quite believing it himself. If she knew, then of course it was because Teddy had told her. "Am I right, Krystal?"

She nodded.

"Well, I'm not on them," he declared. "Just her. For the record."

"They're prescribed," Sylvie mumbled.

"Not to you," said Paul.

"When did Teddy find them?" Paul asked Krystal. He was so hot. It was like his skin was being ironed.

"Maybe two months ago?" said Krystal. "I told him to tell you. He wouldn't; he said not yet. That was part of our fight."

"So he knew before I did?" Paul asked. "I hope you're proud of yourself, Sylvie."

"Okay, I'm an asshole," said Sylvie finally. "Guilty as charged. But pills aside, here we all are, in a place to which I vowed I'd never return, looking for our missing son. Boyfriend for you, Krystal, I guess."

"I dunno. Like I said, we're in a fight—"

"Shut up, both of you!" yelled Paul. An elderly couple walking by in matching baby-blue polo shirts and khaki shorts jumped.

"Sorry," Paul said to them as they passed, cowering. "Krystal's right. We have to find someone to row us over. There have to be shady characters around for that."

"For a thousand dollars a pop, I'm sure," said Sylvie. "Wait, where's Krystal?"

They turned from each other to scan the boardwalk. The water was a deep blue and lapped softly at its edges. People of all shapes, sizes and ages in varying degrees of dress wandered by, all sweating profusely under straw brims and baseball caps. Paul's own cap felt superglued to his forehead.

"There she is, all the way at the end," said Sylvie. "Talking to some guy. I didn't even see her leave."

Paul picked up his giant pack and walked toward her, Sylvie trailing behind him. He hated his wife. Not always, and hopefully not forever, but right now he did. Teddy knew? What must he think? And he hadn't even felt comfortable sharing this information, this load, with his own father? He thought about the text string from T.B.; Teddy's concern. Poor kid. Jesus.

"Y'all wanna go over, it's gonna cost ya," Paul heard the man saying to Krystal as he approached.

He was a very large man, easily over six feet and had to be close to three hundred pounds, Paul calculated as he stared at him. He was freckled from head to toe, orange freckles on pink skin, and shockingly hairless other than the red tufts poking out from the armholes of his navy-blue Bugs Bunny tank top. His hands were as big as catchers' mitts, his nails ragged with rings of black dirt underneath each one. He stood with one tree trunk of a leg in what could best be described as a dinghy and the other propped on the dock. He wore no shoes.

"Hello, I'm Paul." He reached out to shake the man's hand and was met with a vigorous pump that nearly knocked him over.

"I'm Mickey."

"Nice to meet you," said Paul.

"Sounds like y'all are in a bit of a bind," said Mickey.

"I'll say," said Paul. "We've got to get over there to find our son, but we've missed the ferry."

"If we can't get over there in, like, twenty minutes, we may literally be two ships passing in the night. Or the twilight, anyway," interjected Sylvie. "I'm Sylvie, by the way."

"How you figure that, Sylvie?" asked Mickey.

"Well, he may take the last ferry back here, you know? We certainly don't know. And the goal is to get to that ferry to see who's boarding before it leaves. Because if he's back here and we're out there, well, that's just ridiculous," said Sylvie.

Paul had not even considered that Teddy might ferry back here. His son's intention had been to spend the night on the island; he was sure of it. Then again, he was also sure that Teddy was completely ill-equipped to do such a thing. Sylvie was right that he very well could come back.

"Well, like I said, I can getcha there, but it ain't cheap," said Mickey.

"How much are we talking?" asked Paul. "And how much weight can this thing take?"

"Up to a thousand."

"Are you absolutely sure about that?"

"I'm sure."

"Do you have life jackets?" asked Sylvie.

"Yes ma'am."

"So how much, Mickey?" asked Paul.

"Five hundred each."

"Oh, get out of here!" cried Paul. "Five hundred dollars for each of us? Are you nuts? It's, what, a twenty-minute ride? Come on."

"I could lose my license. This is illegal business, you know," said Mickey. "This ain't no grocery run."

"Might you consider lowering your price, considering there's three of us?" asked Sylvie.

"Three fifty each?" countered Krystal.

"Four hundred is my best and final," said Mickey. He spat

an enormous blob of black tar into a plastic NASCAR cup he pulled out from below the steering wheel. The boat rocked in the water.

"We'll take it," said Sylvie. Paul opened his mouth to argue.

"Oh for God's sake, Paul, are we really going to sit here arguing over fifty dollars? We don't have time. We have to go. Now," said Sylvie.

"Okay, it's a deal," said Paul.

"Well, I'm gonna need cash," said Mickey. "Up front."

"Cash! You expect us to have twelve hundred dollars in cash on us? What is this, *Miami Vice*?" asked Sylvie hysterically.

"Is there an ATM nearby?" asked Krystal.

"In the office," said Mickey.

"Okay. We'll be back. Don't go anywhere, okay?" said Sylvie.

"Okay," said Mickey.

"I don't even think we're allowed to take out that much money at once," said Paul as they all jogged back, his ankle throbbing.

"Well, let's try," said Sylvie, panting. "All we can do is try."

The three of them faced the ATM. Sylvie dug through the backpack to find her wallet. She inserted her debit card.

"Oh fuck me, I can only take out four hundred a day," she screeched at the screen. "What are we going to do?"

"Take it out," said Paul. "I have another card we can try."

"What other card?" asked Sylvie as she grabbed her cash and moved out of the way so Paul could punch in his code. "How do you have a debit card that I know nothing about?"

The machine spit out the cash and he grabbed it, stuffing it into his pocket.

"It's for emergencies," Paul replied, not looking at her.

"You have a secret debit card at another bank?" asked Sylvie. "What in the actual fuck? You told me you had cut up all your cards!"

"And you told me you were taking fucking Prozac!" Paul yelled back.

"You guys sure do curse a lot," said Krystal.

"Fuck off, Krystal!" Paul and Sylvie said in unison. She held up her hands and backed away a few steps.

"Okay, I can take out five hundred," said Paul, returning to the screen. "I'll explain it to you later, Sylvie, okay?"

"What now? We only have nine hundred," said Sylvie.

"Thanks, I can add," said Paul.

Krystal approached the machine, a card of her own in her hand.

"No way, you're not making up the rest. You're just a kid. And you can't use your mom's card," said Paul.

"Can't I?" said Krystal, punching in her own PIN and swatting Sylvie away when she reached out to stop her from keying in the numbers. "What else are we going to do? We've got to get on that boat. You'll pay me back. Okay?" The remaining money spat out of the slot.

"Okay," said Paul.

"Okay," said Sylvie. "Does your mom know you have her card?"

"Y'all have your secrets, and I have mine," said Krystal. "Let's go."

Again, they ran, this time back to the enormous red man in his tiny white boat. They shoved the money into his meaty palm and climbed aboard.

"Here's y'alls' life jackets," he said, handing them each a moldy orange vest.

"Where are the straps?"

"Ain't got none on 'em anymore. You fall in, just grab it around you, like a sweater."

"A sweater?" asked Sylvie.

Mickey started the engine.

* * *

PAUL EXTENDED HIS hand to Sylvie, to pull her up and out of the boat. As she took it, he was reminded of their wedding. Her mother and father had walked her down the aisle to him, and at the end of it, he had taken her from them just like this, in just this way. In sickness and in health, 'til death do us part.

When you get married and you recite those vows, do you even really know what they mean? Can you ever really grasp them entirely? To him, on that day, he thought as he pulled her up, sickness meant a cold. And death, that would happen when they were well into their nineties. It did not mean the death of one of their children. Paul could not have even fathomed that scenario on that day. And still. He had lived it, he was living it, and the fact that it was his reality seemed impossible. And yet it would always be fact.

"Thanks," said Sylvie. Paul extended his hand again, this time for Krystal.

"Y'all be careful," said Mickey. "And good luck." He tipped his mesh cap in farewell and sped off into the sea.

For a moment, the three of them stood on the island in silence.

"Look, the ferry!" said Krystal. "It's loading up. Let's go!"

And so they ran. Again. At this point, Paul didn't even feel his ankle, which had been throbbing steadily all day. If they could just find Teddy here, boarding the ferry, and go back with him, Paul would change everything. He would really and truly cut up every single credit card he had, he would transfer the money in his secret bank account, he would be empathic toward his wife instead of wanting to kill her, he would enjoy this Bar Mitzvah instead of just enduring it. He would be a better person. He would get his son into therapy.

"Teddy!" screamed Sylvie as they got close to the ferry.

The line of people boarding, almost all of them dyed red by the sun's relentless rays, turned to witness the spectacle that was the three of them yodeling into the twilight.

"Do you see him?" Krystal yelled. "Has anybody boarded yet?"

"I don't see him," said Paul, panting.

"Excuse me, have they let anybody on yet?" Krystal asked a couple with their little girl at the start of the line.

"Do you think we'd be waiting out here in this oven if they had?" the wife retorted.

"Now, come on, Nicole, enough," said her husband. His eyes were tired, and he was holding their daughter, who was half asleep on his shoulder, her curls tangled under his jaw. "It wasn't all bad."

"Okay, thanks," said Sylvie. She walked down the line, searching for Teddy. Paul followed and then behind him, Krystal.

"He's not here," Paul announced. "Teddy's not here."

"There's still time," said Sylvie. "We'll wait."

"Has anyone drunk a sip of water in the last six hours?" asked Paul. "Here."

He dug through his pack and handed them their bottles before drinking from his own. The water was still cold. He certainly had his many flaws, but damnit, he could pack a bag.

They stood, drinking and looking, looking and drinking, until the last family boarded and the boat began to pull away.

"Shit," said Sylvie, shivering despite the fact that the temperature still hovered around one hundred degrees. "Of all the places to bring us," she said.

"But he didn't bring us," said Paul. "That's the point."

Sylvie looked at him, really looked at him.

"Oh," she said. "Right."

"Guys, where do we start?" asked Krystal. "His phone is still off." She sighed. "Do we think he's on the beach or, like, over there in those ruins or what?"

"Well, you have to figure that he's been here all day. He probably started at the ruins and then made his way to the beach. It's my guess that he's at the camping grounds trying to figure out how and where to sleep," said Paul.

"Paul, it's not even six o'clock," said Sylvie.

"So maybe he's eating over there? I don't know. I just can't imagine him on the beach or exploring for any length of time. Can you? I mean, it's Teddy."

"True, but I also could never have imagined him taking this trip in the first place, so what do we know?" said Sylvie. She began to cry. "This is all my fault."

"Sylvie, it's okay," said Krystal. "We're going to find him." She touched Sylvie's arm. "Maybe he'll get lonely and turn his phone back on. I have an alarm set; we'll know the moment he does, and then we've got him."

"It's like we're tracking some kind of endangered animal," said Paul. "Let's start at the beach. Everybody keep their eyes open. Wait, Krystal. Are you hungry? Shouldn't you eat something?"

"Are *you* hungry?" she asked him back.

"Let's all have a protein bar. Here." He took off his backpack and plucked out three, one for each of them. "Take these and your waters and we'll eat as we walk."

"Do you think Teddy brought enough food?" asked Sylvie, as they began their trek.

"Probably not," said Paul.

They walked. The patchy grass turned into sand. A mosquito buzzed in Paul's ear. He yelled for Sylvie and Krystal to stop again, pulled the bug spray out of his backpack and enveloped them all in a noxious cloud.

Walking again, its metallic taste in the back of his throat, Paul stopped fighting the memories. He had been doing that since he'd put the key in the ignition of the car that morning, and he was tired.

The ferry.

They had taken it over to the island just fine three years ago. If he closed his eyes, the memory of Sylvie pregnant and laughing, a giggly Teddy with fuller cheeks and eyelashes ten miles long swam right up behind his lids. Sitting inside with Teddy beside him, peering through the window at the frothing water as they churned toward the island in the unexpectedly hot sun. It was April, but out of nowhere, the temperature hovered near ninety degrees. At home packing the night before, Paul had glanced at the weather on his phone, shocked by the sudden surge coinciding directly with their plans to spend thirty-six hours outdoors.

"We don't have to go, you know," he had said to Sylvie. He had gone over and over this moment so many times that there was a permanent groove worn into his brain; he was sure of it.

"Don't be ridiculous," she had answered. "Of course we're going. If it's too hot, I'll just lie in the tent and you and Teddy can take turns misting me with water like the beached manatee I am."

Beached manatee. That phrase, though wholly inaccurate because Sylvie had never been more beautiful than when she was pregnant, Paul thought, had stuck with him. And Paul was glad because it allowed him to recall that conversation and cling to it in the days and months afterward, when he had blamed himself for what had happened. He had planned the trip, after all. And if they hadn't gone on it, would Delilah have survived?

But he had given Sylvie the chance to back out. He had not forced her on the trip; she had been excited to go. It was not Paul's fault.

It was the ferry ride back that was burned into his subconscious.

"Paul," Sylvie had whispered.

She had walked over to him at the campground after that long, hot day, grabbing his forearm forcefully as he had begun to take the tent out of its carrying case. Teddy was playing with his LEGO men, lining them up in the underbrush, making explosion noises as he conjured up catastrophes in his nine-year-old brain.

"What?" Paul had looked up from the tent bones he had spread on the dirt in front of him, electrocuted by the worry in her voice. Her eyes were dark. Dark as night.

"Paul, I think I'm having contractions," she had said.

"Are you sure?"

Paul could barely get the question out; the world had gone silent all around him, the birds had stopped chirping, Teddy had stopped chattering, the faint rhythm of a Grateful Dead tune from a nearby campsite cut off at the knees of a note.

"I don't feel right," she had said. And then squeezed his arm again. "There. Just now. It happened again."

Those tiny details, they swam right below the surface of his consciousness; Paul knew this. He very rarely allowed himself to summon them anymore, but here: of course. There was no escape.

He looked over his shoulder at Sylvie, trudging along behind him now. Where was she in her mind? Or was she anywhere at all? Did those pills work like a superhero's shield, deflecting pain in a single bound? Her brow was furrowed as she walked. Who knew? Obviously not him. He turned back, kept his eyes ahead. No Teddy in sight. The path to the beach was deserted except for them.

"Sit down, Syl," Paul had said as calmly as he could that afternoon. "I'm going to take care of us. We're going to get the next ferry back, okay?"

She had nodded, holding her stomach as though it might detach from her body.

"Teddy, buddy, we've got to go," Paul had said next.

"What?" he had asked, his voice on the cusp of a whine. "I don't wanna go! What about camping?" He crossed the cusp into full-fledged, his volume rising too. "I want to sleep in a tent!"

"Teddy." Paul had walked over to his son, crouched down to meet his face. "Mom doesn't feel good. The baby, she may be ready to come out of her tummy. We have to get her to a hospital."

Teddy had looked over Paul's shoulder, to get a better view of his mother. Sylvie paced the campsite slowly, her head down.

"Why does she look like that?" Teddy had asked.

"She's in pain. And she's worried."

"Why is she worried?"

"Because the baby may be coming earlier than she's supposed to." It was hard for Paul to breathe through his own rising panic.

"She's coming now?" Teddy had asked, looking at Paul with alarm. Paul did not have time for an in-depth conversation with a nine-year-old; he did not have the patience it required, but Teddy deserved it. He was confused.

"We don't know, buddy. All we know is that we have to pack up and get on that ferry before it leaves." Teddy had bitten his lip. He had nodded. He had gathered up his LEGOs men.

Paul had flown back to the tent and shoved it into the bag, grateful that he had not yet assembled it. He packed up the rest of their stuff, shoved it into his enormous backpack, all the while keeping his eyes on Sylvie. She had been sitting then, on a picnic bench, as pale as a ghost. Every minute that passed, she seemed to get paler, Paul had thought. Like she was being erased. His breath had caught again, imagining the worst.

He would get them onto that ferry and into their car and then he would race down whatever highway at the speed of light to whatever hospital was closest, and everything was going to be okay. That's what he had told himself, over and over, as he did all those things. Up until the last moment, the moment the ultrasound had confirmed their tragedy.

Paul looked up now. He had reached the shore.

A small figure, knees drawn to his chest, sat in the wet sand about sixty yards in front of him. And a yard or so beyond that, four horses trudged slowly past: heads down, matted tails twitching.

"Teddy!" Sylvie screamed. She sped up beside Paul, grabbing his arm to pull him with her toward their son.

Paul took her hand. Together, they ran to him.

CHAPTER TWENTY-NINE

SYLVIE

Sylvie sat on a picnic bench, watching the sun slowly wake up, turning the black sky to hazy pink and yellow as it rose in the sky. She placed a pill on her tongue, its familiar acidity a comfort.

That they had found Teddy so quickly, that had been a blessing. She had thought it would take them hours, combing through the darkness. But thankfully, for once, a break. She and Paul had scooped him off the sand and drawn him into them, becoming one from three. Krystal, who was much more intuitive than Sylvie could ever have imagined, had stood to the side until they were finished. Watching Teddy walk to her afterward, to engage in the bond they had formed, to accept her comfort as his girlfriend, had unexpectedly comforted Sylvie too. Krystal was not a threat. She was an ally. Sylvie was grateful.

There had been no questions as they made their way to the campsite; it was not the right time for questions. Paul had assembled the tent; Sylvie had treated Teddy's mosquito bites with the hydrocortisone cream she had stashed in her bag at the last minute, before spraying all of them again. They had consumed their necessary nourishment, an odd jumble of trail mix, fruit and protein bar bits.

Finally, their stomachs full, sitting on the blanket Paul had had the good sense to cram into his pack, Sylvie had toyed with the idea of asking her son why but was afraid of the answer. Once again, she was being selfish, which at this point was no surprise to herself but nevertheless depressing.

Finally, Teddy had offered an explanation himself after emitting an enormous sigh, a sigh heavy with emotion. A sigh too big for a thirteen-year-old boy.

"I wanted to come back here, because this is the place where everything changed. I didn't leave this island the same kid I was when I came. Everyone is talking about how this Bar Mitzvah marks the transition from boy to man, but I don't see it that way. For me, it was here."

"But you were only nine," said Sylvie.

"True," said Teddy. "But I don't know a lot of nine-year-olds who have to witness death firsthand."

Paul had scooted over to him on the blanket and put his arm around their son's shoulders.

Sylvie had stayed where she was, numb because of the pill she had just taken secretly, in the darkness of the tent. Her son. Her husband. Delilah's death had not just happened to her; it had happened to all of them. She was a selfish, stupid woman. A selfish, stupid drug addict of a woman.

"I'm glad I came," Teddy had said. "But I'm glad you found me too."

"Has it provided any solace for you?" asked Sylvie. "To be here again?"

"Not really." She watched as he took Krystal's hand; she was sitting on the other side of him. "But I'm remembering things. Things that I think are important to remember before I stand on the bimah and declare my manhood or whatever. This sadness is part of me; it's not going anywhere."

"It's like a limb," offered Krystal. "An extra leg."

"Right," said Teddy. "An extra leg that I need to learn to walk with."

Sylvie couldn't believe this wise person was her Teddy. She was in awe of him. And so disappointed in herself.

They had burrowed into their sleeping bags not long after, she and Paul trying not to touch, and Teddy and Krystal together after all, their limbs entwined like branches when she had gazed at them in the moonlight on her way out of the tent a few hours later. She had not been able to fall asleep.

She had taken the flashlight Paul had packed and wandered to the beach, only slightly scared. The stars in the sky were like a candelabra, pinpoints of light everywhere all at once as she sat, looking up at them. She heard them before she saw them. The horses snorting, their disgruntled whinnies, the *squoosh* of their hooves through the wet sand. And then, there they were. The stuff of her nightmares. Sylvie pinched herself, to make sure she was awake. She was.

In the darkness they were like shadows, only alive in the whites of their eyes, which were like daggers piercing her heart. Sylvie thought she might have a heart attack right there, right then, it hurt so bad. The pain of memory.

From the moment she had set foot on the island three years prior, something had felt off. She had told herself it was the heat. It probably was the heat; it had to have been one hundred degrees in the sun. And so suddenly too, a freak heat wave in April.

Her legs and arms had felt so heavy, like they had been made of lead. But her stomach, it had been as tight as a steel drum. She had pressed it, trying to get the baby to move, to give herself some relief, but nothing. There was no release. No movement. And yet still, she smiled at Teddy skipping through the sand, at Paul nerding out over the remaining architecture of the spooky mansion eroded by time.

She was forty-three; of course this pregnancy was going to be different. It had been different. She would drink her water, she would take it slow, everything was going to be fine.

Except it hadn't been fine for a week. She hadn't felt Delilah move the way she had been; the jigs she would perform in the wee hours of the morning, waking up Sylvie with a start. They had stopped.

But Sylvie had refused to entertain any catastrophic thoughts. She had a full-time job, a son, a husband. She was older. This was to be expected.

On the island three years ago, however, as she and Teddy

and Paul had watched the horses sway by, completely uninterested, likely annoyed by the presence of such useless humans, the tightness had gotten even tighter, like a corset over her swollen midsection. Sylvie had known this feeling before, she had thought, panicking slightly. But it couldn't be. And so she had waited.

When it had become apparent what was going on, when her own denial was no longer a support but a very clear danger, she had finally told Paul. He had moved at the speed of light, getting them out of there. They had boarded the ferry just in time, the three of them shell-shocked. There was no hiding her pain and terror from Teddy, although she would have given anything to be able to. Paul had begun timing her contractions; they were ten minutes apart.

How they had all gotten to the hospital in one piece, how she had ended up in a bed with a gown on, she still had no idea. She had been in so much pain by then that everything other than that pain simply had not existed.

What she did remember, however, was the doctor—a doctor she had never met or even seen before in her life, how could she have, where was she, even?—strapping the electrodes to her stomach. *To hear your baby's heartbeat,* she had said. *You're six centimeters dilated, by the way,* she had said. *Do you want an epidural?*

Sylvie had nodded. Yes. A thousand times yes.

"Isn't it too early?" Paul had asked, as the doctor had turned on the monitor. "Is the baby going to be okay?"

"Let's just get a listen," she had answered. And so they had. But there was nothing to hear.

A contraction had wrecked Sylvie at just the moment the doctor's expression had gone from placid to alarmed, like a bolt of lightning striking the room. Suddenly, techs and doctors invaded, armed with machines and plugs and charts, all on top of her at once. Paul had hovered over her, trying to get to her, but they had asked him to step back, to wait just a moment.

An ultrasound machine had been wheeled in. And on the screen: the outline of Delilah. Floating. Silent.

"I'm so sorry, Mrs. Snow," the doctor had said. "Your daughter. She's not alive."

"She's dead?" Paul had asked, as another contraction raged through Sylvie's body.

"Yes."

The sun was up now. The birds had begun to sing. Sylvie wanted so badly to cry, but no tears came.

That was the thing about grief. It didn't care about when you wanted it. It would show up when it damn well pleased. And it had been showing up and showing up for Sylvie until the pills came along. And then, suddenly, Sylvie had some sort of control.

Except of course, she didn't.

Sylvie had refused the epidural then. It was the last time she would experience her daughter, she had reasoned silently, as Paul and the doctor urged her to reconsider. That, and she wanted to physically punish herself for ignoring Delilah's signs of distress, for not calling her doctor immediately when she stopped feeling her move. For being stupid enough to think everything was okay.

And when she had pushed and pushed until she felt her entire body would just explode right there on that bed in a flurry of flesh shrapnel, guts and blood, Sylvie had held her breath for a second and prayed for a miracle. That somehow her exertion had powered her daughter back on, human electricity through the umbilical cord. But that had not happened.

A pretty bird began to warble in a tree nearby. Goosebumps raised along Sylvie's arms despite the fact that it was already eighty degrees in the shade.

Delilah had been her grandmother's name. Her grandmother had named this bird, the one who sang at the top of its lungs to herald the arrival of spring and wouldn't stop all summer, "pretty bird."

"Listen," her grandmother had told Sylvie when she was tiny, "he's telling us we're pretty." Sylvie had stopped to listen, on the warped sidewalk in Brooklyn with her, holding her hand. She was right; it did sound like that.

"*Prettyyyyy, pretttyyyyy, prettttyyyyyy,*" it had sung.

And it sang now.

Before Delilah had died, Sylvie had believed without question that the soul lived on, even through death. The body expired, but the soul was forever. After Delilah died, Sylvie didn't believe that anymore. Except sometimes, there were moments like this, and she thought maybe she still might.

Behind her, she heard the flaps of the tent rustle.

"Jesus, my back," Paul complained, straightening up slowly and cupping the base of his spine with both hands. "Not what it used to be."

"What is?" asked Sylvie.

He ambled to the bench and sat down beside her, rubbed his eyes.

"My mouth tastes like a sewer," he admitted. "I don't suppose you have any coffee?"

"No, the Starbucks was closed."

"There's a Starbucks?"

"I'm kidding, Paul."

"Right." He circled his neck clockwise. "You're quick this morning."

"I never really slept," Sylvie admitted. "Took a walk to the beach and back."

"Nerves?"

"I guess so. It's kind of awful to be here again. We never did make it to the tent last time, so . . ."

"Yeah. I agree. Who would have thought that Teddy would be the one brave enough to come back?"

"Alone, no less," said Sylvie.

"Who is this kid?" asked Paul. "He's changing every day."

"He's growing up," said Sylvie quietly.

Prettttyyy, prettttyyy, the bird continued to warble, its song echoing off the trees.

"Why didn't we hold her?" asked Sylvie. Paul turned to look at her, processing the context of her question.

"You were adamant," he replied. "I tried to convince you otherwise, but you were adamant. You said you didn't want to know what she looked like. That it would be too hard, that there was no point."

"Did you see her?" Sylvie had never asked him this. She had never wanted to know until this moment.

"I did," Paul answered. He crossed his arms in front of his chest, bracing for impact. "You're finally asking me."

"I am."

"Are you stoned?" he asked her.

"Just a little."

Paul sighed.

"Did she look like me?" Sylvie continued.

"She had your hair. Dark. And your lips."

Sylvie looked up, into the blue sky. She pointed her toes inside her sneakers as hard as she could. Tears filled her eyes.

"I thought she might have," she said.

She wanted Paul to hug her, but he did not move, just stayed sitting with his arms still folded, as stiff as a statue next to her on the bench.

"Why did you refuse the autopsy?" he asked quietly.

"I couldn't face anything, Paul. Not one fact. My heart, my body, my soul: they were all broken. I regret everything."

A sob rose up from the pit of her stomach, like some kind of ancient battle cry, and she released it into the air. The pretty bird flew off its hidden perch and away.

Finally, Paul touched her. He put his warm hand over hers.

"I should have held her. I should have agreed to the autopsy. I should have insisted that we take footprints. I should have taken her ashes home with us," said Sylvie.

"Sylvie," said Paul. He took her hand and threaded his fingers through hers. He was crying too. "You did what you were capable of doing. You were broken. We both were."

"But why didn't you make me!" she sobbed. "Why didn't you talk sense into me! You were all I had!"

"Sylvie. Have I ever been able to talk you into anything you didn't want to do? I tried. God knows, I tried. You wouldn't listen to me. And the things you said to me, the insults you spewed in response, I had no choice but to surrender."

"I spewed insults?"

Paul nodded. "Awful things. You told me it was all my fault. Jesus Christ, Sylvie, why wouldn't you go to therapy with me?" He let go of her hand and stood up. "Here we are, three years later, finally talking about this?"

"I did go to therapy with you," Sylvie said.

"Once! You went once!"

"You went on with your life!" Sylvie yelled. "Three months to the day after she died, and you were back at it. You forgot her."

Paul looked around spastically. "Is there a hidden camera? Is this a fucking joke? Back at it? What are you even talking about? I channeled my grief the best way I knew how. I started exercising because moving was the only thing that made me feel better. I think about her every day, Sylvie. Every day. And you never, not once after those first three months where we sat in the dark inside the house like silent prisoners because you wouldn't even talk about it, would even entertain a conversation about Delilah." He kicked the ground angrily, and clods of dirt splattered all over her shins.

"And by the way, you were back at it too. You went back to work."

"I didn't have a choice."

"What's that supposed to mean?" asked Paul. "I know I

screwed up with the shopping. I lost control. I was trying to fill the hole in my heart, okay? But now, now I'm trying to fix it. And anyway, are you trying to claim that if I made a million dollars, things would have been different? That instead of working you would have gotten the therapy you needed? Give me a break."

"I got fired," Sylvie blurted out.

"What?"

"I was fired on Monday."

Paul stared at her.

The tent flap rustled again, and this time Teddy and Krystal came crouching out.

"Good morning," said Sylvie.

They straightened up, the impossible beauty of their youth like a halo all around them, even in their rumpled, unwashed state. Especially in their rumpled, unwashed state.

"Sounds like the day is off to a great start," said Teddy.

"I'm going to go looking for horses," Krystal announced.

"Okay," said Paul.

"Shouldn't we feed you first?" asked Sylvie.

"I can't take another protein bar," said Krystal. "Maybe I can go scrounge up some powdered donuts or something. Anyway, I'll be back."

"The ferry leaves at ten fifteen," said Paul. He looked at his watch. "Come back in an hour, just to be safe."

"It's seven A.M. We need two hours to pack up the tent and walk to the ferry?"

"Well—"

"I'll be back by eight forty-five. See you."

She gave Teddy a kiss on the cheek and walked off into the woods, looking like the bedazzled fairy that she apparently was, thought Sylvie.

"She's a nice girl," Sylvie said to Teddy.

"You lost your job?" he asked.

"I did. But it's not a big deal," she lied. "I'll get another one." She had no idea if she would get another one, actually. She was old and expensive: the kiss of death.

"Okay," Teddy said. "Dad, do you have any water?" Paul nodded and went back into the tent to retrieve it.

"Was it the pills? Did they get you fired?" Teddy asked her when he was out of earshot.

Sylvie brushed nonexistent dirt off her shins.

"Maybe," she said.

"Here," said Paul, emerging with the bottle and handing it to Teddy.

"Dad, Mom's addicted to those pills the doctor gave you," said Teddy. "But she promised me that she'd stop, after the Bar Mitzvah."

"Wait," said Paul. "You two have talked about this?" He loomed over them.

"I confronted her, yes," said Teddy.

"Wow, Sylvie," said Paul. He raked his hands through his hair. "Just wow. Your own son, staging an intervention with you. Your thirteen-year-old son. I hope you're proud of yourself."

Sylvie looked down into the dirt beneath her feet.

"Dad, stop," said Teddy. "You both have secrets, and I, for whatever reason, feel compelled to keep them for you. Or felt, anyway." He shook his head angrily. "Not anymore. It's not my job."

"You're absolutely right," said Paul.

"What secret do you have?" Sylvie asked Paul.

"Just some text flirtation from one of the women I ride with. Nothing serious and I certainly never considered doing anything about it."

"Oh great," said Sylvie. "That's just great. Mr. High and Mighty over here is sending sexts to twenty-year-olds, and I'm the one who's an asshole."

"I never sent a sext!" Paul yelled.

"That's enough!" Teddy yelled back. "Enough."

"Listen," said Sylvie, "nothing about this brings me anything but mortification and shame, but here we are. And going cold turkey off these things—I'm going to have withdrawal symptoms. I'd rather not do that on the bimah with the Rabbi, you know?"

"Oh, you're not going cold turkey," said Paul. "You're going to rehab."

"I'm not going to rehab, Paul. Don't be ridiculous."

"You're going. I made some calls after David told me."

"David told you?" Teddy asked his father.

"I'm not goi—" Sylvie began.

"You're going!" yelled Paul. A shirtless man, wrapped in a towel on his way to the shower, tripped over his feet nearby, startled by Paul's outburst.

Sylvie put her head in her hands. She did not want to go to rehab. She did not want to sit with a bunch of drug addicts in a sterile room and talk about her feelings.

"Where is it?" she mumbled.

"North Georgia. Monday. It's all set up," said Paul.

"How long is it?" asked Sylvie.

"Ninety days."

"Ninety days! What if I hadn't been fired? How would that have worked out?"

"Good thing you were," said Paul dryly. "It's a sign."

"Shit," said Sylvie.

The three of them sat on the bench, staring at the tent. Teddy passed her the water bottle, and she took a long swig.

"Teddy," said Paul, "are you glad you came here?"

"I am," he answered. "You know, I have memories too, of that trip. They don't just go away."

"I'm so sorry you had to witness that firsthand, Teddy," said Sylvie. "No kid should have to view death up close."

"Well, it's not like it was your fault," said Teddy. "Nobody planned it. It just happened."

"But we could have planned better care for you afterward," said Paul. "We completely dropped the ball. We failed you as parents then, and we've failed you since," he admitted. "I'm sorry for that."

"I was nine. What did I know about therapy?"

"Nothing, and that's the point," said Sylvie. "We were the ones that knew better. And yet, we forgot your pain in the midst of our own, and that's a mistake I can't forgive myself for. That you had to run away, to come back here alone to sort out your emotions, to risk God knows what when all we had to do was find you someone who wasn't us to talk to. We're so selfish. Or I am, rather."

"No, don't do that," said Paul. "I'm to blame too. Passivity is not an attribute. I'm ashamed of myself. I should have insisted, Teddy. I should have insisted about everything. With you too, Sylvie."

"Why didn't we ever talk about it as a family?" asked Teddy.

"That's my fault," said Sylvie. "I wasn't thinking clearly. I thought I was the only one entitled to the pain. Stupid."

"Do you ever wonder what our lives would be like now, if she had lived?" asked Teddy.

"Every day," said Sylvie.

"Me too. I think I probably would be, I dunno, a more normal kid. Less in my head all the time. Maybe I'd have a friend."

"You have friends," insisted Sylvie.

"Not really."

"What about Martin and Raj? They're coming to the Bar Mitzvah."

"Raj is popular now. Basketball," Teddy explained. "And Martin is, like, way into video games. It's all he talks about. Or all he did, anyway. I can't remember the last time we hung out. They're coming?"

"Yes," answered Sylvie.

"Huh."

"You have Krystal," offered Paul.

"Yeah," said Teddy. "That's true. But that's it."

"And your friends from Twilight Manor," said Sylvie. "That Manny guy."

"Mom, they're, like, ninety," said Teddy. "And it's Morty, for the hundredth time."

"No," said Paul, "you were an introspective baby. You are who you are from the moment you're born."

"You think so?" asked Teddy.

"I do."

The only thing Sylvie knew about herself as a baby was what her parents told her: that she was loud and inconsolable much of the time. Well, that tracked, she guessed.

"What do you think Delilah would have been like?" asked Teddy.

"Gosh," said Sylvie. "I have no idea."

"I think she would have been like you, Mom," said Teddy.

"God help her," said Sylvie.

"You're not all bad," said Paul.

Oh Paul, if you only knew, Sylvie thought, thinking about David. She didn't know if their marriage would survive that truth. It was on life support right now as it was.

"Anybody want a clementine?" asked Paul. "There are a couple in the bottom of my backpack."

"Hot clementines?" said Teddy, wrinkling his nose in disgust.

"Guys!" They looked up to see Krystal making her way back to them. "I found donuts!" She held up a box. "Four!"

Sylvie was not going to ask her how or where she had gotten her hands on them. All she knew was that she was starving.

And so they devoured their prey, powdered sugar coating their fingers and mouths like snow in the hot, hot sun.

CHAPTER THIRTY

TEDDY

Teddy looked down into the Torah and began to read. The Hebrew flowed from his mouth, the same passage he had been practicing for nearly twelve months. It filled the synagogue, his voice reverberating off the stained-glass windows. The Rabbi stood behind him. Just the two of them on the bimah and so many, too many, sitting before him.

To be fair, his mother had invited only those he agreed to, but now, it felt like too many. Too many pairs of eyes staring at him in his starched blue shirt and tie, which may as well have been choking him for how tight it felt around his neck. All his mosquito bites itched in fiery protest, but still he read.

He considered all the Jewish boys and girls who had gone before him, reciting this same passage, perhaps, in the same airless sanctuary. Did he feel a bond with them? He guessed so. Did he feel a connection to his Judaism that he hadn't yet felt? Possibly. When his grandfather had given him his tallis that morning, he had felt, quite unexpectedly, a sense of continuity. A sense of obligation to his history. He had wanted to tell his mother this, but she was walking around in a Stepford daze, smiling and nodding at everyone, her eyes dull behind her mask of fake cheer.

And then, he was finished. He stepped back and took what felt like his first breath since he had woken up that morning.

He looked into the audience. Teddy knew it wasn't an audience; technically, it was a congregation, but it felt like an audience. For a brief moment, he entertained the idea of himself at the Oscars, accepting the award for Best Director, and a small smile played across his lips. Lips that just that morning had sported a faint, fuzzy black top hat in the bathroom mirror upon close inspection.

Finally.

Now he saw Morty, shaven and slick in a navy-blue suit. He smiled at Teddy and gave him a thumbs-up sign. Next to him was Beverly, in a black suit of her own. Her lips were crimson. She wore a yarmulke.

"And now, Teddy will share with us his Mitzvah Project," said the Rabbi.

Teddy cleared his throat and pulled his speech, which he had folded into a tidy square, from his pants pocket. He was not carrying his green notebook today and felt naked without it, but his mother had insisted it was "too bulky" for his fancy pants. He unfolded his square of paper, feeling nervous.

But this was it. He just had to get through this speech and he was done.

"Hello, everyone, and thank you for coming today," he read too closely into the microphone. He pulled back a little. Took a deep breath. Continued.

Right in the front, his grandparents. All of them. His Bubbe and Zadie, and his Granny and Pop. Night and day. His Bubbe, dressed in an emerald-green wrap dress and up to her armpits in Spanx, a detail she had shared with Teddy that morning. His Zadie in a tailored black suit, his sunspotted head gleaming in the overhead lights. He didn't say much, his Zadie, but how could he? His Bubbe never stopped talking.

His Granny and Pop looked remarkably uncomfortable in their Saturday best. Granny was happiest in her Bermuda shorts and T-shirts that clung to her plump midsection; her trusty visors of which she had one in every color. His Pop favored cargo shorts and Hawaiian shirts, an Atlanta Braves cap perched on top of his thick head of white hair. Today, Granny was in a floral tent and Pop was in a white long-sleeve button-down, red tie and khakis, all brand-new with the crease folds to prove it. They smiled at him. And there was his aunt Gloria, looking like a praying mantis in a purple minidress. She'd been married two times; Teddy had been the ring bearer at the last one, holding what looked like two tiny circles of tin foil aloft on a white lace pillow as he walked slowly down the makeshift aisle.

Teddy thought it must have been hard for all of them, when his dad had married his mom, someone completely different from them. It was probably still hard.

"Thank you to Rabbi Cohen and to my parents, Sylvie and Paul Snow, for everything you've done for me this year."

He looked up to find his mother dabbing at her eyes with a tissue. Finally, some emotion, Teddy thought. His father sat beside her, in his own starched blue shirt and yellow tie, his hair pushed back off his face. He was not crying, but he nodded his head slightly upon eye contact with Teddy.

"My Mitzvah Project started out one way but ended up being something entirely different. Which, I suppose, is a lot like life," read Teddy. "But in this case, it was for the better, and I want to thank Krystal Platt and her mother, Patty, for that. Also, Jackie Jones, the director of Twilight Manor."

Jackie, dressed in an elegant black pantsuit and a necklace as big as a serving platter, winked at him from the fourth row.

"When this Mitzvah Project came up, I was annoyed. I couldn't believe that I had to do even more work. As if reading a foreign language with no vowels in front of a crowded room in a tie wasn't bad enough."

The music of the congregation's laughter relaxed Teddy. He unfurled his clenched fists.

"So my mom took charge, the way moms do, and set me up at a pet shelter. Now, no offense to dogs and cats, but they're just not my thing. And sure, a mitzvah is to do a nice thing for somebody, or, in this case, some wayward animals, without expecting anything in return, but a mitzvah is something else too. The word itself comes from the Aramaic root *tzavta*, which means connection. There was no connection between those animals and me. It was an empty experience."

Teddy looked up to find his Bubbe whispering to his Zadie.

"What, Bubbe? I did my research!" More laughter. Teddy felt better.

"I don't love animals, but what I do love is movies. I love that for two hours you can escape whatever's bothering you and reside in a completely different world.

"So my girlfriend, Krystal, she told me, if you like movies so much, why don't you share that with others? Let the dog lovers be with the dogs. And she was right."

He found Krystal in the audience, sitting with her mosquito-ravaged legs crossed. She was picking at nails that she had painted blue and white for the occasion.

"The colors of Israel," she had explained to him on the phone the night before.

"Of course," Teddy had agreed, touched by the gesture.

She looked up at the mention of her name and smiled. His savior. Without Krystal, who knew if his parents would ever have found him? And who knew if they would have ever talked about Delilah? And his mom, would she have ever agreed to rehab if they hadn't been there at that exact moment, in that haunted space, together? He was glad he had gone. He was glad they had followed him. Maybe that had been his plan all along.

"Her mother, Patty, is a nurse at Twilight Manor. She got me a meeting with Jackie, who was coo— I mean, kind enough to let me run a movie night once a week, sharing and discussing some of my favorite movies, and that's when I really got what this whole mitzvah thing was all about."

Patty Platt, in a black dress that showed the tops of her

breasts, looked bored. He wished, for her sake, that she had worn a scarf or something, to cover herself, but he had a feeling that Patty Platt couldn't have cared less about the glances the other women in the congregation had given her when she walked in.

"And I'm grateful, because it's been a really special experience."

Teddy paused, took a deep breath. He looked out at his parents again, who smiled up at him.

"I love movies because almost always, there's a neat, happy ending, tied up in a pretty bow. That's what I think everyone wants, after all, to escape from the fact that life not always, almost never, is like that.

"In real life, people die. In real life, people are sad, sometimes forever. In real life, people make big mistakes that have big repercussions, and sometimes those repercussions are impossible to untangle. It's all a big, messy muck. And happy endings are a fantasy."

Teddy kept his eyes trained on his paper.

"But everyone, it seems to me, has their own muck. And the muck can be lonely, but it doesn't have to be. Muck should be shared. Because maybe yours is a lot like somebody else's. Or maybe you have very different mucks, but the connection bridges the gap.

"I'll always love movies for their happy endings, for the hope they provide. But real life has room for hope too, through these kinds of honest and unexpected connections. And as I cross this threshold into my supposed manhood today, I hope I can always believe in this.

"And I guess what I'm saying is that I hope you can too.

"Thank you."

At last, Teddy looked up from his paper, which was damp with the sweat from his palms. The room was quiet. He knew he *had done good,* as Morty would say.

And that was enough.

CHAPTER THIRTY-ONE

SYLVIE

Did you know your son was such a skilled orator?" asked Sylvie's mother as they pulled extra toilet paper from the linen closet.

Sylvie had forgotten to stock the bathrooms before they had left for the synagogue, and now there were so many people, all of whom would need to go at some point during their stay, in her house.

"I mean, can you even?" Sylvie shook her head in wonder as she piled three white cylinders on the shelf over the toilet. "He's changed so much."

"Well, he's becoming the man he's going to be," said her mother, adjusting her necklace in the mirror. "You know, everyone scoffs at this whole rite-of-passage, boy-into-man, girl-into-woman Bar or Bat Mitzvah business, but it's true. It's like clockwork. I swear, on the morning of your Bat Mitzvah, *poof!*, you had breasts."

"Mom, I had breasts at ten," said Sylvie.

"No you didn't."

"Sylvie, the caterer is asking if you have another serving platter?" asked Paul's mother, popping her head in.

"You know, Mary, I didn't have the chance to tell you how much I like your dress," said Sylvie's mother. "Very flattering."

"Barbara, please," said Mary. "Don't bullshit me." Sylvie smiled. Good for Mary.

"Can you believe our boy?" Mary asked her, her eyes twinkling. "Wasn't he just amazing?"

"He really was," agreed Sylvie. "Oh, come on, Mom, can't you laugh?" Barbara sulked by the tub. "Haven't we all known each other long enough by now?"

Her mother sighed. "Well, you didn't have to be rude, Mary."

"Why not? You've been rude for years. And there's no hard feelings, Barbara, really. You're the glamorous grandma, and I shop at Dress Barn. Apples and oranges."

Barbara cracked a small smile.

"Can we get out of here now?" asked Sylvie. "Actually, you two: out. Mom, can you show them where the platters are? I need to pee."

Sylvie closed the door behind them and exhaled deeply. She had only two, three at most, more hours of socializing to endure. She closed the toilet lid and sat down, digging in her pocket for a pill. She took it out and placed it on her tongue.

She stood up and faced herself in the mirror. She was a bona fide mess, but at least her son wasn't. She hadn't screwed him up entirely. His speech, that was proof. She was so proud of him and so sick of herself.

But on Monday she was going to rehab. She could not back out; she could not run away. She had to do what she had promised them she would do. She had let them both down, and now she had to earn their trust back. It was that simple.

Paul knew everything except the one thing that could be the last straw. David. But did she even have to tell him?

"No," she said to herself in the mirror.

"Yes," she said after that.

Neither felt right.

There was a knock at the door. Sylvie opened it to find Beverly from Twilight Manor, a study in graceful aging in her black tailored suit, white bob and red lips.

"Oh hello," said Sylvie.

"Hi," said Beverly. She looked like Lauren Hutton but sounded like Dolly Parton. "Your Teddy gives me hope for the future men of this world."

"Thank you," said Sylvie. "Me too."

She walked out, and Beverly walked in, closed the door behind her. Of course it was yes. She had to tell Paul. How and when was another story.

Sylvie strode into the kitchen and then through the French doors out to the deck, where all the guests mingled and ate from the buffet of bagels and lox and salads and spreads; cucumbers and tomatoes and pickles of every persuasion. Pitchers of orange juice and lemonade; bottles of champagne and vodka for those so inclined; white hydrangeas placed on every available surface.

Paul walked up to her, placed his hand at the small of her back.

"It's a lovely brunch," he told her.

"Drunk guy, one o'clock," Barbara warned them, clattering by on her heels to set her carefully procured plate at a table.

"What?" asked Sylvie.

"Who?" asked Paul.

And then, there he was, lumbering toward them in a too-big gray suit that swallowed him whole, a polyester maroon tie that practically glistened. Sylvie's stomach somersaulted. David had been invited before all the messiness but had never RSVPed. Surely, he won't show up, Sylvie had reasoned. But here he was.

"Amazing the lengths someone will go for a decent whitefish salad," she managed to squeak out to Paul—her attempt to defuse the bomb that was three feet, now two, now directly in front of them.

"Great party," said David, slurring.

"Good to see you," offered Paul. "Do you want to sit down? Here, come with me—"

"Nah, I'm not staying long," he said. He took a swig from his amber bottle of beer, his eyes locked directly into Sylvie's. Her knees felt like jelly. She didn't know who or what to ask for mercy, and she sure as hell didn't deserve it, but she internally uttered a quick *Please, no, don't do this* anyway.

"So the thing is," David began. "About the pills. You know, what I told you about?"

"Yes, I know," said Paul. "Sylvie and I have discussed it, David, and I want to thank you, you know. You saved her. She's going to rehab on Monday."

"Saved me?" asked Sylvie. "Well, I don't know about that—"

"Yeah, well, see, I also fucked her," said David.

All around them, guests mingled and ate. Sylvie could even see Teddy sitting with the long-lost Martin and Raj, Krystal by his side, all of them laughing, their plates scavenged. How stupid Sylvie had been to assume that David would just go away.

"Do what now?" asked Paul. His hand fell from the small of Sylvie's back, and she was certain that it would be the last time he touched her at all. Ever.

"She fucked me for those pills," explained David. His eyes were as flat and lifeless as pebbles. "Offered herself up to me."

"Like a prostitute," said Paul, turning to look at Sylvie in disbelief.

"Yeah, well," said David. "Yeah. But the thing is, see, I took her up on it. I'm just as bad, if not worse than Sylvie here. Because I knew better." David gasped, overcome by a wrenching sob, one that caused everyone around them to stop what they were saying, eating or drinking to take notice. "I'm just so lonely, man," David blubbered.

"Oh God," Sylvie mumbled into the floor of the deck.

"You know what, David, let's get you out of here." Paul would not look at Sylvie. He put his arm around David and walked him off the deck, into the yard and down the driveway, talking about who knew what.

Sylvie stood alone. Paul had handled the situation so deftly that everyone had resumed their activity none the wiser except maybe her mother, who kept staring at her. She turned from her gaze, grabbed a flute of champagne from the bar and continued on into the living room, which was all but deserted. Sylvie sat on the couch, careful not to spill, and took an enormous gulp of her drink.

All things considered, Sylvie felt remarkably peaceful about what had just happened. She had always known that she would have to tell Paul. David had just taken care of it for her. And if she was being honest with herself, which she almost never was, this whole mess had started because she had felt invisible. Now here she was, being seen for the drug addict, prostitute, repressed woman that she was.

She had lost her daughter, and now she was going to lose her son and her husband too.

"Sylvie?" She looked up. It was Ellen, her onetime ally from the PTA.

"I just wanted to say, what a beautiful service. I've never been to a Bar Mitzvah before." She took a sip from her own champagne flute. "Very spiritual."

"I'm addicted to pills," Sylvie told her. "I'm addicted to oxycodone, and I slept with my husband's friend to score some once I ran out of other options. That was him, back there, ratting me out."

Ellen nodded, completely unfazed. "That sucks," she said. "Although: define *addict*."

"What?" asked Sylvie.

"Define *addict*, because I drink a bottle of wine a night and I just call that survival. Although I wouldn't screw the Kroger manager to get it. Is that the difference?"

Sylvie stared at her.

"I'm sorry, I'm making a joke because I'm wildly uncomfortable," said Ellen. She sat down next to Sylvie.

"Why are you telling me this?" asked Ellen.

"I don't know," said Sylvie. "I guess I don't have any friends."

"Well, that's your first problem. Women need friends. You might not have gotten into this mess if you'd had a girlfriend to steer you elsewhere."

"Maybe," said Sylvie. "But probably not. I'm big on self-destruction, it seems."

"I'll be your friend," offered Ellen.

"Okay. But you have three months to prepare for the role. I'm off to rehab on Monday," said Sylvie.

"All right then," said Ellen.

"Excuse me," said Sylvie. "I have to go collect myself. And listen, don't tell anyone, okay?"

"What are friends for?" asked Ellen, raising her glass.

Sylvie walked down the steps and into the far-left corner of the yard. Behind some bushes there was a very small clearing. And in that clearing there was an Adirondack chair and a tiny rattan side table. Sylvie had declared it hers during her nesting phase with Delilah, when she had gone through the entire house and yard throwing out and scrubbing and buying.

She had spent an entire weekend directing Paul, having him pull out shrubs so she could plant ones that didn't require much light. She had bought the chair with Teddy, asking him for his opinion on its color, agreeing on yellow and then paying the exorbitant amount. Paul and Teddy had carried it over and set it down once and then a second and third time, until Sylvie had deemed its placement exactly right. Sylvie had finally accepted the fact that a baby was coming out of her, and her goal had been to be topless and breastfeeding all through the summer, protected from view by the shrubs and trees that remained.

Now the chair was mud splattered and sun bleached. The plants were dead. She hadn't been back here since Delilah had died. Sylvie wiped some debris off the seat and sat down, staring up into the leaves of the trees and beyond, into the blue sky.

It was amazing what one did to survive. Why she had insisted on taking the least noble route was a mystery to her. First, with anger and repression, and then with drugs and alcohol and lies. Why hadn't she gone to counseling like a normal person would have done? Why hadn't she processed her grief with some dignity?

All her decisions, they had been the wrong ones. She had thought being a good mother to Teddy meant chauffeuring him to his various appointments and keeping him fed. Keeping him alive. And in some ways, yes, that was the job description. But it was only a small part of it. She had failed him emotionally because she had failed herself emotionally. And Paul too. She had failed him too.

Long before she had found those pills, she had failed.

She would never know why Delilah had died. Why she

had thrived inside her for eight months and then, not. Sylvie hoped that Delilah had not felt a thing, that there had been no pain. That she had been alive, and then just wasn't.

Sylvie did not want to go to rehab, but she also did. She was scared of who she really was in the inside, but she was also curious to find out. Maybe this place would help her do it.

And who knew what waited for her on the other side? Her marriage could very well be over; she knew that now, and she had known that then, when she got in the car to drive to David's that morning. She hadn't cared, but now she did. Or maybe she had cared in her own misguided, repressed way. Sylvie needed to learn how to care correctly.

Sylvie sat in the chair, looking up into the trees, the hum of party conversation behind her. She hid, and she thought, and she hoped.

And then she got up, dusted herself off and returned, walking with deliberate measure across the lawn toward whatever lay ahead.

EPILOGUE

Sylvie kept her head down as she walked through the hall. The white linoleum floors were polished to an almost blinding sheen, so much so that Sylvie wished for sunglasses. She thought back to how her eyes had felt after detox. They had ached so badly that she could feel their exact circumference inside her skull sockets.

She had been driven here by a husband who was not speaking to her, a son who could barely look at her, silenced by the depths she had plumbed, and still she had shaken off the term *addict*.

She had been admitted into this beautiful place that was technically a rehab but really a prison; strip-searched; her bags turned upside down and inside out; her cell phone taken. She was led to a room she would be sharing with a woman named Kim, who greeted Sylvie by telling her not to touch her shit or else, and still.

She had gotten into her bed, pulled the scratchy covers

over her head, cried just a little and told herself that when she woke up, she would do the program, she would put herself through the paces and the ninety days would be over before she knew it. She was not really an addict. She had temporarily screwed up in an unfortunately extraordinary way.

And then.

The next three days came and went in a blur of nausea, vomiting, shaking, sweating, freezing, every muscle in her body quivering, every bone feeling as brittle as straw, every slam of a door in the entire building reverberating in her head like a gunshot. The dreams wove in and out of her subconscious like a needle, presenting some people long-ago dead and gone and some people who were very much alive, who would no doubt haunt her in some form or another for the rest of her life. David, for example.

When she had awoken, squinting at the ceiling of her room, as thirsty as someone who'd been wandering in the desert for days, finally, Sylvie could no longer deny the truth. Lying, stealing and prostituting herself for pills hadn't convinced her, but this detox had. She was an addict. Finally, she could say it.

And so she had said it out loud, *I'm an addict*, and Kim, her roommate, had said, *No shit, Sherlock*, from across the room where she sat in her bed doing a crossword puzzle. That's when the real work had begun.

It had been forty-four days. The next day she would see Teddy and Paul for the first time since she'd been admitted. Sylvie was nervous to see them, to confront the wreckage of her actions, but she was also excited. She missed them so much. She loved them so much.

"How can you treat the people you love the most the worst?" she had asked one afternoon in Group.

"When you don't like yourself, it's pretty easy," her counselor had answered. That was maybe the truest thing Sylvie had ever heard.

She walked out into the open air and there was just the faintest hint of fall, a crisp edge after an eternity of damp heat. It felt good against her skin. She followed the dirt path, wildflowers nodding around her boots as she made her way. Past the placid lake with its quacking ducks, through the middle of a vegetable garden boasting cucumbers and eggplants, carrots and snap peas, kale and tomatoes that every patient tended to, including herself, toward the barn.

"Hey, Sylvie," said Cynthia, their resident horse whisperer.

Cynthia was a twenty-year recovered heroin addict herself. She stood as erect as a skyscraper in her denim and riding boots. Sylvie pushed her own shoulders back in response.

"We've been waiting for you," said Cynthia. "Come on now, don't be scared. You ain't scared of them, they ain't scared of you."

Sylvie followed her inside, down the aisle through the middle of the horse stalls. The smell of hay and manure, of sweat and animal, almost knocked her off her feet. The horses examined her quizzically, their eyes as big as saucers, their tails swishing lazily. Sylvie told herself to breathe, in and out. Slowly.

"Okay now, Hazel here needs a proper cleaning," said Cynthia. She opened the door to the horse's stall. "Come on, Sylvie. You act like she's a tiger or somethin'."

"Sorry," Sylvie mumbled. "You know from Group how horses freak me out."

"I know," said Cynthia, more gently this time. "I know. But the only way to get over a fear is to face it, right? And Hazel is as gentle as they come." Cynthia stroked the bridge of Hazel's dark-brown nose. Sylvie moved closer.

"Go on, say hello," said Cynthia.

"Hello," said Sylvie.

Cynthia laughed. "Girl, she don't understand English! Touch this damn horse!"

Hazel looked at Sylvie, her eyes calm. This was not the feral beast of before. This was a sweet horse in the present of Sylvie's life, in the very sober reckoning of her now.

With her hand much steadier than she would have imagined, Sylvie reached out.

ACKNOWLEDGMENTS

When I started writing this book, I was living a charmed life. I had known grief on a certain level—the deaths of my grandparents and father-in-law and aunt, for example, but I wasn't intimately acquainted with it. But then that all changed. My beloved husband of eight years, Ronen Shacham, the father of our two very young sons, left for work one morning in June and never came home. He suffered an AVM brain aneurysm and after a week in a coma, died.

As I was in the final stages of copyediting—another thunderbolt of sadness struck. My father, Ethan Fishman, died of heart failure.

The outpouring of love and support from my family, friends and community here in Decatur and Atlanta, as well as in Mobile, Boston and New York, was and continues to be astounding—truly the most humbling experience of my life thus far. The food; the transportation of the boys; the visits; the kindness; the complete selflessness of so many. As a single mother, there is no way I could have written this book or taught my classes without it.

Thank you to my mother, Sue Fishman, and my brother, Brenner Fishman, for uprooting their entire lives and moving to Atlanta. It's astounding, this kind of familial support, and I am so lucky to have it. Thank you as well to my aunt and uncle, Alice Fishman and Michael Dipietro.

I want to thank the Shachams, Nurit, Karen, Michelle, Yaniv and Melissa, for the empathy they've shown me, Ari and Lev despite their own burden of grief in losing a son and brother.

Thank you to Kareen Bronstein and Rainer Madigan for so bravely sharing their stories with me. Sylvie's grief is much more realized as a result of your candor and generosity.

Thank you to my agent, Jessica Regel, whose guidance and support is invaluable. And to my editor, Lucia Macro, whose patience and keen eye are most appreciated.

And finally, to my sons, Ari and Lev: your resilience is spectacular; your big hearts unrivaled. I am so proud of you every single day. Thank you for loving me.

Insights,
Interviews
& More . . .

About the Author

About the Book

Read on

About the author

Meet Zoe Fishman

Karen Shacham

ZOE FISHMAN is the bestselling author of *Inheriting Edith, Driving Lessons, Saving Ruth* and *Balancing Acts.* She's the recipient of myriad awards, including a *New York Post* Pick. She's been profiled in *Publishers Weekly* and The Huffington Post, among other publications. Her writing has been published in the *Atlanta Journal-Constitution* as part of their moving Personal Journeys series. Zoe worked in the New York publishing industry for thirteen years. She was recently the visiting writer at SCAD Atlanta and currently teaches at Emory Continuing Education and the Decatur Writers Studio, at which she is also the executive director. She lives in Decatur, Georgia, with her family.

A Conversation with Zoe Fishman

Q: Opioid addiction is such a crisis today, yet most people likely think of it as either cosmopolitan or rural problems. What made you consider making Sylvie, an upper-middle-class working mother, an addict?

A: The opioid crisis was actually my starting point when the idea for *Invisible as Air* took shape. It's both fascinating and terrifying to me, because this is an addiction that knows no class or race boundaries. And so many stories I read and heard about began with a doctor's prescription. It's a class of drugs that erases physical pain, yes, but it's also an opioid that erases mental anguish.

I chose Sylvie not only because of her significant anguish but because she's the perfect invisible victim. Here's a woman who knows better, who has access to the best psychotherapy around, and yet the ease by which this powerful pill arrives in her life and then takes complete hold of it is astounding and ultimately very true to its danger.

Q: Was it difficult for you to maintain your sympathy toward her?

A: There were moments while I was writing when I thought, *Damnit, Sylvie! You are such a self-involved mess! How* ▸

A Conversation with Zoe Fishman
(continued)

low can you go? And I would be sad for Teddy, mostly. But then I would be sad for her too, because she is so broken and so incapable of fixing herself in any remotely healthy way. The huge void her grief has created within her longs to be filled, preferably by instant gratification. That void is what turns her into an addict. Because an instant is only an instant, and then you're chasing it again, no matter what the cost.

Q: How did Sylvie, Teddy and Paul change or confirm what you might already have known about grief?

A: When I began thinking about this novel, I zeroed in on the idea of a stillbirth. I have always been in awe of the strength of women in this position and heartbroken at just the idea of enduring such an experience, both during and after.

At the time, I was living a pretty charmed life. I had known grief on a certain level—the deaths of my grandparents and my aunt, for example. And I had been party to the grief of close friends and tried my best to be there for them. Around the time my publisher was considering my proposal for this novel, however, that all changed. My beloved husband of eight years, the father of our two very young sons, left for work one morning and never came home. He suffered an AVM brain aneurysm, and after a week in the hospital on life support, he died.

He died.

It still stuns me to type that sentence, even as it is the reality of my everyday existence.

And then, while I was writing *Invisible as Air,* my father fell ill. As I was in the final stages of copyediting, he died as well, from heart failure.

When death happens so close to you, to people you love with every ounce of your being, you are never the same. Every word you speak or write, every interaction you have, every breath you take, is tinted by that loss. The loss of that person, yes, but also the loss of yourself, the you before that.

So although Sylvie and the Snow family's situation is different than mine, it's my hope that by writing myself through grief, I was at least somehow able to write them authentically through it too.

Q: Can you talk a bit about the magic and history of Cumberland Island?

A: Cumberland Island, Georgia, is the largest of the Sea Islands of the southeastern United States, with thirty-six thousand acres of Atlantic beaches, salt marshes and inland forests filled ▸

A Conversation with Zoe Fishman
(continued)

with giant live oaks and palmettos, as well as a vast array of wildlife. A National Seashore, it's probably most known for its feral horses. It also has a very rich history.

Georgia's founder, James Oglethorpe, arrived at the island in 1736, and he built forts and a hunting lodge he named Dungeness. Revolutionary War general Nathanael Greene bought land on Cumberland Island in 1783, and after he died, his widow, Catherine, built her own Dungeness, which was later destroyed by a fire. In the late 1800s came Lucy and Thomas Carnegie, brother of the steel tycoon, who built a grand Dungeness Mansion in 1886. In 1900, the couple built another home, Greyfield, which is an inn today.

Other than the inn and the First African Baptist Church, most famously known for the place where John F. Kennedy Jr. and Carolyn Bessette were secretly married in 1996, almost all of the formerly opulent buildings are in shambles. Wild horses, almost two hundred in all, roam the island and are believed to be the ancestors of horses abandoned by Spanish settlers over five hundred years ago.

Cumberland Island can only be accessed by boat or ferry from St. Marys, Georgia. No driving is allowed.

I visited Cumberland Island with

my husband in April 2015. It was a babymoon of sorts, as our second son was due that June. To say that the island is magical is a gross understatement. Though there are no human inhabitants, you can feel the grandness of what once was in the ruins of Dungeness and the spirit that lives on there. The trees have stories to tell, the marsh and beaches feel somehow frozen in time and the horses, oh, the horses. I remember sitting on the beach and just watching them trot by, completely unfazed by us. I will never forget it.

While I was there, I wanted very much to write about the experience in a book one day. And so, I did.

Q: What's next?

A: Since the death of my husband, I've been thinking a lot about the soul and where it goes once the body's time as a vessel expires. I've also thought a lot about fate and what-ifs. Pretty standard grief thoughts, I suppose. I'd love to explore these themes in a way that perhaps incorporates a little magical realism, but I haven't figured out quite how yet. Or if I'm even ready at this point. Time will tell.

Reading Group Guide

1. What do you think makes Sylvie take her first pill? While only she made that decision, what were factors that went into it?

2. Do you have sympathy for Paul's role in their marital situation? Why or why not?

3. In what ways does Paul's exercise addiction mirror Sylvie's own situation?

4. Teddy is making his Bar Mitzvah, and in doing so, he technically becomes a man. In what ways does he act more like an adult than his own parents?

5. It's never clearly stated in the book, but do you see moments where Sylvie's friends and coworkers are on to her sooner than she thinks?

6. Discuss the symbolism of Teddy's trip to Cumberland Island.

7. At one point Sylvie's friend Ellen says she herself drinks a bottle of wine every day. No one seems to think much of this. Why do you think so many women live lives of quiet desperation?

8. What do you think the future holds for Paul and Sylvie?

9. Sylvie was in denial about her baby's health and continued to be in denial of both her grief and the depth of her addiction. What in her background might have made Sylvie such a world-class avoider?

Read on

Have You Read? More by Zoe Fishman

INHERITING EDITH

A poignant breakout novel, for fans of J. Courtney Sullivan and Elin Hilderbrand, about a single mother who inherits a beautiful beach house with a caveat—she must take care of the ornery elderly woman who lives in it.

For years, Maggie Sheets has been an invisible hand in the glittering homes of wealthy New York City clients, scrubbing, dusting, mopping and doing all she can to keep her head above water as a single mother. Everything changes when a former employer dies, leaving Maggie a staggering inheritance. A house in Sag Harbor. The catch? It comes with an inhabitant: the deceased's eighty-two-year-old mother, Edith.

Edith has Alzheimer's—or so the doctors tell her—but she remembers exactly how her daughter, Liza, could light up a room or bring dark clouds in her wake. And now Liza's gone, by her own hand, and Edith has been left—like a chaise or a strand of pearls—to a poorly dressed young woman with a toddler in tow.

Maggie and Edith are both certain

this arrangement will be an utter disaster. But as summer days wane, a tenuous bond forms, and Edith, who feels the urgency of her diagnosis, shares a secret that she's held close for five decades, launching Maggie on a mission that might just lead them each to what they are looking for.

DRIVING LESSONS

Sometimes life's most fulfilling journeys begin without a map.

As an executive at a New York cosmetics firm, Sarah has had her fill of the interminable hustle of the big city. When her husband, Josh, is offered a new job in suburban Virginia, it feels like the perfect chance to shift gears.

While Josh quickly adapts to their new life, Sarah discovers that having time on her hands is a mixed blessing. Without her everyday urban struggles, who is she? And how can she explain to Josh, who assumes they are on the same page, her ambivalence about starting a family?

It doesn't help that the idea of getting behind the wheel—an absolute necessity of her new life—makes it hard for Sarah to breathe. It's been almost twenty years since she's driven, and just the thought of merging is enough to make her teeth chatter with anxiety. When she signs ▸

Have You Read? ***(continued)***

up for lessons, she begins to feel a bit more like her old self again, but she's still unsure of where she wants to go.

Then a crisis involving her best friend lands Sarah back in New York—a trip to the past filled with unexpected truths about herself, her dear friend and her seemingly perfect sister-in-law . . . and an astonishing surprise that will help her see the way ahead.

SAVING RUTH

Southern fiction with a pungent twist, Saving Ruth *is a wonderfully evocative, delightfully engaging tale that, nonetheless, seriously addresses provocative issues like anorexia, family dynamics and the racial and ethnic tensions of the Deep South.*

Ruth Wasserman has always felt like an outsider in her Alabama town. Being a curly-haired Jewish girl among blond Southern Baptists was never easy, and within her own family she has always played second fiddle to her older brother, a star athlete and student whom her parents adore. So when it came to college, she went as far away as she could get, attending the University of Michigan, a Yankee school that she hoped would open up a new world to her.

But now she's back home for the

summer, and though she may look like a new, wiser woman on the outside, she is struggling with low self-esteem after a dead-end relationship at school and what could quite possibly be the beginnings of a serious eating disorder. And now having experienced a world beyond her muggy, Kool-Aid-soaked hometown, she feels even more removed from her family and friends. She's hoping time at the same summer job as a pool lifeguard and swim coach that she's had for the last few years will center her again. But when one day a child almost drowns on her watch, she discovers the repercussions will push her to confront truths about her parents, her brother and herself that she's been trying to ignore.

BALANCING ACTS

A must for fans of The Friday Night Knitting Club, The Reading Group, The Jane Austen Book Club *and* Girls in Trucks, Balancing Acts *brims with wit, sensitivity and wisdom—with characters women readers can really relate to and take into their hearts.*

Charlie was a woman who seemed to have it all—beauty and brains that led her to a high-paying Wall Street job far away from her simple Midwest upbringing. But in the middle of a "quarter-life crisis," she decided a ▸

banker's life wasn't what she wanted, quit her job and opened her own yoga studio. But like any new business, finding customers is an uphill battle.

When she hears about her college's alumni night, she decides this will be the perfect place to drum up some business. At the alumni night she reconnects with three college classmates—women who, like Charlie before, haven't ended up quite where they wanted to in life. Sabine, a romance book editor, still longs to write the novel brewing inside her. Naomi, a child of the Upper East Side, was an up-and-coming photographer and social darling but now is a single mom who hasn't picked up her camera in years. And Bess dreamed of being the next Christiane Amanpour, but instead finds herself writing snarky captions for a gossip mag, which is neither satisfying nor rewarding.

When Charlie invites all three to a weekly yoga class, they all are looking for something new in their lives. The class, and especially the bonds that form there, help each woman find the life they were looking for as they fall in love, struggle in their careers and come face-to-face with haunting realities.